The Reich Strikes Back

Ableiter pulled the floss backward with a sudden jerk, twisting it until a thin mist of red clouded the white. The mist became a spray. Rosa clawed at the German's arms but missed, her mouth yawning open and pinching shut in a slow-motion parody of a jungle turtle . . .

By the time she hit the floor, her head had been nearly severed.

THE HIMMLER PLAQUE

JACKSON COLLINS

 AVON
PUBLISHERS OF BARD, CAMELOT, DISCUS AND FLARE BOOKS

AVON BOOKS
A division of
The Hearst Corporation
105 Madison Avenue
New York, New York 10016

Published by arrangement with St. Luke's Press
Library of Congress Catalog Card Number: 86-6729
ISBN: 0-380-70324-6

The St. Luke's edition contains the following Library of Congress Cataloging in
Publication Data:

Collins, Jackson, 1939–
  The Himmler Plaque.

  I. Title.
PS3553.0474795H56   1986   813'.54   86-6729

First Avon Printing: September 1987

For John and Carolyn Schisler
who know how long the road has been

and for Carol
who helped me to go the last mile

THE HIMMLER PLAQUE

One

The jungle was silent in the hazy April morning. There were charred animals in the burned places, and suffocated animals in the places where the grass remained. All were beginning to smell. The few palms that stood out from the river's edge leaned in over the carnage, their fronds drooped in sadness and expectancy. Bullet holes yawned in the high limbs of the trees, and the bark on certain trees yawned in the high limbs of the trees, and the bark on certain trees bore a splash of orange color, the feathers of dead parrots. For two days the Germans had killed everything that moved.

At the place where the river curved to the southwest lay a twenty acre triangle of sawgrass, its tan tip pointing toward the camp just beyond the treeline. The camp, a cheerless cluster of seven wood and metal buildings, was painted a mottled green, the stuff of camouflage. Joining the camp to the river was a three-hundred-foot line in the sawgrass carpet. This path led straight to the river, to a small wooden pier that jutted out over the water, its legs awash at a depth of five feet. From the land side six steps led up onto the mesh opening shaded by an ancient and ragged umbrella. Inside the tub and resting on rocks were five of what the natives called *barbamarillo,* yellow whiskers. They were young serpents, but quite deadly. Although the morning was still, they often ran their tongues forward as though trying to sense movement from somewhere nearby.

Beneath the pier, his legs lying numbly in the water, his chest in the soft mud, Tomas Portillo turned his head to look across the river for the hundredth time in the past two days. His neck ached and his feet itched as if they were about to rot away. The water in the tub sloshed just above his head and he trembled. It was not so terrible in the daytime, but now he wondered whether he could endure another night, a third night, hearing that sound. There were other things in the river, things not confined to tubs, and he knew that his luck could not hold forever. The piranha had not yet found him, nor had the anaconda, but it was just a matter of time. The Virgin had been with him, up to now. Rejecting what he knew to be good judgment, he looked around, raised his legs and felt the needles of discomfort boring into his flesh. Mud and silt coldly ran down from his ankles to his knees and he would not allow himself to think of the snakes just now. His trousers, once white, had become green with moss; it was as if the river were absorbing him into itself. Sanchez had told him that it would be at least two days, perhaps even four, and he had agreed because words have no length, no way to mirror the time that they describe. Two days, perhaps four. How simple it had sounded when they had agreed.

As if in rededication, he now gazed at the bundle that lay in the mud just below the pier's steps. Wrapped in a plastic bag and several layers of sacking cloth, its heaviness was all that had sustained him through last night's rain. Touching it in the terrible darkness, he had pretended that it was one of Rosa's hips, had pretended that he could feel her undulate under his caress. She would not have been unhappy with this fantasy of his; after all, the thing being touched was representative of her in other ways. With its promise of wealth he and Rosa would be able to go away and start a new life.

Twenty thousand pesos. That was what Sanchez had promised. It was more money than Tomas had known to exist, except perhaps in the blue and glass *banco* in Ascunsion. It was more than ten times what the Germans had paid him for his two years of loyal service. Now he touched the bundle again, but in daylight the love fantasy would not emanate from the cloth and he felt a little ashamed.

Unable to stand it any longer, he leaned sideways and flipped loose the two bottom buttons of his fly. He reached into the shallow water at his knees, rinsed the mud from his right hand, and began to stroke himself. It would not come up at first because of the cold but, as his hand began to dry and memories of Rosa's soft stomach and black triangle became more real, it began to pulsate. He thought of their first time together, of the bed in her mother's house as the old lady was outside cleaning fish. There had been nine fish, more than enough to allow them time to do it well. An exotic frenzy had overcome him on that day and he had buried his lips between her thighs and had licked her there for a long time. It was a thing that they now did often, and he wondered if other married people did such things. Perhaps he was not a normal man for wanting to place his mouth there; it was a thing that he had never mentioned to anyone, not even to Sanchez. He grunted and spilled his seed in the mud, sighing heavily.

Feeling that nameless disgust that he always experienced after stroking himself, he buttoned his trousers and slid forward in the mud and peered through the low grass at the pier's lower step. A slice of one of the buildings was visible and the almost indiscernible wavings of the grass made the camp appear to sway. There was no human movement; it was a good omen, all this stillness—the Germans had called off the search just as Sanchez had said they would. For all their boasts of their long trek across Russia and Poland, incredible tales of five-day marches on three hours of sleep, they had given up the search for Tomas Portillo after only two days, but now they were paunched, bald, gray. All except Ohlendorf, whose black hair and lean body caused him to appear out of place among the others.

As Tomas thought of Ohlendorf his tongue darted forward drily and involuntarily. If he were caught, it would be Ohlendorf who would have him. Once, when one of the camp roosters attacked Ohlendorf's leg at feeding time, the dark German seized the bird by its spurs and held it, shrieking and flapping in his left hand, as his right continued the feeding—lazily, methodically. He had tied the thrashing legs with a bit of twine and had gone away for what seemed the better part of an hour. When he returned he had two tall sticks with notched ends and a shorter, stout stick and a bit of wire. Only after he had forced the tapered ends of the tall sticks into the soft earth and placed the stout stick in the notched ends did the others become aware of what was about to happen. They were starved for entertainment and they joked in German as Ohlendorf tied the wire around the rooster's legs and hung the bird upside down. The leaves from a dead magniflora burned slowly and it took the bird three hours to die.

The echoes of the bird's shrieks drifted away hollowly down the tunnels of memory and Tomas lay his forehead in the cool earth beneath the steps. The Holy Virgin must have been with him till now, he reasoned, and he whispered her name over and over as he thought of the others. There was Bleure, who had never been heard making a human sound, who stared with evil eyes at the river but really into the cruelties of another time. There was Renck, the tall one whose fan-shaped scar pointed its three prongs toward a Heaven that he could never hope to see. But these were only two of the seven small fish who lived in the fringe camp; the others, possessing names that had never been heard by the natives, lived at the camp that lay a mile farther into the jungle.

Tomas rose on his stiffened elbow, rolled over onto his side. There was activity in the tub above him, but his flesh no longer prickled. The Germans called the serpents *fer-de-lance*, but what did the Germans know? They had a strange name for everything. He squinted at the square of dull, gray light formed by the pier's open side and yearned to swim in the comforting river. The tawny willow that stood directly across from the pier held his attention once again, for it was from there that Sanchez had promised to signal. Still, as ever, nothing.

Now he rolled the heavy bundle to one side and withdrew the plastic bag that had lain beneath it. The bag was not nearly as heavy as it had been two days ago, and he consciously swore to include gluttony as a portion of his next confession. The bread and knockwurst had long since disappeared and the cheese, once a large chunk of yellow, now was a misshapen shard of green. Pretending not to see what his hands did, he removed a maggot and tossed it behind him. It made no sound as it hit the water.

He was halfway through with the cheese when he heard the brush of footsteps on the nearby grass. In his fear his jaw locked and spittle ran warmly from his mouth and down his neck. A shadow crossed his wrist as the man walked up the steps, and Tomas drew his hand away as if from a flame. The heavy boots made a drumming sound as the man walked to the snake tub, paused, strode on to the lip of the pier. This was followed by a brief silence that was devastating. Tomas felt his fingertips dig into the soft mud and then, less than three feet beyond his toes, there began a dull, monotonous spattering of unmistakable origins. Tomas could not recall when he had ever been so happy to be nearly pissed on. There came a soft rush of metallic sound as the man zipped his trousers. The steps retraced themselves to the tub and paused for several seconds. From above came the sound of frenzied splashing as the snakes made a banquet of the minnows that had been poured in their midst. The heavy boots went back down the steps and onto the soft grass. Parting the grass at the bottom step, Tomas saw the familiar buttocks of Renck. The German moved in a laggard and lazy gait back toward the camp, picking his nose as he was swallowed up by the incredible greenery.

Tomas bit into his wrist and felt his body go rigid. It was the better part of a minute before the seizure passed, before logic reasserted itself. He thought of Sanchez. A simple hand signal from the willow across from the pier, that was what Sanchez had said. Tomas felt the desperation easing from his breast as the last of the cheese lurched down his throat. He had forgotten that it was in his mouth.

Now the sun touched the pier and the fog of morning wafted away. The umbrella over the snake tub made a half moon shadow on the river's surface.

He smiled at the half moon on the green water. It was telling him that the mission was half completed, this thing that had begun exactly forty-eight hours ago. It was then that he had laid down the scythe, strode to the well house as if to get a drink, and sneaked into the utility house that sheltered, among other things, a black foot locker. Because it had been there for thirty years and because theft was a thing totally unlikely, they had taped the key to the locker's top. As had been planned in the previous days, Sanchez had placed the plastic cloth and the wrapping cloth just inside the door of the shed. It had taken Tomas seven long and terrible minutes to finish the wrapping and make his departure. By mid-afternoon, when the screaming and shooting had started, he had already been under the pier for five hours—indeed, had already eaten the first of his meals. Although the fear had been benumbing as they passed at times within five feet of him, it did not overshadow his feeling that for the first time in his life he was more than a cutter of grass, a day laborer. He wished that Rosa could have seen it. There would be time enough to tell her later, when they and Sanchez were on the ship.

The soft breath of instinct moved across the back of his neck, and he turned to look at the willow across the river. He blinked his eyes, adapting them to greater distance. The limbs of the willow parted and a human hand made a waving motion. For a long while Tomas merely stared as if stuporous from a garbled dream. In the world of the poor, nothing ever comes to pass as planned, and he was taken aback by the simplicity of the hand that had waved from the willow. Yes, surely he had dreamed it, but he continued to stare.

Again, the hand appeared and motioned.

Sanchez!

Tomas raised a muddy hand and crossed himself. Part of this impending wealth would go to the Holy Virgin but, since she was not greedy, the fifty percent that he had decided upon yesterday now became five percent. A great number of candles could be had for five percent.

He grasped the package and began to slither backwards, the shock of the cold water causing him to gasp.

The needles of pain in his sleeping legs were as lightning bolts, and it came to him that this was an eventuality that even the slippery Sanchez had overlooked in their talks. He looked across the river and saw the hand motion again, this time with the sharp thrust of exasperation. Despising the dullness in his legs, just as he despised the feeling that this was yet another of his life's debacles, he backed farther into the water, his eyes never leaving the horizontal line of brown grass beyond the pier. When the water touched his shoulders, he leaned backward, rested for a moment on his knees, and then turned. Keeping the bundle high as Sanchez had ordered, he began the slow, punishing trek across the river. In another month or so, this would have been impossible, for the expected floods were known to turn the docile green into a torrent. Sanchez had thought of everything.

Four times in the last week he had waded here, always at night, and each stump that now touched his legs was something of a benchmark, a blessed friend that assured him by its pressure that he was yet alive. The current began to assert itself against his right side and he struggled against the steady pressure. Now the surface line moved down his breast to his navel and he knew that if he could but live for another twenty seconds he could live forever. The sensation of being watched by smirking eyes caused his neck hairs to feel cold. Finally his hips were exposed and he waded into the grass beneath the willow and collapsed at the feet of Sanchez.

"Simple," Sanchez whispered, pulling him on into the trees. "Did I not tell you it would be so?"

"Liar," Tomas gasped. "You are late."

"Late, but safe," said the tall one. He pulled a cigarillo from his pocket, thought better of it, replaced it. "Yesterday some of them passed within inches of me."

Tomas was not interested. "Where is the boat?"

Sanchez removed his tan sombrero and wiped sweat from its inner crown. He studied the hat for a time and then looked down at Tomas with pain in his eyes. "They chopped it with axes."

Tomas stood and looked back toward the river. Through the jungle's pores he could see part of the pier and its tub. He felt his legs tighten, and his wet trousers had become colder. "Then how do we meet your contact?"

Sanchez shrugged, but there was impishness in his gesture. "Simple. We walk."

"Through twenty kilometers of swamp? With the leech, the *barbamarillo*?" Even as he spoke he saw his friend begin to smile.

"There is another boat," said Sanchez. "I left the other for the purpose of being found."

Tomas was unable to say anything for a moment. He looked up and watched a macaw nibble at a plum, but his brain saw neither bird nor fruit. Here again was the manner that Tomas had come to despise in his friend. It had been this way for the past several weeks, this imperious manner seasoned with occasional touches of goodness. Several times of late Sanchez had come by the house that Tomas and Rosa shared and had left small offerings of fruit or vegetables, usually when Tomas was at work for the Germans in a distant part of the forest. And then, on their next meeting, Sanchez might be at once nervous, vicious, friendly, suspicious.

"Come, it is time," said Sanchez, already moving away, instantly absorbed by the great fronds of the jungle. Tomas stood, hefted the bundle and looked at the pier and its tub for the last time. He recalled the heat and sweat that had gone into its construction and a wave of nostalgia ran through him, but he also recalled the screams of the rooster, and he pulled a frond down over the scene and ran to catch Sanchez.

"Why do you limp?" Sanchez asked. He had paused to wait for his tardy friend and was pulling grapes from a low vine.

"My legs, the water. It is strange, but my thoughts of the piranha caused my legs to become as steel springs. Now they have the sintomas of my fear. The steel has rusted."

Sanchez smiled at his friend's uncharacteristic foray into humor. "They must be the legs of the hippo now," he said. "We must be at the boat by dark." He spat grape hulls and looked away at the quiet, emerald jungle.

Saying nothing, he moved away and resumed the journey.

It was then that Tomas saw the pistol. The semicircular butt jutted from Sanchez' hip pocket with the graceful and evil curve of a falcon's wing. It had once been of a silver color, but Sanchez had wrapped the grip with black tape for protection against the ever-gnawing rust. At this moment, in which his joy should have been at its highest, there was no joy to be had. Grudgingly, he admitted to himself that, for the first time ever, he was afraid of Sanchez. Switching the bundle from his right arm to his left, Tomas started down the trail and flexed the weight-numbed fingers of his right hand. When this was over, when they arrived in Los Mochis, the place of Rosa's birth, a village off the high western seacoast of Mexico, this hand would do wonders for her thighs, hips, breasts.

They walked for seven miles without talking. The sun reached its greatness and turned the jungle into a cauldron and started down the other side of the tree-shrouded sky. Floral blading cut at their hands and necks, and often they had to move out of the pathway to avoid the drop zone of the lazy python.

After four hours, they paused under a great spreading banyan tree and ate wild bananas. Tomas consumed nine of the yellow-green fruit before kneeling to drink from a nearby stream. He had barely raised himself off his knees when the stomach seizure hit him. Dropping his pants, he relieved himself noisily.

"You are disgusting," said Sanchez, looking away.

"It was the wait between fresh foods," said Tomas apologetically. He did not like this squatting, this having to look up at his partner in helpless, vulgar humiliation. God had made some like Sanchez who never became ill, never farted, never developed nasal incrustations that had to be picked out, never had sprigs of hair that could not be reformed by comb or brush. And then He had made people like Tomas to whom all these outrages were the very stuff that held skin and bone glued together.

"Hurry up," Sanchez ordered. "The smell is worse than tapir guts."

''Then perhaps you should go away for a while,'' Tomas countered angrily. Another seizure hit his bowels and he felt the last of his discomfort drain away.

Sanchez gathered up a wad of jungle grass and exchanged it for the bundle Tomas clutched. As his friend wiped himself, Sanchez tossed the bundle from one hand to another and was thrilled by its weight. He knew enough about gold to realize that even a whisperweight was enough in Yanqui dollars to equal what the Germans paid him in a year.

''Tell me, Tomas,'' he said, his eyes afire with personal visions, ''how far do you think it is to the next river?''

Such a strange question from Sanchez, the brilliant one, the man always a step ahead of mere men and not more than an inch behind God Himself. He seemed confused. No, more than confused—afraid.

Tomas finished wiping himself and said, ''Not more than six kilometers.'' He was pleased with the ring of certitude in his words; for once, he sounded almost like Sanchez. And there was more to this conversation than the casual listener might have inferred: Tomas was now aware that Sanchez had been afraid, confused. And lost. *Si*, that was it. His friend and partner had but one genuine and irreducible flaw. Sanchez had absolutely no sense of direction.

''Are you certain?'' Sanchez asked, handing the bundle back to Tomas. ''I would say fifteen, perhaps.''

''Very well, fifteen.''

Sanchez patted him on the shoulder and said, ''Now we may make jokes. It is six, perhaps seven. I simply wondered if you remembered our hunts here of some years back.''

''I remember well,'' said Tomas. ''If one walks just to the left of the setting sun, the river's curve will be the first opening.''

Sanchez looked away, remembered, nodded. He straightened his back and flexed his arms outward, the action of a preening bird. ''Take care of my little *aguila*.'' He pointed to the bundle.

"Ours," Tomas corrected. Sanchez was already walking away and pretended not to hear.

They had gone only two hundred yards when Sanchez stopped, turned and smiled, "You were right, Tomas. It is only six kilometers. I remember that tree." He pointed away to a place over Tomas' shoulder.

Tomas looked away and saw no unique tree, only the green-black of the forest. A bit of grass had adhered to his buttocks, and he wondered whether he would have enough time to lower his trousers and remove it. Opening his mouth to speak, his gaze returned to Sanchez and he saw the pistol. He had only enough time to gasp.

Sanchez fired. It was a bad shot. The bullet dug a horizontal trench just above Tomas' left ear and the blue-black gash was instantly filled with blood. He screamed and pitched backward onto the damp earth, then tried to roll sideways into the wet brush.

Sanchez fired again and saw Tomas' shirt puff upwards as the echo of the shot carried with it the sound of screaming birds, chittering monkeys. Tomas writhed as a great, languid torrent of blood stained the back of his shirt. His hands twitched slightly, and then he lay still on the grass. The body voided the very last of the green bananas, and the two stains, one red, one brown, met at the small of the back. A fly walked across one of the hands, flew upwards, made several dizzying circles, and landed on the line formed by the juncture of blood and excrement, its tiny arms working feverishly.

Sanchez could hear himself breathing, feel himself sweating. He returned the pistol to his pocket, picked up the bundle and ran, his eyes peering down an imaginary line that lay just to the left of the leeching sun. If he paced himself well, he could be at the boat long before dark.

Two

The swirling hills of central Texas shimmered beneath a yellow sun. Twenty-three days of drought had made the green earth brown and barren. Little animals scurried quickly from one rock to the other and cooled their feet as their tongues hung out limply. The black belt of highway was heavily spotted with their corpses, and they quickly became grease and stench. The sky was pale at the horizon but anemically blue at the outer reaches of the sun's corolla. It was an area that travelers passed through quickly, and with a slight sense of foreboding.

A gray Rolls Royce moved along the highway at seventy miles per hour, its hood ornament glinting dully. The car passed quietly through the ground swells, and the heat waves parted for it like transparent curtains that quickly closed when the winds of passage were stilled.

Inside, dressed in a raw silk suit of gray that matched the car, the driver looked at his platinum wristwatch and slowed the car's pace. He removed the watch, placed it on the burgundy mouton seat, and rubbed his wrist thoughtfully. Although his appointment time was set for an hour hence, he had made the trip from Dallas with some two hours to spare. That meant an hour to kill somehow in this hellhole. It seemed to him that no matter how high up the ladder of success he climbed, by whatever means, the sun and dirt were always going to play a part in any profit that might be destined for his wallet. He looked at the wristwatch lying on the seat and wondered why it did not make him feel successful. Not that it should, since nothing ever had. But, as always, he smiled at the watch, a symbolic act just as the timepiece itself was a symbol. The Texas Jewelers Association had presented it to him three years ago in appreciation for his work as president of their group, had inscribed its back with his initials: AB. As he ran his soft hand through his thinning hair, he wondered if he would ever feel successful. Certainly the watch did not do it, nor did the car. The initials were proper; it was just that they did not represent the proper name. Thirty years ago Arnold Blaustein had become Alan Bond, and it was a thing that had needled him quietly ever since. The membership in the country club was a farce, if not a hypocrisy, for he had served on its board of directors for nine years and had joined in freely when the other moguls had belittled Jews, niggers, wops, and all the other ill-colored but well-to-do candidate fauna whose names had shown up at times. The Rolls was rented, which made it a phony. The initials were real, but phony. And his current expedition was questionable at best, which made it phony. All that was real was the watch, which was owned outright, and he smiled at it as though it were human, an old friend with whom he could eat cheese and drink beer.

The day grew hotter and he eased the Rolls off the highway and into a truck stop. Sipping a cola as he watched the denizens of this godforsaken place speculate in whispers about who he might be, he remained a little distant, even aloof, as they washed the car. The owner asked at proper intervals about what particular cloth to apply to the pearly finish. He delighted in affecting a British accent, explaining that any soft cloth would do.

He paid and left, checking in his rearview mirror to see if they watched him far down the road. They did.

Now that he had killed the better part of an hour he was back on schedule and was thus spared the agony of waiting in the rolling plains country for the bus that carried the Latino. His speed, which was in keeping with the searching eyes of a confused driver, had altered downward to thirty miles per hour. When he saw a great sign advertising Akron Super tires, he knew that he was exactly eleven miles from the meeting point. Touching a button on the armrest of the door, he let all the windows down and smelled the heat.

A slight trickle of sweat had appeared at his temples, and he patted each with the backside of his fingers the way he had once seen George Sanders do in a movie. It was a genteel way to do a rather mundane thing, he thought.

Alan began to look for the landmarks, but the country itself was of no assistance; the land was a mass of khaki ripplings under a stark sky. He momentarily panicked and realized that he had no business out here, city person that he was. Why in God's name did they not get someone else? Yes, he had agreed, but it had made sense at the time. Now he was going to fuck it up for himself and the others, and lose the money in the process.

At last, the sign. It was one of those ancient tire advertisements that featured a little boy in pajamas holding a candle and an auto tire, its calligraphy barely legible. He smiled to himself and let the moment of panic pass, become something else. He had not been fearful at all, he told himself, just apprehensive. Within seconds the apprehension had become mere caution. Yes, he convinced himself, you are prudent, and the terror of two minutes ago was prudence in the throes of creation. His self-esteem having restored itself, he drove two miles beyond the sign and saw the road.

The car moved heavily off the highway, down into the dry ditch and onto the twin wagon ruts that led to the distant butte. The tremor returned to his fingertips and his self assurance began to falter again. This, his source had told him over and over, was the big leagues.

The car pulled along its train of dust at a steady twenty miles per hour. A pair of lizards moved out of the dirt, crossed the road and were gone. He looked into the mirror, saw the last sliver of highway disappear and, instinctively, locked all four doors, his fingertips leaving a telling haze of perspiration on the silver button.

He saw the four posts in the distance and inhaled deeply, easing his foot downward lightly on the accelerator. He stopped the engine, let the drift of dust pass, and got out of the car, the intense heat touching the top of his head like a barber's towel. Walking quickly to the thatch shelter, he looked for snakes and, finding none, went underneath. It was eight feet by five, large enough for a small family who might have wanted nothing more than a brief respite from the pounding sun. He looked about for some trace of them and found nothing.

Five minutes elapsed, ten, fifteen. He returned to the car and started the engine so that the air conditioner could return him to the blue cushion of the twentieth century. He looked at his watch and was disgruntled. He had not wanted to do this in the daylight, and had said so. The tiniest glint seen from the highway would attract a state trooper, traveler, or some curious clown who would ask questions. It would have been better done at night, as he had said, but, looking at the haunting butte and at the dead swirl of hills once again, he was relieved that he had been overruled.

Taking a pair of dark sunglasses from the glove box, he blew the fine skein of dust off their lenses and deftly slipped them over his forehead; it was the kind of thing that he had seen the country club women do when something met their disapproval, an act of elegant pique. For a time it did not occur to him that this was a psychological act, but now he sensed burning on his forehead, a burning that was not of the sun. He felt watched, and the burn had been there for ten minutes without his realizing it. He shrugged it off, but not completely. Logic told him that there was no one here to watch, no one but the bird that rolled magnificently, bloused its wings, and seemed to hang from the sun.

He looked at his timepiece, decided to give his contact exactly thirty minutes more. The fidgets were getting to him.

The hanging vulture suddenly soared downward, flapped its wings, and shrieked at something behind the butte. Struggling skyward a few feet, it wheeled and repeated the process. This time it did not emerge, and Alan Bond felt a sense of disquiet crawl up his spine. He leaned against the seat of the great car and felt perspiration collecting at the base of his sunglasses, but he dared not move; he had been right all along—there was something or someone out there.

Three

Voris Arnold Mohler, universally known as Moe, watched the two snipers working in tandem. They had only one weapon and they shared it with an ease that made Moe aware that this was not the first time that they had been up to such shenanigans. It was the turn of the taller of the two, and the man knelt in the window and steadied himself like a true professional. Moe knew that the man had been an expert marksman with the Marine Corps and that his chances of hitting the target were more than good. From his vantage point behind the door Moe could see the crowd on the street below and wondered whether any would walk into the path of fire at an inopportune moment. The paper could get sued, and just now a lawsuit was all the *Sentinel* needed. Still, he could not take his eyes off the sniper, and it didn't occur to him to stop the proceedings. He looked around to find the hallway behind him still and empty.

"Okay, bastard," said the kneeling man to his partner, "here goes." He drew a bead on the target, pulled the rubber band to the limits of its length, and let fly. The paper clip flew forward in a whiz of dull aluminum and hit the rectangular object called a Bug-O-Cutor. There were sparks and a dull electrical crackling sound as the paper clip found its mark and dropped to the street below.

"Jesus, Roger," said the partner, Henry Underwood, "that's four I owe you."

Roger stood and laid the rubber band on a small wooden table. "Yes it is, Hen. When can I see some money?"

"Payday, like I said. Just don't dog me about it, okay?"

"Henry, dogging you for money is like swatting flies with a paper towel— lots of activity with no results. You now owe me four cheeseburgers. Four times in four days. Why don't you give it up, honcho?"

"I guess I'm just a compulsive gambler, Rog. How about we go double or nothin'?" A flicker of hope darted across Henry's face.

"That ploy is what used to be called Saigon Saturday Night. It indicates desperation. Are you desperate, Henry?"

" No, not really," said Henry, with desperation. "I just think eight cheeseburgers is better than four. It's something to think about."

"Believe me, I've thought about it. Winning bets with you and driving around on OPEC oil are not forays into confidence. Dig?"

"You're needling me again, Rog. Would I fuck you? Would I?"

"Let's just say I run for the Vaseline when I see you coming. Payday, Henry, is ten days off. At this rate, you'll be lucky to get a new chain for your bicycle."

Listening to this, Moe could not help smiling. As the dialogue continued, he heard Roger make one point after another concerning Henry's penchant for financial stalling.

Now Moe looked through the crack again and studied Roger. At six feet, three inches, Roger was the tallest employee on the staff. His brown hair and brown eyes complimented a face that might have, at one time, graced a recruiting poster, were it not for a touch of perpetual sadness that emanated from the eyes; sadness was not an emotion that the Marine Corps desired in its minions. And, too, Roger's pug nose and full lips made him a bit too pretty to convey the necessary pragmatic quality of a potential killer, a defender of the faith. On the other hand, Roger might have looked right at home in a Hong Kong whorehouse, so maybe the Marines had missed a bet with him after all. But Moe knew that these speculations were academic now, since at thirty-four Roger was beginning to develop not only a sea swell of paunch but a few eye wrinkles as well, cosmetic aberrations that could probably be attributed to the reporter's world of greasy meals and deadlines. The main thing that Moe liked about Roger, he admitted to himself, was the brutal honesty that had almost gotten old Rog fired in his early months. It was that same honesty that was now raking Henry over the coals for being a deadbeat. Had Moe been a betting man, he would have bet that Roger would collect the money within the specified time, and with interest.

Having almost forgotten what he came for, Moe was suddenly aware of the piece of paper in his hand, a memo that he had written to himself. He went to the elevator, descended to the city room, and told the switchboard operator to fetch Roger, dropping a broad hint as to his possible whereabouts.

Moe's office was a glassed-in cubicle that stood at the south end of the great room and, even without the glass votive to his rank, it would have been obvious to the casual observer that this was indeed where the buck stopped. The desk held an overflowing dead copy spike and what appeared to be reams of paper of varying sizes and colors. Moe's chair was a swivel job whose naugahyde arms had split down the sides, releasing cotton lint that was forever on his forearms. At the other side of the desk was a small love seat whose butt-sprung cushions spoke of years of torture suffered by those who had been ordered to locate there. The only other furnishings were a metal filing cabinet and a hat rack whose antlers had been standing in plastic omnipotence for as long as Moe could remember. He really had to speak to Lynch about some new furniture but, because of the current financial crisis, this was not the time. Besides, this thing that had come his way this morning had all the earmarks of an occurrence that would allow him to tell Lynch to take it all and shove it up his ass. Moe sat down, opened his desk drawer, and took out a miniature airplane, a World

War II Thunderbolt whose nickname had been "Jug." He spun its little propeller idly and waited for Roger.

"You wanted me, Chief?" Roger asked.

Without looking around, Moe said, "No. I wanted H. L. Mencken, Hodding Carter, and William Allen White. But you'll have to do. Sit down, Roger." He waved lazily toward the love seat.

Roger sat down uneasily and tried to read Moe's face. Expressivity was not one of his boss's strong points. There was a quality about Moe that did not allow extreme emotion to issue forth; at seven in the morning or at ten at night he still had that old long-nosed Schnauzer look of one who had seen it all and is forced to look again.

Moe stopped twirling the plane's little propeller long enough to scratch the top of his balding head, and this spotlighted his rather exotic hair style. Roger had noticed it on the first day that he had hired on. It had reminded him of several stalks of bamboo laid across an empty gymnasium floor, and it still did. Moe's part was slipping farther and farther down the side of his head nowadays, and soon he would be combing his ears if the part got any lower. His nose was flat and its tip made a screeching stop just above his thin lips. This, combined with a somewhat prominent chin, would render him the spitting image of a pelican if he ever lost his teeth. Moe was not pretty, but Roger thought the world of the crazy bastard. Even Moe's predisposition for ass-chewing was tempered with a fairness that left the chewee feeling great guilt and no anger. Voris Mohler was a hell of a city editor.

"What did I fuck up this time? The nephew murder trial?"

"Nope. You did quite well on that one."

Roger watched the airplane. When Moe had the plane out it was indicative of deep thought, usually of a troublesome nature.

"I give. This suspense is killing me. Chew away."

"No chewing, Rog. I tried to get you earlier. Where you been?"

"Upstairs with Henry."

"Doing what?"

"I've been fucking Henry, Moe."

"Funny, you don't look sweaty."

"Not that kind of fucking. The financial kind."

Moe's mouth smiled, but his eyes remained questing, slightly puzzled. It was his act. He loved the moment and decided to pursue it. "Tell me something, Roger, have you ever heard of the clip monster?"

Roger grinned and shook his head with quizzical, jerking motions. "Can't say I have, Moe."

"There is a monster who flies around this building at night and lays paper clips outside on the sidewalk. It had trouble in its chromosomes, though, because all its little clips are coming out bent. A creature like that goes nuts occasionally, I hear, the urge to reproduce being what it is. Maybe you could do a story on it."

"I'd like that, Moe," said Roger, easing into the spirit of the thing, knowing that he had been caught. "Dracula meets the Clip Bird. Sounds like a natural for the drive-ins, don't you think?"

"Uh huh. So from now on you and Henry keep the door closed and I'll pretend you're working on a screenplay. Which is another way of saying don't let brother Lynch catch you. As crotchety as he is these days, it could be fatal."

"Oh? That again?" Roger asked.

"You bet 'that again.' This paper is operating on the thinnest of shoestrings. Circulation is down from last year by a percentage that I don't even want to ponder. And there have been feelers from a chain, I hear."

"I'll go quietly, as long as my last paycheck is enough to put tires on my bicycle. How do you see the bottom line?"

"Don't see any bottom line just yet. That's the hell of being a peon, all eyes and ears and no brain. All I can say is that this paper is down and the count is at about three. If I had my way it'd be all ass and gossip, like the *National Enquirer.*"

Roger laughed at Moe's words. "Yeah, nothing succeeds nowadays like sex-cess. And we have to have a boss who thinks that taking a piss is the act of Satan. I wouldn't mind it if he was a religious nut, but he's just one of those assholes who spouts integrity and does his drinking behind the barn. Pure old Texas Baptist.''

"Yeah,'' said Moe, ''but he's still the asshole we gotta please. Between him and our readership, my job is like carrying a bomb through a snake pit. Bit or blasted, I lose either way.''

"You can have my job, Moe. I'd have already quit, but where else can I make three hundred a month?'' Roger said sarcastically.

"Don't knock it. Any goddam pay raises happen around here, yours truly is first in line. With Edna gone it looks like alimony city for sure. How's Darlene?''

Roger's face clouded slightly as he said, ''Gone, as usual. This time for good, I would imagine. We had a hot one last night. She clipped me with a can opener. Does it show?'' He pointed at an area above his left eye.

"Nah, not much. Kinda red, like you squeezed a pimple. That's what you could say if anybody asks. You learn to make up shit to tell people. Being separated makes you one helluva liar. In your case it matters not, since you two were cohabitating without benefit of clergy, as they say.''

Roger felt himself becoming a little uneasy talking about it. It was time to shift gears in the conversation. "So you sent for me,'' he said. ''What's brewing?''

Moe twirled the prop once, twice, three times. Finally he put the little plane away and placed his elbows on his desk. His old doggy eyes gazed at Roger and through him. ''Did I ever tell you about the ice cream man, Roger?'' he asked.

"Yes, Moe, you have. But I forgot the puncheroo.'' Roger was lying his ass off. He had not forgotten the puncheroo at all, but Moe liked to tell it, and he hated to lessen the old bastard's fun.

"I'll spare you the trivials, then,'' said Moe. ''Just rest assured that Voris Mohler has a sixth sense about certain things. I got a big one for you, Roger. Yes, sir, this is gonna be a big one. You remember Rix?''

"A ranger? Something of a smart ass?''

"The same. Anyhow, Rix owes me a favor. I mentioned his name about six months ago on that Mexican murder ring thing. So old Rix called me about thirty minutes ago and hints broadly about something that may prove to be exclusive. You know the old dirt road that leads to the Hopkins Cattle Pens?''

"Yeah. About twelve miles to the west. All rocks and sage.''

"That's the one. Rix has a scanner in his car. About an hour ago he heard a tow truck driver talking to base. This guy says that there is a car that looks like a Rolls Royce sitting in the boonies about two miles beyond there just off the highway. Being the nosy sort that he is, Rix investigates and calls me. Guess what?''

"A body.''

"Nope. Two. A Mexican and a Caucasian. Gunshots having terminated both. Rix is going to wait for you out there and hold off the dogs as long as possible. There is something brewing on this one that I can't quite fit into the box of logic so far. Rix is not the type to get worked up over nothing, so it must be something. The old two and two adds up, almost. What I can't decipher is just why Rix is being so good to me all of a sudden. Maybe it was an attack of conscience, or something. Anyhow, I want you to get out there right away. He's waiting on you. Take a camera and a van and depart thee from my sight.''

Roger was already moving. "Got you, Chief. Maybe this will get me a day off if I handle it right, huh?''

"That'll be the goddam day,'' Moe growled.

Roger went into the city room and was immediately surrounded by the dull, katydid buzz of another day's news. Cigarette smoke hung like a shroud over the place. Grabbing a set of keys off an old pegboard that hung in a corner near the teletype machine, he winked at Mrs. John Cable, the rewrite lady. She lit another Pall Mall and regarded him as a bit of dust that she really must get around to sweeping up someday. He was aware that she hated everyone generally, and himself specifically, the reason being that she did not like the star quality that Moe had assigned him. Jealousy and cigarettes were all that held the old bitch together, and Roger could not help but strut just a little as he walked past her desk.

In the basement, standing in spiteful semiretirement against a stained concrete wall, loomed a black van that Roger had come to call Nicodemus because of its inherent propensities for being a sputtering, rattling son of a bitch. It had a rusted fender, no hubcaps, and a cracked windshield. Some years ago, when the paper was not in the dire circumstances of the present, Lynch had hired a painter to write the word *Sentinel* on the doors of all the paper's utility vehicles. The man had been a jack leg sort, and cheap paint had been employed, paint that was now mostly gone or indecipherable.

Roger ran a thumbnail under what was left of the second "e" and tore it loose, creating a little snowfall of acrylic on the concrete floor. This ordeal had been his before, and he knew that the TV bastards, prideful and overpaid and overloved as they were, would be there in their sixty-grand rigs complete with cameras, whirling radar screens for storm scan, and all the other accoutrements of the radar age. Roger felt that he was in Matthew Brady's wagon, but the engine roared to life at the first touch of the key and he drove up and out into the June heat.

He got caught in the turgid mid-morning traffic that consisted of housewives who did not know or did not care how to drive, and he did not breathe easily until he was on the northwest side of the city. He wanted to go to his apartment to check on Darlene, but his own good sense and memory of the previous night, coupled with Moe's almost breathless urgency about this story, kept him on the highway. Committed to what he had to do, he eased the accelerator down and went into the baked prairie at eighty miles per hour. If things worked right, he could get the story and be out of the area before the TV crew even got wind of it.

As he was coming from the east, the promontory in the distance seemed to swirl around slowly like the skirt of a lazy flamenco dancer, its pocked face taking on a different touch of shadow with every turn of the highway. He saw the Rolls Royce and one car just behind it and knew that he was either very early or very late. Instinct made him think that he had at last staggered in the right direc-

tion, and that Moe's "big" one was starting out so far
so good.

Easing the van off the highway, he drove along the dry
ditch for a few yards until he found the almost indiscernible ruts of the little road that led to the promontory. The
van protested with steely clatterings and, finally, the swell
of a low brown hill lifted him out of the rocks. In the
near distance a tall man stood beside a white Plymouth
and, just beyond the car was the leanto, a collection of
posts that had once held foliage or perhaps animal skins
as a pitiful respite from the sun. Two lumps, like dis-
carded sacks of rags but unmistakably human, were coiled
under the little shelter. Standing away from this motley
scene like a thoroughbred in a barnyard, the Rolls Royce
glinted imperiously in the morning sun. It was a crazy
scene, but Roger was accustomed to crazy scenes. Stopping the van, allowing the cloud of dust to pass, Roger
hoped that the bodies did not yet smell. He had had
enough of that in Nam.

Stepping down, he approached the tall man and said,
"Brother Rix."

"Brother Wilder," the man answered coldly.

"Whatta we got?"

"What the hell's it look like?" Rix said.

Roger looked at the dead men, sucked the scene in
quickly. One Mex, one Caucasian. Gunshot wounds.
Turning to Rix he said, "The tide comes in, the tide goes
out, but your shit personality goes on forever. I hear
you're outta work. That right?"

"And I hear that rag you work for is about to fold.
Any truth to it?"

"Who knows? They tell me what they want me to
know, which is goddam little. Are you self-employed
now?"

Rix lifted a cowboy boot and ground out a cigarette on
the instep. "You could say that, I guess. I'm trying to
start up my own agency. Private dick."

"Good boy. You'll make it." Roger wondered why he
suddenly felt compassion for this prick. Rix was a sarcastic piece of shit. Being out of work had not knocked

the snot nose out of him. "What do you make of it?"
He nodded at the bodies.

"Long range. Dum dums, I figure. The Mex is missing a good deal of his back. The white one ain't got no
face on the down side. Yeah, dum dums."

"God," said Roger, "whoever it was, he was either
good or close."

"Good, I'd say." Rix pointed at the promontory. "He
hit them from over there from about the crest."

"How do you know?"

"They were standing under that shelter talking. They
both fell away from the hill. The bullet hit the Mex just
above the heart and popped out lower-lung-wise."

Roger studied the bodies again. The Mexican was one
of those nondescript Latinos who might have just stepped
down out of a laborer's truck, except for the dark suit he
was wearing. The Caucasian was dressed in a gray three-
piece suit, something shimmery. Sharkskin. The delicate
way that he held his hands, even in death, indicated that
he had been something of a blueblood. His sparse hair,
rather than having been trimmed, had been downright
sculpted into a suede skullcap.

"Whataya think, M-l?" Roger asked.

"Yeah. Or some other form of 30-30. He meant for
them to twitch not at all. My guess is they were dead
before the sound got here, especially the white one.
There's traces of brain all down his back."

"I smell fag," Roger stated.

"Nope." Rix answered.

"Why not?"

"Can't say, really. Just don't. It's the Mexican that
screws the fag theory."

"So why can't a Mexican be a fag?" Roger asked. Rix
was again relapsing into his arrogant manner; he had a
way of being self-assured to the point of obnoxiousness.

"Just take my word, son, when this is cleared up you'll
find that this was not a fag episode." Rix smiled at him
and lit a filtered Lucky.

Roger turned away to formulate an argument but saw
that two State cars had turned off the highway and were
speeding toward them. Even in the rolling dust Roger

could see that there were two men in each car. They stopped behind the van side by side. All four men alit hurriedly and all wore suits, Stetsons, and cowboy boots. They seemed to tower over the area. It was little wonder that they were the stuff of legend.

"Morning Rix," said the one who was obviously the leader. There was a coolness in his tone and he did not smile. "May I ask what you are doing here?"

"I got a right to be here, Cap, same as you. I'm private now. My scanner works as good as yours."

"So what's a private eye doing here? Gotta be booze or whores to get you up this time of day."

"Allegiance to justice, Cap. I see you haven't lost your ability to be snotty. And I ain't had a drink in sixty days, if it makes you feel any better."

"It don't make me feel nothin'," the captain said, walking on.

Within a matter of seconds the whole Rix thing had been cleared up and Roger congratulated himself on having not pressed Rix about it. Somebody like Rix, bastard though he was, could come in handy down the line if he made a go of his private practice. Boozer, ass chaser, and general fuck-up, Rix was the sort of character who always got rich or got killed before he hit forty. Listening to the whiz of a Japanese camera as one of the Rangers made pictures, Roger watched Rix's mouth contort in rage and shame.

"This is an official investigation, Rix," said the captain, "and you have no part of it other than in a voluntary basis. Do we comply?"

"We comply," Rix acknowledged.

"All right, now that we know who's who, what have you got?"

"Not a lot. One Cauc, one Mex. Possible 30-30 dum dum, maybe not, and maybe. Note that a good deal of one head is missing, though. I go with dum dum fired from that peak over there."

"You'd have made a good Ranger, Rix," said the captain.

"I did, sir. But I guess that's over now." Roger could not determine whether it was a statement or a plea.

"Yes, that's over. Any ideas on this one an old man might overlook?"

"Roger here wants to call it a queer thing, but I say no. You know how these news jackoffs are." He looked at Roger disdainfully.

The captain smiled at Roger and extended his hand. "How's it goin', news jackoff?"

"Very well, Cap. And you?"

"Not bad for an old man with hemorrhoids. You keepin' Moe out of jail?"

"I just stay out of his way, generally speaking."

"So why the queer guess, Roger?"

Roger felt at once very important and very foolish. The captain was seriously asking his opinion. "Just an idea, Cap. Why drive a Rolls full of dope down a country highway? That would be like leading a camel through a synagogue. The Cauc looks a bit effete, too." Roger shrugged. "Just a theory."

"Remind me to buy a dictionary someday. You may be right, but I doubt it." The captain turned to look at the Rolls, and Rix winked at Roger in triumph.

A red-haired Ranger had extracted the wallets of both men and began to read aloud: "Alan Bond. Brown and blue. Age fifty-six. 4334 Lemmon Heights, Dallas." He removed two small sheets of paper from the bill section and studied them. "Looks like he might be a jeweler. Yeah. And the Rolls is rented from Executive Leasing Company."

"Rented?" the captain asked. "Who in hell would rent a Rolls?"

"Somebody that couldn't buy one," said Red.

"Very funny. Read to me about the Mexican."

"Raimundo Gomez. Tijuana, Mexico. *Sinco Sinco. Recuerdo.* I don't read Mex, Cap."

"It's like . . . souvenirs and such," Rix volunteered.

Red stood and handed the captain the wallets. Cap held the leather in his hands and slapped them together as if to spook out clues. "A jeweler and a dealer in souvenirs. Dallas and Tijuana. Jewels and souvenirs. Souvenirs and jewels. Jesus." He squinted off toward the promontory.

Rix suddenly snapped his fingers and said, "Look down at the bottom somewhere on the Mex's cards, Cap. Look for the word *negocios.*"

The captain threw Rix a glare but then did as instructed. "Yeah, here it is."

"So that's it," Rix said with quiet piety. "The man is indeed a dealer in souvenirs."

"Hooray," the captain said without feeling. "So he comes all the way from Tijuana to get shot out here in the boondocks. Why?"

None answered. Roger instinctively took out his note-pad and began to scribble. Up to now the most interesting thing had been the Rolls and its presence in this unlikely surrounding, but now a dose of sinister occurrence had been injected into the matter. The thing was beginning to feel heavy, and he found himself breathing hard. He started to ask the captain to venture an opinion but saw that all eyes were riveted on something behind him. Turning, he saw that three men were staring at them from the great windshield of a monstrous bus, like owls looking down at mice. Roger stifled a groan as he recognized John Holt, newscaster and ego, in that order.

"Oh, Christ," said the captain. "The circus is about to begin."

Holt got out first and his cameraman followed. The driver went to the dark confines of the rear of the bus to serve as engineer. "Captain, sir," Holt greeted. "Get the bodies, White," he ordered the cameraman.

"In answer to your questions, Holt," the captain announced dourly, "no we ain't got a clue, and no, we do not want to go on live camera, and no, we do not want to be taped. Not just yet."

"Fine, Captain, Sir," said Holt with no trace of rejection. He walked over to the Rolls and sat down on the car's fender.

The captain smiled and said, "Holt, that car has not been fingerprinted. If you do not remove your buns from that hood in one second I will have to follow you to San Antone to get the toe of my boot out of your ass. The reason that I am not yelling is that it excites my blood which rushes straight to my hemorrhoids. Do you savvy?''

Holt nodded and got off the fender, looking rather hangdog.

Rix grinned and said, "You want these news jackoffs gone, Sir?" He looked at Holt and at Roger and the grin faded.

"I'll decide that, Rix. Your day of giving orders is over."

"Yes sir," said Rix. He inhaled deeply on his Lucky and looked away.

In an attempt to grease burned egos, Red interjected, "Cap, I smell two killers. Pros, maybe."

The captain forgot Holt and Rix and went over to Red, who was kneeling, country style, his hat pulled down low over his forehead. "I'm up for grabs, Red. Speak."

"Forget that queer thing, Cap. It's dope or jewels."

The captain looked at the other two Rangers who had generally been ignoring the politics of the moment. They were hunkered near the rear fender of the Rolls, sniffing and jabbering. "You guys got anything yet?" he asked.

"Not so much as a whiff, Cap," said one. "Nary a hollow fender, nary a weird hubcap, no new screws, no new paint. It could be in the tires, but I doubt it."

The captain, looking fatigued and hemorrhoidaly pained, said, "What gets me is how the Mexican got here. Damnit, I get the feeling these two met here; they did not come here together. And our third party knew that they were going to be here. Anybody got any ideas?" He rubbed the vicinity of his buttocks, thought better of it, and studied each face.

"Could be the Mex came with the third party and then the third party shot both," Roger offered.

"Nope," said Rix. "There was one set of tire prints when I got here, and they belong to the Rolls. My theory is that he parked on the highway out there, loped to that high spot over there, and waited for a clear shot."

"So how did the Mex get here, then?" the captain asked.

"Who knows?" Red asked. "Anybody know if that little old dip shit bus line runs past here?" Nobody did.

"That could be it, Cap. Whattaya you think, Hardy?" The question was directed to one of the kneeling Rangers.

"I think they are awful dead," said Hardy.

There was heavy laughter all around, but the captain glared at Hardy and the noise died instantly.

"May I offer a theory?" It was Holt.

"Hell, yes. Pot luck me."

"This thing shrieks of double cross. It waves flags, for chrissake. One of these two had a hunk of money for a payoff of some kind. Find the money and you got your killer."

"Brilliant," said the captain. "And how did you come up with that one?"

Holt looked queasy, sweaty. "You got a dead pair with no dope, no jewels, no money. It can't be common shit, or they'd have taken the Cauc's watch, not to mention the Rolls. And it ain't queer, because a queer will always leave his mark in one way or another—it comes with the territory."

"You seem to know a lot about queers," said Hardy, snickering.

"Asshole!" Holt retorted.

"Cut the shit," the captain interrupted. "Maybe Holt is right. And maybe he isn't. Anyhow, here comes the meat wagon. You guys about done?"

"Yep. We can get the Rolls towed in, but I got a sawbuck says we don't find nothing a-tall," said Hardy.

The square ambulance moved toward them, its roof lights blooping soundlessly, redly, foolishly. Feeling the thing slipping away from him, the captain moved toward the promontory as if to gain a new perspective. All followed, except for Hardy, who stayed to supervise the moving of the bodies. After ten minutes of scuffed shoes and ripped pants, all arrived at the crest sweating and wheezing. From this site they could see the distant lizard's tail of highway and then more hills and mesquite. It was pure Texas for a million miles. Hardy and the ambulance men resembled chitinous insects standing hungrily over crumbs.

"Anything?" the captain asked Rix.

"Nope, not that I can see. He was a pro. Not a print, not a casing."

"Captain, sir, could we go on now?"

"On what, Holt?"

"On the air, Sir." He was holding his mobile microphone outward toward the captain's face. The cameraman was lining them up.

"Oh, that. Yeah, I don't see why not. Only it's got to be on tape, not live. There is such a thing as next of kin, you know."

"Yessir, tape it is."

Tired of it all, Roger wandered alone back down the hill and watched as the ambulance moved over the barren landscape and back toward the highway. He said to Hardy, "Whattaya think, honcho?"

"It's a tough one, Rog. But, to be honest, I go with dope all the way. There is a mouton lining in the trunk of this car. Mouton! Can you feature that shit? This thing cost more than I'll make in the next five years. That's why I go with dope."

"But it was rented, Hardy. Why was the goddam thing rented?"

Hardy swatted his shoulder and said, "That's the reporter in you talking. I look at their arms and find no marks, and that is what puzzles me. You look at a rented car and that's what puzzles you. Perspective is a funny thing, ain't it?"

"Yeah. Hilarious."

"They been dead a pretty good while, I'd guess. Two more for the bone yard. Two more Mafia bastards gut shot. *C'est la guerre*, as the Frenchman says."

"What'll happen to the bodies?"

"The usual. A quick runover by the coroner or his assistant, and then shipped out. That Mex will be in Tijuana by sundown. Bet on it."

"And why's that?"

"Because this is Texas," Hardy answered.

"One dead Mexican does not for good relations make, huh?"

"Uh huh. Especially a *nacional*. They hear about it on the Mexican side of town and there'll be a protest march and ninety rumors of racial shit. So we get 'em out as fast as possible. No crap, no hassle.''

"What's the deal on Rix?" Roger asked, knowing part, wanting to know all.

Hardy snickered. "Ass. Booze. Showin' up for work with no shave and no sleep. General infirmities of the spirit, you might say. You ever been to his apartment? Jesus, the pornography! You'd think he had his private supplier, the books and shit he's got."

"In spite of his pricky nature, he seems like a good cop."

"There's more to it than impressing the captain at times like these," Hardy countered a little harshly. "Frankly, I think the bastard is on the take from somebody. Nothing I can prove, just a feeling."

Roger started to speak but saw the others coming down the hill. Holt was interviewing the captain on the run and Rix and Red were making chopping motions with their hands as they talked. The air was aswirl with opinions and Roger was glad that he was not up there among them. A dull despair settled over him as he realized that this would be one of those things that Moe would hang over like a bulldog pawing at an ant hill.

He sat in the van and pretended to write as the Rangers left, followed by the news bus. For a long while he sat and looked at the shelter, at the blood stains and sample scrapings underneath. The Rolls stood in haughty diffidence, like a nun waiting beside a road for a bus that might or might not be coming. Thinking that he had experienced basically all involving the Rolls and the two bodies, he headed back toward town.

Four

The old Dodge was parked on a flat area that stood off the highway by several yards. It was one of the few flat areas to be found and, in the hellish sun, the sand was as warm and as yellow as butcher's salt. The hills and rocks in the distance were yellow in the high areas, orange in the low areas. Orange and yellow were the colors of Mexico, he concluded, and they could keep the whole country. Some fifteen miles to the west the ocean made its sudden thrust against the land and, by straining his eyes, he imagined that he could even see terns hanging above the breakers. Just a mile inland lay the village, a mostly rectangular assortment of adobe and tin that rose from the heated stillness like a series of blisters. Once again he looked to the north and northeast, his blue eyes following the undula of tan highway. Certainly the world's shortage of fuel could not be blamed on the Mexicans, for in his two hours here not one vehicle had passed.

Now an old Mexican appeared from behind a small rising in the floor of the desert, and he watched as the man led a mule over a hill and disappeared behind another. He waited for ten minutes and then stepped down from the car and cupped his hands over his eyes. Walking toward the highway, he wished that he had bought the sombrero in San Luis Potosi. The purchase would have been made, had it not been for the lady with the almond eyes who led him to her hotel room. This was the first time that he had thought of the hat since yesterday, or of the woman. She had been fat and had smelled of sweat and bacon grease.

When the old man saw him, he and the mule paused in the roadway for a moment and then came toward him apprehensively, the old one speaking to the mule as a father might coax a shy child toward a party.

"*Buenos dias,*" the old one whispered.

"Good day, sir. The bus from Tijuana, does it come from that way?" The tall one pointed to the north.

"*¿Norteamericano?*"

"Uh, *si.* Yes. The bus?"

The old man went to the rear end of the mule and looked. He caressed the animal's rump and smiled. "*Si?*"

"No, not the mule. The bus. The . . .ah . .*camion?*"

"Ah, *si.*"

"Good. When?"

The old one paused in his lover's caress of the mule's rump and studied the situation, his old eyes looking first at the sun and then at the highway. He knelt and drew a circle in the dust at the roadside and made tiny clock hands, one at twelve, the shorter at two. "*¿Comprende?*"

"*Si.* At about two o'clock. Thank you. Uh, *buenos dias.*"

The old one smiled, pulled at the rope halter and shuffled away, his head bent slightly as though he were listening to voices from the sand.

The tall one watched him go and rubbed the clock from the dust with his shoe. Again cupping his eyes with his hands, he looked skyward and judged the time to be twelve, perhaps a little after. As he walked back toward the car he cursed himself for having never bothered to learn any but the fundamental Spanish, for having clung to the theory that ascendancy should be the desire of all peoples, especially of Third Worlders. But just now he could not help feeling that his quarter-century of condescension might be catching up with him.

He got into the car, started its engine, and pushed the button designated *Fan.* Since buying the car in Mexico City, he had studied its idiosyncrasies, its acceleration, its penchant for oversteer. It was a good car, and one that would serve his purpose until he got to the United States. He would abandon it at the border and continue the trip by airplane, by rented car. The thought of these impending conveyances thrilled him, but not without somehow carrying with the thrill a touch of sadness at having to abandon this one, the first automobile that he had ever owned. They had warned him back at the camp that a Mexican license plate would never do in the United States, that the American Border Patrol would check him every hundred miles or so. For a people who prided themselves on freedom for all, the Americans indulged in certain hypocrisies that were open to question.

A small bug, red and black, moved across the seat and he watched it for several seconds before crushing it and dropping its body outside. There was a tiny rent in the fabric and he imagined that the bug had been hiding there all this time. With a finger he expanded the tear upward so that it stood like a barn roof, the inverted V of cloth arching starkly over the cotton padding beneath. At once his thoughts carried him back to Russia, to another barn whose roof stood out over a six-inch crust of October snow. The others had gone ahead for the parents, but he had told them that the girl was in the barn, that he would wait for her. They had laughed at that, their laughter clashing in counterpoint to the clatter of their weapons as they ran. He had shivered for two hours, fearful of advancing out of the treeline, across the snow and toward the barn. After two hours the lint of nightstare had begun to fuzz his vision, but it cleared when he saw her. She was less than ten yards from the barn when he fired once and saw her go down, her pistol sliding across the veneer of ice to her front. She was a mass of blood from the stomach downward when he got to her, his feet measuring his slow progress across the snow like a metronome of death. At that moment the others had come back with the parents, a pair of old and bent shadows who breathed heavy steam into the night. After they had questioned the parents and cut their throats, the soldiers had acknowledged his nickname: Ableiter, lightning rod. A private named Mende had said that it was a name he deserved, since that which was sought had come to him. Mende did not know that he had originally acquired the name much earlier in life, and Mende would never know, since Mende was later caught by partisans and beheaded. So much for bugs and barns and beheaded privates.

A tiny glitter of light popped from the northwest and then disappeared. He stared through the windshield and waited and was quickly rewarded with another glitter. It had to be the bus. If one followed the logic of the Mexican bus company, then today had to be the day, since yesterday was not the day, but neither did today have to be the day if sandstorm, flood, riot, or bandits impeded the progress of the bus. It ran every forty-eight hours on perfect schedule, unless it did not. What was amazing was that anyone in Mexico ever arrived anywhere.

He rubbed his wrist and noticed that there was no perspiration, the result of this dry heat, he surmised. It was totally unlike the jungle in every regard, even in how it sucked the life from one's body. Wristwatches were good for only a few months in the jungle, the perspiration from the wrist gnawing upward into the springs. For once he was happy about this, since last month Ohlendorf had won his watch with a pair of *Königon*. Let the homely bastard have the watch; he would get a new one as soon as he got to the United States.

He reached into the back seat and freesnapped the lock on the naugahyde case. Traveling supplies. A pair of white cotton gloves, a small plastic box of dental floss, and a pair of ancient binoculars whose rotator bore a small black *swastika*. Stuffing the first two into pockets of his tan jacket, he lifted the third to his eyes and peered to the north. The bus was red and white, and its top bore chickens in wooden cages. He could even read the name on the hood: REO. He had once seen the name on a bus in Ascuncion but, of late, they were mostly Chevrolets.

When the bus passed he allowed it two minutes and then started his engine and followed, driving slowly. The old man and the mule were still plodding along as he passed, both their heads bobbing in that lazy cadence that he had seen in all brown people who walk toward errands that availed them nothing more than another day in which to live. The sons of *Negerns* were quickly becoming the

Jews of the modern era, leeches here, oil barons there, and he felt a sense of sadness at realizing that he would not be around for their eradication.

The tail of the bus was a tiny square in the distance and he sped slightly, assuring himself that he would not lose sight of it. The ring of hills that separated the sea from the village rose up as he descended and the village loomed larger than he had imagined it from the distance. Each building took on a definite separateness as he neared, and he slowed as the bus turned off the highway and stopped in front of a two story edifice whose side bore the word *Zapateria*. When he was within two hundred yards of the village, he nosed the car off the highway and let the motor idle. After stopping the engine, he picked up the binoculars and watched as the vehicle vomited its passengers.

The first person off the bus was Rosa Portillo. He had seen her perhaps twice in or near the camp, a squatty girl of about twenty-five, sweaty and braided. A small boy was driving a platoon of white ducks along the street and Rosa stepped backward to let them pass. Now the man named Sanchez stepped down and berated the boy, his disdain being directed at the duck shit along the dusty and unpaved driveway. Having proved his allegiance to cleanliness, Sanchez turned and took two suitcases from the driver. The bus groaned and lifted itself onto the highway like a fat man rising from an easy chair, and Rosa and Sanchez walked into the village and were swallowed by its heated alabaster walls.

Ableiter started the car, drove into the village, and parked in the alleyway beside the *Zapateria*. Rosa and Sanchez were now forty meters up the narrow street, the woman waddling, the man straining beneath the suitcases. They paused at a small adobe hut whose only claim to grandeur was a green door. Sanchez dropped the cases, fumbled for a key. When they were inside, the street was empty.

Now Ableiter looked into his rearview mirror and saw that there was nothing behind him. He paused long enough to look again at the scar on his left cheek, a three-pronged fan that was a bit less than one inch long. The years had mellowed it, absorbed it into his skin, but, in his own mind, it was as red and as ugly as the day on which he had suffered it. Rather than being a thing of disgust, it was a personal symbol of pain well borne, almost a rune of survival. He tapped it with his fingertip and felt the dull nervelessness beneath, a ritual that he always honored when about to embark on anything that might cause pain. Nothing could hurt like it had hurt him on that day in 1943 when the Russians had unleashed a barrage of white phosphorous shells, blasting and roasting to death the four who had been in the hole with him. He hadn't screamed, not even when rinsing the sizzling chemical away with the lung blood of a dying corporal. The corporal had stared at him with eyes that were uncomprehending and hating in death glaze. Ableiter had patted the man's hand and thanked him for his blood.

He put on the cotton gloves, tore off a two-foot strand of the dental floss, and stepped into the shadow of the building. As he walked toward the green door, his eyes followed the heat shimmers between each of the houses on either side; it was as though he might be watching a tennis match played with a hand grenade. A goat wandered across his path, its tether rope dangling impotently in the dust, and he shooed the animal into an alley. He stopped in front of the green door, looked down the street at the car, and tapped twice.

"*¿Si?*" It was the voice of the woman.

"*¿Que tal?*" he said softly, hoping that they were the proper words.

A lock snapped from within and the door opened slightly. He kicked the wood at its base and lunged forward, his left hand finding the woman's mouth as the cotton glove muffled her attempt to scream. Her eyes widened in a glare that was both fearful and hating and, as she tried to move backwards, he followed her into the room, his eyes coming to rest on a distant window sill. Sanchez had already gone out the window, but his hand was perched on the sill as he steadied himself in his frenzy of flight.

"Halt!" Ableiter said without emotion, his right hand entwining the floss about the girl's neck. He spun her around and held her between himself and the window, his right hand taking up the slack in the fine white string. The room smelled of old ashes and fresh peppers. The suitcases stood on the floor near a wooden table. For a moment the place was silent.

Sanchez stood, his lithe body shading the openness of the window. It was almost as though a painting had suddenly graced the barren wall, a portrait of a brown man whose desperation with the follies of life had been caught by the artist's brush, even down to the clear sweat that ran from his neck onto his shirt. But it was in the eyes that the sadness was most profound, most visible, for in those brown circles was all the defeat that had ever been suffered by mankind. He looked at the woman as if to ask forgiveness.

"Ist die Frau ihre Freundin?" Ableiter asked.

"Ja," said Sanchez, nodding at her, attempting a smile that did not materialize.

"Then come in, and let us reason together."

Sanchez tiredly lifted one leg and slid across the sill and into the room, his eyes never leaving those of Rosa. He sat at the small table and drummed his fingers across the wooden top. "Thank you for speaking English," he said. "It is easier for me. German is such a difficult thing to understand. As are Germans."

Ableiter let the slur pass and said, "Where is it?"

Sanchez looked at the suitcases and then back at the man. His shoulders sagged slightly and his sweaty face took on a pink tint. It was as though the pride of his blood had cooled and left him to bleach on a shore of hopelessness, like a fish caught and thrown away.

"It is in Tijuana. A man named Gomez has it. He is a seller of . . . *recuerdo*. Will you free her?"

"Of course. *¿Cuanto questa?"* Ableiter's hands fluttered like wasp wings at the woman's neck.

"All the money. All that is left. Nine thousand pesos." He nodded downward at the suitcases. "With the rest we bought clothing, wine, hotels."

Ableiter pulled the floss backward with a sudden jerk, twisting it as he did so, his eyes watching as a thin mist of red clouded the white. Rosa tried to claw at his arms but missed the mark and appeared to relax as the floss bit on through her throat. Sanchez was up and running toward them as the woman's body hit the floor, her mouth yawning and pinching shut in a slow motion parody of the laconic manner of a jungle turtle. Ableiter leaned forward just as Sanchez slammed into him and bounced off. Now the German squared his shoulders and lunged upward, his hands never relaxing their grip on the floss. By the time Sanchez had fallen heavily on his back, groaning, Rosa's head had been nearly severed. Performing a lithe pirouette, Ableiter relaxed his grip, allowed the body to fall to the floor, and kicked Sanchez in the center of his belly, memory reminding him that a belly kick neutralized the power to scream. The Indian gasped once, sweat beadlets appearing on his forehead as he stared at the ceiling joists, at the pinpricks of sunlight whose presence in the rotten roof were as strangely tranquil as votive candles seen from afar. He continued to stare, unable to breathe or even to move in these last seconds, his hands formed as talons over the tormented hollowness where his stomach should have been. He wanted to breathe. He wanted to live. He did not want to die in Mexico. He did not want the huge man, whom he had always hated at the camp and who now stood above him with yet another strand of white, to do what he was about to do. There was so much life left, so many plans dreamed over a thousand nights that were unfulfilled. As the German bent down over him he closed his eyes and saw the face of the Blessed Virgin, saw the tears in her eyes.

Ableiter moved backwards without standing. The pain in his own stomach had flashed, cooled, flashed again. With measured movements, his hands curved over his belly; he was at last able to rise, his staring eyes never leaving the bodies whose necks now appeared to be swaddled in red pennants. One of his hands found the adobe wall and the texture of years of smoke grit felt warm against his palm. It had been well over a third of a century since he had killed, and he had mused often in that time of waiting as to whether it was a skill inherent or acquired, a skill not reflected in the act, but in the subsequent emotion. War killing and civilian killing were the same, he knew at last, lancing and draining one of many mental boils that had been burgeoning for nearly four decades. He removed his hand from the wall, looked at the smoke grit, wiped it on his trousers. It was his left hand. It did not tremble.

He had memorized the sounds and tempos of death a long time ago, and thus it was that he knew already that no one had heard, that no one would be immediately coming. Like swimming or riding a bicycle, killing was a response act whose brain groove remained a clear channel in perpetuity. But it went deeper than that, involved more than the physical act of taking life; yes, he now realized, it was not the killing but the reaction to it that was so extraordinary. That reaction was a warmth on the spirit, a nostalgic yearning for a time when men had been more than mere humans; gods, they had been.

Coming back from memory's soundless caves, he looked down at the dead pair and saw that the universal, ubiquitous, tireless fly walked on Rosa's eyes, pausing occasionally to rub its forelegs together. In Russia, sometimes at twenty below zero, disturbed bodies yielded up flies, especially those body piles whose depth created an abundance of methane.

He lifted Rosa Portillo's skirt and lay it back gently against her belly. She wore white satin panties that had been new perhaps twenty-four hours ago, but which were now piss-soaked and blood-crusted at the edges. Indians were by nature dirty people, especially those of her tribe, and this was possibly the first pair of panties that the cunt had ever owned. It was obviously Sanchez who had bought these garments, his probable motive being the creation of a banana-republic Pygmalion. God, what a distance the world had to go in order to make most of its humans bathe! He kicked down hard with the heel of his shoe, the contact making a dull, explosive sound against her pubic bone. Ignorant, stupid, and unattractive, this one had outwitted her husband, the Indian called Portillo. Even the most stupid of women had one talent that was as natural as bleeding, that talent being the ability to deceive.

Now he looked at her with benevolent eyes. It was the sort of gaze one might affix to a mischievous puppy who had died. Had she not been so treacherously involved in this whole thing, there might have been no way to track Sanchez. So, in effect, this crusted, bruised, malodorous pussy that lay on the floor was the source of his current good fortune. She had been the key to his departure from the jungle, the very linchpin of his own release.

He had known that Tomas Portillo lay under the pier; indeed, he had at one time stifled snickers while pissing over the Indian's feet. During the great hunt, he had staked himself on the pier, allowing no one to come near, directing firing operations from the vicinity of the snake bucket.

He, Ableiter, had known all the time that it would be he who was sent to retrieve the purloined object.

He, Ableiter, had known all the time that he had to get out of the jungle, to get to a Yanqui doctor.

It was downright sinister that all was working so well up to now. One could never loosen his grasp for one moment, never stop planning, though, even when it was working.

It had been a good ten minutes, and a fortunate ten minutes, a time of renewal, resurrection, rededication. All was going to go well. All that now remained was to get to Tijuana, lock in on the trail which would doubtlessly lead into the United States, call Montreal for the name of a "safe" doctor.

He checked his shoes and clothing for blood, took the remaining money from the suitcase, and went outside into the incredible heat of the Mexican afternoon.

Five

Roger parked the van in front of the town house complex and looked at his watch. It was a little after two. He knew without going in that the place was empty, that she and her clothes were gone. It was the thought of seeing the barren closet that bothered him most; a human body could be absent for a million years and leave no haunting, no track, no scent, but an empty closet was one of the most hateful of all voids.

Without looking up, exhibiting a somewhat sad demeanor, he walked among the bicycles, garden hoses, and brown shrubbery to his door. He had been planning for some time to tell the owners of the place to go to hell. His reasoning would have been that the area was never cleaned, mowed, painted, but in his guts he knew that it was the incredible middle-classedness of the place that was getting to him; it was a low income crash zone for middle-class losers like himself. It was shabby without any of the impending luster of Bohemia to which he might someday point with pride at having lived there. Having now dehumanized himself to the point that his nerve endings could stand the emptiness within, he turned the key and entered his apartment.

The place smelled of furniture polish, unvacuumed carpet and that inherently indefinable dullness to the nostrils that rented dwellings never quite dispel. His eyes immediately went to the board and brick bookshelf that they had conceived and stained and stacked together. The picture was gone, as he had known that it would be.

Roger sat in the blue chair with the floral pattern and studied the almost invisible stains on the rounded arms. It was there that she always sat after getting out of the shower. He could never be sure whether it was mere water or a mixture of water and sexual effluvia that had darkened the fabric.

Darlene. Maker of stroganoff, tacos, fondue.

Darlene. Discusser of Albania's position on the Adriatic.

Darlene. Hottest piece of ass in Texas.

Roger knew that he could replace her. Yes, he could. He could, yes, by God, replace her.

No, by God, he could not, he knew just as certainly three seconds later. When it came down to what Moe called the nut cutting, she was at least a number two.

He went to the phone, called in the story, told Mrs. Cable that he might not be in until much later, and hung up before she could relay the message to Moe.

Again, the chair caught his eye. It was in that chair that it had all started, or had begun to end, depending on how he chose to look at it. Three days ago, just as the sun was setting, she had emerged from the shower and had sat on his lap there, naked and dripping. He had licked water off her back, the tiny drops having already acquired, through some osmosis, the hint of her sexuality in the taste. It was a strange thing about her, he recalled, this ability to exude sexuality even through the blandest of occurrences; the tartness of her labia had been there in the untoweled droplets. As his index finger traced an indefinite line from her pubic hair around to the small of her back, he had asked, "Why is this circle here?"

"I don't know," she had answered, shrugging his hand off, a hint of anger and fear in her voice.

It was the shrug that did it, or maybe the anger, or maybe both. He had long ago learned that in this life certain things must entwine in order to present a clear picture; the shrug would not have done it alone, nor would have the anger but, taken together, they were the stuff of evasiveness. Shrug and anger. He had thought of the words while staring at the circle, a slightly pink-red area, already knowing that it had resulted from suction made by a human mouth, a mouth not his own. At that moment, it was as though an unseen hand had touched the place in his manhood at which the emotions were stored, punctured it, freed everything that he had ever felt about himself, about their relationship, let it drain away leaving him hot and empty.

"Want to talk about it?" he had asked.

"Talk about what?" she had asked, pulling the towel around her back, assuming the role of housewife who has been caught nude by a visitor.

"Who is he? It's not that hard to answer, is it?"

She had laughed at him, but it was that dry-throated and insecure laugh that is the way of those who have been caught. Her eyes reddened and she breathed heavily. Her shoulders twitched.

"I said . . ."

"I heard you," she said in a whisper. Twirling the towel like a toreador's cape, she had walked from the room and back to the bath, the pink and supple buttocks that he had learned to kiss and to stroke and to ride smoothly in even the most tumultuous of their couch and bed sessions jutting high in sexy arrogance. He went to the bathroom door and began to hammer just as she locked it. He could hear her crying inside.

He had driven about the city for several hours. When he returned he had found the note. Roger: I'll have my things out by tomorrow afternoon. It was over a long time ago. I hope you have a long and happy life.

Now, feeling a nebulous aloneness that had nothing to do with her absence, he went to the refrigerator and peered inside. Even there he could not escape her, for the first thing that he beheld was ninety degrees of a circle of rat cheese, the missing portion having dissolved last Sunday morning. Onions with cheese and crackers was one of their favorites after screwing; there was something patently French about it that she had once seen in a movie. He noticed that the edges of the cheese were beginning to turn dark, to crack and uglify.

He returned to the living room and sat in the chair, wondering what to do about the stains. He was glad that she was gone, that it was really over at last. He felt relieved. He cried for a long time.

Roger got back to the office just as the staff was leaving. At one side of the city room Brandon Reece sat fidgeting with a dictionary. At the other side Voris Mohler sat glaring at Roger. Roger noticed that Moe was wearing his five o'clock face, a jowly expression that portended evil.

"I do not wish for any shit, Roger," he said.

Roger sat across from Moe and looked away. "Then we shall have none. What did you not like? Did Mrs. Cable forget to dot her T's and cross her I's?"

"The TV bastards are gonna make it their second lead. It was our story and they blew our asses out of the water on it. How come?"

"Because the camera is faster than the typewriter, I suppose. Besides, it's just after five, so how do you know it was their second lead? They don't go on for another twenty minutes."

"Because somebody down in those electronic pits owes me a favor, damnit. I got the word about an hour ago that it'll be second." He ruffled the sheets on his desk with the side of a thumb and then rocked backward, holding his pate in his palms. "Eight pages. I send you out into the boonies and you called in eight pages. Those eight right there. You couldn'ta got ten?"

"No. It wasn't World War II, or anything. Damnit, did it make the street or not?"

"Oh yeah, it made the street. Bottom of page one. Bottom! Lynch wanted the President's speech holding up the masthead. This one came with flags waving, guns firing, and old Lynch puts it on the bottom."

"Well, it was an interesting day. It kept me off the streets, at least."

"Yeah. By the way, where'd you call it in from?"

The question caught Roger completely off guard. "Uh, a phone booth on the outskirts of town. Why?"

"I just wondered. How's Darlene?"

Roger shrugged. "Gone, like I figured."

"Good boy, Rog. You're better off. Did anyone notice you in that phone booth?"

"No. Should they?"

"Yeah. A grown man cryin' his eyes out would attract attention."

"It shows, huh?" Roger found himself staring away.

"Yeah. You were at the apartment getting your shit straight, so don't feed me any lines about any phone booth. It's okay, but I wanted you to know that I knew."

"You're one uncanny bastard, Moe."

"Yeah. I love you, too. When this thing gets rolling you'll know just how uncanny I am. This story ain't over, not by a long shot. Buy you a cup."

"You're on."

They went across the street to Gino's, an oblong place of naugahyde booths, forty weight coffee and rotating waitresses. Moe had once speculated that one might see every waitress who had ever worked in the city if he hung out in Gino's for two years; sooner or later they all made it to this place.

The rear of the cafe abruptly jutted to the right and revealed another series of booths that were apart from the main area. Gino called this his drunk tank, for it was here that he seated late night revelers whose exuberance might offend the more conventional diners. An ancient Stromberg-Carlson television set hovered in a corner, staring at the booths. Moe switched it on and they took a booth nearby.

"Coffees, Moe?" the waitress asked. She was a black girl whose eyes resembled elongated almonds. Moe held up two fingers and smiled at her.

They sipped their coffee slowly through the report of the President's speech, waited through a commercial, and then sat upright as the report of the double murder was aired. Fluffy Holt, boy reporter, did two minutes with the captain, went to a closeup of the Rolls, and then ended with a pontifical phrase, ". . . and here in this desolate area, only the coyotes and the mesquite were witness to this bizarre occurrence. John Holt, action news, on the scene a few miles west of the city."

Moe turned the set off and sat down heavily. "They got a way of making it more than it is and less at the same time," he said. "Tomorrow he'll say the same thing about a dead insurance man or an old woman who found a sack of money. Give me the printed word every time."

Roger wondered whether to say what was on his mind and then drove it in deep. "Face it, Moe, maybe this one was just another murder. Hell, we report two hundred a year, a Mexican here, a pair of black holdup men there. The whole fucking world is armed to the teeth and cutting its own guts out. I mean, let's face it, Moe, two more bodies ain't exactly banner headline stuff no more."

"'Any more,'" Moe corrected. "You gotta clean up your goddam act, Roger."

"Okay, but you're evading what I just said about the story. Damnit, Moe, you're getting downright reachy in your old age. The publish-or-perish thing is caking your mind with canary shit."

Moe gazed at him for a long moment and did not smile, a smile being the reaction that Roger would have considered most likely to be forthcoming. The old honcho stared long enough to embarrass them both and then looked away.

"Hard times coming, Rog," Moe said toward the dead TV set. "The printed word is good, adequate, substantial, and forever. But we are in the age of the spoken word, the age of microchips and quasar bullshit. Do you know where I'm going with all this?"

"Sounds like Lynch has been getting nibbles on the paper again. Am I close?"

"If you were any closer you could smell its breath. A most substantial-looking pair of dudes visited brother Lynch today. No, before you ask, the paper has not been sold. But, brother, the handwriting is on the wall. I think it is time for fear when tyrants seem to kiss, to quote somebody. The tyrants did not kiss today, but they held hands for two hours."

As Roger spoke he felt his throat contract drily. He had been unaware up to now that it had had such an impact on him. "How do you know all this shit? Were you in the room? Maybe they fought, for all you know."

"No, they did not fight. They came out glum, but not mad. Not glum—maybe that's the wrong word." Moe thought about it until Roger interrupted.

"Disappointed?"

"Uh, yeah. But something more. Stalled. Yeah, that's the word. Stalled. Like a farmer going to the house to get a bigger shovel, if you know the look I'm talking about."

"Yeah, I'm afraid the illustration has hit me in my mental gonads. So what does it come up smelling like?"

"Maybe their price wasn't right. Who knows?" Moe grinned and sipped at his coffee.

Roger studied his own cup and looked therein at his reflection. The darkness of the brew made him look fatter, more fatigued, and older than he really was. His ears seemed to flap as the tiny ripples loblollied and then were still.

"I can't stand it any more, Moe. To paraphrase Pogo, I has listened with my good ear, and all it picks up is bad. There are cobras in my bed."

"There are cobras in both our beds. I got more than you. Their names are age and poverty and divorce and a boss who'd piss on his mother's grave if it'd get the paper out of hock. Are you now aware of why I have been adamant about this story?"

Roger looked at his old boss and tried to read between the lines. Moe was saying something without saying it, a lawyer's ploy known in courtrooms as leading the witness. Roger wondered about just where he was being led. Moe stared at the old television receiver and tapped his coffee cup with his spoon.

Six

Two days later, in another part of the city, Edward Rix downed his ninth drink and gagged on it. He wondered whether he might have an ulcer. That would have been a form of primal joke, he figured, since ulcers were usually the stuff of the upper intellect. Ulcers were the stuff of Dior neckties, of Mercedes parked in front of town houses, of steely-eyed men who carried briefcases and were late to business luncheons. He sneered at himself in the mirror and attributed his discomfort to a common belly-ache from too much Cutty Sark.

"Arthur? You wanna help me outside?"

Arthur had seen the symptoms before and quickly came around the bar and led Rix outside. The street had that scent of sundown that streets everywhere emit in the gloaming: exhaust and tar and hot rubber. The traffic was sparse and from somewhere came the trill of a nightbird calling to his lady. The bartender, a stout man in his forties, led Rix to the side of the building and sat him down on a tuft of grass.

"You gonna make it, Rix?"

"Yeah, I'm gonna make it in about two seconds. Stan' back." As Arthur complied, Rix grimaced and spewed forth a mixture of liquid and German sausages, the latter having been the impromptu supper that he had eaten at five o'clock. The sitting position was wrong for a good heave, and he leaned onto the dusty grass, bracing himself with his left forearm and finished the job. A hideous wad of sausage cooled on his trouser leg, and he flicked it away with his free hand.

"You gonna make it?" Arthur asked. "I need to get back inside."

Rix waved him away and listened as Arthur's shoes bit sullenly into the cooling gravel of the parking lot. Now that he was alone, his next project was to arise and try to make it to his apartment, a thing that he would not have attempted had Arthur remained. It was not that he was really drunk, he reasoned, but Arthur might have thought he was, and it was not good to have civilians think that a Texas Ranger would have ever gotten into this shape. There were, after all, traditions to uphold.

Now he recalled that he was no longer a Ranger. Hell, he hadn't been for quite some time now. Easing himself backwards in an action reminiscent of a dog scratching its ass, he soon felt the brick wall of the tavern at his back. By digging his heels into the grass and gravel, he was able to push himself backward and upward, the mortar and bricks eating away at his spine. He stood there for several minutes, uncertain of whether his legs would move. Seven feet away the hood and fenders of a green Buick taunted him, beckoned him onward. Pushing himself away from the wall, he staggered to the car and placed his palms on its warmth. He now knew that he would make it. We Rixes are strong people, his mother was fond of saying.

He sloughed off this last thought; hell, his mother had proved to be the lyingest old bitch in the state anyway, so why bother with anything else that she'd said?

He had learned bitterness early on, at his mother's cotton-patch-scarred knee. At least that is what he told himself. It helped to think of it that way when he was stealing state funds or lying. But he had just killed two men; it did not help when killing was the misconduct at hand. When he gassed up his personal car and charged it to the state, that was one thing; this last one was bugging him, bugging the hell out of him.

He grabbed a lamppost and heaved. A terrible rush of heat coursed through his body. He thought for an instant that it might be a heart attack. And wouldn't that be a bitch, just hours after killing the Mexican and the Dallas bastard?

That damned Gomez was plainly told to deliver the package to Bond; instead he had managed to drop it or stash it someplace.

Face it, Rix, he was thinking now, your mother made you a thief, but it was yourself who made you a murderer and drunk.

He paused, leaned against a hedge, looked behind him. There was nothing there except night and memory. Strange, he could have sworn he felt eyes.

Now, it was less than half a block to his apartment, and he knew that he was going to make it without making an ass of himself. The traffic light was hung on green against him, and he stood wavering for a long time as sweat went down his collar and tickled his back. Every bastard in San Antonio was probably watching, so he lurched off the curb and half loped across to the other side. It had not all come out back at the tavern wall and he was not going to puke in public. For that matter, he was going to do it never again. It was one thing to drink and be a thief, but murder was something else, he thought hazily.

There, he was thinking about it again. An old man who walked by spoke to him and kept walking. Rix turned around to see if the old one was watching him and followed his progress far down the street. Of late he had been careful of everyone with whom he had come in contact. No, not of late, exactly; just the last three days. Three days. God, had it been only three days?

There were myriad other things that he could have thought about, but just now he chose not to. The divorce, the two hundred a month, the dago his wife and child now lived with in Frisco. He wondered why he had never developed any fatherly feeling, but this opened up deeper chasms of his psyche that he chose not to peer into, and he let it pass.

But it did not pass. The very same nothingness of the spirit that kept him from feeling anything toward wife, daughter, parents was that same emptiness of purpose that had sent him to kill the Mexican and Alan Bond, not for

any real gain, a thing that he would not let himself
believe, but because he wanted to feel something. And
that was why he was drunk tonight, because the wash of
booze had never yet laundered away that incredible spot
of nothingness. Edward Rix could not feel anything.

"Except fear," he said to a derelict lying on the street.

"Says whut?" the bum asked. He extended his right
hand and then spat in it and looked at his own sputum in
the anemic yellow haze of the street light. He peered up
at Rix and grinned. "You wasn't, was you?" he asked.

Rix ran. He did not know what the man was talking
about, but he did know that there were more and more
people in the world who were crazier than himself. His
shoulders twitched; he felt out of breath; his mouth tasted
like steel cans and oak leaves.

When he was in front of his apartment building he
slowed, looking over his shoulder, and affected a casual
air. A thing that Edward Rix prided himself on was his
almost uncanny ability to recover from the effects of alcohol. He knew how to act undrunk. Being careful not to
walk too straight (the deadliest of giveaways), he saun-
tered up to his mailbox, got his duns and hardware store
flyers, and went on into the stairwell that smelled the
same now as when he had first come here. Butane, furniture polish, and cleaning fluid hit his nostrils, and he
trotted up the stairs to puke one last time. This time
would get it.

Hanging his head over the commode's cushioned seat,
he strained and urped without results, little rivers of air
escaping his gullet like invisible bats fleeing a rancid
eave. The insides of his jaws were sweating, and he knew
that it was just a matter of minutes. Hell, it was just a
little past nine or so; he might even rinse off and take in
a movie. The night was young. He was feeling better
now, and he resolved not to drink for at least a week, to
maybe give it up altogether. He would return to law
school, get a hold on himself. The ten grand he had been
promised for killing Bond and the Mexican would do it.

In his haste to get to the commode, Rix had gone into
the apartment without closing the door behind him, without turning on any light except the one in the bathroom.

Aggrieved as he was at the moment, he did not hear the door shut, nor was he aware of the sound of feet falling catlike on his carpet.

Rix raised his hand, tongued a rope of spittle off into the water, and glared at his reflection, the malice in his slitted eyes equaling all the self-disgust that commode hugging drunks reserve for the moment. It was after some twenty seconds of this staring that it occurred to him that something was distorting the picture. He cocked his head slightly to the right, then to the left and, for the life of him, he could not imagine what was wrong.

It was there in the commode, a face, smiling, apparitional, gray. Like a fool Rix smiled back, captured by a flight of fancy that he believed to be the result of the whiskey. But the face stopped smiling, and Rix felt a sudden wave of horror shock his upper torso. Torn between reality and illusion, he was aware now that the face was real, that someone was indeed in the room with him. He started to roll off the commode to face his companion but, at that instant, he felt his head being raised by its hair; it was a tight feeling, full of itch, tingle, and pain in his scalp.

He tried to cry out as the lancet of pain encircled his throat, but the sound was cut off. He leaned backward to escape but his attacker leaned with him, and Rix heard the dull roar of death. He felt his hands flutter upward as the sound grew louder and then carried him into an endless tunnel of warmth and darkness.

Roger was dreaming. A group of Basset puppies were jumping about, bouncing balloons off their noses. Roger giggled and hugged his pillow. One of the pups tried to lick Roger's toes and he pulled his feet up under him. The balloons continued to bounce. All the puppies had round white spots at the tops of their heads. The balloons suddenly stopped in mid-flight and hung in the air. They became suspended hand grenades. The puppies looked upward and blinked their eyes. Roger knew that if they jumped up and touched the grenades with their noses, there would be one hell of an explosion and that the shrapnel would clip off his balls. One of the puppies jumped up and Roger screamed.

The phone rang. With trembling hand Roger reached over and picked it up.

"Yeah?"

"Whattaya say, asshole?" It was Moe.

"I almost pissed on myself, Moe. Goddam, remind me to tell you my dream. I think you were in it."

"Go on, Rog, laugh at your old boss, will you!"

"It wasn't a laughing dream. Not exactly." Roger now knew who the puppies represented.

"I ain't talking about your friggin dream. This, Roger, is the happiest day of my life. Ask me why."

"Moe, why is this the happiest day of your life?"

"You ready?"

This was getting tedious. Roger licked his lips. They tasted like a whore's blanket. "Yes, Moe."

"Rix is dead."

Roger felt a jolt of red course down his spine. "Jesus, Moe. Murdered, I take it."

"That's why I love you, Rog, baby. Nobody else on my staff would have surmised that. Murdered big. Guess what the weapon was?"

Roger tried to remember Rix's obnoxious face, and could not. "A mouton bootjack, I guess. How the fuck would I know?" There was something about being caught on his back that was irritating him. He sat up and scratched the puckerline that his shorts had left on his belly.

"Moe?"

"Yeah, Rog."

"I hate it when you do this. What was the weapon?"

"Dental floss."

"How dental floss?"

"Around-the-neck-tight dental floss. Such a novel weapon, don't you think? Stout as tire wire, and ten times as easy to conceal. What do it smell like to you?"

Roger pooched out his lower lip while thinking. He attempted to exhale from his mouth and suck the air into his nostrils at the same time. It was a thing he had done since the sixth grade, the objective being to determine whether one's breath was bad.

"Not Mafia," he said at last. "Nope, not Mafia."

"Why?" Moe was playing questing City Editor again.

Roger shrugged his shoulders, "No guns. No open windows, no trunk of a '64 Pontiac. That's why. They always leave their mark, no matter how small."

"Good for you, Rog. I needed convincing, and you just did it."

"I'm glad, Moe. I really am."

"You ain't awake yet. Go slosh your face and come over here. God, you oughta see it. Rangers, sheriffs, cops all over the place. And hurry."

"Over where?"

"You remember that story about the woman makin' tamales from rats?"

"Yeah."

"Well, this is just two blocks on up the street. Rosewood Apartments. Sleazeville. Just look for half the cop cars in Texas and you've come to the right place. Now goddamnit, move!" Moe slammed the phone down.

"Press," said Roger, fifty minutes later.

"I figured," said the deputy. He motioned Roger up the concrete steps and made a jaunty *pas de deux* as the newcomer passed. It was obvious to Roger that the little short fart did not care to be outside. He looked back and over the man's head and counted nine police vehicles. Moe had exaggerated slightly, a thing he usually did when hyper.

Roger opened one of the twin glass doors and went into the foyer. Down at one end there were enough hats to start a cattle drive, each hat sitting atop a talking head. Boots and suits on a threadbare rug. Hanging over it all was an ox yoke chandelier, only one of whose four bulbs had awakened for the party. The place smelled old and sad and tired. Old Rix had not known the good life, at least not at the end.

"Who the hell are you?" a voice asked from a dark hallway.

"President of the Troy Donahue fan club, asshole. What's happenin', Don?"

The deputy named Don Reed emerged and shook Roger's hand. "I doubt that you can get in. Half of Texas is here."

"So I noticed. What can you tell me before I go to the circus?"

"Not much. Rix is awful dead. The landlady to this dump found him this morning. His door wasn't shut, so she figured something was out of kilter. She was right. I never liked Rix much. Still, that's a helluva way to go."

"Nobody did, and yes it is. Catch you later." Roger took Don's wave off and went down to the scene of the action. A series of flashbulbs went off, and he heard the captain chewing someone's ass. He was doing it quietly, so that the blood would not rush to his hemorrhoids. Roger eased into the room and bobbed like a cork on an ocean of shoulders and arrow-print suit coats. In one corner of the stifling and buzzing apartment Moe was talking to Baker of the city homicide squad. Moe motioned him over and Roger had to step over an empty coffee cup. Old Rix was still in the place somewhere, *morte au naturel*.

"Rog, you know Baker?" Moe asked rhetorically.

"Hi Bako. What's it look like?"

"Looks like a goddam crazy house, that's what," said Baker. "There's more chiefs and fewer Indians here than a Pentagon poker game." Baker scowled across the room and shook his head.

"Anything about jurisdictional boundaries you want us to bitch about?" Roger asked, winking at Moe.

"Nah. Hell, he was one of theirs, at least until lately. This one is show bizzy as hell."

Roger started to speak, but the place was suddenly enveloped in a stark gray light. For a moment he thought that someone was welding something, but it turned out to be the light from the TV camera. One of those sexy blonde newshen types was interviewing the captain. As the cameraman backed away for a medium two shot, she adjusted her stance so that her left hip flowered into full roundness for the viewing public.

"Jesus," said Moe.

"Hollywood," said Roger. "Can we see the deceased?"

"Sure," said Baker. "Why would you be any different than the rest of the hemisphere?"

With Baker leading the way they horse-nosed through the throng and went to the door of the bathroom. "Be prepared," Moe whispered.

The first thing that Roger noticed was that the area had been dusted for prints and then trundled over as if by a herd of longhorns. The effluvia of investigation were everywhere: chalk marks, flashbulbs, fingerprint powder, dirt on the floor. He marvelled that city police perpetually had dirty shoes, and salted the thought away for possible use in the story.

Rix looked downright stupid. His chin hung over the edge of the commode seat and his mouth was twisted in a grotesque grin that was the result of his lower lip having caught on a tooth and dried out. His eyes, fudge-brown and characterless in life, were just as devoid of feeling in death: they stared into the bowl at the rust stains along the water line. Roger remembered that Rix was one of those people whose smile never incorporated his eyes, and somehow it made him feel a little sad. The trousers were stretched tightly over the rump and the hands were placed on the floor palms upward, frog flipper fashion. Having seen several hundred bodies in Nam, Roger was aware of the impossible shapes into which dead bodies could get themselves but, seeing Rix in this posture, made him feel disappointment. For some idiotic reason he had expected a little more from Rix.

"Rumsey said it was a fast death," said Baker, referring to the medical examiner.

"Rix would probably like to grab Rumsey by the balls about now and tell him a thing or two," said Moe. He leaned over and looked straight down at the neck. "Holy shit," he whispered.

Roger leaned in and saw that the crucial matter in all this hubbub was a double strand of dental floss pulled so tightly that there appeared a thin, open area that seemed to separate the neck into two distinct portions. Rix had done his bleeding down the front of his shirt and onto the floor around the left side of the commode. It was then that the smell of human waste drifted into Roger's nostrils, and he quickly leaned back.

"Any ideas?" he asked Baker.

"Yeah. Male."

"Us too," said Moe. He wound his watch, a signal to Roger that it was time for them to be alone.

"Uh, Moe, can I see you outside for a minute?" Roger asked.

When they were on the porch, Moe inhaled noisily. "Had to get the fuck out of there, Rog. You smell it?"

Roger nodded, "Yeah. Seems everybody has to take a shit when they die."

Moe looked about the area as if to see whether they were being eavesdropped. The short deputy was on the street now, sitting on the hood of a county car. "Do you get it?" Moe asked.

"Get what, Moe?"

"I told you three days ago, an' I told you yesterday, an' I'm telling you now. We are the only two people on this earth that have got it tied up."

"Make that one. Frankly, I don't know what in the hell is going on in your head."

"Bond and Gomez, and now Rix." Moe waggled his eyebrows.

"Okay, Moe. Bond and Gomez and Rix. You been in there with all the badge wheels. What do they think of it?"

"That's just it, Rog. They don't. Not even the captain. He's so caught up in the Ranger image thing that his only purpose here is to keep the hearth clean."

"This thing just gets shittier all the time, Moe. Hell, Rix hasn't been a Ranger in months."

"True. Which is why they will soft-pedal it. And the softer they pedal, the harder we pedal. It makes sense now, doesn't it?" He studied Roger's dull face for some landmark of intelligence.

"Good theory," said Roger, trying to get into the swing of it, "but only if we can indeed tie Rix in with those two out there. Which brings us back to square one, namely, why is it just you and no-goddam-body-else who thinks Rix had something to do with Bond and Gomez?"

Moe bit his lower lip and looked away. "Roger," he said quietly, "there are approximately fifteen lawmen in there. There are reporters from the two leading papers in this city who have already come and gone. Only one TV station showed up and, when they air the story, it'll be dead in five seconds after the following commercial. The other papers will print this on page two, count on it. The Ranger force, as has been noted, have their own reason for, shall we say, inattention to detail. Baker, in there, will file this with sixty other unsolved murders. Now here we are—you and I. Just little old us. We are the only two people in the County of Bexar who have even an inkling that two related capstones have been kicked off of . . . something."

Roger felt elated and defeated at once. His passion for Moe's efforts was not so large as to overcome what was now almost certain knowledge that Moe had gone around the bend. But what if Moe was right?

"Okay," Roger said, yielding, confusion wracking his brain. "What next?"

"You're going to Dallas," said Moe.

They stared at each other. Roger felt good fairies stroking his back, and bad trolls placing his balls in a vice. It was the same sensation he had felt on the day eons ago while reading the assignment board at Pendleton. The trolls had won that one.

"When?" he asked.

"Today," said Moe.

There were people gathered at the distant end of the street. A city policeman was talking to them. The civilians wanted to wander past the police cars and see old Rix's body.

"I'll go," said Roger. What the shit, he needed a few days to think things over anyway.

Moe smiled. "Good boy. But you still ain't convinced about all this, are you?"

"I said I'd go," Roger mumbled weakly. An ambulance was approaching, nosing its way through the police cars like a pig cautiously passing through a flock of chickens. It was one of those orange and white panel trucks. Roger decided that he hated those goddam meat wagons, not because of their starkness of purpose but because every time one showed up it meant more work at his desk, more typing, more speculating. The driver and his assistant got out awkwardly and apologetically. Ambulance drivers were always awkwardly apologetic in their movements.

"Some things are about to happen," said Moe, jerking Roger's gaze from the ambulance. "First, the captain is going to approach us and, in so many words, tell us to downplay the story. Do you want to bet a beer on it?"

"Nope," Roger answered.

"Secondly, within forty-eight hours you are going to have a newfound respect for your old goofy boss." Moe pointed a thumb toward his chest and waved it back and forth. Roger noticed that lint from Moe's chair arm was on his shirt sleeve; since Edna was gone, Moe had taken to wearing the same shirt as often as three days in a row.

The ambulance men passed them, nodded, bumped the wheels of the pork wagon on the porch, and rolled it on into the hallway. The buzz of human voices was quelled slightly as the men passed on into the bathroom and then it started up again. Someone inside was actually laughing about something, but it was a quiet, nervous laugh. Roger stared at the street, at the crowd, at the cars, and pondered the sounds and accoutrements of death.

"Moe? How's it going?" a familiar voice asked from the doorway. Roger turned and saw the captain. He was holding a brown grocery sack in his left hand.

"Fine, Cap. Wanted to speak to you earlier, but the circus got in my way." He shook the captain's hand and looked at the sack. "Been pickin' tomatoes?"

"Nope. Rix had some questionable books in his closet. Thought I'd better get 'em out fast. Next of kin stuff, you know."

Moe knew the expression. He had first heard it in the Navy, and it always had sexual connotations. From the outline of what was in the sack it had to be books, probably pornography.

"Roger, how's business?" The captain shook Roger's hand and looked out at the street. "Seems you and I see a lot of each other lately."

"How's the hemorrhoids, Cap?" Roger asked.

"A real sonofabitch, Rog. I got one of those car cushions, but it doesn't help much. Guess I gotta have surgery, like the doctor advised. God, I dread it." He placed the sack beside his foot and straightened slowly. "Moe, I gotta ask you something," he said, looking back over his shoulder.

Moe looked at Roger, a hint of a smirk in his eyes. "Oh? Anything we can help with is our pleasure, Cap."

"Old Rix in there," the captain began slowly, "well, he was a man who had problems. Hell, we all do. I have a feeling that when this is cleared up, it might have to do with a woman, maybe a married woman. It smells like the jealous husband thing. But that's just an idea for right now. Anyhow, what I want to say is, Rix was at one time a part of our little lashup, but he hasn't been on our payroll for some time. He was privately employed at the time of his death. The reporters from the other papers have agreed that it would do no disservice to their readership if his service with us was unmentioned, and I was hoping that maybe you'd feel the same way."

"No problem," said Moe, looking at Roger. "Having been in the paper business for most of my life, I'm aware that sometimes silence serves the cause as readily as reportage does." It was a good speech, even believable. Turning to Roger he said, "Okay, Rog, here it is: there will be no reference to Rix ever having been a Ranger. Got it?"

"Good enough, Moe," said Roger. "By the way, Cap, anything else on those two out on the prairie?"

"Nah. Red says it's dope, but he's got nothin' to go on. He and Hardy went up a blind alley on it. The folks in Dallas are just as stumped as we are as to that jeweler. As far as the Mexican was from home, that takes dope out of the picture. Mexicans do not haul dope out of their own country, they send it."

Moe seemed to glisten as waves of self-righteousness coursed through his marrow. He fought down an impulse to grab Roger by the scruff of the neck and shake him. His voice was only slightly tremulous as he said, "So that one is another bummer, huh?"

"Yeah," the captain answered, adrift on his own thoughts. "We live in a nutty world, Moe. Dope, murder, vice out the ass. Wife swappers, supreme court justices who are ivory tower fools. Shit don't worry me like it used to, though. I guess I'm cracking up."

"The line forms behind me, Cap," said Moe. "Us old farts want stability, and there isn't any. Not anymore."

"Time was," the captain went on, seemingly ignoring Moe's own paean to the past, "a Ranger was one for life. Now look at Rix in there." He shook his head in sadness. "Ah, but what the shit," he adjusted his stance so that his hemorrhoids might align themselves. "Word is, Moe, that your paper might be on the block. Anything to that?"

Moe shrugged. "A shithouse rumor at best. Lynch says no, so for now it's no," he said, lying his ass off.

"Well, I gotta get back to the salt mine," said the captain. He hefted the sack and held it slightly away from his body, as if to keep the substance therein from soiling his clothing. "Stay in touch." He moved down off the porch with cautious, angular steps and went toward the brace of cars.

"There goes the finest kind," said Moe.

"Yep. Him and the longhorns have no place in their own home country anymore," said Roger. "Did you grab what he said about Dallas?"

"Sure, and it couldn't have been better. We know what they don't."

"So, I'm still going?" Roger asked.

"More now than ever. Tell me what you're looking for, Rog." He was back at his old games again, this one called Make the Reporter Think.

"Alan Bond, his life and times. Sounds like one of those cheap biographies." He waited for Moe to laugh. When Moe did not even smile, Roger lurched into the gap of embarrassment by saying "I'm to tie Bond to Rix or bust a gut trying. I am to prove that Alan Bond and Rix are dead because of something that is so big that the cops cannot see it. It is like one of those grade school drawings that says 'Find the hidden rabbits.' That about it?"

Moe turned on Roger coldly. "That sums it up. And there are rabbits because I say there are rabbits. Roger, there is no such thing as extraordinary coincidence."

"So, why not just work on the Rix end of it right here?"

"Several reasons," Moe said quickly, "reasons that I've already chewed over in my head. You start turning over rocks here, the other papers get wind of it and get nosy. That's one. Number two, you stood right here on this porch and heard for yourself; namely, the police powers that be are already pulling the blanket over anything to do with Rix. We'd muddy our own water all to hell for years to come. I promised Cap we'd downplay this, so we will."

"Let me guess on three," said Roger. "It has to do with Lynch in one way or another. Right?"

Moe stirred visibly; his shoulders shook and his eyes seemed to glaze.

"Look at the *Washington Post*, the *Philadelphia Inquirer*. Shut down in a matter of hours. Those were big leaguers. We are not big league, Roger, but we could be. Yeah, the third thing has to do with Lynch. The sonofabitch wants me to run his paper, by God I'm gonna run his paper." He looked at Roger as though he had thrown him a challenge.

"All my fucking life, I've been a canoe locked between battleships," said Roger mournfully. "Just once, I'd like to be one of the goddam people who had my fate in his hands. Now it's you and Lynch."

"You gotta admit your agonies have slown down," said Moe. "In the Marines they had you by the balls and you couldn't quit."

"But my penchant for eating hasn't slown down," said Roger, mimicking Moe's concocted participle.

"Our circulation is down by nineteen percent from last year. Our equipment could stand an overhaul that would make Lady Liberty's look like a lick and a promise."

"Piss poor analogy," said Roger.

"It's a piss poor world, Roger. And getting pissier." Moe placed his hand atop his head and smoothed a sprig-let of hair. No sooner had he removed his hand than the wisp of hair stood up again. Moe hated his balding head, his life, his superiors, and his subordinates. He felt himself, as someone had once said, up to his belly button in pygmies.

"I'm about to speak in diplomatese," said Roger. "Do I have your ear?"

Moe nodded. Roger was about the only person on the *Sentinel* staff who possessed diplomatic immunity with the city editor. And, heretofore, he had used it sparingly and with generally good results. "Bitch on."

"Okay. We are reporters, not creators. In the media world, those who create news by whatever means are usually up to their short hairs in hot water. Dig?"

Moe looked at the people who were assembled at the end of the street. They resembled cattle that wanted feeding. Their open faces looked strangely like those surrealistic World War II paintings of starvation. Moe hated them.

"So you think I'm creating all this, huh?"

Roger shrugged. He felt his temples heat and a definite dry closure in his throat. "Let's just say that the possibility is there, all things considered," he said feebly.

"That's one step. Let's hear some others."

"Sure," said Roger, a little sarcastically. "Why not? If I'm in Dallas, then you've got leverage to stall Lynch from any sudden moves. The potential of a big story is there, the paper is about to be saved from oblivion, so Lynch would not dream of selling. Your sense of timing on this one is impeccable, Moe. Unfortunately, it's transparent as hell."

"So we're back to square one," said Moe. He started to say something else, but a rumbling from within the building interrupted their talk and turned them around. The ambulance attendants were coming out in a low crouch, Rix's white swaddled form on the cart between them. In this attitude, they resembled question marks standing at either end of a blank space, a thing that Roger hoped to work symbolically into the story. He moved with Moe down off the porch and toward the waiting cars.

When they got to Moe's old Valiant, they leaned on a rear fender and watched as the fool's parade wandered out of the apartment.

"Make you feel obsolete?" Moe asked. He nodded toward the gorgeous Cinderella TV lady who, although no coach was in sight, was being borne along by her retinue of rats. Amid her host of admiring badge wearers, she moved down the steps with the fluidity of a cobra on a carpet. The aura of sex hung over the place like mist over a placid creek. As she got into the TV station's Ford Chateau, the deputies and the Rangers went into trances watching her ass. When she was gone, they said nothing. This was that phenomenon known in male circles as: Beautiful Just Is.

"Not obsolete," said Roger. "Just misshapen."

Moe smiled at this, and they watched as the group went into meltdown and dissolved in a flurry of chrome and exhaust fumes. He looked down the street and saw that the civilians had mostly dispersed. When those remaining saw him looking toward their little cluster authoritatively, the last of the gawkers left, all except for one little gray-haired woman. Her beady eyes and circular mouth continued to be locked onto the facade of the apartment building as if drinking something from it. She and Moe stared at each other for a short time. Finally, Moe's eyes got the best of her, and she turned and hobbled away. "There goes your public, Roger, like it or not." he said.

"Yeah, kinda sad, ain't it?" Roger asked rhetorically.

"But it's who we serve," said Moe. "Her and all her tribe who have a quarter to spend."

"What proof do we have that if I go to Dallas——"

"Shut the hell up," Moe interjected. He pushed himself off the Valiant's fender, walked around the hood, and opened the door. "Get to the office. Park your car underground and come to the front door. Don't argue." And, with that, Moe was gone in a roar. The old Valiant had a lot of spunk.

When Moe was gone Roger got into his own car, a nine-year-old Dodge, started the engine, listened to the lap-lap sound start up and then taper off to nothingness.

The car had been making these lap sounds for the past month, sounds that hovered momentarily on starting and then dropped from earshot. Leave it to a goddam Dodge to make such sounds.

By the time Roger got to the *Sentinel* building Moe had already parked and gone upstairs. He parked the Dodge beside Moe's Valiant, dropped his keys on the floorboard and got out. Somewhere down in his guts he felt, or hoped, that he would never see the car again, so what the fuck difference did it make if somebody stole it a few days early? He went up the concrete steps that led from the parking cavern and felt the morning sun needle his cheeks. He reached the sidewalk and considered going up to tell Lynch that Moe was bonkers, but all that would do would be to queer the trip to Dallas. Besides, Lynch was supposed to be out of pocket anyway. He thought of Darlene, and the trip seemed even more dessicate.

"Hey, Rog, Moe said give you this. What is it?"

"Hello, Henry. Tell him I said thanks. None of your business."

Henry was embarrassed, confused, and a little hurt. "I mean, shit, it looks as if you're goin' someplace important. Wisht I was." Henry looked down the street at the traffic. Roger's brusqueness had left red blotches on his neck and cheeks.

"I wish you were too, Hen." He tapped Henry on his incredibly low forehead and said, "How many cheeseburgers is it now?"

Henry smiled. The pressure was off. "Several. I lost count. What's threnodic? Somebody said this town is downright threnodic."

"Pertaining to funeral music," said Roger. "Catch you later." He whirled and went back down the walkway, toward old Nicodemus. Just beyond the ancient van stood two new Dodge Tradesmen. They had been there for the better part of a week. Roger wondered what sort of economic lunacy Lynch was pulling now. Two new vans, and he had to drive to Dallas in black Nick.

Forty-five minutes later, as Roger finished putting three of everything in his suitcase, the phone rang.

"Yeah?"

"Rog? Moe."

"Is it cancelled?"

"Nope. Just got a phone call, Rog. Darlene. She said to tell you she's getting married." There was a pause. "You there Rog?"

"Uh . . . yeah. She say where she was calling from?"

"No. Just sounded long distance, if you know what I mean. You ain't gone yet?"

"Yes, Moe, I'm gone. This is a goddam recording talking to you."

"Needn't get huffy. She ain't worth it, Rog. No piece of ass is."

"Damn straight," said Roger. His cheeks felt hot, scalded. "I'm off to Dallas. Catch you on the other end."

"Rog---"

Roger hung the phone up, his cheeks now numb. He picked up a pair of shorts, saw the faintest trace of lipstick around the flyseam. It had gotten there the night they had driven down to the reservoir. Her kind would not pass this way again. He threw the shorts into the suitcase, looked about the place, and went outside to the van. God, what a morning it had been, and even now it was but a little past eleven. He threw the suitcase to the rear of the decrepit vehicle, listened as the clatter was sucked into the steel walls.

"Shit!" he screamed, starting the motor. If he hung tough, he could be out of this madness by noon and in Dallas by dark.

Seven

The medical center stood at right angles to a monolithic hospital. It was an area of drug stores, drab unpainted nurses' housing and expensive cars whose license plates bore the caduceus. As Ableiter paid the cab driver, he mused that despair and pomposity were forever the opposing indexes of medicine. It would be a thing to think about at another time. The smells of new mown grass and urine samples hung perceptibly in the June heat.

Inside the medical center, affixed to a wall, a plaque offered a variety of medical services. All that could drift asunder in the human body had been catalogued and delegated. He was halfway down the list when he found the name he sought, the name that Montreal had offered as being secure.

Aaron Viorlanska, M.D.

So, he was thinking, we have a Yiddisher. It would be an interesting meeting, he knew already. Here was a man who would have a story to tell.

He took the elevator to the second floor and found the opaque glass door that bore the exotic name. For a moment he looked at the vague misshapenness beyond, as if waiting for ghosts to make themselves known or, perhaps, to discern the whereabouts of snares that might lie within. His fingertips found the scar on his face, drifted over it until a vague anxiety passed. So many old habits were returning from dormancy lately; this scar-touch was a thing that had not leapt from its closet for the better part of a lifetime. He remembered its purpose, but he would think of it later, when there was time.

He went inside, closed the door behind him. An old couple sat on green chairs and scarcely looked at him. It occurred to him that he was a reflection of themselves, now, and that his years in the jungle had not escaped notice by what the Indians called The White Hand. The receptionist, a large bullish lady with false teeth, said, "May I help you?"

"Would you tell the doctor that his old friend Axel is here to see him?"

She leaned to her left and took an index card from a metal box. Pulling a ballpoint pen from her gray bouffanted hair, she said, "Full name and nature of complaint?" Still she had not smiled.

"Would you tell the doctor that his old friend Axel---"

"The doctor is a very busy man, Sir. If you'll just---" Her words stuck there, her wrinkled neck holding them as certainly as the large hand held her neck. He had leaned in with the quickness of a serpent, his upper torso balanced perfectly on the little window's elbow-worn shelf. As quickly as he had seized her he released her, his head turning even as he did so to determine whether the old couple had seen. They had not. He looked back at the woman, his eyes now encircled with the red bloodlines of rage. She knew better than to scream, though how she knew it was as much a mystery to herself as it might have been to the potted plant in the corner. In the refractors of memory she had seen this face before, or had possibly dreamed it; in any case, it was the face of death. She rose and went into the adjoining room and whispered to the doctor, her voice coarse in the warbling and uncontrolled croak that was unmistakably the rasp of fear.

The doctor appeared in the hallway, his own face registering that same fearful scowl of vulnerability. But with the doctor's gaze was something even more profound; it was on open-mouthed inhalation of the fumes of hell. A thin macrame of hair lay across the top of his small round head, and the scalp beneath it was as pink as if newly scorched. And he was short, even for a Jew.

"Axel?" the doctor asked. The nurse emerged from somewhere behind him and went on up the hallway, her lower lip leading the way.

"My good friend," said Ableiter. He moved through the little swinging saloon doors and into the hallway where the doctor stood amid the smells of alcohol and sweat and, for a long moment, they looked at each other as old mates from a long faded class might—dimly, abashedly, confusedly.

"Your face is not familiar," said the old doctor with a mild Yiddish accent, "but your manner is." He gave a sidewise jerk of his head, an indication that Ableiter was to follow. At the far end of the hall the old man turned abruptly to his left and held the door open for his guest. As he heard the door close behind him, Ableiter surveyed the room. Doctor's offices had not changed all that much over the years: cotton swabs, tongue depressors, a plastic mockup of a seahorsey human fetus, a small row of bottles bearing unfathomable names and, in the middle of the floor, the universal examination table. This one had a wide, thin paper over it. Ableiter wondered how long they had been covering exam tables thusly. One could become so out of touch in the jungle.

"I had almost forgotten," said the doctor. "Some twenty years ago another 'old friend Axel' had occasion to visit me. Time and attrition are doing your sort in, it would appear."

Ableiter let the sarcasm pass. Again his eyes met those of the doctor.

"Irony abounds, my friend. We did our best to kill you and now I seek your expertise. It is fortunate that you survived. Where were you?"

"*Maidanek. Treblinka.*" He paused. "And you?"

"Neither of those places. What do they have on you?" He hoped that it was the proper question, and hoped that it was stated properly in Americanese.

"That does not concern you. What is your problem?"

The examination took some twenty minutes. From the first touch to the first reading of a wet X-ray it was foregone. Their animosity laid aside for a moment, the two men looked at the photographs of Ableiter's guts as two old hunters might gaze lovingly at a rack of antlers.

"It is primarily confined to the outer part of the small intestine just now," the doctor said, tracing his words with the yellow pencil that he used as a baton, waving first this way and then that, the litany of death, as ever, camouflaged in mottled verbiage: metastasis, adrenocarcinoma, adherence, adjacent structures. "Usually eleven to sixteen months," he said at last, answering the question that had now been asked.

The German looked away at the plastic fetus. "Usually?" he asked.

The doctor nodded. "Usually." He took down the photograph and replaced it with a second. "Here, this whitish area, is probably mucin. It indicates movement of cells, doubling."

"Which means nothing positive, I imagine?" Ableiter said, almost uninterestedly.

The doctor shrugged. "A twenty-minute office visit leaves much to be desired. Certainly exploratory surgery is called for. I imagine that you do not have time for such matters." It was a declaration that just missed question form.

Ableiter felt slightly chilled. He picked up his shirt, slipped his arms in, buttoned. The doctor switched off the square of light behind the X-ray's ugly amorphousness and sat down at his desk. As a matter of habit he started to write a prescription, but suddenly laid the pen down. He wadded the square of paper and tossed it at a wastebasket. Looking up, he saw that his patient had by now knotted his tie. "My sisters would have been fifty-nine years old tomorrow," he said.

"I see."

"Twins," the doctor said.

"I gathered as much."

"Sophia and Wanda. When they got onto the boxcar they carried matching yellow cases. They waved---" The doctor picked up a pencil, broke it, threw it into the wastebasket. His chin quivered.

"My own mother was probably baked to death in a cellar in Dresden," said the German. "She was there to escape the British and American bombers. Dresden had been tacitly declared an open city. On February 13, 1945, Mister Churchill rendered that tacitness null and void. One hundred and thirty-five thousand people died that night. The flames could be seen from one hundred miles away.'' Ableiter looked at the line of what had been called mucin. Death was everywhere. He looked at the old doctor and saw that the man's gaze had fallen on a pair of lancets that lay in glistening chromium gentility in a red velvet tray. ''*Ich brauche Ihre Hilfe,*'' said Ableiter.

''Of course,'' said the doctor. ''Let us remember that it was all in another time. But I reserve the right to hate your brutal guts to eternal hell.'' The words containing r's had come forth with Yiddish burr and spittle.

''You intrigue me, Herr Doktor. We have more in common than we have apart. Why will you not talk to me about the past? I did not kill your sisters—I could not have. Again I ask, what does . . . Montreal have on you?''

''What does Tel Aviv have on you?'' the doctor retorted defensively.

''I was a member of *Einsatzgruppe B.* Have you heard of that organization?''

''What Russian has not?''

''True, what Russian has not. What was done was done quite well. We were young men, then.''

''Is that some form of apology?''

Ableiter gave him a cursory glance. ''No. Merely a statement. Now, as we said in grammar school, I've shown you mine. May I see yours?''

The old man looked at the door, opened it, closed it. ''Confession is the Catholic method of theological masturbation. It rids one of current tension. How strange that you are the one person on earth that I might use to lessen my tensions. Did Montreal not tell you . . . anything?''

Ableiter shook his head. ''Only that you were a Jewish doctor, that you were safe.''

''Safe.'' The old man uttered the word to the tile floor, watched it wither there. Without looking up he said, ''It was at the end of it all. April, 1945. There was snowy mud. Hauptsturmbannfuhrer Kolb came to the barrack. We were to be evacuated, some of us. Eleven of us were left. He lined us up, told us to race to the end of the barrack and back. Several were so old that they did not bother. I won the race. My feet were as frozen iron, my lungs were screaming, frozen inside my body. We were all shoeless. Then we were led outside. There was a gallows with ten ropes looped at the end. Not nooses, mind you, just strangulation loops. Because I had won the race . . ." He buried his face in his hands and sobbed. "Because I won the race, I was . . . given the honor, as Kolb put it, of hanging the rest. They were stood on inverted buckets. Oh God, I can still hear their gasps!"

Ableiter said nothing. The doctor sobbed for the better part of a minute and then wiped his eyes with the tips of his index fingers.

"I kicked the buckets away one by one, my muddy feet murdering ten harmless old men," the doctor gasped. "Some of the other guards had gathered to watch. They . . . applauded me!" He stood and smoothed his thin hair with his palm. "Within hours we were placed on railroad flatcars and moved west, four guards to a prisoner. So, you see, it was a thinning process. Performance of duty with a minimum of danger. Four guards to one Jew. Such cowards, the *Totenkopf!* And, even in your final moments of glory, you made plans for me, didn't you?"

Ableiter looked at him dully and shook his head. "I don't understand."

"Perhaps you don't. I will clarify things for you. In 1949 while I was at the College of Surgeons in Glasgow a man approached me. He knew of my plans to go to America, knew even of my impending work at the University of Texas. And he asked if my feet were yet bruised by the buckets! I was too stunned to reply. It was night, we were outside a dormitory. His breath came out in frost like smoke from a forgotten hell in the February cold. He said that one day someone called 'my old friend Axel' might need me. And then he walked away."

Ableiter thought these last words the most extraordinary of all. The Order was not dead after all. Its fibers, however worn, burned, blasted, were still holding the body together. He and his group were not isolated pariahs doomed forever to the jungle, but ganglia whose nerve endings spread at least to Montreal and possibly to the earth's farthest reaches! He felt his chest swelling, his scalp tingling.

"And I am the second Axel," Ableiter said.

"And probably my last," said the doctor. "I am to retire in a few months. And you are to die in a few months. We, and all that we represent, are in a state of degeneration. If the Jewish community knew what I have told you, I would be an outcast. I do not plan to be an outcast. Over the years I have wondered just how many survivors like myself are still in your . . . their service."

"And, strangest of all," said Ableiter, "is that, if we went together to the newspaper at this moment and told them about ourselves, we would be thrown into the street as two harmless old fools." He picked up his coat from the table, pulled out his wallet, and handed the doctor two one hundred dollar bills. "One is for the nurse, with my apologies," he said.

"She will recover," the doctor said. "Nurses do. She has been kicked, vomited on, cursed, and threatened. But she has survived. In that way she is much like the Jew."

"Or the German," Ableiter added. He extended his hand. To his surprise, the doctor shook it.

"Strangely, I cannot hate you," said the doctor. "I have tried to see you in your gray-green uniform, the death's head, the lightning insignia, but I cannot. You are an old man who is soon to die of cancer."

"I will not die of cancer," Ableiter stated.

"Oh? And why not?"

Ableiter opened the door and stepped into the hall. "Because I am a soldier. I will die a soldier's death. It is one of those things that one knows beyond the realm of knowing." He closed the door behind him, leaving the doctor alone with his memories.

Eight

Dallas was beginning to stretch and blink its night eyes when Roger saw it from thirty miles out. Like a rhinestoned glove with fingers of varying heights, the city stood out of the prairie starkly and boldly.

He drove through suburbs for a long time before arriving in the guts of the city. It was mostly deserted, except for a few night crawlers. Two black prostitutes tried to flag him down and then gave him the finger. It all made him feel quite the stranger, a feeling that he had known in a score of places over the past few years.

Seeking out human companionship that had no tags attached, he stopped at a small coffee shop and ordered a burger and a cup. The burger tasted good enough to justify another, and he found that he had dawdled away the better part of an hour. Now it was pitch dark outside and it was a strange city and he knew that to go to a motel room would be unthinkable, his onyx-black depression being what it was just now. Dredging up a phone book, he looked up Bond Jewelers and by nine o'clock had parked the van outside the Landmark Hotel. It was in one of those areas that bore all the marks of being torn down or refurbished into cheap tenements. At the base of the hotel and standing to the right of the revolving doors was the gilt inscription, Bond Jewelers. It was dark inside the jewelry shop, and the interior of the hotel appeared to be only a few candle power brighter. Unaware that he was being watched by four pairs of eyes, Roger parked and locked the van and went inside.

All hotels had a scent about them, and this one was no different. Naugahyde furnishings and ancient carpet and undusted potted plants caused his nose to recall certain dingy whorehouses in the Far East. At the left side of the large lobby was the typical alcove with its typical desk clerks, one old and one young, both wearing that look of serene failure that is the way of desk clerks everywhere. Letting his gaze wander, he saw that several vacant and dusty windows stared out at the mezzanine, only a few of which still carried the names of those entrepreneurs who had fled. At the far right corner was a lighted door way that announced OFFEE SHOP. Wondering when they were going to come to replace the C, Roger strode over to Bond's shop and peered in. There were glass cases and a smattering of rings and watches, but it was readily apparent that old Bond was on the skids as a jeweler.

"Plannin' big things?" a voice asked.

Roger turned and saw a black suit and a black hat. Beneath the hat was one of the roundest and reddest faces that he had ever seen. The man was at least six feet, four inches tall and had to weigh well above two-fifty.

"No. Just curious," he answered, feeling an inexplicable chill dart across his shoulders.

"Curious about what?"

"Watches. Rings. Is that all right?"

The man's hammy hand went inside his breast pocket and came out with a badge. "Maybe it is, maybe it ain't."

"Whatever you say." Roger instinctively moved backwards.

"Dave!"

A deputy appeared from the doorway to Roger's right. He wore cowboy attire and a Sam Browne belt. He rested his right hand on the butt of a .38. Roger started to smile, to say something, anything, when he felt someone breathing on his neck. "Whatever you're thinking is wrong," said a soft voice. Roger turned and saw another deputy just as the man stepped back. He was shorter than the other, but his pistol was just as long. The whole thing had taken less than ten seconds.

"Well, it seems that window shopping has its hairy moments in Dallas," said Roger.

"You shut up," said the big man.

"Groucho, Harpo, and Zeppo," Roger said, feeling his throat tighten.

"Well," said the big one, "we know who part of us is, don't we, Charlie." He nodded at the smaller man, and Roger felt himself being frisked.

"A little higher and to the right," said Roger, his hands extended.

"Clean, Mister Sturbridge," said Charlie.

"Real slow now, let's see your wallet," ordered Sturbridge.

Roger eased the bent and ass-sweaty packet out of his hip pocket and handed it over his shoulder. He made a mental note to get a new one as soon as possible. It looked like hell.

"Press, Mister Sturbridge. Roger Wilder of the San Antonio *Sentinel.*" He handed the wallet back over Roger's shoulder.

"You guys ever hear of illegal search?" Roger asked.

"Shut up," said Sturbridge. "Let's us walk over here and talk." He led the group to a modular naugahyde couch and eased his big rump into it. The deputies remained standing. Roger sat across from Sturbridge and noticed that the man licked his lips often, as if to prime himself. The red face and the licking told him a great deal about the old cop, but just now was not the time to play psychiatrist. "Charlie, you go get the lady," the big man said.

Roger heard Charlie leave but dared not look around. He had once seen an Army private look the direction a Saigon cop was pointing, and the cop had used that instant to swing his sap. He had not thought of the incident in years, but now it made him sweat. "So you're Sturbridge and I'm Wilder. What can I do for you?"

"Probably nothin'. But, just for the hell of it, let's say you're a long way from home and just now you've got your hind leg caught in our fence. So why did you happen to come jump our fence?"

Roger felt some of the fear easing off. The back of his head had stopped tingling. "I got ordered here. I'm here to do a story. Guess who about?" When the man nodded toward the jewelry shop, Roger said, "You got it. So I'd appreciate any help you might be able to give me."

"There ain't none. He got done in down your way. We been on this place the better part of two, three days, only it seems longer."

"And I just happened along to break up the monotony," said Roger.

There was the slightest hint of a smile as the big man said, "You ain't the best one that we could get, but so far you're the only one."

"Lucky me. And my boss thinks I'm in expense account heaven about now. Jesus!" The hotel smell was heavy in his nostrils.

The cop started to smile but grimaced instead. It was as though he were attempting to hide an unbearable seizure. Looking up at Dave, he said, "Boy, go to the coffee shop and get me a Coke."

Roger heard Dave move away and now the thing that he had been thinking all along was heavy with credence. Sturbridge was sick, but it was a self-imposed sickness. In spite of the old cop's rather arrogant manner, Roger found himself feeling a little sorry for the bastard. He studied the man's face carefully and judged his age to be in the late fifties. Retirement age.

"What can you tell me about Bond?" Roger asked suddenly, as though to bring Sturbridge back from the hell into which he had drifted.

"Broke. Aging. Maybe a shade crooked. Small time."

"Good. The sort of man who'd be likely to sell his ass on a long shot. Did he leave any tracks?"

Sturbridge looked at Roger for a long moment as if concocting a precision-tooled answer. "No," he said at last.

Roger suddenly felt the strange sense of being had. The cop was definitely hiding something. Maybe it was time to slow down, to temper his questions with a soft glove of subservience. No, that would not be the proper manner either; people like Sturbridge were ever contemptuous of cowards. Entrapped in these thoughts, it came as a sudden mild surprise when Sturbridge volunteered: "There's all he left behind."

Roger looked to his left and saw the small deputy standing with a woman of about forty, maybe forty-five. His first impression was of large brown eyes that were set into a face whose separate parts had meshed into a plainness that no man would ever find attractive. Her nose was a bit too wide and her lips were a bit too thin to register any hint of a voluptuous nature. He tried to see her as unattractive, but that was not the word. It was after a moment of contemplation that the proper word came: careworn. In those eyes was the same despair that he had seen in those photographs of sharecropper women of the 1930's. Here was something beyond mere sorrow at the loss of a relative; here was a woman whose suffering was a life-style. She was of medium height but might have appeared taller had her posture not been slightly stooped, stooped not of fatigue but of acquiescence to something borne since early childhood. Her cheap dress was green, as was the vinyl purse that she held tightly with both hands, and her feet were strapped in green flats of a slightly different shade. As his eyes wandered back to her face he was again stricken by that quality of suffering. She might have been a Russian peasant of another century, a woman brought from the fields to stare at the camera for a moment, so that her presence on this earth might be recorded, if only to prove in some future time that she had indeed lived. Her hair, a predictable medium brown, was pulled back away from her face in a severe chignon, as though to indicate to the casual observer that she had long since admitted her plainness and had chosen to glorify it. Roger thought of Gruschenka, Anastasia and, somewhat seriocomically, Ma Joad.

Sturbridge and Roger stood and smiled at her in that funereal way that all non-sufferers greet the next of kin. "Starla," said Sturbridge, "this is Roger Wilder. He turns out to be a reporter from San Antonio. Sorry we left you outside, but he looked, ah, likely at the time. You understand, I'm sure."

"Hello, Starla," said Roger.

She smiled and continued to clutch tightly at the ugly purse. The big deputy brought Sturbridge's Coke back, and the cop turned it up and inhaled it as the others stared. Handing the glass back he said, "Thanks." There was no emotion in the word. "Bond's niece," he said, never breaking stride. "We just got her off the plane. Figured she might need some protection. Besides, we were gonna go in the place and look it over with her. After all, it's all hers now."

"I see," said Roger. He continued to eye the strange woman, already aware in his subconscious that he had to interview her. She, and not these yokel cops, would be the source of knowledge regarding the real Alan Bond.

Sturbridge motioned, and the group set off across the lobby, Roger and the short deputy bringing up the rear. "Ninety percent of the frigging murders in this state involve Dallas sooner or later," the deputy whispered. "If I had it to do over, I'd get me a job in some small town, drive a prowl car at night, and listen to the crickets chirp."

"We all got our crosses to bear," Roger mumbled back. "I imagine that little lady would trade troubles with you right now."

The deputy said nothing, but Roger noticed that his face reddened a little. As Sturbridge fumbled with the key to the jewelry shop, Roger moved near Starla and tried to get a whiff of perfume. As he expected, there wasn't any.

When they were inside, Sturbridge said, "Hope you won't mind, but we've been over the place pretty good in the last couple of days. No clues. It's all intact."

Such as it is, Roger was thinking. But, if Bond was as broke as it looks like he was, she may wind up having to pay the asshole out of hock. He found himself hating Bond for being such a fourflushing shithook.

"Funny he'd leave a few rings and watches out and hide the others," Dave said.

"Who said he hid any?" Sturbridge asked.

"Well, the place just doesn't look . . . you know."

"I believe the word is 'prosperous'," said Starla, a steeliness in her voice. Dave looked away and feigned interest in a lady's opal ring.

"Well," said Sturbridge, "now that it has been brought up, you'll find he wasn't all that prosperous. Matter of fact, Miss Landau, you may find that all this stuff is in some sort of litigation. Sorry, but that is what our preliminary findings show. I'm afraid Mister Bond was heavily in debt."

"Which either directly or indirectly resulted in his death," said Starla.

"No, ma'am. That ain't always the case. Not always. But it is a thing to be considered."

"I'm sure you'll do your best," said Starla.

"We always do," Sturbridge assured her. "By the way, his name was not Bond, but Blaustein. Do you know of any reason for him to change his name?"

As she smiled for the first time, Roger noticed that her teeth were perfect, even if the smile that revealed them bore a hint of malevolence. "He was Jewish in a non-Jewish setting," she said. "To attempt to explain that to you would take more time than I have just now. Your question, as I undertand it, was whether he might have been hiding from someone. The answer, to be best of my knowledge, would have been no."

Sturbridge licked his lips and rubbed his coat pocket. "You understand we leave no stone unturned in these matters. A man's religion is his own affair, far's I'm concerned."

"I thought we were discussing his name," she said.

"Uh, yeah," the big cop tried to smile and could not. He looked at the deputies and said, "You boys can go on now. We'll wrap up from here."

They nodded and left the store and went out into the night. Roger saw that the big one was still carrying the Coke glass. Petty theft in the first degree.

"Well, this is the place," said the big cop. "We just wanted you to see it. There's an inventory list downtown. You can have a copy, if you want one."

"Possibly," she said. "Tell me, is there anything yet to indicate a motive?"

Sturbridge shook his head, his ears reddening slightly. "Not to my knowledge."

The bastard is lying, Roger was thinking. Why? It was time to try to pull the thing together, but to make no sudden moves in doing so. "Why don't I stand us to a cup of coffee?" he asked.

"I, uh, now where are you going, Miss Landau?" the cop said ignoring Roger's invitation, watching Starla, who had begun to move away.

"I would like to get a room and disappear from the world for a while," said Starla.

"That, uh, sounds like a good idea. There's uh, no reason to feel that you are threatened, none that we can come up with, at any rate. You are gonna handle your uncle's, uh, arrangements."

"Yes. The funeral is in the morning at Beth Rethel. After that, I plan to return home."

"Well, I gotta go get . . . some police work done," said Sturbridge. He nodded toward the door and indicated that they should leave. When they were outside, Sturbridge gave her a card, told her to call him in case of emergeney, and left.

"They kinda let you feel your own way through in Dallas, don't they?" Roger asked.

She nodded and looked inside the shop and the darkness, at the lusterless glass of the display cases. "Strange, isn't it, how a human existence can consist of a bit of glass in a small room. Still, he was more fortunate than the others."

Roger watched her eyes for any trace of theater, but there was none. Here was a woman who wanted to talk, who wanted to deliver something without the usual female bullshit that one had to wade in order to get a story. He found himself liking this not-so-flashy lady, if guardedly.

"What others?" Roger asked.

"His family." She lowered her head, as though trying to remember names, faces. "Our family, I should say. It just occurred to me that I am the last of the Blaustein blood." She looked at Roger to determine whether he understood the weight of this statement.

"I'm sorry to hear it," he said, hoping that the words were not too trite. There was something about her that was like a piece of crystal that was about to shatter; he knew that no matter what in hell he said or did at this time it might be wrong. "Tell you what. I'll stake you to a quick cup. If it's all the same to you."

"You're all I've got at just this minute in time, Mister Wilder, so I'll take you up on it."

They went into the hotel's little coffee shop together, and Roger steered her to a booth. The thought raced across his mind that some eighty percent of his life was spent either at a booth drinking coffee while getting a story or at a typewriter banging it out. She ordered Sanka and he ordered a Coke; the thought of any more Indian bean nauseated him.

"How'd I do?" she asked suddenly.

"About what?"

"With you and them out there."

"You mean the cops? Fine, I guess. Why?"

"Because some of the things that I said and did were totally out of character for me."

Roger smiled. "Yeah, when you were putting the screws to Sturbridge, I seemed to detect a lack of practice. You resembled a housewife on the witness stand, if you know what I mean."

"Does it show that plainly?" she asked.

"What? Timidity? Yeah, but don't feel bad about it. You mind telling me about yourself?"

"There's not a great deal to tell. I'm nobody in a world of somebodies."

"Lady, if that could be bottled and sold, there wouldn't be any takers. It's a bitter wine we've all had to drink at one time or another." He thought of Moe and Lynch and of all the hassles that were raging back in San Antonio and, for the moment, he was happy to be in Dallas.

"It's strange," she said, "but there is a feeling of kinship that I have for you. You have a certain look that I've seen in my own mirror for the better part of my life. You are not all that happy just now either, are you?"

Roger raised his Coke in a mock toast. "Trouble for trouble, I can probably outrun you by miles."

She looked at him, but did not see him. Her eyes found his own, but she was miles away and, again, he was aware of that profound sadness that he had seen outside.

"I'm going to stay here tonight," she said suddenly. "Will you be here in the morning?"

"Sure. What have you got in mind?"

Her eyes explored his as if seeking some form of touchstone. It was a look he had seen on the faces of certain lost or orphaned Vietnamese children. It indicated a complete separation from all that was familiar. He wanted to hug her, but instead he listened and nodded as she said, "I must attend a funeral in the morning. It is the funeral of my last blood relative. I don't want to go alone. Would you go with me?" As he nodded dumbly, she concluded, "Then meet me in the lobby at nine. I've had a long day and I just don't want to talk anymore."

Before he could say anything she was gone. It was a furtive movement of a schoolgirl who has discovered that her dress is improper, a movement made much too quickly for one who was fatigued. For five minutes he rethought the day's craziness.

"Glad to see you're still up and alive," said a familiar voice. Sturbridge eased himself into the booth like an old hippo testing new mud, contentment written all over his face.

"Everything check out?" Roger asked.

"Yup. Van registered to Gaylon Lynch, dba *San Antonio Sentinel*. The lady did not stay long, Wilder. You piss her off?" Sturbridge picked up Starla's coffee cup and sipped.

"Funny you should ask. The lady has the movements of a demented bee. Maybe she's scared of me, which is stupid. Maybe she's scared of whoever killed her uncle, which would be understandable. All I know just now is that I'm supposed to meet her at nine in the morning to go to the funeral. Bond must be getting pretty ripe, I'd guess." He smiled. The cop did not. "Anyhow, I'll give it my best shot."

"Good boy," said the cop. "What do you think you'll find?"

"Don't know just yet. But she's got troubles far and away beyond a dead uncle."

"Yeah, I got that feeling, too. Still, I don't think it's got to do with this Bond thing. Speaking of which, what have you boys in Bexar County come up with?"

"Not as much as you have," Roger said, tonelessly, cryptically.

The cop's eyes narrowed. "Meaning what?"

Roger shrugged. "You tell me."

"You got something to say, let's hear it." There was cop-threat in these words.

"Okay, cards on the table. You didn't come in here to tell me my van checks out. Not likely. Which means you came in here to pick my brain or to tell me something. Since you know damned well I don't know shit, it stands to reason that you came to tell me something. Am I close?"

Sturbridge grinned. "Wilder, I'm liking you better all the time."

Roger grinned back. "Can this be love?"

"Not likely. Okay, you said cards on the table. Yours first."

Roger let it go, all of it. Bond, Rix, the captain, Moe's idiotic intuitions, the whole nine yards. He talked for five minutes, finishing with, "And then I came here and looked in the window out there. That's where you came in."

Sturbridge meditated on it for a time, sipped the cooling Sanka and said, "Sounds logical. You're full of logic, it seems. Tell me, what have you come to think of the whole thing since arriving in Dallas?"

"For some strange reason, I can't get over the feeling that I owe Voris Mohler an apology. Which is another way of saying that whatever it is you came to tell me is going to make this thing a little more bearable. Time for your cards, Sturbridge."

"S'pose I ain't got any. S'pose I just been pickin' your brain, as we say."

Roger felt a slight worm of anger stirring in his guts. "Because you're not that kind of cop. I know things about you already that you'd like to imagine are hidden. They aren't."

"Such as?"

"Such as your buddies the deputies. Let's say there's a cop who's near to retirement, but he had a problem. He drinks. Let's say the sheriff is an old buddy who wants his pal to get his gold watch right on time. The old cop gets assigned to a third rate murder investigation that didn't even occur in his own jurisdiction. Let's say the sheriff knows that this is the old cop's last chance to do right, so he assigns a couple of deputies to, ah, stand by and see that the old one doesn't blow it on booze at the last minute. Am I close?"

The cop's wrinkled face was white. "So close it ain't even funny. I didn't know better, I'd say you was readin' my mind."

Roger laughed. "No, not that good, unfortunately, but I've been watching county and city politics for a long time. Just some twos that added to four. Too much lip licking, honcho. And that Coke the deputy got you iced the cake. How'd you like to have a fifth right now?"

"I could bite the neck off a bottle of Cutty Sark," the cop admitted, half smiling, half grimacing.

"Please don't. Whattaya got left? Three months, four?"

"Six. I been dry for seven. If I make it, it'll be lucky thirteen."

"Just remember, that pension'll buy a lot of booze."

Sturbridge attempted to pick up the cup. His hand trembled, and he placed it back in the saucer. A fine rime of sweat had appeared at his brow. "This one is my last chance. I can't afford to blow it. I got a ball I want to throw in your court." Sturbridge removed his hat and wiped his brow with a hammy fist. "Tell me, Wilder, you ever hear of Elgin Tatum?"

"Seems like he's a music or TV name. Right?"

"Uh huh. What they call acid rock. Jesus, whatever happened to the likes of Teresa Brewer and the Ames Brothers?"

"They went the way of all twentieth-century sweetness. With me it was Elvis and Johnny Mathis. So what's the sudden significance of music in our lives?"

Sturbridge inhaled deeply and stared at the cup. "Today, the local paper said that this Tatum had been spotted at a local hotel. Public interest, gossip stuff. He's not playing a concert here, so his presence ain't all that much to get worked up about."

The cop ran his hand into his coat pocket, thought about it for a moment, pulled out a small piece of paper. It was a three-by-four note card. He handed the card over to Roger. In precise ballpoint someone had written Tatum, Ableiter, Jarvis, Fontana.

Having studied the names for a few seconds, Roger handed the card back. "Fontana is an Italian word meaning fountain. Pete Fountain, maybe?"

Sturbridge shook his head. "Not in this instance. It might be one helluva coincidence, but I don't think so. This Ableiter don't mean shit, but the others are names I can get my teeth into. Interested?"

"More than ever," Roger said, realizing that he had been holding his breath. Exhaling, he said, "Tell me about it."

"Fontana is the name of a local hoodlum who deals in pornography. Jarvis just happens to be the name of a local private detective. And now Elgin Tatum shows up. What does it smell like?"

Roger shrugged. "Could be coincidence."

"Don't think so, no sir. I'll tell you why: I found this in among some checks in Bond's cash drawer. Those checks were all placed there in the last five or six days, according to the dates on each and every one."

"I'm trying to follow you, Sturbridge, but it's not that easy."

"Damnit man, let's see you do two and two again! A broke jeweler would not hold checks would he?"

Roger pursed his lips. "Yeah, I see what you mean. It's like maybe a few checks had no big significance all of a sudden."

"Atta boy. And you can yell coincidence all you want to, but I say these names on this card are golden."

Roger despised himself for saying it, but he blurted, "I'd hate to tell you the number of times a name got pinned on the wrong donkey in my line of work."

Sturbridge drew an imaginary line on the table. "Just how many people you know named Fontana?" he asked.

"Not one. But hell, it could be one of those jackoff liqueurs they advertise in *Playboy*, for all we know."

Sturbridge drew another line, this one vertical, attaching it to the first. "Jarvis?"

"Nobody."

The cop boxed in the bottom. "Tatum?"

"Okay, nobody. But this last one, Ableiter or whatever, leaves your little cage open on one end." Roger leaned back. "But," he went on, "just for the hell of it, let's say I'm gonna listen because I'm a nice, steady guy. Either that or I'm an open-faced moron. You got some names—good. What I need is a clincher."

Sturbridge leaned across the table, his eyes glinting in self-righteous glee. "You want a clincher, son, here it comes: Fontana and Jarvis have disappeared from the face of the earth in the last three days." He leaned back to let it soak in.

Roger felt stunned, speechless, a little foolish. Maybe the old cop was a rumbum, but he was no fool. Now the bones of what Moe had started in San Antonio were finally showing meat.

"Okay, so let's say you've won me over. Even the most dyed-in-the-sheepdip cynic would say that there may be something to this, if indeed it's dependable."

Sturbridge leaned sideways as if to physically let the insult slide by. "It's dependable. One dead, two missing, one shows up in town. The other, this Ableiter, assuming it's a person and not a place or a thing, is all we don't have. Four out of five, honcho, ain't bad odds."

Roger thought it over and finally had to nod. "Okay. But if you know all this shit, how come there's no APB out on Jarvis and Fontana?"

The cop looked over his shoulder and about the place as if searching for unfriendly eyes. "Part of the reason lies in what you have already dredged out of my not-so-happy face. Granted, I'm a drunk. But I'm a cop, and I used to be a good one. I'd like to leave on a high note, if you can understand that. And with a little nudge from you, it could be done.''

"Of all the people in the state of Texas, how'd I get so lucky?''

"One, you're from out of town. Two, you have a vested interest, said interest being a good story to keep your paper afloat. Three, as I said before, I think you can be trusted.''

"You scratch my ass and I scratch yours, then,'' Roger said.

The cop smiled. "Graphically put. And, as irony would have it, you are, right now, ahead of me in this mess.''

"How so?''

"Because, since about two days ago, I have been withholding evidence. Call it a hole card, if you will, but my motive has been to keep this shit to myself until a moment when it might be needed to save my ass. All I'm doing is marking time until something comes along that will make me look good. I followed up on Jarvis and Fontana both, hence my knowledge of their absence. You and I are the only two people on earth who know that they are locked together on this card. When we find out why, we'll be home free.''

"So what if they turn up in the trunk of a '78 Pontiac? Chronologically speaking, that could make you look very bad.''

Sturbridge bit his lip. "I've thought of that. In that eventuality, this card gets burned, and this conversation never happened. I'd know things I couldn't tell to the powers that be. You, on the other hand, have reporter's immunity from divulging sources.''

"The Supreme Court is a little sketchy on that right now,'' said Roger.

"Remember that poor bastard up east who got locked up some time back?''

"Yeah, but it ain't gonna come to that. Right now we are third raters who are sitting on first rate stuff. You know it and so do I. They put me on it because it was going to be a marginal investigation, figured I couldn't fuck it up no matter how drunk I got. But the little tree put out big roots.''

"And my legwork is going to uncover those roots."

"Absolutely. I could go see this Tatum, but somebody might ask why. And, too, as you've said a dozen times. It might just be a terrific coincidence, his being in town."

Roger said, "Tell me about Fontana and Jarvis."

Sturbridge stuck his finger in the cold coffee and licked it off, his eyes sadly contemplating its blandness. "Jarvis, not much to tell. A seedy private eye. Handles divorce shit, does a lot of work for Mexicans over in his section of town. Kind of a loner. Fontana, though, is something else. An ex-mobster from Joizzy. About ten years ago he and some Jew mobster got in some kind of mob scrape back east and got exiled to Texas. Some kind of coup among the greaseball-goombahs, I would imagine. They fell from grace, but not enough to wind up in the East River. Anyhow, they deal in porno stuff, or did. They supposedly fell out some time ago. Fontana is small potatoes in the porno world, which means that he makes about a million a year. He handles films, books, rubber dicks— the kind of stuff you find in those porno houses. If it pertains to ass, Fontana is in on it.''

"A private eye, a porno dealer, and a jeweler," said Roger. "Jesus, how do you tie it together?"

Sturbridge laughed inaudibly. "I don't. You do."

"Thanks. So you think my best bet would be to start with Tatum?"

"Yeah, or with Starla Landau. As my pappy used to say, a bird in the hand beats nothin'."

"Your pappy should have been a reporter," said Roger. "A bird in the bush looks good right now. Most of ours have either flown or died. By the way, who told you my paper was on the skids?"

"It does not take a mental giant to see that. The van told me a lot. Top of the line transportation, it ain't. That was another thing that made me decide to trust you; a man who needs a story will work harder than one who doesn't. Now, Wilder, my ass is in your hands in more ways than one. What say we get a good night's sleep?''

Roger wanted to ask a million questions, but not one emerged just now. His thoughts were a garble of names and coincidences. And he was very tired. Moe's phone call that had awakened him was light years in the past. Sturbridge paid them out, shook his hand, told him to stay in touch, and was gone.

Registering, he paid in advance. One never knew when something as mundane as an unpaid hotel bill might be the catalyst of failure. Twenty-eight bucks seemed an impertinently great sum for what he got, a monk's cell with sagging mattress, bespotted walls, and worn carpet. He threw his bag on the bed and tried to recall whether he had locked the van. He looked out at the street and saw that it was emptier than a whore's soul. It all reminded him of the way he had always felt just before a twenty-mile route march: dazed, crazy, off on a fool's errand.

The shower did no good for his inner being, and he lay on the cool sheets and thought about the whole thing. If there really was reincarnation, then his option for the next go-round would be to return as a mole or a buzzard, something nobody usually fucked with.

Sleep would not come. He thought of Fontana, the name, and it became fontana, a word. Anita Ekberg had waded in a fontana in *La Dolce Vita,* holding a cat, cooing to it. He wondered where old Anita was just now. Probably fat and stretchmarked and in a villa somewhere with a rakish sort named Vito. He wondered about Darlene for a second and put her out of his mind.

Names came and went: Fontana, Rix, Jarvis, Ableiter, Bond. Damnit, fight it as he might, Sturbridge and Moe, in their separate ways, had just about convinced him that this goddam nutty mishmash of events and characters might be something after all, coincidence and clairvoyance notwithstanding. Sturbridge would yield to the booze in a matter of hours, probably, and it was no good trying to convince himself that he would ever get in touch with the old cop again. Roger Wilder, you are one self-serving, unchivalrous bastard.

He rubbed his wet head, flipped his pillow over, fondled himself for a time, and found that it did no good.

All his fantasy women were out on a toot just now, rebushing their cussedness with those thorny things that women did to become cussed and lovable. Inane thoughts, summer dreams. Nothing related to anything else. This morning he had been in hell over Darlene, and now he could barely remember the outline of her nose. Why? Was he cracking up under the strain of it all—the story that meant everything and nothing, the sale of the paper, the loss of Darlene, the loneliness that seemed never to go away?

There had been pornography at Rix's apartment and Fontana was a pornographer. This meant nothing; hell, truth be known, ninety percent of the adult male population had something stashed back in a closet to make it tingle when real bodies weren't around.

He slept, but it was a sweaty, fitful sleep.

Nine

Moe went at it like hell for the first two hours following Roger's departure. Like all who have a natural ability, he worked at his editings almost as an afterthought. Stories flipped past his eyes with the same easy cadence as those lines that delineated the center of a highway. The lead was about the Russians and the U.S. raising hell at the disarmament talks; he gave it a bit of extra time. The other stuff was the pedestrian and bleary-eyed mundane roilings of daily life: water table dropping, zoning commissions, guerilla raids in the Middle East, a kid rescued from a cave in Illinois. And, all the time he worked, he was fully aware that something inside was eating him alive.

"Anything for me before I go to lunch, Moe?" Henry asked.

Moe looked up, as if trying to focus his eyes on a rather unpleasant character in a bad dream. "Yes, Henry. I want you to go to the cashier and get me five one hundred dollar bills."

"Okay. Don't I need a paper or something?"

"No. Tell her Moe said it, and it shall be opened unto ye. Do it, Henry."

"Okay, Moe. You comin' over to Gino's for lunch?"

"No. I'm having tacos, probably."

Henry started to pursue that statement but a crazed look in Moe's eyes made him think better of it. Besides, Moe had turned his back on the world and was twirling the prop of his little airplane.

At 2:00 P.M. Moe was in a Delta 747 high over the wastelands of New Mexico. He ate his free peanuts and was still hungry. The stewardess offered him one of those little miniature whiskey bottles, and he paid his two bucks and drank it straight. The booze did no good, and he ordered another. It was the first time that he had drunk straight whiskey in years, and it went a long way toward relaxing him. He thought of Henry and Gino's and wished that he had taken enough time for a cheeseburger.

By the time the plane was over Arizona the alcohol had, like a buffeting and sheeting rain, washed over his mind and settled in for a long stay. The first two passing sheets were fear and melancholy, and the one that stayed was remembrance.

Middle age. The two words were lodged there like driftwood to be moved out of the way of the flow, and there was nothing to do but move them. You, Voris Arnold Mohler, are aging, he admitted. Face it, you are never going to be all those things that your boyhood dreams painted in the red and yellow hues of life's sunrise. Cowboy, surgeon, president, millionaire. The poet had said it best: "God pity them both and pity us all, who vainly the dreams of youth recall." He could remember neither the poet's name nor the poem, but the long-dead bastard had summed it up beautifully.

And here he was over Arizona, riding on a ticket that was purchased with money that, if not exactly purloined, was at least questionable.

Middle age. God, how had he gotten here? It had been only days, after all, since he had finished high school at Shakeland, Ohio. The Depression had been on, and he had worked as a cleanup boy in a fraternity house at Ohio State, room and board for a buck a week. His first job out of college was driving a truck for a Cleveland concrete tycoon at twenty-six bucks a week, princely money. There was a Sunday, splitting wood for a fireplace, when the girl he had intended to warm came running out, not with the promised cocoa, but with news about an attack on Hawaii. He remembered supervising the bringing ashore of a load of oranges on an island called Peleliu. He had eaten at least eight of the sour bastards, and he hunkered to take a shit beside a shattered stump. He had just dropped his fatigue pants and grunted once when the sniper's bullet tore a freeway through his left hip, ricocheted off the stump, and slapped the hell out of the back of his head.

It seemed that his life had begun again there. This was because of the haze in which he dwelled for seven months. Palm trees, white walls, intercoms calling for doctors.

"Why are you crying?" he asked a nurse. It was the first thing that had emerged from his mouth since October.

"The President is dead," she answered. It was raining to beat hell outside.

"It will ruin Christmas," Moe had said.

"Bullshit. This is April."

"April?"

"April 12, 1945. You are in Bethesda, Maryland."

And so he was. The waking from his lead-induced slumber was a tonic in itself; it was as though the rays of healing entered his body through his eyes and could get there by no other avenue. By early June he was able not only to walk, but to run and drive a vehicle. He and one of the Navy dentists became great pals and Moe got to borrow his jeep whenever he wanted it. It was gray and had a tiny triangular pennant at the front fender. On the pennant was a tooth, a thing they all thought was funny. It was while driving this jeep in Baltimore that Moe met Edna.

"Get in and rest those precious bones," he had said, Navy style. She fooled the hell out of him and did. That was at noon at a busy intersection. By nine that night Voris Arnold Mohler knew that he was going to marry Edna Stein. The last thing that Moe ever did in uniform was to marry Edna the day before Thanksgiving, 1945.

"Would you like another drink, Sir?"

"I do." Moe was still thinking about it all. "I mean, yeah." He looked out the window and saw something that looked like a great yellow sheet with occasional lumps in it. It was called Arizona. Moe wondered why so much of the country looked like something that needed to be rolled in flour and fried.

"Your drink, Sir."

He sipped and forgot Arizona and went to where it was quieter and softer, a place where people like Tex Beneke and Harry Truman called the shots. It was a world that he understood.

Edna could not have children, a thing that did not matter at first. From 1945 to 1960 they were happy and they moved about and they got it on in bed at least three times a week. They complemented each other like few married couples had ever done. They had had a good marriage.

The change had begun during the Kennedy-Nixon thing in the summer of '60. He had been sent away to Jersey and then up to Hyannis Port by his Indianapolis paper, one of a herd of journalistic cattle who mooed all over that particular election, the last of the really fun elections. Even the songs from that year: Elvis doing something about it's now or never, a bunch of smooth blacks saying save the last dance for me, a kid named Sedaka singing you mean everything to me—they were, if not great, at least memorable, and you could understand the goddam words.

"I've been with another man," she had said. Even now, with the soft suck of the jet engines barely audible, he could hear her words like something from outside a window.

"Been?"

"Yes, been. Do you want me to use the word?"

Moe shook his head and they did not speak again for two weeks. It was as if they entered a fog together and had emerged wearing different faces. Whether or not she ever made it again with another man, he could never tell for sure. They had gone from Cleveland to Indianapolis to Dubuque to Saint Louis and finally to San Antonio. They had a Cadillac and a '64 Valiant clunker. Two weeks ago Edna had taken the Cadillac and her clothes and had gone to her parents' home in North Dakota.

Voris Arnold Mohler looked out the window at yellow and lumpy America and wondered where it had all gone.

The stewardess tapped his shoulder and told him they were stairstepping into San Diego.

There was a burst of warmth as he alighted from the plane, a warmth that seemed to say that here at last was California. It was yellow and pink with just a horizontal line of blue, the very colors that might be created if roses and ocean water could be spun into fine powder. It was the same California of the forties, but it was a little cracked around the edges. Moe inhaled and caught the acrid burn of auto exhaust and human sweat, and some of the pink and blue paled a bit. He did not want to believe that anything had changed. He hailed a cab and, within minutes, was hurtling toward the border. The driver was a Mexican who spoke of "hungriness" and tried to steer Moe to his great-uncle's hostel. Moe did not understand.

Tijuana was a great deal different than he had imagined it. The American and the Mexican influences coexisted while fighting each other, like the richest kid in school posing with his foot on the spine of the poorest kid. There were Coke signs, but they were dusty; there were American hamburger joints, but all were being run by dark people who looked as if they themselves might have provided the dark, flyblown meat that mouldered in the windows. The city appeared to know the words but not the music. A sign reading *Lecheria* turned out to be a dairy shop, and its neighbor *carniceria* was a butchery. Moe wondered whether they were killed and milked or milked and killed. "*¿Adonde va?*"

"Uh . . . Gomez. Souvenirio?" He cringed as the driver looked at him blankly. "Pull over," Moe ordered at last. He indicated for the man to wait while he flagged a cabful of American sailors. "You gobs know this town?" he asked.

"Sure, Dad," said a young seaman with beer tracks in his eyes. "You want your knob polished?" His buddies laughed.

"No thanks," Moe said playfully. "Where would I find the shop of a Raimundo Gomez?"

"Wasn't he an old movie fart?"

"Not the same one," said Moe.

"Look in the phone book," suggested one of the sailors as they drove away.

Moe went over to a pair of old tourists who turned out to be retired schoolteachers from Wisconsin. They had studied Mexico all their lives and had saved like hell to get to it. They were completely disillusioned and wanted to go home, but the tour they were with still had five days to run. The main thing was that they spoke perfect Mexican and, with the help of a phone book, soon had Moe on the right track. He reentered the cab with the correct address.

The place at which the cab stopped was at least two miles off the general tourist run; it was an area of bars, two story hotels and parts stores. Moe wondered who in hell in Mexico needed auto parts, since every car that he had seen had an American license plate. The object of Moe's cab ride was a shabby edifice whose entire facade was no longer than thirty feet. It would seem that whatever Gomez did, he had not been all that successful at it; the place looked like it could do with a barrel of scrub and a bushel of paint. The whole street shrouded itself in grit and despair. The sky that had been so blue in California was gut gray over here, and he felt a rush of superstitious allegiance to America. The third world trolls were fucking up his mind, making the skies change color, bringing out the bigot where none had existed before. Well, not much.

He got out, paid the driver twenty dollars, which he knew to be too much, and felt his kneecaps jellify as the cab pulled away. Even Edna's departure had not given him the sense of loneliness that he felt here.

"*¿Peso?*" a small voice murmured. Moe turned and saw a dark and dirty lad of about ten. His white cotton trousers were chopped off at the knees, and his ankles were so dark from filth that he appeared to be wearing leg irons. Noticing that Moe gazed at the store, the boy said, "*Me duele mucho el pio.*"

Moe handed him a dollar and said, "Gomez?"

"*Si.*"

"Where the hell are they?" Moe whispered under his breath.

"The old man is dead," said the boy. "His daughter is in there."

"You talk pretty good," said Moe.

"So do you," said the boy.

"What do you know about the man?"

"He died in Texas. That's what they say. You a cop?"

"No. A friend. Where is everybody?"

"Siesta. See you around."

Moe wanted to talk further but the boy whizzed away like a track star. Now he turned his attention to the dusty glass. Beyond it and running the length of the store was a cheaply paneled wall. That wall stood about six feet beyond the glass and gave the place the appearance of a doctor's front office or a photographer's anteroom. Down on the far end was a white door.

Moe walked down to the white door and suddenly felt benumbed by something that was not readily apparent. It was not that he felt watched; that feeling always raised the hairs at the back of his neck. And it was not that he felt threatened, for he was not sweating at the temples. No, something else was wrong here, and it took a good thirty seconds of wandering around barefoot in his cluttered attic of memory to bring it into perspective. And suddenly he had it: the white door itself—that was what it was. And memory. 1940. An Ohio farmhouse. Voris Mohler, cub reporter, has been sent to talk to a farmer. The smell of soured apples hangs in the air. The beetles of summer buzz and rustle under the mulch grass, in the fruit trees, along the eaves of the house. There is an old wagon, an old plow, a small barn whose windows bear the pleasant and amusing heads of cows. It is a nice day. He is very happy as only a young man can be in the springtime. He knocks on the door, finds that the door is slightly ajar. He shoves the door open. A bed is shoved against a far wall. In the bed is what is left of a body. The body had blown its head off with a shotgun several days earlier. Maggots cover the body and make a white geyser up the wall while eating spattered brains. Voris Mohler screams.

Shaking the memory aside, he knocked at the door facing and said, "Hola." After living in San Antonio all these years, one would have thought that Spanish would be a second nature thing. With Moe it was not.

The door opened just enough to allow passage of the long nose of a .22.

"Speak," said a female voice, a voice fearful and deadly.

"I, uh, want . . . uh, Gomez?"

"Who are you?" The voice was thick with an accent.

"Mohler. *San Antonio Sentinel.* A newspaper." Moe felt himself sweating. He thought of maggots.

The sound of a hammer release came from within the room, the pistol's snout lowering at the same moment. A coolness emanated from within the place as the door opened.

"I am Bonita Gomez," said the woman.

As beautiful as the woman was, it was quite obvious that someone had worked her over to a degree that her attempts with makeup, rather than camouflaging her contusions, heightened their harlequinate presence. Her mouth had been full and pouty in its natural state, but now the split lower lip had a bedsack effect about it; her left eye was red about the cornea, and twin black circles, dime-sized in mirror image of knuckles, hovered over her right eye. The pistol was now self-explanatory, at least to the degree that she was scared down in her taco-stuffed guts.

"All I want from you is a fucking story," he said, regaining his composure.

She did not open the door, but moved away from it, her absence on the other side leaving the dark slash of openness somehow more of a vacancy than it might have been had she never been there at all. He knew that he was beyond danger now, that the pistol had been the woman's ploy not of aggression, a thing of which women are basically incapable, but of acquiescence to her own weakness. Rather than appearing dangerous, she had been somewhat pitiful. It must be hell indeed being a woman, Moe was thinking as he opened the door.

They shut Tijuana out and Moe was amazed at the elegance of Bonita's living quarters. Where he had expected to see cornstalk hutches and a fire-blackened hearth afizz with chili beans and tortillas, there was instead American

Drew and floral Broyhill. Grasscloth and walnut paneling vied for attention on the walls and, without looking, Moe could sense that the nap of the carpeting was heavy and expensive. Poor greasers the Gomezes were not. She pointed to a chair and seated herself on the couch. Moe had no sooner located in the chair than the eyes of Raimundo Gomez met his own. Gomez, subject of a technically imperfect painting, stood above the couch, his hand touching a short Corinthian pedestal. Roger's description of the dead man had been close, but the painter, having had a live subject off whom to bounce his imageries, had been able to capture an essence that the printed word would never surpass. In this case, the essence was in the eyes; cold, cruel, beady Mestizo eyes, but with just the tiniest irridescence of youth. He could not help but look one last time, and the face that he saw belonged to a priest in a whorehouse or to a doctor who loved torture and pain. Incongruity, that was what was there. Raimundo Gomez had once owned a damned interesting face.

"You are here because of what they said about him," she said accusingly.

"Perhaps," he answered, not knowing what in hell she was talking about, but aware that she needed someone just now. It was going well, much better than an untrained eye might have surmised. "Our cloth and buttons are what people say of us," he volunteered. "The real self has to come from the self. Your father is dead. I can never ask him about his real self."

The woman listened to these words, looked at the round and dull American eyes that touched on her every move. Without knowing how he was doing it, she was aware that this American was mesmerizing his way into her confidence. An older man, a docile man in spite of his little tirade at the front door, he reminded her of what an uncle might have been like had she been born Gringo. Bonita smiled at him, and there was a warmth in the room.

"I will talk to you," she said.

Moe nodded. "Good enough." He looked again at the painting. "Tell me about him."

"He was a good man, not a *pornógrafo* as some have said. He knew priests, bankers, lawyers. He was welcome in the society of this city. He was a father who carried me on his shoulder, who always had candies for all my friends. I once saw him cry at Christmas mass." She looked down, away, into the past.

"Who called him a *pornógrafo?*" Moe asked, a tone of disdain in his words.

"A woman at his funeral. An old puta. The worst kind—the reformed, renewed, virginal puta." Again she looked away at nothing, but this time there were tears in her eyes.

"This woman," said Moe, "did you know her?"

Bonita shook her head, her dark hair becoming darker with movement. It was as though the woman were a living covenant with sadness. "One of the old faces in the town. A crazy woman. They made her to be silent. Someone took her away."

Moe looked down at his nails, back up at the painting of Gomez. Probably the woman was not as crazy as Bonita was making her out to be. In a long and unsheltered life, Moe had discovered that funerals were often as excellent a catalyst as bourbon in the release of truth. Still, it was going well up to now, and it certainly was not time to make any sudden moves.

He laughed a pained, embarrassed laugh and said, "Lady are you saying your father was called a pornographer?"

Bonita's eyes raked him up and down for the slightest clue that might reveal malice, treachery. What she saw instead was an open-faced American who probably had a Cadillac and a mansion and blonde children who attended Harvard. But no, there was a haggardness about the eyes of this man that no actor could ever have accomplished without the most able of makeup men. Voris Mohler was what he said he was. If not, it would come out later in the interview; she could deal with it then.

"Yes," she answered.

Moe felt a sensation like dipping a boot in ice water. Unexpected. He could have lived with dope, gun running, hot cars, prostitution, funny jewelry, or funny cigarettes. But pornography. Somehow it did not smell of heavy things, murderous things. It was boys jacking off behind the barn, cheap shit, petty shit. He felt the trip, and the paper, and his job, slipping away. Ice water in a boot. This morning, a million years ago it seemed, they had found some pornography in Rix's digs. And somebody had said that every man in America had some such shit stashed somewhere. Looking at it that way, there might be money involved on a rather large scale. But, no, this Gomez thing was not about something so simple as dirty pictures. Or was it? Damnit, the man was a *pornógrafo*, a pornographer. But it did not mean anything. Or did it?

"And there were others who thought as much?" Moe asked, dipping his toes in it.

Without the slightest of emotional preambles she began to cry. It had all those face dissolving fluidities about it that convinced him that here was no act, that the lady was in real pain over her father's past. He looked at the pistol that lay on the couch beside her.

When he looked up, she was staring at him. She ran a fingertip across a cut on her upper lip. He wondered how much time had elapsed, probably less than three minutes.

"Yes," she said. "There are others who thought as much."

"There are times," he began with numbing slowness, "when that which is unpleasant must be dredged up and looked at. To realize that our relatives were less than perfect should in no way diminish our love for them." He hoped that the words were comforting, without betraying his real feeling at this moment, that feeling being that Gomez was indeed a shit. And probably a crooked shit as well.

"I must ask what you think," she said, flexing her neck as if to strike.

God, Moe was thinking, so many moods, "I think nothing. As I have told you, I am here to get a story."

"And you have not heard the *pornógrafo* stories?"

"As God is my witness I had not heard such a thing until you said it. Are you afraid that I might say things about your father that are not true?"

She looked at him with the eyes of a fawn who has heard the gentle snap of a limb behind her. His final question was heavy with accusation, but it was gentle accusation. Gringo bastard that he might be, this Mohler had her respect and even a good deal of her admiration.

"Wait here," she said, rising quickly, exiting by a side door.

Moe sat in the quiet room and looked at the pistol. Gomez stared down at him in unctuous rancor, a father staring at a suitor who had stayed past midnight. Now, with the slightest movement of his head, Moe caused the light against the painting to move with an almost ectoplasmic subtlety, and the face was not at all malicious; indeed, Gomez's expression was that of one who holds a toy out toward an infant who must smile for his reward. Beg, even. Goddamnit, this painting was disconcerting. You sonofabitch. Gomez was saying now, you are leading my daughter down the path to save your fucking paper. Yes, fucking paper. We men can say these things now, can't we? So why don't you get your Yanqui ass up and leave? Moe shook his head, changed the lightfall, and Gomez just as quickly said, Hey, Moe, I was kidding.

The door opened and Bonita reentered. She had washed her face, applied lipstick, tied a white ribbon in her hair. It was a good sign; an even better one was the manila envelope she held in her hand.

The envelope held a sheet of paper. Blue, cheap paper. There were four sentences written in black ink, the holography long and angular, as though written by a methodical drunk, or by one who thinks that this which he writes is potentially dangerous. Although the sentences were in Spanish, the proper nouns were readily recognizable.

Jarvis. Ableiter. Grossman. Molly.

As far as Moe was concerned, the rest was hieroglyphics. "Would you read it?" he asked.

Bonita did not bother to get up. "I have read it fifty times in the past three days. It says that Grossman has the money, that Jarvis and Ableiter are at odds, that

Molly will care for the object well and, before you ask, I know nothing about the meanings.''

"How did you come to have this letter?" Moe asked.

"That is strange. He wrote the letter and for three days studied it. As simple as it is, he would go to it, open it, reread it. It was as if he were trying to decide . . . something. He had ceased to be the . . . *broma* that he was so capable of being in those last few days."

"Broma?"

"Yes, a . . ." she made circles with her hands. "A fooler at times. In America there is a name. A maker of foolish traps."

"A practical joker?" offered Moe. His eyes crawled up the painting. He and Gomez now understood each other. That was what the Mexican had been trying to tell him all the time. There was life there in that long-dried oil, a life that none but Moe himself could see. Bonita's little practical joker anecdote was bound to have spilled forth. Moe smiled at the painted face and was not at all surprised when chills clutched at his back, for the light was creating the strangest thing of all.

"Is something wrong?" Bonita was asking.

"Uh, no. I'd like to know why you told me that before the moment passes."

"What?"

"The *broma*, uh, jokester thing."

"I don't know. Is it important?"

Moe ran his hand across his thinning hair and wanted to shout. The thing was here, the thing that had always hit him at some moment in a story, the wrenching of the guts that told him that his nose had not lied to him. Hell yes, he was a million miles from figuring out what in hell was happening but, by God, something was happening.

"No," Moe said, "what is important is Grossman, Molly, Jarvis, and Ableiter. 'Molly will care for the object well.'" Moe looked away, down, at the ceiling. "What object?" When Bonita shook her head, he asked, "Object. Objection. Are you sure your context is right? I mean, Spanish into English?"

"Yes," she said, "I'm positive."

For a full minute they stared at each other, and each of the sixty seconds was a flower of incredible color for Moe. In spite of himself he felt his palms sweating, his armpits adrip as though he had been caught up in a frenzy of writing. Ink was his religion, and the revival ceremony that had been announced by the deaths of Bond and Gomez was just beginning. It was time now for a little bloodletting.

"Tell me about the past week," Moe said.

"You are looking at my cuts."

"For a fact. Can we talk about the past week?"

She shrugged. "My father was murdered, and I was beaten. It was not a typical week."

"Now we're getting somewhere," Moe said.

"You want to know about the beating?"

He smiled wryly. "Look, I've been here less than thirty minutes, and I've already developed eyestrain looking away from your contusions. May I assume that they have to do with your father's death?"

She folded her arms and rubbed opposing biceps with opposing hands, a traditional female reaction to concern. Moe had seen it in the islands, in hospital wards, in death houses. But he had never before been aware that it was such a universal thing. Hate it as he might, deny it as he might, he was getting bad vibrations from her. Here was a perturbed woman, and perturbed women will lie. The big thing with her was her father; it was regarding old Gomez himself that he now had to be careful. The story was here, a living, almost-audibly-breathing thing. Careful, Moe, careful.

"You may assume that," she said at last.

"You were beaten over your father? Over something he did?"

She sat back onto the couch's cushions, her shoulders making rotating motions as though she desired to become a burrowing creature of that sort whose only defense is disappearance, a sand viper etching its delicate curvings on the floor of the Sahara. Unable to disappear, unable to dispel the cold that emanated from her own memories, chilled visibly, she began to speak.

"My father was a good man. I will tolerate no suggestions otherwise." It was a threat, a challenge, a request that he pounce in and say something, anything, that would keep her from having to talk, to vomit it out at last. Moe hung tough this time, however, and Bonita knew that at last it was coming to the fore. There were no more good father jibes behind which to hide. "And he was killed. And I do not know why he was killed; I can only speculate. There were times in which he held expensive items for a short while. A pawned bauble, perhaps. But you do not wish to hear of that." She looked at him accusingly. He allowed his expression to change not at all; it was one of those hallowed moments when art and truth were merging, even while being at odds.

"And he was killed," Moe said, leaving it open-ended.

"And he left here on a plane. Five days later he was brought back and buried here. And your country speaks of its laws and of its constitution and of freedom for all men. You send us songs of our Tijuana Jail, pictures of us eating chili beans and going to sleep under cactus. But for all your glory you could not protect the life of one innocent Mexican. What hypocrites you are!" There were sudden indentations in her chin. Moe thought that she might be about to spit at him. He would just have to let her; this thing was getting better all the time.

"I apologize for your father's death having occurred in my country," he said.

"But not for your country," she accused again.

"No," he said, shaking his head, "not for my country. It is a good country in most ways, just as your own is. There is evil everywhere, Bonita. It has jumped every fence ever built around it."

She stood, went into a bedroom and came back with a box of tissue. Wetting the tip of one with a small vial of something clear and viscous, she daubed it against one of the cuts on her lip. She went to the door, looked out toward the street, and closed the door.

"He came the same afternoon in which my father left," she said, her eyes watching the door. "A tall man. White hair. A fan scar here." She touched her cheek. "He was nice enough at the beginning, and then he began to suggest that I was lying. I did not know where my father had gone, and told him so.''

"How long was he here before he started to threaten?" Moe asked.

She shook her head, looked toward the ceiling as though that particular memory were an elusive bird. "Five minutes? Ten? I do not know. Why do you ask?"

"If he got here just as your father left, he probably was incredibly unlucky. If he did not seem to be in a hurry, then he had no knowledge of your father's recent departure.''

"Which means?"

"Which means he was, and probably is, working alone. A spy in the street would have stopped the gray man and led him to your father." Having said this, Moe leaned back and listened to his tympanic heartbeats. And Gomez would never have made it to San Antonio, and I wouldn't be here on this story, he admitted to himself.

"He thought that we had someone else," she said.

"What do you mean by that?"

"He said *'Uh amigo tuyo Ascunsion Prescindir de.'* At some time while he was slapping me he said that.''

"And it means?"

She smirked slightly, lumping him for a moment with all Caucasians. "It means, in bad Spanish, 'You will now have to get along without your friend in Ascunsion.'''

"Paraguay," Moe interjected. "Who did your father know in Paraguay?"

"No one. To my knowledge, he had never been to Paraguay.''

"Then what did the man mean?"

"The Britisher? Who but himself can know? My father had something that he wanted.''

It was painfully still in the room. They stared at each other as if a third person had made these last statements. "Why did you call him a Britisher?" Moe asked.

"I did, didn't I?" she exclaimed. "I had not been aware of it until now. That was what was different, his accent! All this time I have thought of him as American. He was British!''

"Can you be specific?" Moe asked.

She retreated into her memories for a moment and then shook her head. "No. Just certain words were . . . British."

"Okay," said Moe, "good enough for the moment. We've got a tall Britisher with white hair and a fanshaped scar. He's slapping you. Words. Names. Places. Think! He's hitting you!"

"Sanchez," she hissed, the pain on her lips causing her to squint. "He wanted to know when Sanchez had been here. I don't know any Sanchez."

"So what did you tell him to make him stop hitting you?"

"What could I tell him? I showed him the stuff of my father's business, the stuff of *guerra tela.*"

"*¿Guerra tela?*" Moe questioned. In spite of her thunderously heavy accent, it still came as a jolt to him when she had to occasionally resort to her native tongue.

She came off the couch and motioned for him to follow. Their route included a small kitchen whose sink was piled with the dishes of her recent despair.

Embroiled in thought, Moe paid no attention as she motioned him into a great dark room and stepped aside as he entered. He was making plans for telling the human race what a dirty piece of shit it really was when he felt a human shoulder in the darkness.

The electricity of fear stunned him, chilled his blood in his arteries, froze it in the wider seas that were his veins. Again he listened for his heartbeat and was not amazed that he could not hear it. It was drowned out by the sound of his breathing.

His hand did not move. The shoulder did not move. There were slappings on the wall behind him, the wings of a bat whose twin syringes were prepared for his jugular vein. His eyes were becoming adjusted to the dark, when reality asserted itself and he could see that the party whose shoulder he touched was wearing some sort of military cap. Further reality transformed the bat's wings into Bonita's hand that slapped over the wall in quest of the light switch. Now, most horrible of all, Moe saw that beyond the man whose shoulder he held were many other men! Not a few men, but a dozen or more!

Moe felt his bowels churn. There was a violent lurch in the lower part of his torso as raw fear tore out the circuitry of his nerve endings. Still the people did not move. In all, ten seconds had slithered by, now fifteen, thirty. Bonita's hand still slapped about, the light switch making itself a part of the wall's flatness.

"Ah," she said. The great room was suddenly filled with light.

Moe gasped, stepping backward even though his legs were without feeling. The men stared at him with dull blue eyes, all twenty pairs of eyes. Their lips were unsmiling and their noses, angled perfectly to point straight at Moe, portrayed a flawless, patrician primness that made them appear malignantly homosexual, iniquitous. All wore the very same face, the same combed eyebrows of blonde-brown, the same blonde hair. Now he saw that they were not looking at him, but through him, and that which held their dead attention was, he found in turning, a portrait of Adolf Hitler.

"God," said Moe, "a platoon of SS troops!"

"Yes," said Bonita, waving her hand at the room's openness, "this is what I wanted to tell you. My father sold the stuff of war. These mannequins are his Aryan models."

"Souvenirs." Roger had mentioned this fact only casually in his original story of the murder. But, at that time, Bond had been the big news, not some dead Mexican. Feeling queasy at the stares of the SS platoon whose presence had scared the wind out of him, Moe stepped out of their sight line and made an impromptu tour of the place. A hundred feet long, eighty feet wide, musty-dusty with the coolness that is always the way of stored materials, the room was rather like a museum whose curator had lost interest. At one time there had been cataloging, oiling, cleaning, brushing, but now there were evidences that even common dusting had gone undone. What did it mean? That Gomez had indeed gone into something more lucrative? Moe walked the length of the place down one side, up the other, his heavy shoes funereally observant of the horrors that these things had wrought, tracks in the dusty floor being created for those who would never again make tracks. There were racks of Nazi flags; "jingling Johnny," the Romanesque fur-draped guidons of the *Schutzstaffeln* legions; wallboard after wallboard hung with iron crosses and swastikas of various sizes. Hemingway had said somewhere that all things truly wicked start from an innocence, but Moe could have traced forever before finding anything innocent about racks of bayonets, Lugers, Walther PPK pistols whose lethality against Jewish skulls in Russian and Czech forests had been documented by some of his bedmates during his recuperation. World War II was alive for him once again as he walked, and the voices of FDR, Kaltenborn, Heatter, Fulton Lewis and the legions of others echoed in his thoughts. Beyond the bayonets there were hundreds of propaganda posters, the most dubious of which pictured a muscular blonde mother offering up her infant to Adolf Hitler. Helmets stacked to the wall, belts, *Wehrmacht* uniforms by the score. Moe had seen enough. In cruel obeisance, the SS troops stared at the distant oil of Adolf Hitler, and he could emphathize with how one entrapped in a police state would keep one's goddamned mouth shut; he realized that there was a mendacity in uniforms that he had never seen before, not even in his sailor days.

"Did he have an office?" Moe asked.

"Yes."

"May we?"

She nodded. "You may. I have never been in my father's office. It was not allowed. Are you finished here?"

Moe took a last look about the cavernous place. The SS troops were still sizing him up, their faggot eyes wanting not his prick but his very soul. Say what one would, they nearly whipped the world.

"I have never left there without feeling cold," she said.

"Yeah." He followed her down the hallway past the kitchen door. She stopped, pointed to a key hanging from a nail over a doorway at the end of the unlighted hall. Whatever else one said about the Gomez tribe, they believed in saving electricity. Moe went on, took down the key, heard her close the kitchen door.

The office was about a ten-by-twelve. Stark wooden desk, old swivel chair something like his own, except that

Gomez's was solid wood. Metal filing cabinet. And map on the wall. World map, courtesy Rand McNally, captioned under its two globes *Orbis Terrarum Descriptio Dubois Planis Hemispharis*. Fancy. Someone had done the map in decoupage and added the verbiage in cheap gilt. There were short pins stuck in several places on the map: Stockholm, Los Angeles, Düsseldorf, Berlin. They meant nothing to Moe, never would without Gomez along to help, something damned unlikely. Some were blue, some were red.

The filing cabinet contained four drawers. The top three were empty. The fourth proved that Gomez was what his daughter professed that he was not—a *pornógrafo*. If not a pornographer, then certainly a man whose past had dealt with the more questionable uses of a camera. From several jacket files there fell bookkeeping paraphernalia, tax papers, a nail file, but from two fell a spate of photographs. In one of these a once famous European actress was being serviced by two blacks who were dressed in the uniform of the U.S. Navy. One worked her mouth, the other her anus. She did not appear to be enjoying any of this; rather, she looked off as if trying to recall whether she had added bleach to her last load of towels. This might have constituted heavy blackmail stuff years ago, but now it was the sort of thing one could pick up on almost any newsstand. There were varied groupings and proddings by other sorts of humanity in the other pictures, and Moe found himself yawning before he had gotten halfway through. He dropped the photographs back into their file folders and shut the bottom drawer on all that was left of the life of Raimundo Gomez.

Gomez and Bond. Rix. Tijuana. Britisher. Paraguay. War souvenirs. Pornography.

Nothing. Bonita had thrice denied that her father was a pornographer, but the sonofabitch was, or at least had been. Nothing to chew on there, just a daughter's shame.

He opened the door, looked over the office one last time, hung the key on the nail, and returned to the living room. Bonita sat on the sofa. She did not look at him. The smell of hot tea emanated from somewhere. Moe looked at her right and saw a small pot standing on a hot plate. There were two cups beside the hot plate.

"You have stared at me for a full minute," she said. "Is there something you wish to know?"

He nodded.

"You want to know whether I have lied to you?"

He smiled. "I came as a friend. I'd like to leave as a friend. I came for a story. So far there is little reason for me to have made the trip."

She went to the core of her memory and talked for twenty minutes. They had not always lived in such circumstances; at one time, life had been not only good but, by Mexican standards, downright enviable. She had known, at a tender age, that her father had dealt in erotic playing cards and Tijuana bibles, eight pagers featuring poorly-drawn cartoon characters from the legitimate newspapers. The forties, fifties and part of the sixties had been good years for the Gomez family, and they had traveled extensively: Europe, the Orient, America. She had attended school at UCLA. Then, in her senior year, her mother died; this brought her home to care for her bereaved father. Gomez tried to pull himself out of the vacuum of despair but, by the time he got around to it, America had discovered its own abilities at creating pornography and did not need him any more. Subsequently, he had bought some war supplies. And, for the past decade, this had been the business of Raimundo Gomez, a business conducted for the most part through small ads placed just within the back covers of male-oriented magazines. The large dollars had never come.

Moe was silent for two minutes. Even when she stood and poured tea and placed the cups, he said nothing.

"Convergent!" said Moe. He picked up his teacup, sipped, and winked.

"What?" she asked.

"I was thinking aloud, Bonita. It wasn't divergent at all, but convergent. The man who came here, your father's departure, the death of Rix. Convergent occurrences." He smacked his lips and winked at her again.

Convinced that she was in the presence of one who had suddenly become distracted, her voice quaking with dread, she asked, "Will you be a bit more . . ."

"Lucid?" Moe interjected. "Hell, yes." He stood, walked the length of the great room, looked at Gomez's oily face, pointed at it, left his finger in the air for a moment. "Tell me again the basic things the man said," he commanded.

She complied, triple trenches of memory forming between her eyebrows. Bad Spanish, Ascunsion, Sanchez. She shook her head, shrugged, could think of nothing else.

"He killed Rix," Moe said. "I'm right. I gotta be."

"And my father?"

Moe stopped his pacing, looked up at the painting and returned to his chair. Sipping his tea, he said, "No. Your father was killed by a man named Rix. Rix himself was killed by the man who hammered on you." He placed the cup in its saucer and slammed a fist into his palm. "Why, goddamnit, why?"

"Why what?"

"Why several things. For openers, why didn't he kill you? All I can figure is that he wanted you alive so that you could describe him. Now why in hell would he do that, unless he wanted someone on his trail to know what he looked like?"

"Perhaps you are missing the obvious," said Bonita. "Perhaps, by killing me, he would have lost the thing he was looking for, the thing my father had. If I were dead, of course, my father would have returned to Tijuana but, by then, this thing or these things would have been sold. Or destroyed. Would you turn over this thing after your daughter had been murdered?"

"No," Moe answered thinly, feeling some of the power go out of some of his speculations. "I think you've got me there. Still, I think there was some deeper reason for his not killing you. It's almost like he wanted to follow your father into the States, convergent and convergent." Again Moe picked up his cup, found that it was cold, waved off a warmup.

"Tell me about this Rix," said Bonita. "I want to know what he looked like so that I can hate him."

"He wasn't so despicable as you might like to imagine, just another human grabbing for something that wasn't there. An ex-policeman who drank, who saw his life slipping away, who tried one heavy time to pick up the big money." Moe remembered the smell in the Rix apartment. God, was that only this morning in San Antonio?

"And you are sure that he is the one who killed my father?"

Moe shook his head. He was suddenly very tired. On a small ring binder tablet he scribbled many things: words, names, impressions. Somewhere there were answers to all the questions. For now it would be enough just to return to San Antonio. He put the tablet in his pocket and lurched to his feet like an old fighter who must go one more round but has forgotten why.

"Fairly sure, Bonita. Is there anything else you can recall? Anything at all?" The question was exhaled in a vapor of fatigue.

"Nothing. I'll call you at your paper if anything recurs. But it won't. He wasn't here for . . . me." She came across the room and led him to the door. She was smaller and even more vulnerable than she had seemed nearly two hours ago. He wanted to shake her hand but that was not appropriate. He did not know what to do, so he smiled at her, nodded, and went into the street with its browns and tans, that for whatever reason are forever the colors of poverty.

Two hours later, Moe watched the canteloupe slice of Pacific sunset disappear under the plane's wing as the Braniff swung out over the ocean and then back inland. He was very tired, very confused and, strangely, very happy.

Ten

Elgin Tatum stirred. He was in a white place, but from somewhere the smell of pink wafted in. What in hell, he asked himself, was the smell of pink? He had been strung out of late, admittedly, but even for old weird Elgin this was walking the border. If he knew his name, which was Elgin Tatum and, if he knew the name of the song that was coming into the room from a radio, then it stood to reason that he should know all the other things that were bugging him. City: unknown. Time: ditto. If I could find my neck, he reasoned, then I could lift my head. My eyes are in my head and, thus, if they were elevated, they could see where my ass and feet are. Logic conquers all.

His neck did its thing, and he remembered it all in a flash. The pink smell was sex. Or, more specifically, vagina, one or both of the two that were in bed with him, bracketing his body like twisted bookends. The song, just ending, was called "Green Dolphin Street," an evergreen from a way back. The city was Dallas, and the hotel was the Winston. The grass had been gray-green, and the coke had been white, and the pills had been yellow jackets. Testing his voice, he said in a whisper, "My name is Elgin Tatum. I am thirty-four years old, and live in Trancas Canyon, which is somewhere in Southern California, and I have two million dollars in the Cal-West Savings and Loan, not to mention properties in the Philippines and Hawaii. It is all straight except for two things: who are these two girls in bed with me, and what am I doing in Dallas?"

One of the girls moaned and snorted. Elgin tried to move his arms, but they were gone. Gone? Oh, Jesus Christ, there's been an accident. He lifted his head and saw that each arm was pinned by a female torso, saw that his arms were not only asleep but probably atrophied as well. He thrust his torso forward and grimaced as needles of pain coursed through his hands and biceps. The girls continued to snore and to salivate in an excess of unconscious ecstasy. One, a redhead whose back was specked with freckles, had bled slightly, the rusty crust of blood making a Rorschach of an electric chair on her leg. He rose, hurried to the bathroom, and pissed like a race horse, the smell of his own urine burning his nostrils. His tingling hands betrayed his aim, and the stream hit the commode lid, and ricocheted off onto his knees. A two-minute shower reclaimed his body but his mind was still floating as freely and as volitionless as a scud cloud before a storm.

Standing before the mirror as he toweled off, he looked into his own brown eyes and saw his curly hair. Famous curly hair. His gaze wandered to his chest where there was silver among the black, and he promised himself to get an appointment with Henri as soon as he got back to L.A. The chest was one thing, but never, ever, as his agent had put it, should his fans see gray among his upper locks.

"So, why are you in Dallas, asshole?" he asked his image.

And then he remembered the phone call from Eddie the Freak, as the man was known in L.A. Forty-eight hours ago Eddie had said that a big skin deal was going down in Dallas and that Elgin should waste no time in getting there. The deal was one of the biggest, said old reliable Eddie, and it would take at least two hundred thou. Elgin had commented that for that kind of money it had better be Jackie O blowing a horse. Eddie had laughed and said that the man to see was one Perry Jarvis. Period.

Two hundred thousand dollars for perhaps one dirty picture, or maybe a film. Eddie had been necessarily hazy, but the bastard had always come through before, so it must be the ultimate, whatever that could be. After all, it was Eddie who had set up the Oscar orgy of 1977, a party at which two Oscar winning females from Hollywood's past had been on hand. One, a brunette lady who had won in the late fifties, was still a queen naked, and she had given the best head in the house.

He looked again at the image in the mirror and saw the rudimentary wings of fat that had begun to emerge at his sides, flesh that was somehow more shiny than the rest. Why did the human body always wear its failures like a red hat? Why did buck teeth shine? Why did fat always glow?

He lathered, shaved down with the grain, lathered again, and shaved up against it. Drying off, he patted his cheeks with a concoction called *Couchage le Dame* which meant, ingenuously, bed the lady. He had given sixty dollars for the two ounce bottle, not because of the scent but because of the price and because of the name. Such shit meant nothing anymore. It was ironic that money lessened its power by growing larger.

Pouring the *Couchage* down the commode, he mulled over where enough had become too much. In a country that had promised to the millions but had awarded to the tens, he had beaten the odds. It worried the shit out of him.

That was where the sex came in, and the worry, feeding on each other like two nameless creatures locked in some dark arena and taking occasional bites out of each other for sustenance, neither really liking it but neither knowing just how to end the cycle of bite and pain. He and some of his honchos had bought half the whores in Vegas and Beverly Hills, coveys of them, bevys. The worry had started ten months ago when a pair of blonde twins had taken turns licking his prick and balls for six hours. He had been unable to walk for twelve hours after that one and, for that twelve hours, he lay on the dark bed and wondered why he no longer felt satisfied. It was his feeling that the sexual orange should give up both pulp and juice but, since that time with the blondes, the pulp always remained behind, a softly taunting thing that would not go away, no matter who or what he rammed. He had told his shrink that he was a sexual arthritic, one whose pain never quite leaves. The shrink had gotten a chuckle out of that one. It was the first time that he had ever heard a psychiatrist laugh, and it bothered him a little, this ability to penetrate aloofness. Certain people, he reasoned, should be above laughter, for it is axiomatic that one never laughs when another's guts are on the fence.

Leaving the bathroom reeking of laythelady, he reentered the cavernous suite and took in its blues and ivories, its touches of mahogany. The goddam draperies alone probably cost what his old man had made the year Elgin was born, and he walked over and pissed a yellow stream up and down their folds, lazily smiling as the liquid pattered to the carpet. One thing about dope, you never had to worry about the ability to piss.

Now he looked at the other girl. She was a brunette of about twenty, and she needed a shave in her armpits. She lay on her right side with her left leg drawn up, and he knelt beside the bed and examined her. A fine patina of semen had dried in her pubic hairs, and they were a dull gray near the labia. He stopped his exam and rolled her over onto her back, thus creating the perspective that all mankind loved, a naked and total vulnerable female body. Jesus, the ways that women could turn you on just by turning themselves. Twitchy asses, soft tits, tears and tongues like the very satins of Valhalla. Thirty seconds before he would have refused to piss in the river for all of womankind, and now he felt himself getting hard. But no more, not with these two at any rate. Shaking them, he wished that he could remember how it had been. The dope thing had to go. Hell, look at Janis, Jimi, Elvis.

"Sha' doin'?" the redhead growled.

"Milkin' time, your ladyship. You gotta get out of here."

"Where's that bastard that was gonna pay us? We ain't leaving without our money."

"Oh, who's that?"

"You know, your flunky, the one got us up here. Hey, you're smaller on stage than in person. Hell, you're fat."

He seized her by the ankle and dragged her off the bed, her lower quarters leaving a light pink trail of blood on the sheets. Too groggy to scream, she merely stared at him with her face contorted in rage as he pulled her across the carpet. Within seconds the friction got to her, and she squealed and twisted sideways, grabbing the leg of an ornate marble table, thus halting all forward progress.

"You bastard, you burned my ass!" she spat viciously.

"So sue me, whore. By the way, was I good last night?"

"Good what? You were zonked all to hell. You never even rose up a hard. I hate your ass, an' I'm gonna tell all my friends."

He laughed and dropped her leg. She noticed her own blood and reddened about the cheeks. It was a very human thing, almost pathetic, this facial scalding, and Elgin looked away as if busying himself with the other one.

"You wanta roust out, cunt?" he asked. The brunette nodded hazily.

Ten minutes later they were gone, each with her hundred dollar bill picked up from the floor. It was a thing that Elgin always did to prostitutes, this throwing of the bills onto the floor. He liked the obvious symbolism, liked the way they always looked up just as they grabbed the money. They did it that way every time; it was as if they thought they were to be kicked in the face.

He went to the closet and took out a black satin shirt and white trousers, his trademark. Hell, he might as well be seen in Dallas, since the local papers had blown his cover yesterday afternoon anyway. At seven last night he had counted the phone calls from the desk and got as high as seventy before smiling and stopping. Whoever had said that fame and attention were narcotics had been right on target. He gulped a yellow and a blue and put on his sunglasses. Feeling high, good, euphoric, he sat on the bed and drew the covers over the blood. The first goddam reporter who knocked at his door would get a story. After all, those insignificant bastards had to eat too.

In those last two minutes of his life Elgin Tatum speculated again as to why he was in Dallas. Eddie the Freak. White hot porno. And, most of all, that dreamy thrust that he would find in new pictures or a new film, that ultimate rush that would take him to sexual never-land. In the house in Trancas Canyon there were one hundred and twenty thousand dollars worth of plain old pictures, not a one of which had ever sent him totally over the top. Even Wona Bawwett had mentioned it in her column, a blind item, of course, but all the show biz types knew exactly who was being nailed.

There was a knock at the door. It would probably be Norton Fine, his confidante and road manager and the goofy bastard who had brought the two hookers up last night to meet the star. Reaching for the knob, he wondered who Norton had brought up now.

Eleven

The little Jewish cemetery lay off the freeway about six hundred yards. Nestled among sad and stunted oaks, it was two acres surrounded by a wrought iron fence. Roger read the names: Stein, Rusen, Cohn, Blintkamp. Sophie here and Maurice there. Counting the rabbi, there were exactly twenty people in attendance. The old man wore a powder blue yarmulke and Roger remembered the coke lid beanies of his youth. It was all he could do to keep from yawning. A bluejay alighted in one of the shorter trees, and Roger watched it for a long time.

"Let us pray," said the rabbi. As the rabbi droned in Hebrew, Roger eased himself backward and watched those assembled. All were older, mostly male and, could demeanor be trusted, extremely attuned to the service at hand. Starla was the youngest woman there, a fact that made her also the prettiest, comparison being the malleable curve on which he graded women. She wore a gray dress with a wide white belt, white high heels, and a gray pillbox hat. It was as if she had stepped out of the fifties for the ceremony. Dour, drab, dumb: still, there was something about her that his reporter's eye yet found interesting. He had called her room at seven and invited her to breakfast, and they had sat in the hotel restaurant yawning at each other over bacon and eggs. Roger had noticed that at least two men in the restaurant had found her worth a second glance, a thing that puzzled him. Perhaps old weird Darlene had soured him to a point whereon he was no longer objective. He had returned to his room on the third floor long enough to pack and, by the time that he was able to check out, she was already gone. He had circled Dallas at least once before the little cemetery presented itself, and he was almost late for the service.

The rabbi went into Bond's personal history, and painted a picture of a giving and caring man whose destiny was cut short by the hand of an assassin. Roger watched all the faces and hands on that one, and detected nothing at all. Clench and tremor had sent more than one murderer up, but there was no Charlie Chan stuff to be had here. He looked and saw that the bird was gone, and he was saddened by its absence.

The service ended less than ten minutes after it had begun, the Kaddish having been gibberish to Roger. He was trying, without much success, to feel Jewish. The way things were stacking up, he would be out of Dallas and on his way back to San Antonio by noon.

"Miss Landau, may I have a minute with you?" he whispered sarcastically.

"You don't quit, do you?" she snapped.

"No, I don't. You want that man they are reeling down to be avenged. It could start here."

"The police are all waiting with bated breath, Mister Wilder. With you on the job, I suppose they can go home."

"Look, goddamnit, I'll give you a ride to the airport. It's free. Gratis. Get it? You bugged out on me and took a taxi here from the hotel. I suppose it had to do with some ingrained pride thing, but it was still dumb." He started to say more, but some of the dry-eyed mourners passed nearby and went down the little gravel road and past the trees and into the street. They both watched the others go; it dawned on him that not one person had known or cared who they were.

"Very well," she said at last, her words quivering in the cemetery's stillness.

They followed the others down the road and by the time they got to the van, the street was mostly empty. Neither of them noticed the dark Mercedes at the distant end of the street.

As Roger started the engine and eased onto the street he said, "Listen, about last night, or this morning at breakfast, or whenever it was, I apologize."

"For what?"

"For whatever I did that is making you act this way. Honest to God, Miss Landau, I'm a pretty decent human being when given a chance. I even had a dog and a bike once."

"I didn't," she said quietly staring ahead.

Roger felt the old stir of a clue being handed to him. "Oh? Why not?"

She shook her head. "It's a long story. Too much for a ride to the airport. We'll have to go to the hotel to get my bags. Do you mind?" When he did not answer, she looked over and saw that he was preoccupied with the rearview mirror.

"Something tells me that if you're expecting to leave today, don't," he said absently.

"And why not?"

"Let's just say the story I'm on has suddenly taken on new life."

"I'm not sure I know what's going on."

"Me neither. But we've got a tail."

She turned and saw the car. It trailed at a discreet two hundred yards and, when Roger steered the van onto a side street and turned left onto another, the Mercedes followed. An arrow indicated that the freeway was off to the right and he eased the van up the ramp and into the moderate mid-morning traffic. The Mercedes still hung back.

"Who do you think . . . ?" Her voice trailed off.

"I don't think, Mademoiselle, I know. Whoever it is has got the power. I'm open for suggestions. We can run and attract a cop or we can try to get to the hotel." He felt his cheeks begin to sting. Why was it that practicality in front of a woman always smelled like cowardice? He was not really afraid, but he would have readily admitted to apprehension. For the first time, he found himself admitting absolutely that Moe's hunch was right after all.

"Maybe it's a coincidence," she offered, still looking out the van's back window. "Maybe it was one of Uncle Alan's friends who wanted to talk to me."

"Maybe it's the King of Denmark, but don't count on it."

Roger shoved the gas pedal down and watched the approaching skyline. The indicator moved from forty to sixty, and the old engine began to protest. At seventy, a buffeting action started, and he let off the pedal, his foot twitching.

"I don't really think you should---"

"Shut up and hang on, kiddo. Old dad's gonna save your ass from the green meanies." He hit the gas pedal again and swerved to the left, the front bumper barely missing the tail of a Chrysler. The old van now seemed to dredge a second wind from within itself. The motor baritoned as the wind bracketed its square body. Checking the mirror again, he saw that the Mercedes was easing up on the Chrysler, at first blocked by it and then emerging steadily around it. The concrete pickets at the side of the road were clicking past like the ruffle of heavy playing cards, and Starla gripped the seat on either side of her hips, her face as white and as still as that of a porcelain Madonna. Roger checked the left lane and saw two cars about a hundred yards ahead. While in the center lane, some two hundred yards to his front, was a semi, its great smokestack firing a dark plume three feet into the gray sky. Now, to his right, was a regular convoy of about seven cars led by an old pickup truck that was itself some ten feet behind and to the right of the truck. The place was like a moving checkerboard. By judging the speed of the two cars in the left lane he calculated that they would be even with the big truck in about another half mile. The Mercedes was back about a quarter but moving up fast and, if he were going to do it, it would have to be now. He checked out the right lane group again and saw that, in fourth place back, were two bearded morons in a Trans-Am. At that moment, they looked beautiful. If his plan worked, he might have to whip their grungy asses. Now, the two to the left were almost closing the slot on that side, and Roger acted, praying a little. He slowed beside the Trans-Am, gave the startled driver the finger and formed the words "mother fucker" silently, fiendishly.

Now he rammed the van between the old pickup and the semi and saw that the Trans-Am was right on his bumper, the two drivers screaming and fanning the air with their own middle fingers. One of them was having real difficulty, as there was a beer can in the proffered hand. "Ain't this some shit?" he chortled to Starla. She stared straight ahead, frozen in fear.

The Mercedes was now frustrated on all three lanes of traffic and hung far back in the center. Roger knew that, as soon as the two in the far lane passed the semi, this particular part of the jig would be up, so he figured on about forty-five seconds worth of free time in which to calculate. The sports model with the enraged drunks was now even with the door of the huge truck, the front fender and cowls of the leftmost car were just emerging. Ahead was a crosspatch of overpasses where the freeway waved its cement flags at the rising city. Think, Roger, think. Now the second of the leftmost was coming out from behind the truck, which meant that the Mercedes would be right on their tails, especially if the driver thought that Roger was going to make a pure and simple run for it. Glancing at the speedometer, he saw that he and the truck were at sixty-five. The Pontiac with its hoodlums was being held in perfect check, which meant that the two right lanes were blocked out. The rear of the leftmost car was coming now from behind the truck, and the Mercedes had disappeared from his rearview, meaning that it was now in the far left lane beyond the great semi. The next front end to emerge from over there would have to be the dark snout of the Mercedes, and Roger steeled himself for his next foray into madness.

"You wanna get in the back?" he screamed. "It might be a nickel's worth of safer back there!"

"I can't move," she yelled back, "so save your nickel."

He grinned at her, and she rolled her eyes upward. Here was a woman with guts, almost balls. Roger liked the hell out of her, and wished that he knew her better. But there was no time to think of that just now; the nose of the Mercedes was coming out just as Roger had calculated.

"Hang on!" he commanded. Grabbing the wheel like a bull rope, hands crossed, he jerked the van to the left and found himself within inches of the great truck's front bumper. There was a dizzying blur of cars and colors and auto horns as the whole freeway seemed to erupt into bedlam. The cars that had been led by the pickup were swerving in all directions, the truck was moving sideways into the left lane, its horn bawling like that of a demented milk cow, and the Mercedes was yawing off to its right to elude the truck. In the dead center of it all, Roger Wilder was grinning like an idiot at seventy miles per hour. He wheeled in beside the Mercedes and saw that it was being driven by a wide-eyed black man, a slender and bald human who was just as frightened as was Starla. They could have reached out and touched the dark car.

"Hang tough, lady, we're gonna hit!" Roger ordered. He brought the van level with the Mercedes and checked out the mayhem behind him in the rearview mirror. Most of the traffic had slid to a stop, pointing at weird angles toward the truck, and now he swung toward the Mercedes again, and the black man slammed on his brakes and let the van slice past.

"The bastard's good," Roger said. No sooner had he said it than the Trans-Am was at his own left side, a fist waving angrily out its window. Better a fist fight than a bullet in the head, he mused, and old Blackie in the Mercedes would not dare start anything now. He slowed the van and pulled onto the side of the freeway.

"When I get out, you lock the door behind me," he ordered, already stepping out, feeling as if his legs might go at any second; his knees were fairly palpitating. He started to look around for the Mercedes, but the two scroungies had jumped from the sports model and were running toward him. One was carrying a short wrench. The other one got to him first, and Roger simply bent over and gave a full shoulder-tackle's lunge into his midriff, driving him back into his buddy and onto his haunches. All three went into the gravel and Roger smelled the reassuring odor of beer. This would be a cinch. He quickly arose, kicked the wrench holder in the chest, and grabbed the heavy steel from his hand. "Bad boy better stay on the ground," he said quietly.

They stared at him for a moment, gasping, and then looked beyond him, through his braced legs. "Who the hell are you?" Wrenchy asked sullenly.

"I'm his bodyguard," a male voice answered.

"We ain't done nothin' to him," said the other scrounge. His face reminded Roger of certain breeds of terriers, those who yip and then run.

"And you ain't gonna. Now you white boys be nice and leave. You hear?" The two scrounges got up and ran to their car.

Roger felt the hair at his neck tingle; it was as if a sword were about to touch him there. For some reason, he could not bring himself to turn around. The big truck and the other cars were passing now, and horns and extended middle fingers seemed to fill the Texas air. Everybody in Dallas hated Roger Wilder, and not one of the bastards knew or cared that he was about to die.

Fighting down an impulse to call the uglies back, he watched them drive away, both giving him the finger.

Turning, he saw that the black man was about six feet tall, and dressed in white, except for a black bow tie. A smile played across his dark lips, and he pointed a thumb backwards at the van. "Your box there does good, boy." Hundreds of years of understanding flew between them on the cold wings of the word "boy."

"I guess so. I didn't know niggers could drive so well. Run, maybe, but not drive."

The man laughed, and the tone was one of genuine mirth. "We don't swim so hot, either. You wanta come nice, or you wanta fight?"

"Depends. Who in hell are you?" Roger spread his legs and prepared to lunge again.

The black man extended his hands, palms outward. "That won't feed the baby, man. I've whipped half of Folsom in my time. All I want is to take you to my boss."

Interesting. Roger shared the ubiquitous Caucasian-American opinion that nearly all the black males in the country had been in the slammer at least once and, if this one was telling the truth, then the karate stance was real and therefore potentially lethal. There was but one way to find out. He leaned his upper torso forward, moved quickly in toward the black man, and was just about to feint to the left when something exploded at the back of his head. His neck hurt, and he smelled the rocks and dirt of the road's shoulder.

"Good white boy," said the black man, his voice coming from miles above. Cars went by, slowed, sped onward. "I love white boys who agree with me. Wanta come on now?"

Recalling Alfonso Bedoya pleading for his sombrero while about to be shot, Roger asked, "Do I bring the van?" He was wheezing and hated himself for it.

"Sure. I have a feelin' you're gonna need it. The lady can ride with me. That way your creativity will be minimal."

Rising sheepishly, rubbing his outraged occipital region, Roger was thinking, Good English. This is no cotton patch nigger. He waved meekly at Starla to convey, if dubiously, that all was well. She waved back meekly, her face drawn in fear.

"You got a name or just a fist?"

"Perkins. At your service."

"First or last?"

"Only. Those Rabbis do drone on, don't they?" He smiled.

Roger limped to the van, and Starla rolled down the window. "I think we got a live one here," he whispered. "He seems okay so far. You ride with him, and I'll follow in the van."

"Not on your mother's grave," she gasped.

"My mother is more alive than I am right now. He is not a human to be messed with, as you might have noticed. Just do it. It's all we got, there ain't no more." He frowned and shrugged.

She climbed down and went to the Mercedes, Perkins following at a distance that was meant to show that the nice white lady was safe.

Roger tagged along in stepchild glumness as the Mercedes moved into the downtown area of Dallas, veered onto a side street, and came up onto another freeway. After five minutes the car sloped down into a slum area of honky tonks, shine parlors, and unpainted and unzoned housing. Obviously Perkins had taken a somewhat circuitous route; it was only toward the end of the journey that Roger realized the black man was shaking any would-be followers.

A seven-foot-wide alley yawned bleakly between a shoe store and a porno movie house; the Mercedes abruptly turned into it and disappeared. A black youth who appeared to be leaning in slumber against the facade of the movie house gave Perkins a perfunctory wave and nodded as Perkins indicated that Roger was to follow. As quickly as he had come to life the young man resumed his dozing posture.

Unable to match the pace that Perkins set through the alley, Roger slowed to a crawl lest the van scrape the dirty bricks on either side. The alley's entire eighty-foot length was over-topped by a roof, and the darkness was that of an exquisitely short night. As he burst out into the light at the other end, he tapped his brake and heard himself inhale deeply.

A courtyard, complete with geysering fountain, fronted a most fabulous dwelling, an angel food apparition. Two story, white with red Spanish tile roof, the place was resplendent with palatially tall windows, lush manicured lawn, and finely pruned shrubbery. A wide stairway led from the courtyard up some thirty feet to the twin oak doors, each of which was fitted with a heavy brass knocker. Surrounded as it was by the squalor from which they had just emerged, the place resembled a wedding cake laid in camouflage in a garbage dump. With the exception of Starla and Perkins, there was no sign of activity about the place; however, Roger could not shake the feeling of being watched.

"Quite a foxhole," he said, approaching the pair.

"We make do," said Perkins. He led them up the concrete steps and into a marbled entryway in whose shadows seraphs and cherubs were carved delicately into the dull whiteness. The entryway alone outvalued everything that Roger owned, and he was hard pressed to keep his admiration to himself lest he appear cloddish. A cavernous sitting room lay before them, and its domed ceiling was centered with a lavish chandelier that hung in rococo icicles over a meadow of white carpet. A Steinway grand stood in the center of the carpet and along the surrounding walls were three mammoth sofas and several overstuffed chairs all done in soft beige patterns. On the far wall from where they stood was hung, incongruously, a painting that caught the eyes of both visitors and dazzled them. Six-by-eight feet, framed in gold leaf and burled walnut, the artwork was of a human female's buttocks against a blue background. Nice, Roger was thinking.

Perkins smiled and said, "Don't be surprised at anything you see here. It gets better," and he looked at Starla, "or worse, depending on your viewpoint."

"Liberace is eating his liver," said Roger.

"Mister Grossman is a man of many facets," said Perkins.

"Grossman, huh? I was beginning to wonder if this joint was yours."

"Dese ol' black hands would have to pick a lot of cotton for dat," said Perkins, a strange coldness suddenly in his voice. "Now follow me, and keep your wisecracks to a minimum." With that, he led them to a white staircase whose presence had been obscured by the piano's luted lid. Roger bit his lip to keep from laughing or commenting, for the stair wall was papered in an expensively tufted design of nudes holding grapes out to passersby, their shamelessness made palpable in the fact that their pubic hair was real hair. Roger knew this to be a fact, for he felt several of them on the way up; the natural effect was striking, enough so that he found himself getting a slight hard on. This Grossman, whatever else he was, was no slouch when it came to wallpaper.

The stairway curved to the right into a darkened area and, as they made the turn, Roger looked back at the living room. From this high vantage point the place looked even more white, even more sterile. Certainly, it was a place that had not endured the ravages of children or pets, and probably it had known damned few friendly conversations. It reconjured the ice palace out of the Zhivago movie, a place of frozen somberness. In spite of its beauty, it yet exhibited that aura of pomposity that had always made him feel a bit insecure in such pristine surroundings. The rich really are different from you and me, he was thinking.

Perkins paused at the last door to the left and knocked softly. "Remember," he whispered, "this is a person who prefers an orderly demeanor."

"No wise ass?" Roger asked.

"No wise ass," Perkins affirmed.

A buzzer sounded and the door popped open. "They are here, Sir," said Perkins. He motioned for them to enter, made a sharp, militaristic left face, and went back down the hallway.

Sitting behind a six-by-ten oak desk was a bald gnome of a man whose tiny hands nervously masturbated a ball point pen. He wore a dark coat, white shirt, and a black bow tie identical to Perkins's own. His head, volleyball round, was mostly pink, but blotches of red betrayed nervousness. With the beady eyes of an aging rat focusing on their faces, he said, "Come in." It was a powerful voice, and did not match the face that held it.

They entered and sat on a silver-gray mouton couch that faced the desk. The walls were crazy-patched with hundreds of photos of naked girls, and Roger pretended not to notice; besides, they were by now getting to be old hat in this place. Behind the photos was stark walnut paneling, and the room's single window was blacked out by a dark shade. A wall lamp provided the only light in the place, a pale light.

"If I am not addressing Roger Wilder and Starla Landau, then Perkins is slipping," the gnome said. They both smiled and nodded and he continued, "My Perkins is most able. We've been together for a long time."

"That is . . . good," said Starla.

"Yes it is. And so was your uncle. Good, I mean. He will be missed. Was it a nice service?"

"How nice can a funeral be?" she asked.

"A fine point. My relatives are in a mass grave somewhere in Poland. No funeral, just a fire, I suppose, but who am I to say?"

Roger felt amusedly uneasy. He wished that the bastard would come to the point. In his dementia he wondered whether a naked girl might come sauntering in; this was sure as hell the place for it.

"Tell me, Roger, how is Moe?" the gnome asked suddenly.

"Adequate, Mister Grossman."

Grossman laughed and the gold in his teeth glowed dully. "Good for you. A bright boy. How did you know who I was?"

"We have our ways," he said, hoping to be at once profound, friendly, and sinister. Perkins's slip of the tongue had made flowers grow.

"Let's lay our cards on the table shall we? I hate to wade diplomatic dung on the way to the seed of truth." He laid the pen down and picked it up again. Studying its contour, he said, "Too bad about Tatum, don't you think?"

"I'm afraid you're one up on us," said Roger. "What about Tatum?" He looked at Starla, as if to find a buttress for his ignorance.

"About three hours ago one Elgin Tatum fell or was pushed to his death from the balcony of the hotel where he was staying. The radio says he fell. We know better, don't we?"

"I don't know," Roger was confused, almost shocked. "What is it that we know better?"

"Cards on the table?" Grossman asked.

Roger yielded, aware that there was nothing else to do. "Cards on the table." It was the same expression that Sturbridge had used.

"Then deal," said Grossman.

"First off, are we going to get out of here? You can beat the hell out of me, or kill me, I guess, but she doesn't know anything about anything. Why not let her go?" He nodded toward the frightened Starla.

"Nothing physical is going to happen to either of you. What I am about to propose is a pact that may benefit us all. Be assured, your bodies are safer right now than they have been since you got to Dallas."

"Okay, here it is," said Roger. "A few days ago my boss sent me into the prairie to cover a murder. Bond and a Mexican named Gomez. No big shit, really, or so I thought. Some time later, a man named Rix was murdered in his apartment. My boss let his wheels turn on that one like crazy, and the bastard decided that the iceberg was showing more than its tip. He holy-wedlocked the three killings, and he's an opinionated bastard who never changes his mind. So, here I am in Dallas doing a follow-up on Bond, or trying to. I was going to interview his niece, Starla, and beat it back to San Antone to look for a job. Last night, a detective named Sturbridge casually mentioned Elgin Tatum, and now Tatum's dead, so you tell me. Your man Perkins hauled us in here, and here we are." Roger relaxed in his seat but noted that his hands were trembling; it spoiled the desired effect.

Grossman nodded. "Good man, and I thank you. What you have said tallies exactly with what I have so far, with a few minor additions, one addition being that I am next on the hit list. Does that surprise you?"

"Nope, not any more. Nothing that has happened in the last three days makes bat sense, or surprises me." He thought of Moe on the porch of Rix's apartment, and mentally saluted the loveable bastard.

"Then read my cards. Last week I got a call from a private detective named Perry Jarvis, a seedy character who hangs around the Dallas fringes and barely makes a living. He handles mostly divorce and surveillance work. Jarvis told me that a man named Gomez was coming here from Tijuana with the ultimate in goods." He looked at Starla and pointed to the pictures behind him. "My metier is, shall we say, that which titillates the great masses. It was going to be an auction, of sorts, and many well-to-do people were to be in contention. Jarvis mentioned Fontana, myself, Elgin Tatum, and then asked who might be available to go to San Antonio to get . . . the goods. I recommended Alan Bond as being the most trustworthy of my associates, and the pickup was set. Jarvis, fool that he is, apparently told Fontana. Are you following the chain of events so far?"

Roger smiled wanly, wishing to God that he had the guts to pull out pad and pencil and write all this down. He would have to go the memory route. "Yes, except for this fabled Fontana. What's the scam on him?"

Grossman laughed softly and folded his hands, as if building a tent in which to store memories. "Mister Fontana and I started out together in Dallas. We were sent here ten years ago by, shall we say, certain interests in the east."

"The mob," Roger said, needling.

"Uh, shall we say, persons who are not known to take losses of faith or capital magnanimously." The red blotches got redder.

"Shall we say, the mob?" Roger asked, rather bluntly now.

"No. Let it sit quietly, Mister Wilder," Grossman warned. "Continuing my tale, Fontana and I were found by our superiors to be marginal employees in a business where the marginal is lethal, at times. Too astute to kill and too stupid to be given higher authority." He laughed at his own failings, and went on. "We were sent to Dallas to form a drop zone for the book and picture trade. Do you have any idea of just how large that trade is, Mister Wilder?"

"Two, three hundred bucks a year," said Roger.

"Try a billion or more per year, Mister Wilder. When the gates of middle-class morality developed cracks in the late sixties, there were certain elements who saw in this laxity a veritable platinum mine. These were men of vision. It is these same men who are prepared to introduce marijuana to the buying public as soon as it is made legal. Do you believe that such things exist, Mister Wilder?"

"We try not to," Starla interjected.

"A commendable comment, Miss Landau, but not at all in keeping with the world as it is today. Are you recording this, Mister Wilder?"

Roger looked at Grossman with mouth utterly agape, and his eyes were as big as bottle caps. "Uh, yeah, a word now and then," he said.

"Good man! Feel free to use it later in your story. Now, getting on with it, Fontana and I had a falling out a couple of years ago. He got greedy, or so I thought, and I got belligerent, or so he thought. I was not about to leave Dallas, and neither was he. I could not buy a house in a desirable area, due to my trade and reputation, so I decided to build my own palace in the very heart of the boil itself." He waved a hand about the room and toward the downstairs area. "So you see, I did not need society or Fontana either one."

"Pardon me for being facetious," said Roger, "but what started out as a house has the look of a fortress. This place was not structured for ice cream parties, but to withstand siege. Just who is it that you're afraid of?"

Grossman looked at him for a long moment before answering. His eyes bore that look of a man emerging from a deep prayer. "I am afraid of the same thing that Fontana was afraid of," he said.

"Which is?"

"Which is who or what killed Rix and Tatum."

"Any ideas?" Roger asked

The old man nodded. "He is not of this world."

Roger smiled. "This is already off the back of the paper and approaching page one. A ghost, huh?"

"In one sense, yes. Oh, he is human enough, but uncannily so. For instance, the powers of communication as we know them are of absolutely no use in determining who he is."

"Whose powers of communication? The mobs?"

"Mister Fontana is in parts unknown at this time," Grossman said, evading Roger's question. "He, too, was unable to find the name of this spectral being."

"Seems pretty sensible to me," said Roger. "Easy. It was a bid situation. You and Tatum and Fontana were not the only people offered the bidding rights. The weirdest thing of all, though, is that not one of you knows what the hell he is bidding on. Okay, so it was some sort of pornography. Big friggin' deal. If it's worth bumpoff city, it must be something to get on the crap table with."

"But not worth dying over," said Grossman languidly. "Nothing is worth that."

"I thought you people were tough and evil," said the almost forgotten Starla. "I seem to detect a quest for something broader in your life."

"Evil, yes. Tough?" Grossman stuck out his lower lip and mused over the statement. "Even Meyer Lansky prayed. So did Anastasia. So did Patton. Prayer and mayhem are not incompatible in the human mind."

"So we're all religious, and scared," said Roger. "And we are all in Dallas about some pornography that nobody but the Mexican ever saw and four people are dead over. So why are Starla and I here?"

"Because, as the man said about the mountain, you are here. Which is another way of saying that you are probably the only people who can safely go after it and not be endangered."

"It?" Starla asked.

"Yes. It. Whatever it is," said Grossman.

"This thing gets crazier and crazier," said Roger. "An hour ago I was afraid I was gonna die. Now I'm scared I'm not, if you get my drift." No one laughed, and he felt embarrassed.

"Let's see what we have," Grossman said. "'We have an object so volatile that four people are dead over its presence, or lack of presence. People do not kill over nothing, so we must assume value. It was broadly hinted at as being something in the line of pornography, so we might assume that the killings have something to do with blackmail. Remember, these are assumptions. Fontana, who was to bid, has found it convenient to vaporize for the duration. I, who am old but fond of the chase, am just curious enough to pay someone to seek out this object d'art." He looked at each face as if seeking reflections of greed.

"Someone meaning us?" Roger asked.

Grossman nodded and started to speak, but Perkins came into the office carrying coffee and condiments. Roger noticed that the tray and spoons were solid silver. Good stuff just had that look. As the black man placed the tray on the desk, Roger asked, "Why not send Perkins? Isn't he a full-timer here?"

Grossman's eyes clouded and he said, "That will be all, Perkins."

"Yes, Sir."

When Perkins was gone, Grossman laser-beamed at Roger and said, "Now you listen to me: do not ever again in your life suggest that a servant perform a duty in the presence of that servant's employer. You have just revealed your ignorance of all that is genteel in the spirit of American propriety. Really, you should apologize." The room seemed aglitter with fire and ice.

"I will apologize," said Roger, "when you apologize to Starla here for being a part of what killed her uncle, for scaring the hell out of her with a blatant kidnapping, for roughshodding her shy ways with a wall full of naked whores. Don't speak to me of gentility, Herr Grossman. You just don't pack the gear to be . . . genteel, I believe your word was. If I am the quintessential American clod, then you are the quintessential American cutthroat and liar." He glared at the old man and felt his eyes burning around the rims, a thing that always happened when he felt wrongfully disparaged.

"I could have you killed, Wilder," said Grossman, drily.

"Maybe you should. After all, if we want to press it, you have a kidnapping charge hanging over you."

"Don't be a damned fool," Grossman snapped.

It was Starla who played the role of arbiter. She said: "Mister Grossman, my only relative in the world was buried this morning. Perhaps you can understand the depth of my feelings at this moment. I ask you, please don't argue with Roger" . . . she looked at Roger.

Roger waited for her to cry, but it did not happen; rather, she pleadingly looked at Grossman. The room was very silent for a time, and then Starla stood and fixed herself a cup of coffee off the tray, and her hands shook not at all.

"You are right, Starla," said Grossman "Will you accept an old man's apology?" Instead of a pornographer, he now became George Burns in the God movie.

She did not answer.

"Okay," said Roger, "maybe I got a little out of hand a minute ago. All I meant was, why not the manservant within thy gates? I guess I can say it, now that he's not here."

Grossman poured coffee for Roger and himself and sat back down. "Because, Herr Wilder, he is a known personage in the Dallas area. He has been with me for years and cannot indulge in the simple bliss of going unnoticed. That is where you and Starla come in."

Roger sipped his coffee, grimaced at the heat and said, "I don't think I'm gonna like this."

"Would you like it ten thousand dollars worth?" Grossman asked.

"I like it better," Roger said.

"Very well. Here is the proposal: you and Starla leave Dallas and go to a distant city to look for a certain woman. If Mister Gomez was truthful with Jarvis, then the object, or objects, are now in that city in her keeping. There is one disturbing thing that Jarvis said, however, a thing that has stayed with me since our talk. He spoke of Gomez as a great jokester, one who delighted in creating the chase for its own sake. The woman mentioned, if indeed she is the woman we seek, was named Molly. That was what Gomez told Jarvis by phone just hours before he died. 'Molly has it at her breast.' What sort of image does that conjure for you?" He again folded his hands into that tent of thought.

Roger placed his cup on the desk and pondered the words. He wished Moe was around to think for him. He really had to call the bastard, provided he still worked for the same paper. "'Molly has it at her breast,'" Roger repeated. "Some sort of sexual connotation, I suppose. Just who is this Molly, anyway?"

Grossman extended his palms outward and looked as if he were about to fly. It was the classic gesture of bewilderment. "Some five years ago there was a movie actress in this city by the name of Molly Wren. She became addicted to heroin and left the trade. At last word, she lived in Memphis, Tennessee. That is the 'distant city.' My sources in Memphis now tell me that she lives in the downtown area and frequents Negro bars. She is a hooker." He looked at Starla, and his face showed a dim veneer of red disgust.

"I didn't know they did movies in Dallas," said Roger skeptically.

"Look around you," said Grossman, indicating the room and the house. "Believe me, there is a lucrative trade in movies in this part of the country, and getting bigger all the time."

"Oh," said Roger. "That kind of movies. I should have known."

"Not really. But you can now begin to see why neither Perkins nor myself can seek out this Molly. There are competitors out there who would like nothing better than to get a clear shot at me. And they know that Perkins, if kidnapped, would bring a dear ransom."

"You weren't so scared of his getting lifted an hour ago," said Roger.

"A matter of expediency, I assure you. Being my most trusted accomplice, it naturally fell to his lot to carry out your arrival here. And, he was there not only to get you but to protect you."

"Protect?" Roger asked. "From whom?"

"Not you," said Grossman. He pointed at Starla. "Her."

Her eyes dulled with concern and she looked at Roger for guidance. "Why me?" she asked.

"Because you are Alan Bond's niece. He was in my employ. Because I made the firmest offer on the object and, because I can be trusted, Jarvis allowed me to send Bond. It was only after Bond had left that I heard about Molly and the object. By then it was too late."

"I don't understand," said Starla. "How am I in danger over something that my Uncle Alan was involved in?"

Grossman shrugged. "Why is Rix dead? Why was Tatum thrown from the hotel this morning? The first part I can answer. Rix was in the employ of Fontana, my ex-associate."

Roger waited for him to go on, scarcely believing what he was hearing. He had known Rix, though certainly not intimately, for some several years. How could it be that the bastard was in cahoots with a Dallas pornographer? It was best not to let on to Grossman that he had rung any bells in Roger's head.

Seeing that he had Roger's plenary attention, Grossman went on: "Rix was no mental giant as a cop, and he was not the most courageous man in the world. But, once given an order, nothing could deter him from it. He had been ordered to kill them both and take the object. He killed them, but Gomez had pulled a fast one; the Mexican was no fool. By the time Gomez told Jarvis that Molly had the object, Rix was already in his sniper's post, I imagine."

Roger was still skeptical. "Just how do you know all this shit? I stood right there and looked at the bodies and watched Rangers examine the scene, and you know more than all the king's horses. You are clairvoyant, I presume?"

"The word is informed, Mister Wilder."

"And that's another goddam thing—call me Roger. I don't like this Mister Wilder crap. It makes me think I'm applying for a loan, or something."

"Very well, Roger, your question was a legitimate one and I'll try to answer it. Perry Jarvis, Dallas's most seedy private eye, is the hinge to this whole thing. It was he who was entrusted by Gomez to get together the ablest bidders. Ablest, meaning wealthiest. Rix wanted to do things the abrupt way. And look where it got him, head down in a commode." Grossman grimaced at the thought.

"So who killed Rix?"

Grossman was despondently honest. "If only we knew. We, meaning anyone who might be able to put out feelers on this person. Jarvis called him The Scotsman."

"Why?" Roger asked.

"Because Gomez had made a deal of his own, apparently. At any rate, Jarvis mentioned that Gomez said there would be a fourth party interested. And, sure enough, the party called and wanted to know who and what."

"Wait, let me guess: this Scotsman called Jarvis and Jarvis told him the whole shooting match. Right?"

"As far as I can determine, that is it, up to now. And now there are dead people all over Texas, and the police are still unable to tie it all together. Jarvis has hidden out,

Fontana is in parts unknown, Tatum is dead, and the Scotsman is out there doing his lethal thing."

"And nobody has any idea as to who he is?" Roger asked.

Grossman looked at Starla and shook his head. "And that is why the lady here is in danger, innocent as hell though she may be. This person is quite deadly and is quite determined to have it." Somewhat nervously he concluded, "Whatever it is."

"One dead and two out of pocket, as far as the bidders go. That leaves you. Why didn't you run for it like Fontana?" Starla asked, her tone uncharacteristically harsh.

"Because I would no more run from this moment than Muhammad Ali would run from one last fight." The old man's chest puffed.

"Once a collector, always one, huh?" Roger asked, looking at the photos. God, where did those women all come from?

"Yes, I'm afraid so. Fontana is a business man who goes home to his Elektra fortress and forgets the day's work. Forgive me for this admission, Starla, but I happen to be in love with the naked human female body. Whatever this thing is that we all seek, I must have it, if only for a minute." He grinned in abashed silence, his head becoming crimson.

"Hell, it might be two goats getting it on," said Roger, looking askance at Starla. She was showing less embarrassment than usual, and Roger was beginning to think of her as one of the boys.

"It could be, but it is not likely," said Grossman. "People do not kill over goats fucking." He, too, looked at Starla.

Roger found himself laughing. The thing had become totally maudlin.

Grossman and Starla, infected by Roger's cackling, began to laugh also. The old one attempted to sip his coffee and could not. Roger had to put his cup on the desk so that he might let it all out, and in a second he was bellowing. It was the first happy moment that he had experienced in three days, and it rolled on for a full minute. As it began to abate and he was able to see, he recognized Perkins standing inside the doorway, his great piano-key teeth sparkling.

"Well," Grossman said at last, "it seems that we have something in common after all. That being what Sam Levenson called the gift of laughter."

As the sweet moment passed, Roger said, "So you want us to go to Memphis and find this Molly. And, when we do, we simply take the thing from her and bring it back to Dallas and hand it to you. Jesus, the simplicity of it!"

"That's all," said Grossman. "When in doubt, send the best."

"Flattery will get you naught, friend," said Roger. "Why don't you just call some of your counterparts in Chicago or wherever and have the thing done? It'd save a hell of a lot of wear and tear on my van."

"Because they might not deliver the thing," said Grossman.

"Honor among thieves?" Roger asked.

"Not at all," said Grossman. "There is no honor to it. The buzz is in my bones on this one. I wish I could go with you, to be there at the magic moment."

"I take it from that you have us on the boat already," said Roger.

"Ten thousand," said Grossman.

"Up front," Roger blurted.

"No deal," the old one shook his head.

"Fine." Roger stood and motioned for Starla to follow him. He saw Perkins blocking the door.

"Mister Grossman?" the black man said.

"They cannot leave, Perkins. Not now."

"So what if I get lucky and deck Perkins?" Roger asked.

"You won't," said Perkins.

"You see, Roger, Perkins learned his rather substantial ways at Folsom Prison. Things learned there have a way of gaining permanence in a person's repertoire." Grossman grinned maliciously.

"Yeah. Perk and I have already met. You'd let him kill me?"

"Something like that," said Grossman.

"We'll do it," said Starla. Again, the men had forgotten her.

"Are you speaking for me, too?" Roger asked.

"Yes."

He grinned at her awkwardly. "Thanks, but go to hell, lady."

"You have no choice. It is the money now or the money later. If he was going to kill us, he could do it now." She looked away at nothing.

Roger thought it over. Damnit, she had a point. He still felt used, ordered about, intimidated and inferior. "I see what you mean, Herr Grossman," he said at last. He sat down, defeated.

"Fine. Now when do you want to leave?"

"How about October?" Roger said, smiling viciously.

"How about now?" Grossman asked. "It is a little past one. You could conceivably be in Memphis by the wee hours."

"We could get there faster if you wanted to turn over a couple of thou for a plane ticket," said Roger.

"You aren't thinking, Roger," said Grossman. "Have you ever heard of airport security?"

"A word now and then. I don't get your point."

"My point is that no matter what you find in Memphis, chances are good that the size might be prohibitive. Or, worse yet, it might be metallic. Whatever it is, I don't want the damned FBI to get their hands on it."

"Not likely. We are looking for porn, right? Why would it involve metal?"

"Probably it does not. But I've stayed alive for sixty years and prospered by following my own penchant for common sense. Let's do it my way." That evil look had come back into Grossman's eyes, and Roger knew that it was useless to argue.

"Our moneys are about depleted," said Roger. "I don't know about the lady here, but after gas and hotel I'll have about enough for a moon pie and a Dr. Pepper."

Grossman stood and went to a large mahogany box that reposed near a closet door. Its delicate etchwork depicted a nymph firing arrows at a flight of swans. Grossman knelt, opened the door, and revealed a gray safe. He twisted the dial quickly and withdrew a packet of bills. Peeling off five, he handed them to Roger.

"Five hundred bucks?" Roger asked, looking at the money as if it were the body of a dead bird. "Can we get across Arkansas on that?"

"You'd better," Grossman said with venality. "You are now in my employ. We have a contract."

"Says who?"

"When I say contract, it has rather a more substantial meaning behind it than you might imagine." The old man smiled.

"Oh," said Roger, "that kind of contract."

"I want that object," Grossman said coldly. "I intend to have it."

"We'll do what we can," said Roger, fully intending to let the thing go to hell as soon as he got to the street and safety.

"Another thing. Do not cross me. You will go to Memphis and you will report religiously." The old man sat again and made a hand tent. "A lot is riding on this, Roger."

"Why do I feel so involved when I am not involved?" Roger asked rhetorically.

"You are involved. We are involved. Goodbye and godspeed."

Roger nodded.

"I will expect a phone call from you tomorrow no later than 5:00 P.M. From Memphis." The old man smiled up over his fingers. "And, Roger . . ."

"Yes?"

"I am not a man who handles disappointment well."

"We'll do what we can, Grossman. That's all we can do. Now let it rest." Starla followed him to the door. She placed her hand on his elbow, and he felt the warmth through the cloth of his coat.

"5:00 P.M. Tomorrow." Grossman handed him a small card with a phone number printed in silver gilt.

"See you in the funnies," said Roger.

"Ten thousand dollars buys a lot of funnies," answered Grossman.

The pair went out and moved down the hallway without saying a word, like children who have received a teacher's stern warning.

When they were outside and in the van, Roger said: "I don't know about you, but I am about to starve. How's about I treat us to a meal?"

"So we can talk it over?" she asked.

He nodded. "So we can talk it over."

She tongued her upper lip, and there were tears in her eyes. "Just get me out of here," she said, eyeing the courtyard, the shrubbery, the mansion.

Roger drove them through the tunnel and into the early afternoon sunlight. The nodding young black was now across the street, still doing his lazy act, still very much aware of all that was going on in the neighborhood.

Roger rubbed the back of his neck as if to disperse small things crawling there, and he wanted very much to get back to a world where people were average and devoid of any sinister motives. He kicked the word average around for three blocks and finally came to wonder if anyone or anything was.

Twelve

Coinciding with that moment in which Roger had been stirring in his hotel room preparing to get to Bond's funeral, Voris Mohler was in San Antonio sliding backwards in his bed. He had had a wet dream. This had not happened since his bobbings on the Arabella, the supply ship that had taken him to war. That was in 1944. Now, years later, he felt the same galling sense of shame. Half crazy in his sleep, he did not want Edna to see the spot on the sheet.

He raised himself up and remembered that Edna was in North Dakota. Rushing to the bathroom, he rinsed off and dried with toilet paper. After stripping the sheets from the bed he took them to the washer and dropped in a cupful of soap.

He looked at the clock. 7:05. Since this time yesterday morning, he had lived eleven lifetimes. Now he knew what they meant by jet lag. In his mind was a crazy swirl of visions and memories and smells. Just twenty-four hours ago he and Roger were on a porch over at Rix's apartment surrounded by half the cops in Bexar County. Since then, two plane trips, to and from Tijuana. He went to the jacket that lay over a chair back and felt for the small tablet on which was written the guts and hair of the trip. Little as it was, it was something to show Lynch.

He showered, shaved, squeezed a blackhead, and farted several times while rinsing his face. "Voris Arnold Mohler," he said to the old man in the mirror, "you are exquisitely complex. You are middle-aged, separated from

149

your wife, and about to lose your job to either your own
stupidity or to the attrition of one third-rate newspaper
called the *Sentinel*. Thou art blessed among men.'' The
words seemed to echo through the house with a dullness
that was the bastard child of loneliness. "Admit it," he
continued, whispering now, "you are scared shitless."

It was beginning to hurt, to hit him in the heart and
not just the face. He left the bathroom and went into the
living room where there was lint in the corners of the
ceiling and unspeakable crud matted into the carpet.
Switching on the TV, he turned down the sound and
flipped from one channel to the other: Little Rascals,
David Hartman with his Hereford face, preachers waving
their Bibles, local newsmen with lacquered hair giving the
farm market reports. He turned it off and looked at his
watch. 7:32. There was a fine powder of dust on the glass
face of the TV, and Moe fingered into it a message that
he had once seen in a Cleveland restaurant: Bloom Where
You Are Planted.

"How does one bloom in so-called middle age?" he
asked the glass. He wiped away the message, rinsed his
hands off, and went outside to the Valiant.

The first person he saw in the *Sentinel* office was Mrs.
Wainwright. She was watering a plant that stood by the
glass door. "Lynch wants to see you," she said with a
hint of smugness in her voice.

"How's the weather?" Moe asked.

"A little cloudy," she said. She dribbled water around
the base of the plant and rubbed dust off the leaves.

"What happened yesterday? Anything important?"

She paused and ruminated over the question. "Not
really. We got a paper out." As acting sports editor, she
was drunk with her newly achieved importance. She had
tenure. It was rumored that she had come with the building. Moe hated her, but one does not fire old women with
tenure.

Moe went into his office and closed the door. He saw
a dozen sheets on his desk, each doubtlessly containing
earth-ripping questions that his keen mind had to answer,
but he ignored them and took out his little airplane.
Holding it aloft in a child's parody of flight, he made

buzzing sounds. Therapy. He left his office. Pressing the elevator button, he looked around, and the same flurry of activity that had greeted him was resumed. Every face in the room was exhibiting that industrious commitment that is the way of all who strive in the straight and narrow. Moe decided then and there that he hated every god-damned one of them, the phony, boss-licking bastards.

Up one floor. Left two doors. Knock, knock.

"Yes?"

Moe went in. Gaylon Lynch was reading an old copy of *Esquire*.

"You wanted to see me?"

"Yes, but I hadn't sent for you yet," said Lynch, somewhat imperiously.

"I came early."

"Yes," said Lynch. "Yes, you did." He flipped a page, and another. "Would I look better in gray or in blue, Moe?"

"Depends on whether you are walking around or laid out for burial. Personally, I prefer blue."

"The New York boys say that stripes and checks are all right, if the colors match." He laughed.

"Yes. I suppose so."

"Where did you go yesterday?" Lynch asked. He did not look up, but kept turning pages.

"I went to Tijuana, Mexico. On your money. Had the time of my life." Moe's tone was half taunting, half fearful.

Lynch turned the magazine around and showed Moe a photo of a comely brunette in stockings and garter belt. "Nice, huh? Why?"

"She just is."

"No. I mean why did you go to TJ?"

"To gather news. Gathering news is my life's work. I have been doing it for all my adult life, ergo, my life's work."

"Why are you being defensive?" Lynch asked.

"Because I have known my employer for many moons. When he is about to blow the birdies from the trees, he steps into the forest very quietly."

"That was the old employer. That was the young and vibrant Gaylon Lynch. That was the Lynch whose father left him oil wells, all of which dried up in the sixties. That was the Lynch who once bought his wife a Mercedes on a whim."

"I . . . see," said Moe.

Lynch laid the magazine down and scratched an eyebrow. "No, Moe, you don't. I spent the night walking up and down the couch cushions until my feet itched. Why, I kept saying. Why?"

"And did you come up with an answer?" Moe asked. Here it comes, he was thinking.

"Yes I did. Moe went because he loves his work and because he is on to something. And if God would send me four more Voris Mohlers, then this paper would not be on the verge of folding. Does that surprise you?"

Moe leaned back in the chair and tried to find a place to put his hands. "Yes, it does." He touched his pocket and felt the little airplane. It represented flight. Freud would have been ecstatic.

"Well, rest easy. What did you find on my five hundred bucks?"

"I think that I found that the murder of that Mexican and that jeweler is heavy stuff. Pulitzer stuff."

"And I can infer, correctly, that this is why brother Wilder is now in Dallas with my van and two hundred bucks of my money?"

"Yessir. I see Henry the Horrible has been talking again."

"He's afraid not to. And what did my Moe find?"

"In a nutshell, war stuff, a beaten Mexican lady, and pornography. Something worth at least three murders."

Lynch's eyebrows lifted slightly. "Three?"

"Yup. Rix, who is now on a slab someplace, died of the same disease."

"Funny, the story you filed yesterday before bugging out did not mention any tie-in." Lynch ran his fingers around the edges of the magazine. "Things need a pattern, and I find none here."

"Goddamnit, Lynch, the Rix thing ties in. Mark my words."

"What you're saying is that all we really have is Mohler's famous intuition. That about it?"

"Nope. What we started with was Mohler intuition. Let me read you some stuff." Moe started to reach for the tablet.

"Never mind," said Lynch, waving his hand. "If you say it's good enough, then it is. But from now on, you clear any trips beyond the restroom with me. Am I getting through?"

"Very well, very loud, very clear. Just mark my words, this one needs a cool guiding hand. It may run on for another two weeks before it breaks clear."

"Why is it that the other papers have not shown interest in this? Why, for instance, did our nearest rival put Rix's death on page four?"

"I call it the Eyes-of-Texas syndrome. They are in tighter with the power than we are. A canned Ranger does not look good. A dead canned Ranger, especially a murdered one, is infamata."

Lynch thought it over. "You may be right. Close ranks for the old school tie, and all that shit?"

"And all that shit," Moe echoed. "To those who have the means, this is a common news story. I have my means here." Moe pointed to his temple.

"Your ego notwithstanding, it still comes out sketchy. Can you see it from my viewpoint?"

"Yup. We lost six thousand in circulation in the last eight months. Ad revenues dropped off by eighteen percent just last year, and it ain't gettin' no better. I do read the paper now and then myself. Wanna talk about it?"

Lynch looked tired, sweaty, defeated. "I'm open for suggestions."

"You have a failing paper. It is not your fault. We have a habit of picking unpopular political candidates and standing by them. Strike one. We do not run pictures of girls in bikinis. Strike two. We have had some setbacks in our financial picture. Strike two and a half."

"Foul ball. Which means that we have one strike coming. Right?"

Moe nodded. "Roger Wilder is in Dallas right now dusting our plate off, and there is a momentary lull in the game."

"What if Roger is not the batter you think he is?"

"Then you can fire me this minute and no hard feelings."

"You are that confident of his abilities?"

"You bet your ass I am. This paper is a good paper. It can be a better paper, but we have just had some bad breaks. It can happen to anyone."

"Moe?" Lynch said, a hint of plea in his voice. "Moe, make it go. Can you?"

"I'll do my best, brother Lynch," said Moe. He rose and started for the door. Halting, he turned to his pale superior, "You ain't such a bastard after all, Lynch."

"I'm in bastard limbo," said Lynch. "Too rich to be a common shit and too near poverty to be the arrogant bastard I can be. You like me better this way?" He grinned.

Moe gave him the thumbs up sign and left the office.

He took the elevator down to his office. Polly Pearl followed him in. "You want me to go on with this thing about the Iranians?" she asked.

"Sure. Why not?"

"I dunno. I figured we'd have a new boss'd wanta kill the story. You know how Lynch is about the Iranians."

"Is Lynch your boss?"

"Nope. You is."

"For a fact. Do the story. We have a paper to get out." He looked at her for a heavy moment and she glared back. She was once employed by the *New York Times*, or so she had said. Forty, single, ugly, Polly Pearl was one of those reporters who seemingly never had time to do a story if there was something else begging for attention. The whole staff needed firing, but today was not the time.

When Polly was gone, there was a weighty run on what would fit where, each candidate for a by-line telling Moe with little subtle hints that this story was worthy of banner headlines. Before he knew it, the hour had melded into four. Voris Mohler's guts rumbled in protest, and it was by God time to go to Gino's. On the way out the door, he started to pinch a leaf off old Bitchipoo's plant, but thought better of it.

The restaurant dozed in the two o'clock dullies that Moe detested. He just had to find another place to eat. Like a divorcee with a new hair style, his foray into singlehood would begin with a new greasy spoon, the nearest of which was almost two blocks away. But he ordered a cheeseburger and a cup of coffee with the sad and sinking feeling that tomorrow would be soon enough to think about traumatizing his system with new poisons.

He was halfway through his sandwich when the man entered, looked at him, sat in a nearby booth. The fellow was of average height, slender and ill-dressed. His yellow shirt and black trousers might have come from a rummage sale, as neither carried the remotest hue of newness. His hat was sweat stained, a straw job that was darkened at the front with fingerprints. He continued to look at Moe for several seconds and then turned away sharply as though to affirm his lack of interest. After two minutes of looking out the window at the passing traffic, he got up and approached Moe's booth. "You Mohler?"

"What's left of him. Sit down." Moe wondered why he had begun to perspire. His reporter's nose was twitching as the man slid into the opposite seat.

"My name is Jarvis, Perry Jarvis."

"Hello Jarvis Perry Jarvis. How'd a little feller like you get saddled with so many names?" Moe felt the old heat lightning blasting its shrapnel around inside his head. The face of Gomez smiled again from the painting. Good shit was coming down, as Roger would say.

Jarvis's eyes smiled and his mouth attempted to follow suit, but his was a troubled face, and the smile failed. "Perry will do. How's it going?"

"Fine, frog hair fine. Coffee?" Jarvis nodded, and Moe ordered him a cup from a passing waitress.

Jarvis squirmed, looked out the window and back at Moe. "I hear you had a killing here recently," he said.

Moe nodded with fatigue. "I guess so. We also have sandstorms and abortion clinics. It's a great place to live, but I wouldn't wanta work here." He finished the last of his sandwich and accepted a refill from the waitress who brought Jarvis's coffee. As the woman walked away, Moe checked out her ass and found it to be too skinny. It was the first time in days that he had thought of women as sex objects, and he wondered just where his mind had been when the wet dream occurred.

"I'm from Dallas," said Jarvis.

I know, asshole, Moe was thinking, and you have no idea of how important you are just now in my life. But he said, "Oh? And how are things in the big city?"

"Not so hot. I talked to Ray Wilson of the *Times-Herald* and he said you were a guy that could be trusted."

"Ray always was an idiot. Trusted with what?"

"With what I know."

"Which is?"

"You got a reporter in Dallas right now. Guy named Wilder. Right?"

"Maybe. I haven't checked the jails or the whorehouses today, so I ain't so sure."

"You wanta talk or you wanta wiseass?"

Moe added cream and sugar and stirred slowly. "It would appear that you're the one who wants to talk, so talk."

Jarvis leaned back and licked his lips, an unplanned mimicry of a viper preparing to strike. "I hear you're a wheel at the paper over there, that you have access to the vault, so to speak."

Moe smiled at him.

"Is it true?"

"Maybe. Why don't you come to the point?"

Jarvis turned away and looked out the window in his shame. "About three hundred oughta do it."

"Do what?"

"Okay, two fifty. I ain't greedy. Just enough to get me a room for a few days. He's in Dallas, you know."

"He who?" Moe asked.

Jarvis tapped his cup as if for luck and sipped. "The bastard who's after it."

"Oh, that bastard. So far so good, except I don't know what in the hell you're talking about." This bit of word sparring was Moe's way of leeching all that he could from the man without having to twist the lion's already sore tail for money; he sensed in his heart of hearts, however, that Jarvis, scared though he was, would never spill all the soup without a coin or two on the old barrelhead.

"Two fifty, Mohler. And let's can the shit. Okay?"

"I'm not sure you've got a goddam thing worth two fifty. Tell you what I can do—I'll take it to the power. If it's worth it, you'll have your two fifty. That's my offer. Deal?"

Jarvis looked away for a moment and then said, "I admire your gall, Moe. Can I call you Moe?"

Moe nodded. "Everybody does." Something about Jarvis had hit an identifiable chord in Moe. He was tired of being a shit. Less than five hours ago he was on the hook himself and now here he was lording over this quivering bit of humanity like a fucking Nazi. "Okay, my man, you're the owner of my ears and hopefully my heart. Thou may jabber on," he said, smiling.

"The bastard is about to fix all our wagons," said Jarvis. "Even from the grave."

"By bastard, do we mean Gomez?"

"Yep. You hear about Tatum?"

"Nope. Who's Tatum?"

"A rock star. He fell from his hotel room this morning, so they say." He gave Moe an all knowing look.

Moe tried to mirror the gaze but finally gave in. "Start from scratch, Jarvis. And don't leave out a thing."

Jarvis doffed his hat, revealing a bald dome. There were little sweat droplets at the crest of his head and he rubbed them away and looked at his hand. "Sweat of the brow. Old Adam should have lived nowadays to know what that really meant."

"Things are tough all over," said Moe.

Jarvis lifted his cup and took a long hard pull at the coffee. It was as if he expected never to taste liquid again and had to make this one draught last into eternity. When he had put the cup down, he looked into it for a few seconds and then raised his eyes to face the world as it was. He looked through Moe, remembering.

"Some two weeks ago, maybe a hair longer, I got a call from one Raimundo Gomez of Tijuana. . . . He said he had something for me. Something big. He said there was five grand in it for me. As you can see, I didn't collect." Jarvis looked down and flipped a fingernail at a bit of lint on his shirt. "Anyway," he said it was something that required the assemblage of several big boys. Sellers or collectors, either one. The bidding was to be done at some place as yet undisclosed."

"Hold it," said Moe. "Sellers or collectors you said. Sellers or collectors of what?" His brain was about to explode. There was only one word in the language that would do now.

"Pornography," answered Jarvis.

Moe leaned forward, heart pounding. That was the word. Bingo! The story was sex and the story was his, and the paper and his job were safe.

"You okay?" Jarvis was asking.

"Uh, yeah, go on."

"These are the sort of folks you don't mess with and ever come out on top," Jarvis said. "I did my part, told them to rake up two hundred and fifty grand apiece. Then, fool that I am, I told them where the pickup was to be made. At a spot a few miles out of San Antonio. Hell, I just threw it in as an afterthought." He slapped the table in the manner of a wronged schoolboy.

Moe licked his lips. He had been unaware that his palate, tongue, and lips were dry. "That interests me," he said. "Why there? Why not the River Walk or Brooks Hospital? Or even the Alamo, for Chrissake?"

Jarvis grinned lopsidedly. "Who can figure Mexicans? See, I knew Gomez. As much as an Anglo can know a Mexican, that is. They're weird people, treacherous sometimes. But Gomez was goofier than usual, always pulling a joke when he could. He loved America, loved Europe, but always the obscure places. It's almost like he hated cities, one of those off-the-beaten-path types, he was. Maybe that's all there was to it. One thing sure, we'll never know now, will we?"

Moe did not comment. Everything was tallying with what he had learned from Bonita, even her father's practical joker's streak, a thing that he had almost forgotten. "Okay, we go from Gomez to Bond. How did Bond get into the picture?"

"He was a stooge for one of Dallas's luminaries, an old porno dealer named Grossman." Jarvis thought that he saw Moe shudder.

"Grossman, huh?" Moe asked.

Jarvis nodded. "You know the man?"

"Nope. Just the name." Two of the four names on Bonita's paper were now brought to light. Not bad at all for less than twenty-four hours. "Real slow like, tell me about this unholy duo," Moe said.

"Well, like I was sayin', Bond was into hock to Grossman. He had a little nit-shit jewelry shop down in the seedy part of town. Actually, it used to be a pretty good part of town, but the whites moved out and the watermelon and frijole bit started, if you follow my drift. The jewelry shop was on the skids, but Bond was the type who might go without groceries as long as his shirts had the proper crease. A phony bastard. So I tell Grossman where the pickup is to be made. Trouble is, I also told Fontana."

"Hold it," said Moe. "Who's Fontana?"

"Another Dallas pornographer, another of my intended bidders."

Jarvis nodded. "Yeah, intended. He's taken off for parts unknown. Maybe Tahoe, maybe Detroit, maybe even goddam Brussels. Who knows? Anyhow I made the mistake of telling Fontana about the pickup, where and when and who, the whole nine yards. Mea culpa. That was how Rix came to get dead." He waited for Moe to comment on the solemnity of all this masterful planning, on the portent of all that was happening.

"Brother Rix," said Moe, recalling his visit to the morbid apartment, an occurrence that now seemed eons ago. "Tell me about his initiation into this little fraternity."

"You know why he was fired from the Ranger force, don't you?"

"Word was, general incompetence brought on by booze and women. Your classic fuckup?"

"I know better," said Jarvis. "Rix had begun to deal in porno on the side for Fontana. The Rangers are a funny bunch—they tolerate some things, frown at others. The porno thing smelled like Mafia and that's all it took. Grossman and Fontana were exiled from up north years back by the mob. Had their buttons clipped and their swords broken and were hurled out of camp, so to speak."

"So they came to Texas to give their expertise to the Lone Star State. Thoughty of them."

Jarvis let it pass. "They fell out some time back, don't even speak now. They are rivals, but respectful rivals. Sort of an old school tie thing. Got more goddamn money than they could spend in ten lifetimes and still got fingers in the Dallas porno trade." He shook his head and looked down at his shabby shirt front.

Moe thought it over for a moment and then asked, "Why would Rix kill Bond and Gomez? Why not hold them up and take the . . . whatever it was and light out for parts unknown?"

"That's a poser," said Jarvis. "I do have an idea."

"Fire away."

"Fontana couldn't squawk too loud or it would draw attention to himself. Rix knew this and figured to grab the gravy for himself. See, if Fontana is quiet, his world is serene. It's when his type makes noise that certain powers begin to get testy."

"Who are these powers?"

Jarvis turned his hands palms upward. "The establishment. The mob. The papers. You name it. *Omerta*. The old silence. It was just the way he was trained. With Fontana here in Texas, Rix possibly figured that he could put his own screws into the old mobster and do it without getting his own hair mussed."

Moe tapped his fingers on the table, and the waitress at the far end of the place put down her nail file and came to refill their cups. When she was gone, he said, "Of course, that last part is all speculation on your part."

"Yep," said Jarvis. "But damned good speculation."

"So we're down to the nut cuttin'," said Moe. "Who killed Rix?"

"The same bastard that killed Tatum in Dallas this morning. If all runs true to form, then I figure I'm next. That is why yours truly is here with you at this glorious moment in time. Frankly, I'm scared shitless." Jarvis tried to smile, but again could not.

"Yeah, it would make a feller a little queasy," said Moe. "For the life of me I can't figure out who this guy is or how he knows so much."

Jarvis pointed a thumb at himself. "You're looking at it. I got a phone call a day or so after Gomez called. This guy with a British accent—I guess it was Scotch-like—said that Gomez had decided to cut him in on the bidding. And here's the clincher—that he, the Britisher, would pay me ten grand just for the right to come and bid."

"Let me guess," said Moe. "You told him the whole scoop."

Jarvis looked positively nauseated. "You got it. I mean, what the hell, ten grand just to be allowed to bid. I told him who the others were, the expected amounts, the whole shootin' match. I mean, Jesus, here I was in tall cotton for the first time in my life, big money comin' into town from every direction, and old Perry Jarvis was the goddamn ringmaster. But I had second thoughts, see, because this Britisher was an outsider, so I called Gomez in Tijuana. Finally got through. This girl at his place said he'd bugged out the previous day."

The girl had to be Bonita, Moe decided. "So you never heard from Gomez again?" he asked.

"Strangely enough, I did. The day before he died, if my calculations are correct, I had a weird call from Gomez. He was a strange duck to the end. It was like he was afraid his call was going to be traced, he talked so fast. 'This is Gomez. Molly has it at her breast.' That's all he said. And he hung up."

Moe leaned back in his booth and pulled in his lips, biting hard. Molly. The third name had surfaced. Bonita's little letter had said "Molly will care for the object well." Keeping his poker face imbecilically straight, Moe said, "Tell me about Molly."

"Shit, you tell me," said Jarvis. "It was right about there that the goddamn mess began to swarm. All of a sudden I was out of my league."

"So what happened then?"

"Nothin', for a couple of days. I read that Bond and Gomez are found dead here in San Antone. Then, this Britisher calls me that same day and wants to know what in hell is going on. In a panic I tell him my theory about Rix being the culprit, that Elgin Tatum is holed up in a Dallas hotel waiting for the bidding to begin. See, I'm scared shitless, and this guy out there with ten grand seems like an old long lost pal under the circumstances."

"And Rix winds up with a dental floss necktie, and Tatum goes out a hotel window," Moe concluded.

"That wasn't none of my doin'," said Jarvis without much conviction in his voice. "At least, I didn't think so up to now." He looked at Moe for confirmation of his innocence.

"The Britisher is our man," said Moe. "What I can't figure is how you think the mob isn't involved."

Jarvis's words came with professional exasperation: "Think just a little, goddamnit. Fontana and Grossman are old mob hands all the way back. They are willing to bid a quarter of a million on something that is downright one of a kind. If the boys who are still pulling their strings got wind of that, it'd be the Jersey swamps for sure!"

"I thought they were outcasts, exiled to Texas and all that shit." Moe was trying to poke a hole in Jarvis's story and halfway hoping that he could not.

"Look," said Jarvis, as if addressing a recalcitrant child, "porno is a five billion a year business. Okay, Fontana and Grossman are shipped out to Texas, but they still deal with Jersey City, you can bet on that. No, if it was the Mob, this thing wouldn't have gotten so out of hand so fast. Bodies lying around are bad for business."

Picking a bit of chair lint from his sleeve, Moe said, "What about Grossman? Tell me about his Sunday School party."

"Not much to tell. He's an old weird Jew who lives in the heart of niggertown in Dallas. Keeps bucks around for protection. They say he lives in a castle at the end of a long alleyway. Word once was that he has pictures of naked women on his walls.''

Moe grinned, ''So why didn't he run like his ex-buddy Fontana did?''

''Good question. He's old, which might mean he's gotten a little flaky. But not that old. From what I gather, he's considered sharper than Fontana. That was a good trick, sending Bond rather than one of his house boys. Cushion against obvious involvement, you could call it.''

Moe looked outside and saw the afternoon winding down anemically. He and Jarvis emptied their cups. He thought of the word ''convergent.'' ''Just for the record,'' he said at last, ''why are the police so inattentive in your opinion?''

''They just don't know as much as we do,'' said Jarvis. ''Tatum will go on the books as a freak who committed suicide on a dope trip—that's already being speculated. The Presley, Joplin, Belushi thing, you know. And you know damned well why the Rix thing is being soft pedaled, his being an ex-Ranger and all.''

Moe nodded, feeling a definite kinship to the speaker. ''As of this minute, two people in the state know the ropes. And they are sitting in this booth.''

Moe stood. Needles of pain ran the circuits from his toes to his thighs. ''Be right back,'' he said. He passed the waitress, ordered two refills and went to the restroom. The bastard was on the up and up. Three names that had been on the Gomez note had now been illuminated: Grossman, Jarvis, Molly. He tried to recall the fourth but could not. Besides, it had seemed more like a word than a name. Yes, he had to get Jarvis his two-fifty so the man could hole up for a spell; that much he owed the seedy wretch.

When Moe got back to the booth Jarvis was noshing a King Don, a dark confection filled with white cream. The cups had been refilled, and Jarvis hand-rubbed his lips and wadded the transparent wrapping paper. Moe knew instinctively that here was a man who had spent his life grabbing a sandwich there, a cookie here, a man who ate not for taste but for survival.

"Well?" Jarvis said.

"Well what?"

"Do I get it?"

Moe nodded. "This Britisher worries the shit out of me. I've got Roger Wilder in Dallas nosing around. If he kicks over the wrong rock, he might get bitten."

"He's not a Britisher," said Jarvis quietly, almost as an afterthought. His eyes were the cheerless orbs of one who has looked into his own soul and found it empty.

"Maybe you'd like to clarify that," said Moe.

"He's German," said Jarvis. He looked up at Moe with the lazy gaze of one who had decided to reveal a hidden card.

Something clicked in Moe's head, and a golden door opened. SS uniforms. Photographs of Adolph Hitler. The material of the Third Reich in a warehouse. Paraguay. Ascunsion. ". . . in bad Spanish it means . . ." And, too, he now remembered the fourth word, or name: Ableiter.

"Well I'll be a sonofabitch," he said to Jarvis.

"Oh? Why's that?"

"Nothing you'd understand. For a crazy second there I knew everything and nothing. Now, back to you: you been holding out on me?"

Jarvis smiled in his lopsided, mirthless way. "Uh huh. I had to know if I was gonna get the two-fifty. You pissed?"

"Nope. We all gotta deal in what we got. What is it you've got?" Moe leaned back in the booth again, his hands resting behind his pate. The little restaurant was blessedly empty of other patrons and the outside world did not exist. This was one of those moments that were as rare as diamonds in a newsman's life, a moment that was to be savored and tongued as deliciously as a fine wine. A moment that made all the hours of drudgery and sweat worthwhile. Jarvis had that look of a bootlegger coming to the Cross.

"I am about to tell you the damndest story that you've ever heard," said Jarvis at last.

Moe nodded. He was afraid to speak lest the crystal-line purity of the moment become opaque.

Jarvis inhaled heavily and began to speak: "Sometime in late 1944, a special SS courier left Auschwitz carrying a heavy package. He left by night and went by closed car. Late the next day he arrived at a prearranged meeting place in Cottbus, in Eastern Germany. He gave the package to Heinrich Himmler. With a guard of several men, Himmler took a special train to Berchtesgaden. In a private ceremony, he presented the contents of the package to Hitler."

Here Jarvis paused, rubbed his elbows, and stared away. Still Moe could not speak. Nearly a minute passed before Jarvis continued: "Sometime after the war, by whatever means, the thing wound up in Paraguay. And there it stayed until a few weeks ago. I guess you know now what all the sweating and killing has been about." He looked up at Moe and his eyes were stark, glassy.

"Jesus Christ," said Moe.

"The Himmler Plaque. Anyhow, that's what I call it. Gomez described it to me. Set in a gold base with a teakwood back is another slab of pure gold about eight-by-eleven, maybe a quarter-inch thick. In the upright gold slab, each about six inches high, are two lightning flashes, insignia of the SS, both flashes encrusted with diamonds. At the top is a golden eagle's head, the bird's eyes consisting of two large rubies."

Moe saw Jarvis lean away and collapse onto himself as if the last of a series of ruinous bones had been pulled from his body. There was a look of rapturous melancholy on his face. Speaking almost inaudibly, Moe said, "I can see now why we've got four dead people."

"Maybe five," said Jarvis, pointing at himself.

"Yeah. But from what you describe, that must be worth at least a million bucks."

"That would be about two dollars a life, figured conservatively," said Jarvis.

"I don't seem to be following you," said Moe.

"The gold, those diamonds, the whole goddam thing is made from the teeth of half a million dead Jews, mostly Hungarians. It was not the money value that Himmler was giving his boss, don't you see? It was a talisman, rune, symbol of a promise fulfilled. Hungary was the last major country whose Jews were exterminated, starting in the summer of '44. It was the essence of Judenrein Europa.''

''Judenrein?''

'''Jew free.' Himmler might have waited until '45 to give Hitler the thing, but Normandy on one side and Zhukov on the other were making things a bit hectic at about that time.''

Moe ran his hands over the top of his head and felt the dampness there. He wondered whether he glistened as so many bald men did.

''There's one major thing I don't understand,'' he said at last.

Jarvis grinned. ''I bet I know what it is.''

''Good,'' said Moe. ''Hit me with it so I won't think I'm the only one going crazy.''

''Why pornographers?'' Jarvis asked, already shaking his head even as the words emerged.

''Right,'' said Moe. ''This pornography thing has been waving its flags all the goddam way, and now you tell me we're after gold and diamonds. So what the fuck gives?''

Jarvis continued to shake his head. ''The jokester in our dead Mexican, I guess. I never had the presence of mind to ask him why pornographers. Maybe he was one of those hippie types who see war as the ultimate obscenity.''

Moe thought this over and said, ''Nope. Wrong country, wrong decade, wrong age. The bastard was tweaking us all the way through, and still is.'' He remembered the painting that appeared to smile and felt a cold rigor in his neck and shoulders. ''Tatum, how did he get into the picture?'' He asked suddenly, graspingly.

''The insiders say he was the king of Hollywood's crotch crickets. I know this sleazy bastard in L.A. called Eddie the Freak. I told him to put Tatum into the inner circle.''

''Does this Eddie know anything?''

Jarvis shook his head. ''I didn't tell the whole fucking world everything. Give me a little credit.''

''So we're back to square one,'' said Moe. ''Why pornographers?'' The two men looked at each other for a short time and then looked away, embarrassed by their shared ineptitude.

"Jesus," said Jarvis, "the funny turns your life takes. I was broke ten years ago when I took my first job for Gomez and here I am still broke, still involved with Gomez."

"What was the job?"

"No big shit, really. I did some quiet work for him on a hijacking. Somebody took off with a load of German swords as I recall. He was uptight about getting his crap into Mexico without any duties, so silence was valuable to him. Anyway, that's how he came to call on me. He always liked me, the friendly Gringo who never put him down. Turned out a bunch of teenage kids did the thing. We got the stuff back, and he paid me a C-note. Nothing monumental."

"Okay," said Moe. "It's tally time, and I dread it. We've got a Nazi plaque and several dead people. We've got a woman named Molly who has the plaque but she ain't to be had, not just yet. We've got Fontana hiding and Grossman in his palace in Dallas, as far as we know. And we've got one damned lethal German of the SS variety who is in on the whole thing. Jesus Christ, Jarvis, all we need are the Budweiser draft horses to make this cockamamie thing complete."

Jarvis laughed for the first time. "Yep, but you left out some more of the goodies. Why not a meeting of diamond merchants? Gold merchants? Hell, why not the Smithsonian Institute? The thing has got to be worth at least a million, so why the bids of $250,000?"

"Maybe that one is not so difficult," said Moe. "One, we're dealing with stolen goods. Two, if you were a Jew who'd lost his family at Auschwitz, would you want to think that there was a museum who had your uncle's teeth on display? Hell no, you'd raise hell until the damned thing was melted down in Israel to buy rockets and assault rifles. And three, Gomez was feeling some heat that he had not expected to feel from our Nazi pal. Gomez made the wise move, offering it fast and privately to people who could afford it without the sale ever making the papers."

"Yeah," said Jarvis after a moment of thought, "you got good points. The original thief was an Indian who had been with the Germans for years. He's the bastard that got this shit to the fan."

"I'd bet a nickel to a monkey fart that the Indian is dead now," said Moe.

"That would make five," Jarvis said nervously. "I'd like to see that it doesn't become six, if you get my drift."

Moe started to reassure Jarvis, but the waitress interrupted them: "Hey, Moe! You got a long distance call!"

"Wait here!" Moe commanded. "Do not move." He trotted to the far end of the place and grabbed the phone. "Moe here."

"Moe? Rog."

"Hi, shithook. Where you been?"

"Dallas. Where else? Hey Moe, I'm on to something hot."

"As long as you've got a change of socks stay with it."

"Cut the crap, Moe. You ever hear of a man named Grossman?"

"About an hour's worth. You ever hear of a private dick named Jarvis?"

"Matter of fact, yeah."

"Well, I'm having my fifth or so cup with him right now. And you thought old Moe was full of shit about this thing! Didn't I tell you it was gonna turn hot? You know what it is we're after?"

"No. But Grossman thinks he knows who's got it!"

"Let me guess: A woman named Molly. Right?"

After a brief silence, Roger said, "Jesus, Moe, why was I off on this goddam snipe hunt when the tooth fairy brings you all the news?"

"We also serve who merely meditate, Rog. By the way, the paper's not gonna be sold anytime soon, so we better pursue this one to the limit."

"That was my next question. How is brother Lynch?"

"Magnanimous and benevolent. At least he was some six hours ago." Moe looked down the length of the restaurant and saw Jarvis brooding over his cup. "This Jarvis is a gold mine of info, Rog."

"Such as?"

"Such as a gold Nazi plaque topped with an eagle's head and fronted with SS lightning made of diamonds. That, me boy, is what we seek."

Roger emitted a long, low whistle. "God, Moe, that is heavy stuff. But my feeble little mind is suffering van lag. Give me all you got."

"It's gonna take a good ten minutes, Rog, but here goes." It took ten minutes and then some. By the time he had finished his ankles itched from immobile standing.

"Holy Christ," said Roger. "And I thought I'd lived two lifetimes in the past thirty-six hours! But there's something I don't get, Moe, one minor thing that ain't so minor."

"Let me guess. Why pornographers?"

"That's why I love you, Voris. Why pornographers?"

"That one would ice the cake, Rog."

"Not even one idea, huh? You say this Gomez was a goofy sort, maybe it's all bullshit."

"Nope, Jarvis and I have plowed that field into bug dust. There's something here under our very goddamn noses that we are too smart to see."

"Maybe. Now listen up, because I have something of my own that is enticing. Grossman has offered me ten grand to go to Memphis to find a certain Molly. He's convinced that she's the Molly we seek."

Moe noted a certain unhealthy boyish enthusiasm in Roger's voice and said, "I'd be watching my ass if I were you, Rog. Jarvis gives even money that Grossman winds up with this plaque one way or another anyway, and that's what got Bond into the skull orchard. Now he's got you out doing his shit. See any patterns there?"

"Sure. So the old fart is cautious. Big deal. He's already given me five hundred for expenses. So why don't Starla and I trot over to Memphis and find this Molly? The story goes on and not a cent out of Lynch's pocket."

"Roger?"

"Yes Moe."

Moe rubbed his head slowly. "Roger, who the hell is Starla?"

"Oh, yeah, I didn't tell you that. Bond's niece. She was there last night when Sturbridge came and we all went to the jewelry shop. Then I went to the coffee shop, and Sturbridge and I talked. Then this morning we went to Bond's funeral, and Grossman's black servant rousted us and took us to Grossman's. Now we're at the hotel getting her bags. Got all that?"

"A word here and there. Any romantic entanglement here?"

"Nah. She's nice, plain, a little weird. You remember that waitress at Gino's you used to call Baby Bullshit?"

"That bad, huh?"

"Not really bad. Just, like I said, plain. Well bred in a poverty-stricken way. Sort of a silent Blanche Dubois."

"So, what's your plan, Rog?"

"You haven't said yet about Memphis. Do we go? Remember, it's paid for. The ten grand might or might not be there if I score, but that'd be gravy above and beyond the story. Grossman thinks we'll be safe since we're outsiders."

"I'm not so sure. I take it you've given some thought to one Elgin Tatum."

"Yeah, too bad. The TV in the lobby said he made quite a splat."

"So far it's only been assholes who've bitten the dust. This German is good, Rog. Damned good."

"What do you know about him?"

"Almost nothing. He should be older, tough as nails, probably a jungle dweller for the past thirty or so years. And, I think I know his name: Ableiter. That's gotta be him." Moe felt himself sweating like a country preacher.

"Ableiter, huh? And you think he did the trick on Tatum?"

"No doubt. He's got a British accent, according to all sources. With a little help from Gomez and Jarvis, and a little deduction, he got to Rix and Tatum both in a little over twenty-four hours."

"But he doesn't know Roger Wilder from Adam's other ox. Goddamnit, do I go to Memphis or not?"

Moe looked back at Jarvis. The aged, frightened, and unkempt detective was looking out at the afternoon traffic. Several patrons had sneaked into the place and were engaged in animated conversations over hamburgers. Their sounds and their actions made Jarvis appear twice as lonely as before. He admitted to himself that he was going to pay Jarvis with his own money, a remuneration that would break him down to his sock tops. Paying with the paper's money would mean that Jarvis existed, a thing that Moe wanted to keep from the world just now.

"Roger?"

"Yes Moe?"

"You just watch your ass and make damned sure you find this Molly, and another thing: stay in touch!"

"Your reassurance is heartwarming, as the piggy said to the lion. . . . Moe?"

"Yes, Roger."

"Remember that time we traced that hush money all the way to the sheriff's office and then found that the sheriff was gone all that week?"

"Yeah. But I don't get---"

"That's what I'm feeling right now. Damnit, why not gold dealers or diamond merchants? Why pornographers?"

Moe felt his nerve endings being grated by that resurgent question. Like an old tom cat whose first paw thrust has not pulled from the dark can all that he knows to be there, Moe knew in his guts that this plaque thing was more interesting in what was not yet known rather than in what was.

"Moe? You there?"

"Yes, Roger. I can't answer you. All I know is to keep punching."

"Okay, pard. We're burnin' daylight, as John Wayne said, so I'm headin' out for Memphis."

"Spare me your cowpoke allusions, Roger. Just watch your ass and report to me at least once a day."

"Good enough. See you, Moe."

"I hope so."

Moe replaced the receiver and impulsively patted it in the manner of a youth bidding farewell to a favorite pup.

His head swam in eddys of nausea and, for a short time, he feared that he was going to heave coffee all over Gino's wall. The sensation passed, leaving him clammy and disconsolate. After inhaling deeply several times, he was able to walk back to the booth. Too much coffee, too much stress—it always did him this way.

"I envy your importance," said Jarvis. "I've sat for days waiting for my phone to ring."

"Yeah," Moe wheezed as he entered the booth, "us dynamic news types are in a perpetual whirligig." He thought of the Valiant and hoped that it would get him through another month.

"You okay?" Jarvis's tone relayed honest concern.

"I'm bifurcated both physically and emotionally just now," said Moe. "Don't ask me what it means; look it up."

Jarvis motioned toward the phone. "Anything there about our little party?"

"Nope. One of the ladies in the place is our current sports editor, needed some info." A twinge of ingratitude bit into Moe's soul as he lied but, by God, it was time he started playing this thing close to his own chest and to hell with the world.

"Lady sports editors. Jesus, our world has changed, huh?"

"Yeah." Grungy thoughts clouded Moe's mind. He wished that Jarvis would just disappear.

"You married?" the detective asked.

"Separated. Divorce probable. You?"

"A two-time loser. Last one was twenty-nine. My occupation and my age don't do much for swingers."

"Twenty-nine? You shoulda known better," said Moe, feeling a keen envy.

Jarvis said, "You sleep with the same woman for twenty years and sex gets to be going from one position to another like sleep walking. Stretch marks and wrinkles creep up like clouds on a hot afternoon. One day a doll winks and you wink back. Next thing you know you're living with her. Every trouble a man has in his life can sooner or later be traced to the head of his prick."

Moe smiled. "What's it like living alone full-time?"

"Just like part-time, only more of it." When Moe did not smile, Jarvis said, "Yeah, I know what you mean, the pain thing. Well, it gets less painful as time goes on. You get used to it, but you never learn to like it." Jarvis suddenly looked ten years older than when he had come into the place.

Moe leaned forward, took out his smooth and hip-bent wallet, removed a blank check. As he wrote with a theatrical flourish, he tried not to read the bank's blurb at the top: Voris or Edna Mohler. Somehow this bordered on sacrilege, for it was Edna herself who had forever told him to keep a blank check for emergencies. As he handed the check to Jarvis, he said, "If this thing washes in our favor I'll see that you get one thousand dollars. You have my word on it."

Jarvis started to speak, but his embarrassment dissolved the words. He stood, extended his hand, and the men shook, a symbol of camaraderie. "Where's a good cheap flophouse?" he asked.

"Try the Cotton Hotel about six blocks down," said Moe.

"Sounds lavish," Jarvis said, trying on his wobbly smile.

"They change the sheets on cloudy Thursdays, I'm told. The main thing is, lay low. You got that?"

"Sweat it not," said Jarvis. "Anything comes up that I need to know, that's where I'll be, or I'll tell you otherwise."

Moe watched as Jarvis went outside, got into his car, and turned left into the pismire crawl of afternoon traffic. Something told him beyond question that he would never see Perry Jarvis again.

He paid, went across the street, and felt the pallid warmth of late afternoon. San Antonio had an afternoon wanness about it that was a direct result of all that had happened today. He hoped only that the check did not bounce.

The paper had been placed in the street racks in front of the *Sentinel* building and that would mean that the vans were gone as would be most of the office staff. Entering the city room, Moe halfway entertained the thought of just sleeping at his desk on this night; it would beat going to that damned empty house.

Mrs. Cable met him at the door. "There was a man here to see you a minute ago. He said he'd go over to your house." She was using polish remover on her nails, and an aura of alcohol and perfume hung heavily about her.

"Who was he?"

"A Ranger. Willard, I think he said."

"Doesn't sound local. I know most of the local boys."

"I don't. Cops give me the willies. See you tomorrow."

"Sure," said Moe. "Tomorrow."

Forty minutes later he wheeled the old Valiant into the driveway and watched as a lanky man got out of a gray, unmarked car across the street. Stetson, boots, black suit. Ranger.

"Are you Voris Mohler?" the man asked.

As they shook hands, Moe said, "What's left of him. You're Willard, mostly."

The Ranger smiled. "Mostly. Got a few minutes?"

When they were in the house, Moe fixed each a bourbon and Coke, and they settled in the cluttered living room. Willard came directly to the point: "You got a man in Dallas on the Bond thing. Any particular reason?"

"No."

"No what?"

Moe shrugged and feigned embarrassment. "It ain't panning out. Seems Bond was a four-flusher. The hot copy planned for has cooled."

Willard stared into his drink and said, "Perturbs me. Yessir, it does. A jeweler and a Mexican meet halfway from nowhere and get shot. Your San Antone locals have got other goats to rope, so I get sent down from Austin. I read your paper and the police reports. So far, zero minus nothin'. Did you do anything on the Mexican?"

Moe felt strangely trapped, chastized. "No, not really."

"Always go with the big money or no money—those are the tree roots of any murder case. That's why I did some research on the Mexican. Left Tijuana six days ago, turns up dead three days ago. A three-day gap there. Interesting?"

Moe nodded. "Interesting."

Willard leaned forward and placed his glass on the coffee table. "I got a friend in Arizona can move like grease through a goose, if I ask him to. He says Gomez flew to Flagstaff, disappeared two, three days, then caught a flight out of there to Austin. Caught a bus from Austin to Hondo and got off the bus out there in the middle of snake and rock country. Any ideas?"

Moe sipped at his drink and shook his head. "People do nutty things," he said. "That's what keeps you and me both in business." He felt a twinge of sorrow for Willard. The Ranger was about forty-eight hours behind him.

"Nutty things, indeed," said Willard. "You went to Tijuana on this thing." Willard's eyes were like cobra noses.

"You know about that, huh?"

"The way to get somewhere is to start somewhere, Mohler. So let's start: Rix murdered Bond and Gomez; I know it, and you know it, and so does Austin. Stupid bastard used his own rifle. Ballistics. He was a good man at one time, but he went off the hind side of the horse. Everybody smells dope, but it's not dope. Frankly, I laid awake last night counting my ceiling tiles over this one. If you're withholding evidence it could get hairy."

Moe tried to smile but could not. "Is that a threat?"

Willard tried not to smile but did. "Just a possibility."

Moe removed a shoe, scratched at the bottom of his foot, and said, "Willard, when I was a kid I was sick one summer and laid in bed for three weeks. There was an ice cream man who made deliveries in our neighborhood. At the end of that three weeks I knew who he was screwing, trying to screw, or had screwed, and was no longer screwing. No brag, just fact. Call it sixth sense or deduction or just damned good guesswork. Right now I'm just in the guessing stage of this thing. Rix was at the murder scene, and then Rix was dead in his own bathroom, and things began to click and would not stay unclicked." He looked down and saw that his sock had a hole in it; he could only hope that his story did not have a hole in it. There had been no mention of Grossman, Molly, Fontana, pornography, or the plaque. His armpits felt hot, mushy, and probably smelly.

Willard lifted his hat from his head, fingered the brim, put the hat back on, and stood. ''Anything comes around that I oughta know, you will get in touch,'' he said, emphasizing the ''will.''

''You got it,'' said Moe. They shook hands, and Moe watched the tall Ranger amble down to his car and drive off into the magenta light of late afternoon.

He locked the door, vacuumed, dusted, straightened this, cursed at that. Four more bourbon and Cokes were sweated off as quickly as he imbibed them and, by the time he showered and fell into bed exhausted, it was well past ten o'clock. Rather than going immediately to sleep, he was beset by that lap dog of the worrier, insomnia. The day had consisted of too much and too many: Lynch, Jarvis, Willard; Mexicans, plaques, Flagstaff, Roger. Faces, some only half formed, came and went.

His last thought before sleeping was of Edna. He missed her not at all, and this confused him even further.

Thirteen

The digital clock on the Southwestern Branch of Commerce Bank stood at 11:39 when Perry Jarvis drove his old Plymouth into Dallas. His tie seemed about to cut his throat, and he fumbled with sweaty, oily fingers to loosen it. Fatigue had come on him suddenly and, for the first time in nearly three days, its motioning hands beckoned from the smouldering ashes of what had been his fear, a fear comparable to combat psychosis. And now his thousand yard stare emanated from eyes darkly circled, gritty, and red. He turned on his windshield wipers, removed his hat, placed it on the seat, and worked off first one shoe and then the other. The floor and the gas pedal were sensuous to his feet, and all that bothered him were the choleric odor of his own body and a toothaching need to piss.

But his agonies were not all temporal. Riding in the old car in spectral silence were shadows whose forms were the shapeless and unlighted presence of human conscience. Jarvis had lied to Moe, however slightly. But self-justification, that horse that can seat but one rider, was with him as he recounted the things that he would be able to do with the Mohler money, and it was momentarily a good thing that he had done. It was he who had been the crux of the gathering, served as its pivotal bearing. It was he who had taken Gomez out of harm's way in Mexico, albeit inadvertently; what had happened to Gomez on the prairie had been of his own doing. It was he who had given Mohler all the information that would enable the newspaper to have a story of monumental bloom once the thing was resolved. So he had lied to Moe about one little thing.

He probably knew who Molly was! Some years back she had been an old porno star in Dallas, had shown a marked preference for dark skin in her matings. Yes, it had to be the same Molly, famous in the Mex and Black sections of Dallas. Now the old bitch was in Memphis somewhere, and Perry Jarvis was probably the only person who knew this. Say what one might, Perry Jarvis was one hell of a detective.

The two fifty was travel money for his Memphis trip. The jaunt to San Antonio had gotten him out of the city. Safety and profit and a sightseeing tour besides! Hell, it had been a good day. Now for a quick run by the office to see whether the insurance company had sent the three hundred for a minor snoop job back in April, and it was on to Memphis. Hell, he might even be as far as Texarkana by sunup. Things were indeed looking up for Perry Jarvis! He owed Mohler nothing, he concluded, and that was that! Tit for tat. The plaque was his—first come, first served. His fatigue was magically gone but, God, he needed to piss.

Orange and yellow neon glimmered and fluttered. Cut-rate furniture stores, unpainted churches, deserted truckyards went by blurrily. The fabulously rich Texas of song and folklore was not represented here. Dull-eyed black men cruised by in white Cadillacs with leopard skin seats while, on every other corner, girls the color of melba toast hailed passing cars. After a lifetime of this sleaze it was time to move on to the grandeur that could be had in the real Texas. The check in the glove compartment and the other that was supposed to have arrived at his office today could be converted to long green at Sandy's Bar just ten blocks away, and the danger factor from Mohler's fearsome German would be minimal at best. Five hundred and fifty dollars. It was the most that he had seen in one wad in ages.

Turning right, he drove two blocks and saw the familiar sign *Arcade Hotel*. The pathetic flophouse was dimly illuminated by a single yellow bulb that hung from a steel question mark. For several years he had noted the obvious symbolism of the question mark, and now the question was answered. Buttressing the hotel's left side, like a scruffy calf nuzzling its mother, was his own office. He drove some fifty feet past the place and parked behind a dirty pickup that bore Oklahoma license plates. It probably belonged to some Okie boy who was getting laid upstairs. Perry smiled.

By now his kidneys were afizz with lightning, and he quick-stepped down the sidewalk. As always when time was of the essence, he could not find the proper key. Cursing, he finally managed to let himself in and ran through the small anteroom, unzipping as he trotted. There was no time to lift the lid, and he sagged and sighed in the splendor of relief as he sprayed the porcelain seat in the darkness, his socks absorbing the spillover.

Upon entering his dark office he touched the light switch and was only mildly angry to find that the lights would not come on. He went back up the hallway to the anteroom and found that this switch also failed to respond. It was then that he saw the small white rectangle taped to his door. In the glare of the yellow light he read: Sorry, but we have had to interrupt your service. Shoeless, unshaven, dirty, and without light, Perry Jarvis banged the door glass with his fist. The floor beneath the letter drop was empty of anything but grit and shadow. No insurance check.

He brailled the dark hallway, felt his way to his desk, and sat down to brood. Cupping his face in his hands, he stared down at the dark desk top. It was then that he smelled the slight odor. His eyes ran over the hazy outlines of all that lay in the overly large twenty-by-thirty foot area, an area that he had tried to fill over the years with the stuff of function: metal filing cabinet, kitchen table with coffee pot, another totally unnecessary desk that he had bought at a fire sale, a steel-pipe coat rack on rollers. This last object might have been the source of the odor, since it now strained under the weight of several winter suits and topcoats. They had not felt the touch of the dry cleaner's art in some time. But no, this was not coagulate body odor, but something else, something familiar but teasingly disguised by the darkness. Then, through the haze of his fatigue, the simplicity of the smell revealed itself: gasoline.

"Do not move," said a male voice.

Jarvis felt his throat tighten. "I won't," he whispered.

"I have a gun. If you move at all, I will kill you."

Jarvis let his eyes wander about the room. The intruder had to be behind the filing cabinet, under the other desk, or behind the soiled clothing, none of these three positions being to Perry's advantage. He kept a .32 automatic in the bottom drawer of his desk but, because his permit had expired, he had neglected to carry it. Perry Richard Jarvis is about to die, he was thinking and in the dark. For some idiotic reason he just hated to die in the dark.

"I said don't move," the voice announced with impatience. "Lean forward and put your forehead on the desk," it commanded.

Perry did as instructed and felt the cool caress of the varnish on his face. A dozen images raced through his mind, the most absurd of which had the police pondering why he had died with his shoes off. They would figure that it was some bizarre sort of sex crime. Absurd. He heard footsteps accompanied by the bell clink of a few barren coat hangers and congratulated himself on having been thirty-three percent right, a percentage of rightness that was in excess of his life's norm. Here lies Thirty-Three Percent Jarvis, his tombstone might say.

The intruder took Perry's wrists and gently affixed them to the chair's arms, an act so barren of evil intent that it almost duplicated the nudgings of a kindly old barber. The alien hands began to make tying motions at the left wrist, but the material being used was so light, so gossamer in its touch that Perry felt as though he were indulging a child in a pantomime of bondage. Suddenly, the hands made a jerking motion, and the top of Perry's wrist felt as if it had been slashed by an extremely keen razor. He jerked slightly and the voice said, "Steady," the speaker already moving around the chair to the right wrist. When both wrists were secured, Perry felt his ankles being crossed, tied. The end of the material was then lashed to the chair's left leg. The bonding had taken less than three minutes. Perry wondered why his captor had not mentioned his shoeless feet.

"You may not raise your head. If you raise your head I will certainly kill you," the voice warned with diminishing volume. The man returned to the shadows. When he was again secreted, he said, "Now you may raise your head."

As he came up slowly, Perry found that the world was even darker, that the objects in the room were now misshapen and made grotesque by his fear. Sensing the stupidity of his words, even before they were uttered, he asked, "What do you want?"

"I have who I want for the time being, Mister Jarvis."

"I don't have it."

There was a stifled laugh followed by, "I know Mister Jarvis, I know."

"Then bug out of here and I'll never tell. Swear to God." He felt a droplet of sweat meander down his right side, and he squirmed against the ironic sensation of being tickled.

The man emitted a sarcastic chuckle. "Come, Mister Jarvis, an enterprising person like yourself? After all, did not Senor Gomez choose you to do his work?"

It was then that Perry knew without question that it was the German. He had pronounced that last word "wairk;" Scotland, with just a touch of guttural Germanic. To now, it had all been English that was a bit too precise, and Perry wondered whether the man was losing his allegiance to theater along with his patience. His cheeks burned as he admitted to himself that he was truly afraid now, gut scared, downright panicky. He tried to work his wrists free, but the binding merely seared and embedded itself in his skin. Allowing himself one quick glance downward, he could see the tiniest white threads holding him, and he knew from his talk with Mohler what it was: dental floss.

"Cut me loose, and I'll steer you on the bastards who have it. You won't gain anything if I die."

"My ambitions do not require your demise, Mister Jarvis; however, neither do they tend to flourish by your staying alive."

Now Perry felt that the sonofawhore was merely torturing him for the pure hell of it. There was an extension of life to be had from all this delaying chatter, Perry knew but, at the same time, it did not diminish his curiosity as to what the German's next move was to be. Maybe the kraut really was being lazily cruel just for the raw hell of being cruel; maybe the logic here was to be found in the absence of logic. Whatever the German was thinking, he was taking his damned good time. Perry tried to remember the name so that things might be put on a personal basis, but all that he could resurrect in his fear was that it began with "A."

"Keep it simple," said Perry.

"I said that you may or may not get out of here alive," said the German.

"Just for the record, who are you?"

The man laughed softly, "If the others did not know, then why should you? Is the identity of one's savior necessary? I think not—it is the salvation itself that is necessary. Shall we talk of our salvation?"

Perry's feet were beginning to go to sleep, and he tried to rub his ankles together. He thought of the movie serials that he had seen as a boy, ill-scripted and underacted affairs in which the hero always had a crowbar or a hidden razor handy; from here on, he promised with rather baseless optimism, he would carry his gun at all times, and to hell with licenses.

"You talk and I'll listen," he said.

"Excellent, Mister Jarvis. I am seeking access to a Mister Grossman. Could you tell me about his current location?"

"I don't have the remotest idea. He bugged out."

"Come now, Mister Jarvis. You two had such a rapport until just recently. When I talked with you on the phone, you indicated that Grossman, Fontana, and Tatum were the very racks on which your future hung; I must admit to having felt a sense of pique. You do understand that, if I cannot have Grossman and Fontana, I must settle for second best."

"And I'm it, huh?" He knew that he was dead, that the man whose name began with "A" had no real interest in his remaining alive. It is over, he admitted with an absence of passion. The smell of the gasoline again assailed his nostrils and he speculated on the presence of such an odor. Desiring to have the thing over and finished, he taunted, "I think you're bluffing to beat hell, Kraut."

There was a moment of stillness in the room, a quiet that was almost phantasmagoric, macabre. The light of a match erupted throwing an orange glow against the wall. The flame survived no more than three seconds and, in the last instant of its existence, a wisp of cigarette smoke blossomed upward through the small circle of light.

"Do you smoke, Mister Jarvis?"

"Huh, no, thanks," said Perry, feeling foolish at this natural, gracious refusal.

"Within two minutes, Mister Jarvis, a cigarette is going to be the most important thing in your life. Do you believe me?"

"I . . . don't know," said Perry, wondering where this was all leading.

The figure approached, his left hand carrying a square white object, while his right held the cigarette high and away from his body. It occurred to Perry that he was keeping the two objects as far apart as was possible, and this attitude of approach made him appear as a demented angel in full wingspread. After placing the white object on the desk directly to Perry's front, the interloper laid the cigarette end-out at one corner of the desk. As the man began to rummage through his pockets, Perry leaned forward and identified the white thing as a common plastic jug. He sagged backward as the stench of gasoline emanated outward from the container.

"I have in my hand a book of matches and some tape, Mister Jarvis. A tiny slit has been cut in the neck of the jug. Do you know what is in this jug?"

Perry tried to speak but was able only to nod.

"Correct. Gasoline." The man picked up the cigarette, opened the book of matches, and placed the butt of the glowing thin tube over the match heads. Snapping off a bit of tape, he carefully laid the matchbook over the area of the slit and connected the objects. As he hastily moved back to the shadows, Perry saw that the result of the German's efforts was an ugly and lethal firebomb that had been concocted of the commonest of goods, untraceable goods.

"The brand is called Virginia Slims, Mister Jarvis. Extra long and even burning. What do you suppose will happen when the glow touches the first match?"

Perry felt all defiance leaving him. The word darted through his mind like a spear point. Incinerated.

"Okay, what do you want to know?" he said breathlessly, realizing at once the inaneness of the question.

"I want to know where it is," said the other, quite matter of factly.

"And how do we bargain?" Jarvis asked, watching the glow of the cigarette.

"You are in no position to bargain. I will put out the cigarette, leave you tied, and depart. Your friends will find you in the morning." And then, tauntingly, "Your trip to the urinal was well advised."

"Cut the bullshit and start asking your questions," Jarvis said.

The hidden one sighed heavily and said, "Many years ago I learned a good deal about humans under duress, not the least of which was that a man allowed to talk will reveal much more than one who is asked questions. The question method is so . . . limiting."

"Okay. I'm talking! The thing has ballooned into a bunch of small timers: Mohler of the *Sentinel*, a reporter, Bond's niece."

"Their names?"

Perry looked at the orange ash. There were now less than two inches of life left. "The reporter is Wilder. Roger Wilder." Ableiter stepped from the shadows and shined a pen light against the jug, the pale periphery arcing Perry's sweating face and wild eyes. Perry used the instant to look at his wrists and saw again the threads of dental floss. If he tried to break free, it could cut him to ribbons. The bastard was shrewd: he had forgotten nothing.

"We have time," the man said without emotion.

"You may have time, asshole, but I got the length of half a cigarette."

"Where is it?" the voice asked with no hint of impatience.

"It's supposed to be in Memphis, Tennessee. An old whore named Molly is our chief suspect. A white woman. I got that from Mohler, for what it's worth," he lied.

"Many years ago, while studying your rather quaint language, I learned that when an American says 'for what it's worth,' the worth is usually questionable."

"It's all I got," Perry said angrily.

"This Molly: does she have another name?"

"No. I mean, not that I know of. Grossman got the name from Gomez. She used to work in porno films. You got enough now?" He saw another bit of ash begin to bend downward.

"Molly in Memphis, Tennessee, Roger Wilder, and Bond's niece," the man recounted. "Ah, how the thrill of the chase is flourishing with these revelations."

"I got enough thrills to last me a lifetime, fella. How about doing something to this cigarette like we said?"

"Very well," said the captor, his words coming a bit too readily, as though he had been aware all along that the time for such agreement was at hand. He came forward and moved around behind Perry. Convinced that he was about to experience release, Perry opened his mouth and exhaled heavily. Just as he did so the wide hands shoved a piece of cloth into his mouth and pulled a handkerchief around his lips. Perry tried to scream, but the cloth in his mouth flipped one of its corners against his palate as he inhaled and he became still, aware that anything more than steady nasal breathing would instantly suffocate him. Like a man leaning away from the face of a viper, he eased himself back in the chair and stared hollowly at the distant haze of yellow light at the end of the hallway. An urge to vomit seized him, and he fought it back and thought of sand, cactus, openness of sky and desert; his imagery would not allow any thought of liquid at just this moment, lest he heave. He willed the feeling away.

"You have been most helpful, Mister Jarvis," said the captor.

Blinded now by his own sweat, blinking away both tears and perspiration, Perry watched as the presence walked up the hallway and disappeared through the door and into the night. Through the gauzelike saltwater on his eyelids he could see that the man was about six feet, three inches tall and had shoulders that were at least forty inches across. His suit had been dark, and it was a darkness that was accented by a shock of white hair that was combed back in that ancient style called a pompadour. The old giant had turned right, as if to avoid the hotel's yellow light, as if to rebuff the question mark from which it hung.

Perry had filed these impressions as a matter of habit, but his awareness of the glowing cigarette quickly brought him back to the impending terror. There was less than half an inch remaining outside the matchbook cover, and the dullness of orange behind its ash showed no sign of going out. He twisted his wrists and found the pain to be excruciating, a slickness on the floss making him aware that he had already cut himself. His feet were completely asleep now, and the tiniest movement drove needles of pain into his instep. He shrugged against the pain but, in doing so, the fluttering piece of cloth stirred itself in his throat and the vomit frenzy almost overtook him again. Gag just once, he told himself, and it is all over; but, then it is anyway. Somewhere in his brain that computer which deals with alternatives was telling him that he could strangle, burn to death, or go through life without hands, provided he could muster enough strength to break the thin bonds, and provided he did not bleed to death in the process. Survive and think, said an inner voice, and it was instantly contradicted by another that said, no, think and survive.

Relaxing, his head making a perfunctory nod to something, as if in acquiescence to its unquestionable power, Perry yielded at last to the commonness that had been his life. He had fought failure all the way, swatting at it as he ran, like a man tormented by unseen bees, but now he was at last aware that it would never let off. Such a thought from a man about to die, he admitted, again fighting down an urge to vomit.

The glow disappeared at last. Perry looked away and closed his eyes. His fingertips twitched.

Captain Wallace Derry of the Dallas Fire Department staggered out of the charred tunnel and back into the street. The chopping and hosing minions under his command merely smiled at each other and continued working; they had seen it before. Derry's inability to remain around charred flesh was legendary. He leaned against the door of the great red engine and vomited the pizza that he had just enjoyed with his wife. It had been an impromptu anniversary supper that they shared with the troops.

"You okay, Cap?" a fireman asked.

"Not by a damn sight, Woody. Get a body bag and go into that back office. There's roast in the oven." He looked up and away with bleary eyes. A semicircle of gawking civilians looked at the scene with faces like misshapen balloons. Here and there patrolmen made upward chopping motions with their hands. Derry wondered why people were turned on to fire. One old tall bastard with a shock of white hair actually seemed to be smiling.

"You got it iced down?" Woody asked a hoseman.

"Yeah. Nothin' left but a chunk about so long. Get Berger to help on this one," said the hoseman. He had shared the pizza.

Woody summoned one of the axemen and shined a flashlight into what had once been an office. Experience told him that such things did not improve with hesitation, and he moved forward, his wet boots sluffing across the floor like wiper blades. He kicked two pieces that had once been a wooden desk and played the light against the ceiling to check for ashfall. Following the beam downward, he saw that a coat rack had been melted by the heat, the wire hangers bronzed and contorted into strange shapes. A chair leg with a tiny thread of something white caught his eye for an instant and he continued to look at it while feeling about with his feet. When he found it and kicked it sideways, the heavy and soggy thing sizzled as water flowed beneath it. The hoseman had been right: it was a chunk about so long.

Outside, Captain Derry was more tyrannical than usual. He chewed out a hoseman for removing a water-soaked boot. When the pressures of the moment were gone, they would rib him about the pizza, carry his ass high. The chastened hoseman looked at one of his knowledgeable buddies and winked embarrassedly.

The drunks and whores began to return to the hotel, and the crowd stared until the ambulance took the chunk away. Moving with the dispersing crowds, the tall observer with white hair walked to a distant corner, paused under a street light for a moment, and then walked away into the night.

Fourteen

At that moment in which Perry Jarvis had been halfway between San Antonio and Dallas, Roger and Starla were watching the sun go down beyond the windows of a roadside diner called Marie's American. He had sandwiched the van in among a labyrinth of great diesels whose muttering exhaust pipes spoke to each other of the wonderful places that they had been. This, orchestrated with the clang of tire tools, squeal of pigs, stenches of cow dung, had given him a tingle that had lasted for the better part of thirty minutes. For the first time in weeks he was consciously happy. He even found himself liking the truckers, gritty and bearded fellows, most attired in cowboy garb. The juke box sobbed out the offerings of Nashville, plaintive and lonely stuff about crying angels and beer joints and forgotten farms. Roger Wilder was experiencing a oneness with America that he had not felt since Viet Nam.

Starla, on the other hand, was continuing the almost rude speechlessness that had been her way since they had gathered up their possessions at the hotel. For two hundred miles she had barely spoken, and then it had only come as a command for a rest stop.

"Want to talk about it?" Roger asked. He stirred his iced tea and touched the bun on his burger. It was still too hot to eat.

"Not really," she answered. "It has nothing to do with you, if that is what's worrying you."

"To look at us, you'd think we were a married couple having a spat," he said acknowledging the yawning and scratching truckers. He picked up the burger and bit into it. Disappointing, not nearly as great as those that he had eaten yesterday. As he chewed he watched Starla toy with her noodle soup. She slowly ran the spoon around in it as if seeking foreign matter.

"They would be wrong," she said. As she lifted a spoonful her hand quaked slightly and a noodle fell back into the bowl.

"Look, if it's really me that's got you all agog, you can tell me about it," he said. "If it's the man-woman thing, you don't have to worry. I'm normal, usually, and I don't rape people. You and I are going to be together for quite some time, so these little questions might as well be laid to rest. We slept in separate rooms last night and that's the way I assume it will be. Okay?"

She looked at him with exasperation. "It's not that. If I didn't trust you I wouldn't have ridden in that van half-way across the world today."

"Fair enough," he said. "So what is it?"

"It's a million things and nothing. Do you know the feeling?"

"Yeah. I've been on night patrols. Behind every bush is Charlie with a machete. You think you've got the market cornered on suspicion?"

She smiled and shook her head. For a moment he thought that she was going to speak, but she only opened a packet of crackers and started on the soup. When they had finished eating, the waitress refilled their tea glasses and they stared out the window at the schools of ever-moving trucks.

"Do you believe in prescience?" she asked, turning her gaze back to Roger.

"I'm supposed to be a writer, but can you define that one for me?" he asked, feeling a little embarrassed.

"Clairvoyant. Able to see things that are . . . unseeable."

"Not really. I leave that up to Moe."

"But that could have been the result of fearing that the paper is in trouble, as you've explained, a bureaucrat justifying his job by creating trouble where none exists. This time he guessed right."

"Boy, did he ever," said Roger. "So what's with your prescience?"

She shuddered. "I don't know, really. Maybe it's genetic memory. Maybe it's just my Jewishness."

"Do Jews all harbor feelings of impending disaster?" he asked. It was the first time that he had used the word Jew in her presence.

"By and large, yes," she said. "This Nazi thing has torn open some old scar tissue that I had forgotten, stuff from my childhood." Suddenly she said, "Why have you not asked me anything about myself?"

"I figured there was time for it later. My plan was to get all I could between the cemetery and the hotel. But we got sidetracked a little. A freeway chase, a judo chop from Perkins, Grossman. God, all that seems like a million years ago, and it was just today. The more time we spend together, the less able I am to dig into you personally. Does that make sense?"

"Yes." She sipped her tea and never took her eyes off his own. "Tell me, have you ever heard of Ravensbruck?"

His mind went back to some of his military history lessons. "A concentration camp, I believe."

She nodded. "I was born there."

Roger stared at her for a long moment, his eyes trying to determine whether this was some form of perverse theater. Unless his books had been all wrong, unless World War II was a bit of fiction that the world had thrown at him to confuse him further, she would have died there. But born? No.

"Maybe you'd better be a little more specific," he said.

"I really was. Has it not occurred to you that Uncle Alan and I were not very close? A Jewish merchant in Dallas and only one relative shows up at his funeral. The relative does not know the few other people there and does not bother to ask who they were. All the trappings of the funeral of a very lonely man."

"Now that you mention it, I did notice that you didn't cry."

"One of the things that has run across my mind over the last few hours on the road is that perhaps you are not a motivated reporter. No insult intended."

"None taken. I've had a few emotional wrenches myself in the last few days. I'm off my feed somewhat, reporterwise. So how does Uncle Alan tie in with Ravensbruck?"

"My mother was named Tzipora Blaustein. All I've been able to come up with over a lifetime of halfhearted digging is that she was a Polish Jew. And a very beautiful woman."

"And she was Alan Bond's sister?"

Starla nodded. "He came to this country with an uncle of theirs in the twenties. The uncle was a *diamantenschneider*, as the Germans might call it, a diamond cutter."

"So the old uncle died and Alan was in the diamond business for life," Roger said.

"A fair summation," said Starla. "I don't know how he came to see Texas as the place for him, because I don't know that much about his history. Anyway, he settled in Dallas and was safe from the pogroms. The classic story of the wandering Jew."

"And your mother?"

Starla sighed heavily, a preparatory act of one who is about to embark on a long and painful oral journey. "What I am about to tell you is the result of hearsay, old letters, people who survived. My mother was a *Gefaengnisfrau*, Jew or not."

"Forgive me, but I don't speak German."

"Neither do I. But I've made it a point to study the whole idiocy of the holocaust and certain words just stand out. Ironically enough, they are better than their English translations, or kinder, I should say. That word means . . . prison woman. It was a kind way of saying prostitute, if you can imagine the SS ever being kind."

"She had no choice," Roger said.

"Jews never have had," she answered, "and it is for that reason that we, we meaning Jews, tend to despise those of our number who indulge in the totally human act of being cowardly. My mother was cowardly, it would seem. You can almost envision her, a terrified, hungry, bedraggled young Polish girl just off a train where no telling how many babies had died either of heat, cold, or starvation, where old people died standing up because there was no place to lie down. You can almost envision her getting off the train and instantly smelling the ashes and rot of that corner of hell. I have assumed, in my lifetime of fantasy, that it was at that moment wherein her choices were offered: work, death, or prostitution to SS officers. She took the human way out, and thereby denounced her Jewish birthright, that right being to suffer the agonies of death or being worked to death on a bowl of thin soup, one per customer per day.'' She paused here and glared at him as if he might have been one of the Aryan group who had engendered such a policy.

"I'm sorry for it, Starla. I really am, for you, I mean.''

"Everybody is. The men who swing their golf clubs on country club greens and then vote non-Jewish membership are sorry for it. The DAR types with purple hair who sniff in the presence of Jews are sorry for it. The salesman down the street who tells a kike joke is sorry for it. The world is sorry for it, but it never ends. And it is going on now. This Nazi who is after the same thing that we are after is a real person! He is real, and I am real, and there is no fantasy. Now do you see why a lifetime of wondering who and what I am had been gnawing on me?''

Roger bit his lip. "Yeah, it's getting clearer. And last night Sturbridge rubbed the old sore with his *faux pas* about Bond's being Jewish.''

"Yes, fool that he and his kind are, well meaning fools all.''

Wanting to reel her anger in slowly, like a kite that has strayed into dense skies, he said, "But you have not told me yet why you and Bond were not all that compatible. My God, with you being his only living relative, it would seem----''

"You still don't grasp it, do you? Don't you know who I am? I am a bastard child. I am the result of Tzipora

Blaustein's absorption of Nazi semen. The name, rank, or serial number of my father is irrelevant. I am half pure Aryan and half Polish Jew. If you can perceive of the agonies of the mulatto child in the deep South, then you can understand what I am to my own people, whoever they are.'' She looked out the window and wiped her eyes with her fingertips.

Roger had seen the photographs, but until this moment they were mannequins in a play that had been produced in a less enlightened millennium. The hanged, starved, tortured, electrocuted, and gassed had never been real people until now. It was as though he looked upon a ghost, a reincarnation of all the suffering that had occurred in distant places with names like Maidanek, Treblinka, Auschwitz, Ravensbruck. He wanted to ask the questions that yet puzzled him, but he waited for a full two minutes before speaking at all. From somewhere deep within him an angry worm of guilt was stirring, moving itself upward so that it could lodge in his throat and choke him. He wondered why.

"We don't have to continue this if you don't want to," he said at last.

"Don't you want to know the rest?" she asked, her composure now intact.

"Yes. My original question had to do with your survival. If it's not too hard for you, I'd like to hear about it."

"Up to age four or five I can only manufacture a scenario for you. Polish Jew has officer's baby on or about the time the camp was liberated. British or Russian soldier takes the baby to a Red Cross lady. Red Cross flies baby to England, or wherever. After a couple of years the baby is brought to America by the Jewish Welfare League. My first adoptive parents were a couple named Weintraub. I lived with them in Passaic, New Jersey until I was nine. They died. Everybody dies, in my world, anyway. After that it was a series of foster homes up and down the Atlantic Coast. I was in one house for all of three weeks. I don't remember the names of those people, if you can believe that, but they had an older daughter who kept hitting me. Her, I remember. The last one lasted from when I was twelve to nineteen, a dear old lady named Sarah Cohn. She had enough money to get me a year at Yeshiva University, and then she, too, died.''

Roger stirred his tea, saw that all the ice had melted. From what seemed to be a great distance came a slow song about someone hitching a ride to Tulsa.

"So, how did you find out about Bond at all?" he asked.

"Bits and pieces. Here and there. Some twenty years ago Sarah received a letter from B'Nai B'Rith. Those people do a wonderful job; in their own way they rival the CIA. It said that Tzipora had a relative who was a jeweler in Dallas. From there it was as simple as a series of phone calls."

"And Bond didn't respond?"

"Oh, he responded. In six short minutes he called my mother everything but human, said that he never wanted to see me. But he did."

"Oh? How did that happen?"

"About five years ago he was in Cincinnati on business. I guess you could call it an undeniable blood impulse, but he looked me up. We spent one horrid hour trying to make conversation. It was in a coffee shop similar to this. I'll never forget his last words, his last action. He laid down his spoon and stared at me and said, 'There is no way that you are of me, for me, or by me. If I predecease you, you may have what is mine. You are in my will, but that is all of my life that you will ever be able to claim.' And with that he walked out."

"So you had one shot at him. One blood relative, one time. Jesus, what a story."

"So now you know why I came to Dallas. I don't know even now if my act was emotional or mercenary. As it turns out, neither was monumental."

"So today you saw the last of your roots buried forever. I admire you, lady."

She gazed at him with a mixture of compassion and loathing. It was as if she were a mother looking at a drunken son, a beloved and despicable part of herself that would forever be a part of her sufferings. ''Don't admire me; rather, understand me,'' she said.

''I think I do, now. A little better, at least. And, too, I can now understand your apprehensions in this matter. Up to now it has been something of a game with me, a vacation from the city room and Moe. They are going to murder you all, and you are the last of the living, which makes you next. Yeah, I can understand your use of the word prescience.''

''Thank you,'' she said. ''Now, if you will excuse me for a minute.'' She arose and went to the rest room, her passage creating only mild interest for the truckers.

The worm of shame continued to stir in Roger as he awaited her return.

She came back wiping her hands with a Kleenex. As she approached him the same uninterested drivers again looked and again confirmed their uninterest.

''I wish you wouldn't stare,'' she said.

''I wasn't staring. I was thinking.''

''About what I said?''

''Partly, and partly not.''

''Tell me the partly not.''

''Why would Grossman be so kind to us? Are we being had?''

''I hope not.''

Roger started to follow up on it but decided that enough of the night had been devoted to confession, cheap food, worry. Before she could sit down he stood, and they went to the register together. When he had paid, Starla handed him three one dollar bills without comment. He knew by the way she handed the money over that it would be useless to comment, useless to offer it back. Here was a woman who had paid her own way all her life, and there was no nonsense about her. Roger found himself liking her more all the time, and to hell with what the truckers thought.

When they were on the road again, he told her about Darlene and about Nam. He was on the verge of asking her about her own romantic life, not for any leading purposes, really, but in order to better understand how her birth and childhood had affected her viewpoints toward men. He looked over and saw that she had sagged against the door and was asleep. He wished that he had a blanket to put over her, and the mere fact of wishing it made him feel better about himself.

In the damp fog that threw a sheet over midnight the towns bypassed by the great highway—Hope, Prescott, Hot Springs—glowed in soft, amorphic light that rose from behind the trees that flanged the road. A faint scent of pines and night dampness intermingled in the Arkansas night, and bugs died quietly against the windshield.

A row of pines opened, and the yawning, starflicker giant that was Little Rock splayed out to the north in yellows and reds.

He convinced himself that he was hungry and steered the van into an all night eatery called The Green Duck. It was a nice place of big windows and big trucks. A gas station adjoined the place, and he parked the van on the dark side so that Starla could sleep undisturbed by light or activity. Night moths fluttered in the light and then stood on the great windows.

Linda Ronstadt was singing an old Hank Williams song to the assembled truckers. Roger took a back booth and rubbed his eyes with his fingertips.

A waitress came, and he ordered ham and eggs. He went off into a fatigue funk for a few minutes, drifted away, and was resurrected only by the scent of the breakfast as the woman put it on the table.

"If I'se you, I'd get a room," the waitress advised. He smiled up at her and saw that she had a wart on her left cheek and a grandmotherly smile.

When he had finished the meal, he leaned back and instinctively reached for his shirt pocket. It was a thing that he had not done in two years. Looking about the place at the wreaths of smoke, he halfway envied the truckers their impending bouts with lung cancer and emphysema; hell, there were times when health was a goddamn drag, and a 3:00 A.M. breakfast was one of them. He went outside, and the night air hit him again, and he knew that he could go for another five or six hours

In those last few feet that led him to the van he marvelled at the simplicities of the good life. A cigarette here, a piece of unexpected ass there, the rewatching of a Bogey movie with somebody that you cared for. And a cigarette. As soon as this shit was over, he was going to take up Pall Malls again, and the Surgeon General could go fuck himself. He opened his mouth, sucked in night air mightily, and exhaled. Hell yes, he was good for another three hundred miles.

Starla was gone.

He jerked open the van's door, looked down its stubby cavern, and saw only the suitcases. It was a moment that was part emptiness, part madness, part anger.

"Godfuckingdamn," he said, slamming the door. He had just started to run back toward the restaurant to do he knew not what when he saw the heads. They were just visible above the roof line of a white Cadillac Seville. There was something familiar about the black head. He homed in like the deadliest of missiles toward the target, and felt the old ecstasy of being on a search and kill mission. The black man moved to his left and, in a fraction of a second, Roger altered his course and moved in straight toward the car, for the black man had placed his back directly in front of the car's left front fender. Now all that stood between them was the car's hood.

Six inches short of the car's right front fender, Roger leapt upward and soared across the elegant hood and caught the man in the small of his back. He heard Starla gasp as they hit the pavement, and his nostrils picked up the intermingled scents of old dust and newly spilled gasoline. He rolled once, was on his feet and ready. The black man stayed down, his hand lifted toward the light in a gesture that was part beseechment, part warning.

"Perkins! What in hell are you doing here?" Roger said. He started to step forward but recalled his humiliation on the Dallas freeway. It would be better to let Perkins make the first move. His chest muscles strained and throbbed in anticipation.

But Perkins did not move. "I was talking with the lady, Roger. Just talking."

"Roger, why don't you let him talk?" she said.

Roger was gallingly aware that he had made an ass of himself.

"Do I get up deadly or friendly?" Perkins asked. The words came easily. They were the words of a man who did not really care whether he was to kill or to be killed, to maim or to receive maiming.

Roger had waded in and was not to be swayed. "I don't know, asshole, but why don't you just do whatever it is that you are capable of?" He leaned in on the balls of his feet and waited. He was hurting in the lower part of his back, and his breath was coming in spurts, gasps. Starla stared, as did the black man.

"All right," said Perkins. "I say we are even. Mind if I get up?"

It was then that Roger felt a strange sense of having been beaten. True, Perkins was on the pavement, was asking to be allowed to stand, but there was something in his manner that was almost mocking.

"Sure, get up," said Roger. He even approached and extended his hand. Perkins's own hand was somehow smaller than he had remembered it from the freeway yesterday. Backing away, watching Perkins dust his seat off, Roger asked, "Now, just what in hell are you doing in this neck of the woods?"

Perkins nodded to Starla. "Let the lady tell you."

"I'm not sure I'll get it right," she said.

"Give it a shot," said Roger.

"He's here to go to Memphis with us. He wants to visit a cousin."

Roger rolled his eyes upward. "Thank God. It occurred to me for a second there that he might be about to lie to us."

Perkins ignored the sarcasm and walked around the front of the car. When he was halfway to the restaurant, his pace slowed, and he turned to face them. Because the light was behind and to the right of him, Roger could not see Perkins's face, but there was real tension in his voice as the dark man said, "I would take it kindly if you would have food with me." The words trailed out across the damp and dark pavement and were sucked into another vortex of sound as a great truck lumbered across the area.

"Can you figure this bastard?" Roger whispered to Starla.

"I'll tell you all about it later," she said. "Frankly, I believe him."

"So what do we do?"

"Scared?" Starla asked

"Yes and no," said Roger, feeling the familiar bite of female taunt.

"I suppose there's an answer in there someplace," she said. "The only thing he said to me was that he was going to Memphis to visit his cousin. He made it appear incidental to our being here."

"And you wonder why I'm scared," Roger answered. "I got a black hit man doggin' me. Goddamnit, lady, this is no coincidence." He looked and saw that Perkins had gone to the door of the restaurant and was looking inside. "Well, let's plug him and see if he's ripe," he said to Starla at last. "One thing's for sure, he won't kill us inside the restaurant."

They went to the door, and Perkins stood smiling at them. "Happy to have you," he said.

"Oh that it were mutual," said Roger. "I hope you are ready to chat, fella, for I feel that we have a lot to talk about."

When they were inside, Roger led them to the booth, found that the waitress had cleaned it off. For the first time, he noticed that the table was red. It indicated to him that at last he was fully awake, that he had eaten not from hunger but from boredom.

Perkins had seated himself across from them.

"Let's start fresh," said Roger. "What in the fuck are you doing here?"

Perkins started to say something, but a waitress came and stared above and beyond them in that waitress-way. He and Starla ordered pancakes.

"If I talk, I do so without interruption," said Perkins. "Is that agreeable to those assembled?" He smiled at Roger.

"Fire all your cannons," said Roger.

"Very well. First, your safety is assured, at least as far as I am concerned. If I had intended to harm either of you I could have done it while I was outside alone with Starla. The reason I asked her to talk to me alone was that I knew damned well I'd never be able to reason with you together." He looked at Roger to let the words hang their hooks in. "What I was halfway into with Starla was the purpose of my being here. I really do have a cousin in Memphis. His name is Noble Johnson. I want to see him, and I don't want to see him, a thing that will be explained in good time. When you two were gone, Mister Grossman suddenly recalled my occasional letters from Memphis and decided that this would be a good time for me to take a trip. I don't know if I am here to protect you or to kill you, and that is the truth. His words were, 'This will bear watching.' But I got the feeling that I was supposed to simply be in Memphis, if you know what I mean. As a sort of backup if you needed me, muscle if he needed me."

"I hear you, which does not mean I understand or believe you," Roger interrupted.

"Oh, Roger," Starla interjected, "let him live. Like he's already said, he could have killed us hours ago if he'd wanted to."

"You're a fool if you don't take this matter seriously," said Perkins. "This German is good. Frankly, Mister Grossman is frightened, and when he is, I am. This Nazi bastard is not one of the more predictable opponents I have ever faced. He tends to come in from the blind side."

"So does every other sonofabitch in this caper," said Roger, "including our bald Mister Grossman."

Perkins nodded. "Which proves my point exactly. You are afraid of me, and I am afraid of damned near everything. If we go to Memphis in convoy, always keeping tabs on each other, then the beer joint backup is in effect."

"What is a beer joint backup?" Starla asked.

"A thing women don't usually get involved in having to learn," said Roger, giving Perkins a genuine wink. "When two buddies get assaulted in a beer joint, they get back to back to ward off unseen attacks. Perkins is saying that he wants to stand at our back, Starla. What do you think?''

"Well, giving credit where it's due, he's about the first person to offer any help in the whole matter. He . . .'' Her words were cut short as the waitress brought their food. One comment led to another, syrup was passed, coffee was dolloped with cream, and a sudden ravenous silence passed over the table. Perkins and Starla turned to their food, and the great trucks outside flowed across pavement seas soundlessly.

Roger was glad to watch them eat. It gave him a chance to think. He was gut haggard, bone weary, and plain aggravated. It would not do to remain that way, he remembered from his basic training lectures, because it was at just that moment that your enemy would chop the hell out of you.

Perkins shoved his plate away, dabbed his mouth delicately with his napkin, and said, "So do we go to Memphis alone or convoy?''

"It's beginning to look like I'm going to wind up as dead as her uncle and all the others anyway," said Roger. "And, besides, some of the shit you've been whipping out makes sense.'' The words tasted sour.

"Most," Starla corrected. She smiled at them both and shoved her plate away as if food no longer mattered now that the crisis had passed.

"One thing," said Roger, "and I'm sure there will be others—what about this cousin?''

Perkins tried to smile, but his lips died on his face. "What do you want to know?''

"For openers, what's his romance with Grossman?''

"No romance. No Grossman. No nothing. He's a means to an end. Mister Grossman sent me to see him as a rot gut excuse to get me in Memphis.''

Roger thought it over and found that it made sense. "So your love for your cousin is not adequate to even merit a free couple of days off? Frankly, there's something about this cousin that seems to scare you more than Grossman does.''

"For the first time, Roger, you have sounded like a reporter and not some damned red neck. Yes, I am not too crazy about my cousin."

"But you said that he often wrote to you," said Starla.

Perkins laughed the quiet, frustrated laugh of a man whose life is a series of miscalculations. "My dear cousin is a thief, my friends. More specifically, a robber. For two years he has wanted me to pull a heist with him. And damn my soul if I'm not a little interested."

"Why?" Starla asked, her voice tinged with shrillness. "Where is the logic?"

"There is no logic. It's more of a feeling, an emotional thing, like going back on dope or back into a bad marriage that'll always be bad. In Folsom at least a fourth of the people I knew couldn't wait to get back on the street to cop that first boost of horse."

Roger said, "I understand. Fire horse syndrome. You're feeling free for the first time in years and the old trade beckons. You got a Cadillac and no boss and a relative to impress."

"Maybe. Who can say? I read a ton of psychology books in stir and right now I can't remember a word from any of them. Maybe it's just that I crave a last hurrah." He smiled at the statement.

"This thing that landed you in Folsom didn't cure the urge, huh?" Roger asked.

"That was a necessary thing, or so it seemed at the time. I held up a liquor store and still don't know why I shot that guy in the guts; all these years later it puzzles me. He's still in a wheelchair, which is why I went the whole nine yards. If I'd killed him, I'd have been out in seven. Figure our courts if you can." Perkins looked out the window at a cattle truck. Dung and urine were strung down the lattice-work sides, and noses protruded here and there. He winced and turned away. "So he's in a wheelchair and here I am in an Arkansas truck stop. Strange." He considered the word and tried it again: "Strange."

Starla said, "When we get to Memphis, maybe you'd better stay with us."

"No thanks. Remember, I'm supposed to be on surveillance, not hobnobbing with those who are under scrutiny. If it ever comes up, you two have not seen me here in this restaurant. Besides, Noble knows I'm on the way and that can't be changed now. Mister Grossman has his phone number. Even when I'm free, I'm locked in. My plan is to get Noble's help in finding this Molly. If she crawls out from under a rock, I'll get the word on to you."

Roger's tone was sinister as he said, "Sounds almost like you're about to sell Grossman out to us."

Perkins looked at the refuse in his plate and absently ran a fork through a napkin. "Does that seem to come out of my words?" he asked.

"Uh huh. And my advice is, don't. This robbery thing won't prove your manhood, won't prove to Noble he's got a blood tie with a wheel. Shit, you watch TV. It's a different world! They've got computers and cameras and lasers and, besides, it's a strange city. Suppose he gets shot, and you have to do the driving. Have you thought of that?"

"Yeah. I've thought of all that." Perkins was becoming a bit defensive.

Roger said, "So we go to Memphis together. What we do when we get there is still conjectural. Right?"

"I'm gonna help find this thing. That's where Noble will come in handy. Whether or not I choose to . . . repay him is something else," said Perkins. He looked at Starla and saw sadness and confusion in her eyes.

When they had paid and gone from the restaurant, the fog had tapestried and its tentacles reached out for passing trucks. Roger's thoughts were troubled as the little convoy passed a sign that read *Memphis 134.* He looked in his mirror and saw that the Seville trailed near and yet far, like a pilot fish that has not yet determined its attack point. In spite of the minor degree of trust that had been established back at the restaurant, and for reasons that he could not quite put a conscious finger on, he slowed and let Perkins pass and take the lead. He did not want the Seville behind him.

Fifteen

"What do they call you, Honey?" the woman asked.

"Honey," Ableiter answered.

She giggled at this and touched her tongue to a hair that was standing up and away from the others. He still smelled of soap. There were so many who would not shower, for whatever reason, and it was good to find one who not only would, but demanded that they do it together. After twelve years in the business, she was aware that it was the older men who possessed the greatest sense of respect for themselves. Perhaps it had something to do with the dignity of old age. But it was not a thing to ponder just now, not with work to be done.

"I'll bet you're a mechanic," she whispered. "Am I right?"

"Yes. How did you know?"

"Your hands smell like gasoline. I noticed it earlier."

He smiled down at her in the wan light and recorded this for future use: clues come in all shapes and from all directions.

"Are you an Englishman?"

"No."

"A Scotchman? You sound like it."

He placed his palms on either side of her head and forced her face down to her work. Like all the rented women that he'd ever known, she thought that she had to ice the cake by being interesting. It was strange that they never learned that the best orgasm is the quiet orgasm.

Her tongue, though hot and wet, was ineffective, and he turned to watch a jet gleam by the window, its great winking tail standing in the night's wetness like a dorsal fin. The distant control tower winked back, and he was reminded of a flashlight signalling to other planes in another time. It was a night landing in Russia, a desperation landing, and three of the planes had been lost. He had helped to pull out several of the bodies, not from any sense of humanity, but because it had placed him close to the door. The cargo had been overcoats and galoshes, and he had gotten first grab. His hands had been sticky with blood from the arm stump of a crewman.

Now another plane came in, but the rain had begun to gauze the window. He looked down at her head, at its circling blonde roundness, and he relaxed because the pressure was off. She had fifty dollars for an hour, and he had forty-five minutes to go. There was plenty of time to think.

He struggled to recall whether the overcoat planes had come in late '42 or early '43 and decided at last that it had to have been in '42, for it was in January of '43 that he had worn it on his westward trek out of Russia, the sleeves heavy with mud.

Lifting his left hand, sniffing the gasoline, he looked at it as though confronting an old friend who had come to speak with him of that other time. His fingertips went into their little tremulous dance, and he allowed himself to return to Russia.

"Furchtbar," the Hauptman had said, holding his jaw, wincing as the cold air touched the tooth. That was what had started it. They were standing on a hill whose crest bore three trees. There was snow everywhere, except for the dark mound of earth that loomed alongside the trench. *"Untersturmfuhrer!"*

"Da!"

"What is it, honey?" the blonde asked.

He touched the back of her head, patted it, pushed her gently back to her work. Tasting her own spittle, smelling its mild smegmatic odor, she knew that she was in for a long session and resolved not to question him again.

"This tooth is killing me. Take over."

That was all. He watched the captain walk up the frozen hill to the tracked vehicle that stood on the other side and listened as it roared away. Ableiter turned to his new command and looked at the others, a few sergeants, several privates behind their machine guns, some seventy in all. They were all good men, these soldiers of *Einsatzgruppe B*, well trained and silent. They had done this before.

The strong ones, chosen to dig the trench, were shot first. That was the signal for the others to be brought over from the far side of the hill, from where the tracked vehicles had surrounded them. There were cloud puffs of winter breath as they came, four abreast, the old, male and female, the young and the infants, sexless in their winter garb. Two thousand, give or take a few. Some were naked and bleeding from cuts across the back. Troublemakers from the village, these would have to go first. He ordered them to come to the trench and line up. One young girl rubbed a foot against the back of her leg as if to warm it and, as she did so, a private laughed and shot her in the pubic hair, its black triangle making an easy target in the white world. She screamed and went over into the trench.

"Fool!" he had screamed at this idiot who had made a mockery of his command. It required three shots from his own pistol to end her screams, the last shot tearing away an eye and the bridge of her nose. Some of the men were snickering behind him and, when he turned, their smiles faded as if absorbed by the snow. It was time to assert command. He would show them.

That was how it had begun. He knew himself to be an excellent marksman with the pistol, but his hand had been cold. In order to emphasize his excellence, he loaded the pistol with a fresh clip and, from ten feet away, finished the others with his left hand. The other Jews were moaning and sobbing now, and the few who broke ranks and ran were shot by the sentries at the outer perimeters of the hillock.

He ordered a sergeant to pass among the soldiers and collect a *reichsmark* from each. When the money was collected, he made the sergeant wrap it in a blanket.

"I will kill seven hundred today, and I will miss not once," he said, "and I will do it with my left hand. If I miss even once, I will match what is on the blanket."

There were no smiles this time, but some of the troops rolled their eyes in smug derision.

That was at nine in the morning. By noon he had killed four hundred, and his left forearm was twitching from the pain. They ate their noon meal in rotation, but he had his sausage while standing in the same spot, empty hulls and clips creating a metallic mound about his muddy boots. Heads, chests, and faces exploded and went over backwards into the trench. Some cursed, some cried, but all formed a perfect line of ten when ordered to do so.

At three in the afternoon, he said: "I count seven hundred."

None argued. He had to be helped to one of the trucks by a private. His left arm hung limply. They brought the money and placed it in the floor of the truck. He massaged his arm and listened to the screams as the machine gunners finished the rest. The arm hurt for weeks afterward.

"You're not trying," the woman said. She raised her head and massaged her jaw hinges with her fingertips. "Are you sick?"

"No."

"Your hand has been jerking like crazy. Have I been hurting?"

"No."

She went into the bathroom, rinsed her mouth, and returned with a washcloth. The laving of his belly, penis and testicles took only seconds. She dropped the cloth on the carpet and again buried her face out of his sight. She was going lower this time, no doubt hoping that he was the sort who liked to be tongued there. When it did not move him, she lay her head on his thigh and breathed quietly in her frustration.

He was unaware that she had stopped. He was in Hanau, and it was 1930. A blue and black storm came over the meadow wearing its lightning like epaulets. The girl was frightened. Her name was either Hanna or Heidi, he could not remember which. He had caressed her hair and laughed at her fear. The only nearby edifice was an empty country school. They stood in its doorway and watched the world turn darker, and his hand strayed down her back and felt the warmth of her fear that emanated from her round and trembling hips. She shoved him away and cursed him. Enpurpled with embarrassment, he chose to lessen its sting by mocking her fear. He climbed the chinked bricks at the doorway, got onto the roof of the school, and catwalked on all fours to the chimney. It was a short chimney, and he stepped onto its top, his feet bracketing the dark, rectangular hole.

"What are you doing?" she screamed.

"*Ich bin* Ableiter," he had called down. I am a lightning rod.

In the fall the story had made its way to the rims of the town's gossip, and by winter to its core. He was brave, according to some; insane, according to others. "Sobriquet" is reflection in sound, he came to know, and he cultivated the incident, and the name.

In the echo of memory his father spoke, and it was two years later. "You will leave here in your shame. I have enrolled you in a school in Scotland. Perhaps you will gain your manhood there, among men. The maid who will bear your child has no such choice."

Ableiter had no answer: in those times, a father's word was law.

The school was on a rocky hill near a village called McBairn. The headmasters were Germanic in their sternness. He stayed for two years and then sneaked back into Germany. It was in that summer of 1934 that he learned that his father had died in the previous year. He felt no sense of loss.

"What are you thinking about?" the blonde cooed.

"The telescope that is memory," he said.

" What do you mean?" her fingers played trace games on his flaccid penis.

"Nothing. And everything." He touched the dull hardness in his belly.

"Don't you like me?"

"Yes."

"Is fifty too much?" A strange question for a whore to ask. "No."

"I'd give back half, if I could, only my man wouldn't like it."

"Why do you need a man like that?" he asked, only mildly curious.

"A woman just does."

He rubbed his stomach again. There was a mild inner twinge that stung as suddenly as shrapnel.

"Do you want me to leave?" she asked.

"No."

"What do you want me to do?"

"I want you to be silent."

She placed her head sideways on his thigh and began to nurse him again, hoping that her jaws would not crack before he had finished.

He looked at the fogged window, at yet another shadowy, silvery plane. The Americans bemoaned the incredible cost of fuel, but still they continued to fly like wasps, always abuzz. Somehow the bastards would win the energy war and they would look back on this time with pride. And, having won, they would flaunt the victory in that ironic, self-effacing manner that was forever their way. They had a way with luck, and it was unforeseen luck that always got them through. At Midway, at the Bulge, at Anzio when there was no way off the beach, they had characteristically turned inferior numbers to their own advantage. It was a disturbing thing to reckon with, this American way with fortune, and it could prove to be the unknown and lethal factor in his quest for the plaque. He tried to envision this Roger Wilder, and saw a tall man with blue eyes, definitely an *uebermensch*. A lucky man, perhaps.

"What are you thinking about?" she asked.

"Luck," he said.

"Yeah. Some got it and some ain't," she answered. "You want me to keep doing this?"

He looked at his watch. 3:23. His flight for Memphis was due to depart at 5:40. "No."

"Maybe next time," she said, resting her head on his thigh again.

"Yes," he said, "the next time."

"Do you get to Dallas often?"

"No."

"My name is Helen. I don't usually work the airport but, if we should happen to meet again, I'd be glad to try to . . . you know."

"Yes. I know."

"I meet a lot of people, but not very many as nice as you."

"Thank you."

She went into the bathroom and showered. He went to the window and looked out at the incessant blinks and reflections and slitherings of the great wet airport in the distance. Rain light had a different texture than dry light, he realized for the first time in his life. Strange, the things that he had come to notice of late. Shirttails, blowing leaves, soap bubbles. He wondered whether all who are told that their insides have begun to rot away begin to notice things.

He rubbed sweat from the pane so that he could see the airliners and dried his palm in his pubic hairs. Her spittle welcomed the dampness and absorbed it as hay absorbs dew.

Somewhere in the last few days he had seen one of those humorous signs of which the Americans were so fond: Nothing Ever Quite Works Out. That was America for you: in the face of success they always acknowledged the specter of failure, while in the throes of failure they forever had that enraging assurance of success. They thought like no other group on earth, fought like no other, killed with a smirking savagery, and then instantly fed and tended the injured enemy. He again thought of Roger Wilder, and wondered whether Wilder was a soldier. How exotic to know the name and not the face or features of one that was to be the ultimate enemy. Perhaps this Wilder was younger than himself, and thus stronger. If it was to be guns, then he would defeat and kill Wilder; if Wilder had no gun, then it would be physical force. Acknowledging the sounds of an inner voice, he already knew that he would be a soldier when the time came; it was a thing that he had to prove for the glory of the Old Order.

She came from the shower and was drying herself with a towel. An ugly and discolored V of stretch marks meandered from her navel to her pubic mound. She had combed her hair and reapplied her lipstick. All human females had a way of looking angelic immediately after the act of sex, no matter what eccentric practices had transacted. It was always so. Men, on the other hand, always had that drained appearance. Within twenty minutes she would be fully dressed and again in the airport lounge where he had met her, and she would resemble a minister's wife awaiting her husband's plane.

"Are you mad at me?" she asked.

"No."

"You was staring at me funny."

"I'm apologetic."

She laughed softly. "I never heard it said that way." She gathered her clothes, dressed, kissed his cheek and, was gone.

From down the hallway came the sound of a group of drunks. They were warbling a song that was a typically American thing, the tempo being of that stressful and fixed recurrence that so smacked of Africa. If only Americans knew just how lethally the rest of the world was affixed into their systems, like parasites in the belly of a great animal who knew not that it was diseased, condemned. And America had done it to itself with kindness and courts. The drunks were closer now, and he could hear that the song was something about a town called Lodi. He wondered where Lodi was. Probably it was one of those middle-class factory towns somewhere in the northeast. America did so pride itself on its northeast.

The song resurrected a furlough in April, 1944. A drunken private named Prench had been singing on the day they brought the Jewish girl back to the camp. All in the hut were enjoying the erotic song when it was announced that the tables had been placed together, that the ceremony was about to commence. The song was about a virgin who met a soldier, and there were double meanings that concerned the length of his bayonet. The

announcement came before the twelfth inch of the bayonet was accounted for.

They had assembled the entire camp for the occasion.
All the inmates were on their knees in the mud, and some
fell forward and died in place. He estimated that at least
eight thousand people were there for the ceremony. He
was slightly drunk, and the whole scene was something
of a blur. It was as he tried to focus his eyes that he saw
the tables.

In the center of this human quadrangle, in an area that
was mirrored by mud puddles, there were four small
tables, and they had been arranged in the form of a T.

He had stood with his hands placed against the back of
an *Untersturmfuhrer* until he could get his bearings. The
half pint of schnapps was hazing him and would not go
away. He had seen many things in the past few years,
but never had he seen tables arranged in the form of a T.
It was not the sort of thing that would have made sense
to him sober and, therefore, it could not begin to be logical while he was drunk. The thought of all this made him
laugh. Those clustered about him also laughed, but nervously and without joy. They knew something about the
joke of which he was unaware. It made him feel like a
youth at some sort of esoteric initiation rite.

"They are coming," someone had said.

He wavered a bit, raised his eyes tenuously against the
gray glare of a spring morning and saw the SS wardress
and two SS sergeants. The girl who walked in their midst
was so small that at first he saw her not at all. When the
wardress moved past and the girl was visible, he saw that
she was no more than fifteen years old, and she was
naked except for sacking that was tied about her feet.
There were blue marks about her buttocks and upper
thighs.

When they were at the tables, one of the SS men
picked the girl up and laid her hips at the base of the
center table. They pulled her arms outward and her legs
downward and belted her securely in place. The wardress
pulled the tables apart as far as possible, so that there
were now little four-inch spaces between them. The girl

looked skyward and did not blink her eyes for a long while.

That which happened next he had forever wished that he had seen plainly or not at all. For more than forty years he had wondered about it, and each time his wonderment left him feeling confused about what had happened. From somewhere one of the SS men produced a crowbar and swung four times, his arms and the instrument combining to make a series of metallic gray semicircles that were so swift as to appear interlocked within their slightly divergent arcs. Each of the four times the rounded neck of the crowbar found flesh and bone at the openings between the tables, and the girl's arms and legs were smashed with dull butcher block blasts of sound. The girl's eyes continued to look skyward. There was moaning from the assemblage, and someone shouted for silence. As quickly as she had been affixed to the table she was loosened by the wardress. The straps hung awkwardly. One of the legs thrashed sideways and hung off the base table, the foot pointing back toward the distant gate.

"Escape is punished by death," the wardress said. "Four left, and three are dead; soon, this one, too, will be dead. There is no escape from this camp."

A kapo ran forward with a small two-wheeled cart, and he and the men picked the girl up and threw her onto the cart. As the cart passed him he could see that she still stared skyward. The wheels made oozing sounds in the mud.

"This is illogical," Ableiter said to Prench.

"What is?" Prench had asked.

"The wardress spoke. She did not shout. They could not hear her."

"They heard," said Prench, smiling.

"But they could not," Ableiter protested. "What is the use of talking when it is shouting that is necessary?"

"Would you like to watch the gassing?" Prench asked.

"Why do you not answer my question?"

"Be silent," Prench had said.

He had not gone to watch the gassing. Instead, he had gone back to the barrack and had gotten quite drunk. The barrack was located above a dungeon that contained starvation cells. Certain prisoners were starved to death there, out of sight of the camp in order to set examples. He could not understand why setting of an example was done out of sight of those who were supposed to learn from the example. When Prench and the others came back from the gassing, he asked Prench about this.

"Be silent," Prench had said, grinning in his ingenuous way.

April, 1944. Time and Memory.

He went to his bed and lay on it for a long time, his hands touching first his penis and then his stomach. That which had once been so alive was now dead, and that which was newly living in him was death itself. Prick to cancer, Alpha to Omega. Be silent.

After he had showered and dressed, he looked about the room. He would not pass this way again. The bed seemed to nod to him. Perhaps Roger Wilder was in a room like this somewhere. A young man, Wilder would have a woman with him. The bed would be sagging under their thrusts, creaking, yielding. The woman would be staring upward.

He looked at his watch. Within one hour he would be in the drenched and cold sky on his way to Memphis. If there was a white prostitute there named Molly, he would find her. It would probably be there, also, that he would find Roger Wilder. It was to be hoped that Wilder was a soldier. It would be good to face a soldier once again.

Sixteen

It might have been the weather that did it. On that particular night there were a great many people who slept not well or not at all. Voris Mohler was one of them. He had awakened out of his bourbon stupor at eleven to the sound of heavy thunder, and he had clung to his mattress like a rat clings to a floating limb. In no particular order, there were three things that scared hell out of him: storms, snakes, and being broke. Just now there were no snakes in the room but, during the lightning flashes, he found himself watching the floor just in case.

Yielding to a nameless impulse born of his loneliness and fear, he quickly dialed the eleven digit number and waited as the phone rang four times. The lightning passed on, and the heavy rain started, and he could hear it hitting the mower that he had forgotten to cover. Another ninety bucks shot to hell.

"Yes?" Her voice was gravely with sleep.

"Edna? Moe."

"Hello, Moe."

"It's storming here."

"I see."

"I mean, it woke me up, and I forgot for a second where you were and all. So how's things with you?"

"So, so."

"That all you got to say?"

"No. But this is not the time to tell you about it."

He felt his scrotum tighten. There was a nuance there that smacked of disaster, upheaval, finality. His stomach churned and his temples burned.

"Give me a hint."

"There is no hint. I won't be back, Moe." She suddenly began to cry.

"Is that final?"

"I . . . yes"

The hot iron of despair scorched his back, cheeks, and shoulders.

"I'm sorry, Edna. I guess I knew all the time."

"I'm sorry too, Moe. We gave it hell trying though, didn't we?"

"Yes. Is there . . . anyone else?"

She had regained her composure enough to affect an exquisite female haughtiness in her tone. "No. But even if there is, I won't tell you about him."

He wondered what in the hell that meant. Women had a way of torturing with words that mere men could only admire. She had said nothing definite, but the inference was a mile wide. "Well, I hope you're . . . happy. Goodnight----" He started to say either bitch or Edna, but neither of the sparring words had time to crystallize in his dry mouth, for she had hung up. Elated that it was settled, he cried.

He spent the rest of the night in that mattress-madness that is partly wakefulness or wakefulness that is interspersed with sleep. At five in the morning he gave it up, rose, showered, ate a loaf of Wonder Bread, and arrived at the office at seven thirty, exhausted.

"That man is here again," said Mrs. Cable. She looked at her nails and went to her desk.

He mistakenly thought of Jarvis and remembered the check. It had bounced bigger than hell, and now the world, including Jarvis, would know what a goddam four-flusher he was. The itshay was about to hit the anfay. Half way to his cubbyhole, he was surprised and relieved to find Willard waiting. The Ranger did not look happy but, then, Rangers seldom did.

"I'll go quietly," Moe said. He sat down, took out his airplane, and twirled its propeller.

Willard watched with emotionless eyes and then said, "A P-38?"

"Nope. That was a twin-tail. This is a Thunderbolt, commonly called a Jug. Were you in the big one?"

Willard shook his head. "Korea. A crunchy. Actually, an MP."

"Figured." They stared at each other for a few seconds, and then Moe put the plane back into his desk. This smelled serious. "The last time I got that look it was from a husband who did not understand. Since I don't know your wife, what is it that you do not understand?"

"Tell me about Perry Jarvis, Moe."

Moe tried to grin but gave it up. A tangible chill had come into the office. "Like what?"

"Like a check dated just yesterday. Your check, signed by you."

"Okay, so I wrote him a check. Maybe I postdated it and mailed it to him."

"Not so hot. About fifteen hours ago you spoon-fed me a bunch of shit about an ice cream man you got to be buddies with. Remember?"

"Uh huh."

"I'm my own ice cream man, Moe. You held out on me yesterday, didn't you?"

Moe felt the story going down the tube. All this work and sweat and double dealing was going to be blown because of one goddamn check. In the back of his mind he wondered just how in hell Willard had found out about the check, but that seemed irrelevant just now. "A little. I had a scared man on my hands yesterday, Willard, a man who made me promise that nobody on God's earth would know of his presence. I talked to him less than an hour before I talked to you. He'll back it up. He's right down the street in the Cotton Hotel."

"I'm laying twenty to one he ain't," Willard said sternly.

"I'll prove it." Moe picked up his phone book and began to flip toward the yellow pages.

"Put the book down, Moe. Perry Jarvis was roasted to death in his office in Dallas at around midnight.

Moe heard the words flutter batlike over his head. He looked at the desk almost catatonically and wondered when he had put the phone book down; certainly his brain did not recall when his hands had moved in that direction. He studied his fingernails, vainly hoping that the proper words might be etched there; he suffered an insane desire to apologize to somebody for something.

"How'd it happen?" he managed to ask, his bread lumping in his belly.

"Gasoline explosion. Fire lab says it was a plastic jug, probably a milk jug or a cooking oil thing."

"Any ideas?" Moe asked, stalling.

"Yep. Same as yours. Don't take it personal, Moe, but there is an outside chance that if you had come clean with me yesterday he might be alive."

"So, he's dead because of me. No, I wouldn't dream of taking that personal."

Willard tilted his head sideways in cop stare. His eyes were spear points of accusation. "Well, the man is gone for whatever reason, so it's time we scraped the shit out of the way and looked at each other's boots. Deal?"

"You're on."

"Start talking."

Moe talked for ten minutes. When he had finished and was pausing to determine whether any loose ends were dangling, Willard interjected: "Jesus, you had the whole recipe yesterday."

"Yep. And I fed you two pickles hoping that it would hold you until the banquet. But do you see why I did it?"

"Yeah. And what you have told me will be in the strictest of confidence, especially the part about the paper being in hock."

"How're you gonna help keep the lid on without jeopardizing your job, for Christ's sake?" Moe asked.

"I'm the head knocker on this investigation. Remember?"

Moe smiled. "Yeah, I guess I overlooked that tiny point. So where do we go from here?"

"While you were talking I totted up a few basic facts. This damn Ableiter is fingerprintless and faceless. But he's not infallible—he left scratches on the door where he worked Jarvis's lock. Nobody's made any real stink out of that. Yet. They don't think I know you from Hogan's goat; as far as they know, this is our first meeting. Helluva coincidence, but a lucky one, that I called in this morning. They wanted to know why a check from one Voris Mohler was in the dead man's car. Now, instead of Mohler and Wilder, we can add another name to what is transpiring, that name being Willard."

"Sounds like a law firm," Moe smirked.

"A two-edged law firm. One side of it is withholding evidence, if you want to stretch the point. The other side is doing an investigation into the deaths of Bond, Gomez, and Rix."

"What about Tatum?"

Willard was a little exasperated by the question. "So far I got nine yards of paperwork about the others. You and I know about Tatum, and that is adequate. Let the Dallas city boys worry about that fruit guitar picker."

"Fair enough," said Moe. "Now that you have all this stuff, what are you going to do with it?"

"I was coming to that. Wilder and his lady friend are in Memphis looking for this Molly. We can assume that Ableiter scared that fact out of Jarvis before he died."

"How can you be sure of that?"

"A logical hunch. If you were about to be fried with gas, would you talk?" Moe thought it over and shuddered. "You got a point."

"You bet your ass I got a point. We could have the Memphis police pick up this Molly on a trumpup, but we'd blow the whole thing for you and drive the bastard to cover. We could do the same to Roger and the girl, then this Molly would get her own ass roasted. I could fly to Memphis, but it might be too late."

Moe was angry at his own confusion. "So what's the goddamn bottom line?"

Willard removed his hat and touched its brim. "The bottom line is waiting to be written, Moe. This Ableiter is as sharp as a two-headed rat. To put it in perspective, he holds the same cards over us that you held over me yesterday. He's faceless, nameless---"

"----and printless," Moe interrupted. "Yeah, it's beginning to come full circle. So what you are saying is let Roger and his girl get to Molly and, hopefully, get the plaque, or try like hell. And if they don't?"

"Then Ableiter will. And some old whore named Molly will be dead, and the plaque will disappear back into Naziland under the palms."

Moe wondered whether he should say it, and then went ahead. "You don't have a lot of compassion for the human race, do you?"

"Not a helluva lot, no. It's a bunch of pack dogs tearing each other's throats out for a gold bone, as far as I'm concerned. Every sonofabitch in this mess has a vested interest, me included. You want your Pulitzer, Roger wants his story, and these other jackoffs wanted the gold. Looking at it from those peepholes, you can almost make Ableiter the hero. At least to him it is a sort of holy object."

"Holy like shit! The gold from the teeth of fifty-thousand gassed Jews does not a holy object make."

Willard looked embarrassed. "Yeah, I guess I tripped on that one. But you know what I mean."

"Yep, but there is one thing that you have still tripped over, and I'm a little surprised that you've made no hay of it. I told Roger from day one that the goddamn thing is more than the gold or the diamonds. Even before I knew what it was, there has been one crazy fucking question that will not lie down and die. Why pornographers?"

"It's no big shit," said Willard. "You think the Smithsonian would want it? The National Gallery? Hell, its historical value is probably a million bucks, conservatively. Why go off on this pornographer tangent?" There was overt sarcasm in his words. He had no way of knowing that Moe and Jarvis had said basically the same things.

Willard placed his hat on the back of his head. He resembled an aging country singer listening to a playback of his latest effort. "I'm going to my motel room and make out a report. Tonight will be something else."

"Meaning what?" Moe asked.

"Meaning things are going to pop in Memphis one way or another. Somebody is gonna find something or find out something that will break this thing. Or give it a good bending." He closed his eyes and nodded, as though answering a private voice.

"I'd bet a five, as broke as I am, that you are right," said Moe. "But we sit here like a couple of demented jackasses and don't do a damned thing."

"You can't afford to, and I ain't allowed to," Willard said. "So we hang tough. We say a little prayer for Roger and hope that he gets the plaque and heads back here and all bodes well." After thinking these words over, Willard admitted, "I don't think all will end happily, but we can hope."

"And the dead will bury the dead," said Moe.

"Maybe there won't be any dead," said Willard, without much conviction.

Moe looked at his phone. "Call me Roger. Call, baby."

"What would you say if he did?"

"I'd double warn him about Ableiter. Jesus, he's off on what he thinks is a lark. He can't know about Jarvis, which means that he's wide open. Oh, Jesus."

They both looked at the phone, until Willard realized the foolishness of it and said, "If he calls, you know who to call next."

"None other than thyself," said Moe. "Where will you be?"

"You don't find me, I find you," said Willard.

"I like that," said Moe. "Gives it the Bogart touch."

"I'll call you about every two hours today. You are gonna get sick of the sound of my voice."

"I already am. I got a paper to run. Nothing personal, but we have talked up the better part of an hour. By the time I get this paper into some sort of readable shape, it will be the shank of the afternoon."

"Nothing personal," Willard echoed. He straightened his hat and shook Moe's hand on his way out of the office. Several pairs of eyes watched his departure and then quickly went back to the drudgery of free pressdom.

When Willard was out of the city room, Moe reviewed their dialogue. Something that the Ranger had said was still nagging, but the entry of Polly Pearl blew it all down, and he bent to his work as a City Editor. She left him a sheaf of notes and memos, none of which were of great import, but all of which needed his attention.

It was at about 11:15 when the thought came back to him. He was reading a story about a house fire in Arizona, a tragedy that had taken the lives of four construction workers. The proper noun Arizona kept popping up at him like one of those rubber balls attached to a paddle bat. Every time he saw the name something disquieting stirred in his mush brain.

"Jesus," he said aloud. "That's it!"

And it was. Willard had casually said that his pal in Arizona had traced Gomez to Flagstaff and then picked up his trail again after a two-or-three day layover. It had seemed insignificant at the time, especially to Willard, who was a state line chauvinist of the old school. Willard did not give a diddly shit about Gomez's itinerary, only about his body being found in Texas. Christ, maybe there was nothing at all here, but it was worth a throw. And Willard had said it not today but yesterday, hence its puckish nature.

"HENRY!"

Henry came running. He had a piece of toilet paper stuck over a newly picked pimple, and a drop of blood showed through and gave his ugly face a certain rakish character.

"What is it, Mister Mohler?"

"Go around and sit down, Henry." He grinned inwardly as the flunky tiptoed to the old chair and flopped backward. "How are things, Henry?"

"Very good up to now, Mister Mohler," he said uneasily.

"Man once jumped out of a ten story building. As he passed the fifth floor someone heard him say, 'So far so good.' Pretty fucking funny, don't you think?"

"Uh . . . yeah." Henry tried to smile.

"How long you been here, Henry?"

"Three, four months, I guess."

"Do you like me, Henry?"

"Uh . . . I guess so."

"Good sharp answer. Shows tact, character, wit, and diplomacy. I like you too, Henry. When you came here you didn't know an offset from a shoelace, and just look at you now. I've been watching you. Are you ready for your first outside assignment?"

"Jesus, Moe . . . I mean Mister Mohler. Do you mean it?"

"Yeah. Though you would be the man for the job. But it requires absolute secrecy. And I goddamn mean absolute. Got me?"

Henry nodded. His chest appeared to swell a bit as he leaned in toward the desk.

"You are to go to the city library. You are to get me everything you can check out on Northern Arizona. Especially Flagstaff."

"What about the Grand Canyon?"

Moe replied churlishly, "What the fuck has the Grand Canyon got to do with it?"

"It's just north of Flagstaff. I did a book report on it once."

"I thought it was at the other end of the state." Moe said, feeling a bit knuckleheaded. "Yeah, that too. But mostly Flagstaff. Now get on it. If you don't fuck it up I'll put you on a real honest-to-God story within a month."

Henry was alight with impending glory. "I'll do it or die, Mister Mohler."

"Henry?"

"Yes Sir?"

Moe winked. "From now on I'm Moe."

There were tears in Henry's eyes. "Sure . . . Moe"

Moe went to Gino's, fought the noon crowd, and ordered a cheeseburger. Edna crossed his mind, as did Willard, Roger, and Ableiter. Reasoner, Rather, Peter Jennings, and the whole goddamn New York crowd were in there, too. When he went forth to accept the Pulitzer, they would all shake his old sweaty paw and fawn like puppies. When he at last wolfed the sandwich, it was cold. He paid, looked across the place at the hoglike diners, and went back to the *Sentinel* feeling on top of the whole frigging Universe. There was not a doubt in his mind that Willard had been right—today was going to be the day. Moe knew it in his guts.

At just after two, the paper had been bedded and the staff had started on tomorrow's stuff. Recipes, grocery ad corrections, some idiot pictured holding a mammoth carrot, another idiot holding a dead rattler. Newspaper high, newspaper low. Moe had all but forgotten his Pulitzer fantasy when he sensed someone standing behind him.

"Here it is, Moe," said Henry. He was holding three books and a dozen magazines. "Everything you ever wanted to know about Flagstaff. Everything that I could carry and that was relevant, that is."

"Relevant. I like that. Put them there and leave." He pointed to his littered desk.

In the shutdown gloaming of late afternoon Moe began to pore over the books. It was mostly Chamber of Commerce crap that made Arizona sound like paradise found. Pictures of cacti, water skiers, skylines. Not much to be had there. He went to the magazines and found several articles on Flagstaff, none of which rang any bells. In spite of the lightness of the sandwich a private pain hit him, and he grabbed up a *National Geographic* and headed for the men's room. He dropped his pants, felt the porcelain coolness on his hips, and began to flip idly through the magazine, his ardor for Arizona waning quickly. It was amazing how the human mind could go from a Valhalla of expectancy to pigsty of despair and back again in a matter of hours. At just this moment the only worthwhile thing in the world was being allowed to take an undisturbed shit. Yes, Moe, he was saying to himself, as his free mind wandered and his occupied mind thumbed idly through the pages of *National Geographic*, you are packing your life in cotton wool like all those other old bastards. Geritol and Lawrence Welk and orthopedic goddamn socks lay just beyond the periphery of this moment, and the only good thing in the world was a simple shit.

He lost his place, cursed, and started back through the magazine. Something in his lower back told him that he would be here a while, so it was best to settle in and roll with life's punches. Pages thirty-two and thirty-three featured a mostly dun-colored map of the Canyon, with traces of black and blue here and there illustrating the Colorado River or incredibly deep ravines. Moe's old tired eyes took a poor man's vacation to the places that he would never see: Havasu Canyon, Rampart Cave, Granite Narrows, Powell Plateau. Viewed casually, the place looked like a twisted and possibly cancerous chicken gut.

Another place name drifted past his eyes and he was just about to close the magazine when his breath came in a rush. His temples, suddenly burned; his eyebrows twitched; he felt as though he had been slapped. The name had been right there on page thirty-two but, for some incredible reason, he had ignored it for the better part of two minutes. He looked up and away, fearful that it might have been an illusion. Slowly, fear and hope urging his hands, forcing them, he opened the page again. There, as if God himself had stepped forward and changed history and nomenclature just for this moment, was the name that he had thought that he had seen, a name given a minor peak in the Grand Canyon.

"By God!" he said, hearing his voice reverberating against the tile floor. He wanted to say the words, to read them aloud, but further sound from his blasphemous and dry throat might have broken the deified spell of the moment. It required a full minute for his dessicated larynx to loosen itself from the sweet shock of realization and, in that minute, several beautiful thoughts sprang forward like jubilant children emerging from hiding places. He was again ahead of Willard! The story was more alive now than ever! Roger was in exactly the wrong part of the country! Gomez was more of a jokester than he had imagined! Molly was not a person but a place! His shocked mind repeated this last fact several times; Molly is not a person but a place!

And now he coaxed himself to read it aloud, an unused but viable part of his mind giving shameless thanks to a

God who really did work in mysterious ways. "'Molly's Nipple, 5,551 feet!' Gomez the jokester! He did it to us all! 'Molly's Nipple, 5,551 feet!' Well I'll be a sonofabitch!''

Seventeen

Martin Luther King appeared to be crying. The billboard that bore his cocoa features in a poorly done painting stood beneath the eaves of a two story house. The place obviously had been empty for a long time and old guttering had broken loose and stood away from the eaves, its snout hovering over the billboard in aluminate lethargy. Most of the rain fell directly from the roof to the ground, but enough found its way into the pipe to spew a small stream onto the top of the billboard. From there, it coursed downward past the painted eyes and onto the ground.

Although Perkins was not usually given to acknowledging symbolic occurrences, this one seemed to semaphore for recognition. By turning ever so slightly to his left and looking across this ugly slice of Memphis, he could see that the slain leader had a good deal to weep about. The entire area was a depressing olio of bicycle frames, overturned garbage cans, and yawning autos, whose hoods pointed toward the gray firmament like the beaks of beseeching birds.

Now, turning farther to his left, he saw the place across the street, a large one story shack of gray boards and ripped screens. The roof had once been covered with shingling of hexagonal green, but the green was for the most part gone and, in its place, was black tar overtacked in spots with scrap aluminum.

"That it?" he asked.

"Gotta be. They described it perfect," Noble Johnson answered.

Perkins sighed and turned back to face his cousin. Noble and this place were both what he had imagined the South to be; dark, sad, dangerous. He had first detected his cousin's body odor at 5:00 A.M. It had been one of those doorway backslaps that are ever the manner of old friends meeting anew, and the stench of armpit had made him queasy. A superficial glance at Noble's place had revealed wine bottles, torn furniture, and a backed-up commode. There was a shower stall in the place, but it was apparent that Noble utilized it for little more than hanging up damp socks. He now wondered why he had imagined for some twenty years that his cousin was superior to what now squatted in the seat beside him. With snaggled yellow teeth, and scars at the chin from a youthful encounter with a razor, Noble Johnson was what the Aryan Brotherhood at Folsom would have instantly pegged as a bad nigger.

Noble started to speak, but Perkins held up an imperious palm and the only sound was of rain striking the windshield and the billboard. It was a bit of pompous fakery, but it had to be done. The truth was that Perkins was suffering a sudden seige of nausea. He turned to face the windshield and the dead street, as if to trim the edges from the tapestry of some great thought, and inhaled through his mouth heavily. As he touched the window button, the Seville's glass slid downward, and he was grateful for the rush of wet air.

"What're you lookin' for, man?" Noble asked.

"The man," Perkins answered. It was a stock answer that all blacks understood. In spite of himself, he felt a yearning for Dallas, for sunlight, for Grossman's mansion and, yes, even for his white coat, that dubious badge of his low station. That was his real world now. This was but a bad dream.

"She turns tricks for twenty, they say." Noble continued. "She was easy to find." He laughed at this, and his teeth were a yellow accent against the gray of the car's window. Grabbing Perkins's palm, he slapped it and said, "Hey, man, Jesus it's good that you're here."

Perkins tried to smile. "Yeah. It's been a lifetime, ain't it?"

They got out of the car, and Noble ran to the door, dodging mud puddles and bread wrappers. Perkins looked skyward and saw a slate dome of darkness and clouds that poured cooling droplets onto his face, and he knew beyond the realm of his consciousness that he was standing in the center of his heritage. He knew also that on this day he would affirm either good or evil as being the history that his presence on this earth would scribble into the book of free will. As expected, they had not been together for thirty minutes when Noble had suggested a robbery.

"Hey, man, you're gettin' wet!" Noble called.

Noble was already inside when Perkins entered the place. The odors of old carpet and cooking grease hung in the hallway. A single yellow light bulb dangled from a cord and outlined generations of handprints on the faded wallpaper. At the end of the hallway, a little mulatto boy of about five looked at them, one bare foot placed atop the other. He smiled.

"Come here, Oreo," said Noble.

The boy looked frightened and disappeared into one of the several doorways. Music came from somewhere, and Perkins recognized the song as "Cherish," an evergreen from the sixties by a group called The Association. He had heard it often at Folsom. The place was closing in on him. "Hey," he said, "let's do it and get it over with. And don't call any more kids Oreo. Got me?"

Noble looked at Perkins as he might scowl at a fine China cup whose handle has suddenly broken off. "Why . . . sure. I just wanted to ask about Molly."

"Your man said the second door on the right. Here it is. Knock on it. 'Egress is assured.'"

Noble touched his scarred chin and laughed as he knocked. "Man, it is good to be with a person who talks like that. "Egress is assured."

The door opened a few inches, and a white woman looked at them over the top of the taut chain latch. She was about fifty but looked older. Her disheveled blonde hair spoke of recent sleep and an unrecent dye job; a streak of black roots coursed from her forehead to her crown. Her skin bore an alabaster starkness that was heightened by the wrinkles at her mouth and around her eyes. She wore a blue housecoat whose upper reaches were coffee stained. The smells of coffee and human body emanated from the room.

"Are you Miss Molly?" Noble asked, suddenly affecting a hat-in-hand attitude.

"Yeah. Ain't it kinda early?" Her voice was a coarse whiskey croak.

"Yes. But this gentleman here wanted to see you. Can you let us in? We come as friends." Noble looked around at Perkins and winked as she closed the door and removed the chain latch.

Perkins was revolted by the clutter. A coffee table sagged under whiskey glasses, old magazines, bobby pins, and a filthy hairbrush. Ashtrays abounded in the room and the stench of cigarettes was oppressive. A towel here, a man's sock there. A tiny puppy trotted from behind a chair and disappeared into another room.

"Pardon the mess," she said mouthing a cigarette and looking them over.

"It's fine," said Perkins. He shoved a magazine aside and sat down on the couch.

"I'll wait in the car," said Noble.

"Fine. I'll be out in a minute."

The woman watched Noble go and then dumped one of the ashtrays into another. With a naked foot she rubbed dog piss from the chair leg and massaged the ball of her foot on a dirty throw rug. "You here about a date?"

"Actually, no. I'm here about Gomez."

Lighting a cigarette with a wooden match, she stared into the flame and watched it burn to within a centimeter of her finger. Exhaling smoke, she said, "Gomez who?"

"The Mister Gomez who gave you the package to keep. He sent me for it."

"He did? Now why would he do that?" She scratched the side of her head with a thumbnail and stared across the room through the smoke.

"All right, if it's verification you want, he told me to mention a Mister Grossman to you."

''Where you from, boy?''

Perkins felt his fists clench. Fighting for self-control, he looked about the room and smiled at the light fixture. A cobweb undulated there in serpentine twirls. ''My name is Perkins, *sil vous plait*. Where would I be from?''

''Maybe southwest of here?''

''Uh huh. Maybe Dallas. I believe that you are familiar with Dallas.''

''Yeah. And Grossman. How is the old bastard?''

''Mister Grossman is enjoying good health.''

''And good wealth, I bet. What is the most outstanding thing about his office?''

''You mean the pictures of naked girls, I take it?''

She smiled. ''Okay, I guess you are from Grossman, but I don't know any Garcia.''

''Gomez.''

''Gomez, schomez. I don't know the gent.'' She dragged on the cigarette and looked at him as if to melt his reserve, to reduce him to a niggerness that she could handle.

''It is very important. There are some people who will do you injury if they think that you have it. I hope that you believe me.''

''What about you? You gonna beat me? Is that how you get it off?''

''No ma'am. And I am not going to tie you and search your place. You would be too smart to have it here. I drove all night from Dallas, so I probably couldn't whip you anyway.'' They laughed together, relaxing the tension in the air.

''Maybe you are on the up and up after all. I'm sorry I called you boy. I was just lifting your fur a little.''

He nodded and smiled. ''I understand.''

''How'd you find me?''

Perkins told her of Noble's three phone calls. He did not tell her that a white woman who turned black tricks in Memphis was something of a novelty whose fame was assured.

''I gotta change my name. Molly. I guess I'm gettin' to be too well known by that.''

"I can honestly say that your name has been mentioned at length in Dallas in the past few days. There are those who think that you are a very rich woman."

She looked at the room, at the clutter. "Yeah. Me and Princess Di have tea together here every Thursday. Are you a religious man?" she asked suddenly.

"No, not really. I have prayed, but I don't know if it ever was heard." He looked away, wondering why he felt bested.

She quickly exhaled some smoke and laughed. "Yeah, me too. Well, let me tell you one, and listen carefully. I have a disease called lymphoma. I might make it, and I might not. The doc says it's no go. So I am telling you, on my death bed and before God, that I don't know this Gomez." She stared at the half-burned cigarette and then crushed it out. It was as though the act were somehow meant to prolong her life.

"I believe you," Perkins said quietly. He wished that there was more to be said.

"Thanks. And if you wonder why I talk of God and turn tricks at the same time, it's that I'd rather do anything than starve. I had enough of that growing up."

"Me too," said Perkins. "And I don't pass judgment on anyone."

"You ain't such a bad guy. May I ask what is supposed to be in this package?"

He shook his head. "If I told you, then you'd know. And, if you knew that, they could beat just enough out of you to think you knew more."

"Makes sense. My female curiosity is eating me up, though."

"That's human, not just female."

She looked at him for a long moment and then began to cry. Wiping her eyes with the back of her hand, she said at last, "Those movies. Are they still around?"

"Which movies?"

"Of me. Years ago."

"Probably not. Old film, old negatives you know. And there are so many new ones."

She nodded and looked at him with red eyes. "Thanks, even if it might not be true."

"It's true. And now I am going to suggest something."

"Which is?"

"Go away for a few days. I'm telling you that for your own good." He stood, walked across the room, and handed her two one hundred dollar bills.

She looked at the money and then up at him. "This is your own money, ain't it?"

"No," he lied. It was in fact part of the thousand dollars that Grossman had given him for expenses. "Do you promise to use it for that purpose?"

"Yeah. God knows I need a rest from this place. I can take a bus to my sister's in Saint----"

"I don't want to hear where," he said. "They might beat me, too." She smiled knowingly and followed him to the door. They looked at each other and the tacit message was there, a soundless moment during which there were no barriers of race, time, corruption, or sin. She pulled his face down and kissed him on the cheek.

"When you get to Dallas, give Grossman a message for me."

"Very well."

"Tell him I forgive him." She closed the door, and he heard the chain lock slide back into place.

He stood in the hallway for a time and looked toward the street, his view thwarted by the dirty door glass, except for a triangular place where it had been broken.

"Man, that was fast," Noble said. Perkins started the Seville's engine and drove out of the place and into the gray, slick thoroughfare that was Crump Boulevard. Off to his left, almost obscured by the low hanging scud clouds, stood the saurian skeleton of the Arkansas Bridge. It had looked good last night because it signaled the end of his journey; it looked twice as good now because it signaled the beginning of a new one, a journey that would take him home to Dallas.

"She give you what you wanted?" Noble asked. When Perkins nodded, the cousin said, "She must be some piece if you come from Texas to get it."

"That was not what it was about," Perkins said coldly.

When they had ridden for two miles and were nearing Noble's apartment, he said to Perkins, "I got it all staked out. Seven o'clock tonight we go. You want the scam?"

"No."

Noble looked over and faked a chuckle. "No? Man, that's just a few hours away. We gotta talk stash and split and getaway, just to mention a few minor items. I got a car treed that we can boost in a minute. A Buick."

Perkins drove the Seville into the driveway and stopped the motor. A group of wet black children were rolling an old tire through the mud at the side of the building, and their clothing was rain-plastered to their backs. Perkins remembered the feeling and shivered.

Noble's eyes clouded slightly in his discomfort and confusion, and he asked, "What's up? You got a plan? It's okay! You are the honcho, the old man. The master!"

Perkins regarded his cousin with the sort of gaze that he might have used while looking at a hyena caught in a barbed wire: compassion, tempered with loathing.

Noble becoming mildly angry, said "So?"

Perkins looked at the rain-dulled windshield and spoke softly, methodically: "Last night, when I got to your house, you called me 'blood,' an indication that our skin and our common relatives have established something insurmountable and irrevocably unbreakable. If you want to call me blood, that is up to you. As far as we know we have no living relatives, alcohol, syphilis, and poverty in its many garbs having taken them away. And now, you want to add a new dimension to our failure as a family, as a people. No, I won't go with you on a robbery or on anything else. You are a loser, not because you are black, but in spite of it. You are a fool who does not have to be a fool, and you are a failure because that is the path that you have chosen for yourself. It is for that reason, primarily, that I want you out of my life. You are not to write me again, nor are you to call me. Not ever! I am not blood, Noble, not any more. Goodbye, and good luck."

Noble stared at his cousin for a time and his dark hand toyed with the door handle. A thin roll of sweat beads appeared at his forehead and upper lip. His eyes sparkled redly. "You got it, man," he said, opening the door, disappearing into the rain. His odor left the car with him, like a dirty smoke wafting away from a dying fire. He had not even bothered to close the door.

Perkins backed the car away, tapped the brake, and let the door slam shut of its own weight. There was a cell-door finality to the sound that made him feel extremely hot, and he opened a window to allow the rain to touch his cheeks. He sang all the way down Crump Boulevard. The song was "Cherish." Now it was a good song, the song of a free man.

Eighteen

Roger saw the light against the wall and instantly recognized it as noon yellow. Although the curtains were
tightly drawn, a shard of sun had sliced through and was
creating a somewhat overstuffed banana superimposed
against the floral wallpaper. In his groggy state he wondered why no one in the history of the world had ever
made a study of the sun's different shadings against walls.
You just knew by looking what time it was, and to study
such a thing might help blind people, bedfast people; hell,
it might even help to beat the Commies. Without a doubt,
this was noongold. He tossed the word around in his
brain: noongold. It sounded like a brand of beer, or a
Jewish musician, perhaps. Arnie Noongold and his magic
violin. Jesus, Wilder, he thought with a queasy feeling,
you're headed for electroshock city.

Having been asleep on his left arm, a position that
caused heart problems, according to Henry, he was unable to feel whether he was wearing his watch; besides,
that would somehow take the fun out of it. Struggling to
his feet and feeling the arm hang as limply as a nun's tit,
he went to the window and stuck his face through the part
in the curtains. Blue-gray scud clouds moved here and
there like small fish attempting to keep up with a vaster
and more ominous school of clouds that moved to the
east. The entire city was shinily wet, and the flat, short
black roof that jutted from the building just below his
window held several glassy puddles. A damned good rain
had come and gone while he slept; he felt vaguely sad

and left out at having missed it. A city in sunlight was just a city, but a city in rain seemed to take on a cloak of character that revealed its true self. He had always loved rain and, groggily, in his hazy state he wondered why.

"Shit!" he said. That summed it up. He lifted his left hand with his right, felt the pin-pricks in his awakening arm, and looked at his watch. It was 12:45 in the afternoon. This meant that he had slept almost eight hours. It was the first decent sleep that he had allowed himself since the blowup with Darlene.

He showered, shaved, and got dressed in his last clean clothes. A gamy odor was beginning to blossom from the used shorts and socks in his suitcase, and he halfway considered taking an hour to find a laundromat. There was something about a disheveled suitcase that made the most hardened traveler an angry, defeated, malodorous wretch. He banged his fist into a pillow and lay back down on his bed, his thoughts idly going to Moe. Brother Mohler would chew his ass to tatters when he called. No doubt he was in the cubbyhole office playing with that goddamn airplane and steaming. Roger reached for the phone, thought better of it, and lay back again.

When the phone rang, he reached for it with his good arm. It could not possibly be anyone from whom he wanted to hear, those possibilities being Starla or Perkins, neither of whom was a mental giant. Once, just once, he mused, pulling the receiver to his ear languidly, I would like to tie up with people who were the ball carriers.

"Yeah?"

"Roger? Perkins here."

"Yeah, Perk, good to hear from you. How in hell did you find me?"

"This is my eleventh place to call. This town has more hotels than gas stations."

"We were lucky," said Roger. "It was my fault not telling you last night where we'd go. Hell, I didn't know myself. I was getting ready to try this Noble Johnson. That was the name wasn't it?"

"Yeah. Maybe it's a good thing you didn't try him. He and I are quits."

"From what you told us last night, I'm glad to hear it. Did he try you on the robbery thing?"

"Uh huh. But he was damned helpful to me and my purpose, which makes me something of an ingrate, I guess."

"You found Molly?" Roger asked excitedly.

"Yep. Guess what?"

"Oh shit, she's dead. Right?"

"Nope. Very much alive. But here's the clincher—she does not know a frigging thing about what we are looking for."

"Do you trust her?" Roger asked, feeling his rib cage cave in.

"Yeah, I do." From here, Perkins went into a detailed account of the rainsoaked visit and of Molly's imminent death. He concluded with, "I'm at a motel near the bridge. I'm going to try to get to Texarkana before I collapse."

Roger thought it over and found himself tortured by a feeling of new distrust for Perkins. Since last night he had come to think of the black man as not only trustworthy but as something of a friend. Hating himself for it in a manner that defied definition, he now caught himself regarding Perkins as a black man. Still, Perkins was all he had out there in the great city, and he had to handle the thing in a way that would not burn any bridges.

"When you get back to Dallas, what're you gonna tell Grossman? He will not be pleased, stating it mildly."

"I'm going to tell him just what I told you. And then I am going to get a date with a woman and try to be a man for the first time in too long." Perkins laughed, his embarrassment and his humanness renewing his credibility.

"I hope you get a doll. You don't think you'll lose your job, do you?"

"Let's hope not. He's old, and I'm about all he's got that's of a substantial nature. Nah, he may yell a little, but I've been yelled at by professionals. I'm in his will big. I'll go, and I'll stay."

"If you ever need a job, why not come to San Antonio?" Roger said, feeling a tiny inner pinprick of phoniness. Here he was, within an angel's sneeze of being unemployed himself, and he was big-timing it like an oil baron.

"Thanks, but Dallas is my town now. You need to ask me anything else?"

"No, I guess not. Luck, Perkins."

"I'll need it on these highways alone." There was a pause and then he said, "Roger?"

"Yeah?"

"I'm sorry about that set-to we had on the freeway. I don't like to hit anybody. Especially friends."

"No sweat, old pal. See you around."

"You too, Rog. So long."

Roger replaced the phone with a sigh of woe. An emptiness burned quietly in his collapsed rib cage. Too, there was still a feeling of foreboding about whether Perkins had just plain lied to him. He picked up the phone again and started to call Noble Johnson. The city directory lay within his grasp and he looked at it for a long moment and then replaced the receiver. Hell no, Perkins was not lying, you jackass, a voice from within said mockingly.

But if Molly did not have the plaque, then where was the goddamned thing? Gomez had said Molly had it. Period. The rest had been speculation on all their parts. She had been a long shot that had missed. Some old whore with the name Molly had waltzed geriatrically through the senile minds of Grossman and Gomez and here was Roger Wilder in a motel in Memphis. Lynch was going to have a field day screaming about this one. The dull buzz of failure hung over Roger's bed, like flies over dog shit.

So where was the plaque? The question would not go away.

A soft tapping came at his door and he forgot his misery and ran over. "Yeah?"

"It's Starla. Are you decent?"

He released the chain latch and let her in. "Actually, no, my dear. That blue haze you see in the air is the effluvia of a recent mental outburst. How long have you been up?"

"Since about ten. I was getting a little worried about you."

"Yeah, well, there's something else you can worry about. Perkins just called. What we came for is not in Memphis." He saw a bit of light go out of her eyes. "Me too, kid. Our trip was for nothing, and I guess it's back to Texas. That is, if you want to go." The words lacked substance; there was no reason for her to go back to Texas. They both knew that what might have been a major adventure was suddenly no more than ashes. "You can, I mean," he said.

"I think that Texas is a place that I can dispense with from now on," she said. "All that I had there, such as it was, is gone. I'm going to Boston."

"Oh? Why Boston?"

"Several reasons. I found, via a phone call this morning, that I am no longer employed." She moved across the room, sat in one of the naugahyde chairs, and let one of her hands touch the Gideon Bible. "Just like that. After eleven years. They never did really . . . like me." Rage alloyed with sarcasm was in her voice as she said, "It's funny how we delude ourselves, isn't it? I've been a nobody at a dead-end job for eleven years, and I always knew it. But I kept hoping that I might get promoted. Not that I worked for it; it was just a fantasy I had. And now I'm going to Boston because a girl that I was raised near is married and living there. It's almost as if I thought that she'd be glad to see me."

Roger wanted to hold her, comfort her, but logic warned against it.

"The world is made up of nobodies, kid. *People* magazine gets rich selling stories of somebodies to us nobodies. Any fool knows it couldn't work the other way around. Hell, at any given moment, there ain't a thousand famous people in the world, movie stars and politicos included. We empty dust pans and fix cars and sell blouses and write shit stories for shit newspapers. If you're on the pity binge, you came to the wrong boy; I got my own crosses to bear just now." He hoped that the words might bite into her guts and pull her together.

"You're right, of course," she said, unmoved. "It's just the impact of it hasn't hit me. I wanted to spill it to someone, and you are all I have."

A wave of shame washed over the room and he said, "Well, you're just seeing a side of me that I've tried to keep hidden. Hell, I gotta call my boss on the phone and tell him I rode hard and came up empty. A lot more than you know was riding on this one, kid. You and I shared some fear, some sandwiches, and a long, hard ride in a van. I guess I'm just getting cynical in my old age, but right now forgive me if I don't get emotional about anybody else's troubles. You dig?"

"I dig. I dig a scared man whom I would like to befriend in our last moments together. We've been at each other's nerve endings for three days and nights in one way or another. If you want to pour it out, I'll listen."

"What's to pour out?" Roger asked, settling himself on the bed and leaning back against the headboard. "I'm pushing forty, probably out of work, no woman, no kids, no prospects. I didn't plan my phenomenal success; I just lucked into it." He mulled over these words and began to laugh. It was a contagious moment, and they laughed together for the better part of two minutes, the ironies of their lives bouncing off each other.

When the moment had passed, she said, "Then it's not just me?"

"Not just you what?"

"That has kept you keyed up. During all our time together. I thought it was."

"Nope. Like all women, you took it personal. If half the housewives in the country knew what their men go through, the divorce rate would be cut by ninety percent. That is not original, but an observation made often by my old lovable boss. Life as you and I know it is a shredder of egos and golden dreams. I knew a kid in Nam . . ." He stopped and looked at her as if to apologize for going on so long.

"Tell me about him," she said.

"No, it's not important. It seems that lately all the references that I make either openly or to myself have to do with people I knew in Nam. I wonder why that is?"

"Maybe it was the time in your life that you felt like somebody."

He thought about this for a few seconds and replied, "Yeah, maybe in your unembellished words you've summed me up. God knows that I haven't felt like somebody in a long time. Maybe that's why I didn't come on to you; I guess it's time we discussed that. You are a nice woman, Starla, and I knew that from the minute I saw you in the hotel lobby. I also knew that you were something of a private person, the type who falls hard. Jesus, why am I telling you this? Anyway, I did not have the time or the inclination to get anything started. I know that I've basically been a hard-driving bastard for the last three days, but I do have a kind side. It's just that I don't get to show it so often in my line of work. I'm not ego-tripping, but I've gotta ask: did you ever have . . . feelings about us?"

She nodded, but her awkward smile removed the heaviness from her words. "Last night when we were in that little cafe talking to Perkins I had a fantasy about us. If you would know women, know their fantasies."

He chuckled at this and felt a pang of embarrassment. "I think that this is a thing that should not be pursued. You're a helluva gal, Starla, and I wish you luck."

"You too, Roger. Write sometime."

"No, you write. Gloria Steinem says it's okay now. Besides, I don't know where you're gonna be. If I'm lucky I'll be at the *Sentinel*."

"Fair enough," she said.

They looked at each other for a time, and dreams, ego, and pride hovered in the short distance between them. Roger knew that it could be done now, but he did not allow himself to do it. Her memories would be greater if he let the moment pass.

He picked up the phone, lifted his eyebrows toward her in mock apprehension, and dialed the string of numbers that would put him in touch with Moe. It crossed his mind that this would be one of the more memorable phone calls that he would ever make, and he was glad that he had done it impulsively. That would take a great deal of the sting out of it. Starla looked away, and he felt some of his uneasiness pass.

"*Sentinel*," said Polly Pearl.

"Polly, Roger here. I'm on LD, so give me Moe fast."

Moe picked up on the first ring. "Yeah, Willard, nothing new."

"This ain't Willard. Who's Willard?"

"That you Roger? Jesus, am I glad to hear from you. Willard's a Ranger who's dogging our tracks."

"It's over, Moe. The Memphis thing is a bummer." He braced himself.

"Not so fast, me boy. I took a shit about twenty minutes ago that was monumental in scope."

"Jesus, Moe, have you cracked up? I said that the woman named Molly is out to lunch. It's no show. Dig?" He glanced at Starla and saw that she was still looking away. It was a gentle attempt to spare some of his dignity in this dark moment.

"I've sent Mrs. Wainwright to the Western Union office with three bills just for you, baby. The folk in Memphis are probably getting the message rat now. Money, Rog. You are broke, ain't you?"

"No, but I'm damn badly bent. I paid for this room in advance, so as not to wash any dishes. I may have about two bills left. Thanks for the dough, Moe."

"Think nothing of it. Lynch yells, fuck him."

Roger's mind was reeling. Great rocks were falling from his chest, and he could breathe again. Still, he could not begin to decipher what Moe was raving about. "How about starting from the front, Moe?"

"Molly is not a goddamn person, Roger. It's a place!"

"Well I'll be a sonofabitch," Roger said blankly. He looked at Starla and smiled in oafish confusion.

"I couldn't figure why Gomez would take extra days to get from Tijuana to San Antonio. It ran me nutsy. It wasn't a conscious thing, just something that was there. Hell, we stumbled all over it, fools that we were."

"Speak for yourself, Moe. You were on the Gomez end; I was on the Molly end."

"Veddy well, Rog. And you did a damned good job of it, too."

"Save your flag waving for later. Now tell me this shit before I go nuts."

"Okay, hang tight to my words. Gomez flew to Flagstaff and disafuckingppeared, two, three days. I sent Henry, bless his retarded soul, down to get some books and magazines at the library. Flagstaff became very interesting to me. But it was not Flagstaff, Rog, not on your tintype. It was the Grand Canyon. That was where Gomez went. The sonofawhore was a practical joker to the end."

"I'll be damned. So he hid the plaque at the Grand Canyon!" He saw Starla lean off her chair now, and her eyes were agleam with shared joy.

"You got it. I was looking at a map of the canyon while taking a crap and guess what?"

"I give."

"There is a peak there called Molly's Nipple. And there, me boy, is where you will find the Himmler Plaque, or my name is not Voris Arnold Mohler."

Roger felt his ear burning, and he shifted the receiver to the other side of his head. Sweat was forming on his forehead, and his heart was pounding.

"I love you, Moe, you ugly bastard."

"Me too you, Rog. So we got our story still, and Lynch has a paper, and that means we still get to buy groceries and stale coffee at Gino's."

"Yeah, but this Willard scares me. You say he's on our trail hot and heavy?"

"Yeah, but for reasons I will not go into just now, he has reasons for not dogging us too hard. How do you feel?"

"Nine feet tall and rich. But my better judgment is beginning to come into play and I've got a few questions. First is the biggie that has tortured us all the way: Why pornographers?"

"Don't know, Rog. But that makes it even spicier, don't you think? It's something else to chew on."

"My jaw hinges have about numbed out from all this chewing. Next, and this is minor, what about this bastard who's killing folks off right and left?"

There was a slight pause from the other end, and then Moe said, "I wish you hadn't brought that one up. It takes a little of the sparkle out of the day. I have reason to believe that he may be hot on your trail." Here Moe took three minutes to tell of Jarvis, of the fire. "So, you see, Willard and I think that Jarvis might have talked. If so, then this Ableiter knows who you are and where you are."

Roger felt a cat's claw of fear ripping through his back and legs. "Maybe not. If this happened last night it would take damned near a super sleuth to get to Memphis and tie things together."

There was exasperation in Moe's voice as he stressed, "Roger, the bastard is good. He got Rix, Tatum, and Jarvis with nary a break in his stride. Willard would bet his mother's tombstone that Jarvis told Ableiter about you and Starla, where you were going, Molly, the whole shooting match. Is any of this shit getting through to you?"

"Yeah, more all the time. Let me get this straight; I ease out of this room, get the Western Union money, fly to Arizona, get a car in Flagstaff, fly to Molly's Nipple." He winked toward Starla's sheepish reaction to this strange name. "Am I close?"

"No, you are perfect, not at all the re-tard that you can be at times, Roggo. If I had two more like you, I could make the *Washington Post* look like The Basket Weaver's Quarterly. Now, back to our invisible friend, Ableiter; he would be well advised to wait for you to get the plaque from Molly, and then get it from you. The fact that you don't have it might buy some time. Notice, I said might."

"Let us remain calm, Moe, even in this, our hour of peril. We've got it by the gonads, so to speak. The buck stopped when you did your *Geographic* bit in the crapper. God, I'm hot as a fox! Can you ever forgive me for doubting you on old Rix's front porch?"

"I'll work on it. Now get out of that goddamn room, Roger! Every minute counts!" Roger regarded the command fuzzily and could gather no sense from it. "Why the incredible hurry, Moe?"

"Because, if I know you, you registered under your own name."

"Jesus, I hadn't thought of that," said Roger. If Perkins could locate him, why not Ableiter? So simple, so deadly. "A minor oversight, Moe," he said a little defensively.

"No such animal in this game, Rog. If the right one don't get you, then the left one will. This lion bites hard and for keeps. He roasted Jarvis for some information. Imagine what he'd do to you for that which he seeks."

"Uh huh. And just telling him where it is wouldn't save my ass, either." He recalled the smell of burned flesh in the hooches in the Mekong Delta. He trembled visibly.

"Okay, enough said. I'm flying Henry to Memphis to drive the van back. He ought to meet you at the airport but, knowing Henry, he couldn't find a sea lion in a swimming pool. Just leave the van unlocked at the airport, and the keys under the floor mat."

"It ain't got a floor mat. It's barely got a floor."

"Yeah, well you know what I mean, in case Hen misses you or what not. We're coming into the home stretch, Rog, and we are leading by a mile. Let us not get panicky and do dumb things."

"This is the king you are talkin' to Moe. Remember?"

"The king registered under his own name. That is what I remember right now. Now tell the lady goodbye and get the frig out of that room. I mean now."

Roger ran his fingers through his hair. "See you within four days, Moe. With the plaque."

"Okay, hot shit, you are committed. Now get off the line."

"See you Moe."

He replaced the phone and positively beamed at Starla. Her lips were straight and firmly pulled against her teeth in a smile that was no smile at all but the grimace of a woman who is about to cry and knows that she must not. To bridge this pit of emotion, she employed the eternally pathetic planking that is all that humans have in such moments, that planking being words.

"I'm happy that you were able to . . . accomplish your mission."

Roger laughed heartily. "I like that. 'Accomplish your mission.' Baby girl, friend of mine, it ain't accomplished yet, but the sweet smell of success is beginning to blow out of the distant desert." He leapt off the bed, grabbed her up, and swung her around and around until both were dizzy and her shoes had flown to the carpet. Still laughing, he dropped her onto her chair like a rag doll and collapsed on the bed, wheezing. He looked at her and saw that there were tears in her eyes. She had picked up her shoes and was rubbing imaginary dust from the toes, her eyes fixed on the shoes but not seeing them. He wanted to go to her and hold her, but again realized that he must not. Roger conceded to himself that, after three days, he not only did not know her, but did not want to know her. She had been a passenger in the van. A hitchhiker. End it—let it go.

"Well, it's been quite a trip," he said.

"Yes." She dropped the shoes to the floor and worked her feet into them quickly. "I'll need to check out myself. According to the sign on the door, we're already an hour over." It was the nervous patter that parting people always use when there is so much more to be said.

"Uh, yeah. I got some stuff in the bathroom," said Roger. He went into the bathroom and collected his toilet articles. He was dropping a little plastic bottle of shaving lotion into the case and wondering whether he should kiss her on the cheek or shake her hand when he heard the door open and close. When he came out she was gone. He wanted to smile, but did not; somehow it would have seemed like betrayal.

It required less than two minutes for him to make a tourist's sortie around the room to look for truant articles, to close his suitcase, and to leave. The hallway was eerily quiet; it appeared to nap before the arrival of the next spate of travelers. Roger experienced a feeling reminiscent of being caught in an art gallery after closing; the numbered doorways were portraits of despair. Not only did he not know which room was hers, but to say anything more would only prolong her dismal mood. He went to the elevator and pushed the down button, unaware that he was being watched from a distant stairwell. He went into the elevator and dropped his suitcase beside his foot. The sliding metal door shut away some of his melancholy and, as the cubicle descended, his spirits rose.

Unlike Roger, Ableiter knew the exact whereabouts of Starla's room. Too, his vantage point had allowed him to observe his prey without being observed. After all, the tall and rather handsome young man who had just caught the elevator had to be Wilder, did he not?

Feeling his heart race, feeling the old involuntary twitching in his left hand, Ableiter heard the music of old glories, saw its windwhipped banners. Here lay a new glory, a greater glory, for Wilder was *untermensch* as the Poles and Russians had been, but an American. Also, he was a soldier, an officer—his ramrod stance and disciplined bearing while awaiting the elevator had proven that. Audacity—that was what Wilder has exuded, an aura of daring, of temerity, of impending violence. Wilder's chin, mouth, and eyes were those finely chiseled features from one of the SS mountain divisions, faces that appeared to be forever looking upward as if to capture a bit of the sun. It would be good to meet this Wilder in combat.

He waited, his ankles itching from his long stand on the concrete.

The woman named Starla had not stirred from her room. If it was a trap, they were taking their time. If it was not a trap, she would be no problem. The Portillo woman in Mexico had reached over her shoulder as if to claw him, but she had been an Indian. Unpredictable womankind. Bonita Gomez, on the other hand, had resisted not at all, and that was why she had remained alive. (But was it really? *Nein*! As he had beaten her, a voice from the Old Order had come to him, via a channel long undredged, a bit of guttural sarcasm cocooned in contempt that said 'go and tell the others that we have passed this way.' It was a thing that certain *Einsatzgruppe* commanders often ordered a chosen survivor of a mass shooting, a taunt in its purest sense, an offer of war. Yes, that was why Bonita Gomez remained alive—to tell them who had passed this way, to tell them who was loose on the land.)

It was time. Wilder had not sprung his trap; therefore there was no trap. Wilder obviously had gone into the city to find the woman named Molly. But why had he taken his suitcase? A minor point, so minor as to eschew reckoning.

Lifting one foot and then the other, he rubbed his ankles into wakefulness and limped slightly as he went down the hallway. He knocked twice.

"Yes?" the woman called.

"Manager," he said, trying to sound American. A snail of perspiration zigzagged down his cheek and stopped at his chin. Wiping it away, he pressed his eye to the door's peephole and smiled benevolently. He heard the sound of the chain latch being removed. His left hand, the hand that had splayed brain, lung, and blood over the steppes, was very still.

"I was going to check out earlier but . . ."

Even as she spoke he lifted his left forearm and waltzed her into the room, his right hand closing the door behind him. Her eyes, red and puffed from weeping, now took on that timeless fawnlike vulnerability that is the look of women frozen in fear. The waltz continued up to the bed as they stared at each other like lovers transfixed in an ethereal moment that had not been before and whose intensity could never come again.

"If you scream it will put us both at a great disadvantage," he said, hovering, crossing her wrists with one hand, grasping toward his coat pocket with the other. She looked from side to side as if to determine whether someone might be watching; it was an action not of fear but of embarrassment. Hearing the Scots burr in his voice, seeing at last the fan-shaped scar, she held her wrists high in surrender and watched with emotionless doll's eyes as he wound the dental floss around, threaded it through, and tied it off. From the time she had opened the door, less than one minute had passed.

"The greatest detriment to a successful inquisition is a lack of understanding between the parties. Do you agree?" he asked.

She nodded.

"Where is Wilder?"

She shook her head. Her throat was closed. Dry. Dessicate.

With the lazy perturbation of a mechanic slapping a fly away from a stalled machine he swung downward with his left hand and hit her a glancing blow that caught a bit of cheek and the bridge of her nose, the impact knocking her onto the bed.

"When will he be back?"

"He won't," she whispered, a rasp in her voice. She was not certain that he had heard, for even as she answered he had begun to cross and tie her ankles with the fine thread ffom the little white box. In her early childhood she had watched an ancient and wrinkled seamstress whose hands moved with a deftness that blurred the old fingers into a ballet of flesh tone. So quickly did he do his tying that the image returned. Now, he shoved the box into his pocket, sat on the bed beside her, and rubbed the blanket as if washing his hands. She noticed that his left hand trembled in what she took to be age palsy. He looked at the floor, about the room, back at the floor. A smile flickered on his face and then abruptly died. Something, a memory, perhaps, had taken her from his thoughts for a few seconds. He rubbed his middle and lower belly, inhaled deeply, exhaled. A spindrift of sweat glowed at his left temple. He was exhibiting all the signs of someone in great pain.

"As one of your presidents was wont to say, let us reason together," he said to the carpet. He turned to face her and ran a finger gently along the red puffiness of her injured cheek. "Tell me about Roger Wilder."

"He's . . . a friend," she said.

Ableiter nodded. "And where is she?"

Starla's eyes were gaunt, puzzled. "Where is who?"

He went to the door, placed the chain latch roller in its little slot, moved it to the right. Had Rix done that in San Antonio he might be alive now, he was thinking. Little things and little things and little things. He looked at his watch and gave the thing ten minutes—plenty of time. If the staff and management of the Holiday Inns of America would allow him a mere ten minutes, then he might make his return to Paraguay in a matter of hours. At most, it would be a matter of two days. No, he corrected himself, the package would be in Paraguay in two days. Having felt the Great Spear in his stomach while tying her, it had occurred to him that he would not go back there to die. It was the package they wanted, not himself. He felt lonely, isolated, angry.

On returning to the bed he stood over his quarry and studied her for The Sign. At Kastle Hartheim, a school for SS inquisitors, it had been stated almost as one of the Holy Commandments that frightened human beings would sooner or later betray themselves by The Sign. A twitch of the eyelids. A sudden lick of the lips. An overwhelming interest in some uninteresting object. Seek a moment of vulnerability. As yet this lady had not exhibited The Sign and it intrigued him. As Bond's niece she had to be in large measure Jewish, in which case the thing would take less than ten minutes, probably less than four. There had been a story of an old Rabbi at Chelmno who had seven fingers broken with pliers, three sawed off, and his beard burned off. He had not talked. The sergeant who told the story had thought the old man senile, incoherent. A sane Jew will talk, the sergeant had said.

Ableiter looked at his watch and saw that two of his ten minutes had passed. Reaching into his other pocket he removed the roll of adhesive tape and tore off a four inch strip. She offered no resistance as he covered her mouth.

"It never changes," he said quietly, like a professor of mathematics expounding on certainties. "We pretend that we are creatures of great ability to withstand pain. Pretense and pomp. Those are the two words that most readily define the moldy fabric of human cloth. We are all afraid of something." He smiled down at her to determine whether she had absorbed the gravity of his statement. She looked sideways toward a pillow.

"Very well," he said. He pulled her skirt up and saw her eyes widen. For the first time since being bound, her hands lurched upward as if to thwart his exploration. Blocking her with his left forearm, his right hand pulled at the elastic of her panties. The hand went down, around and behind her. Lifting her off the bed, rolling and pushing downward as he did so against the filmy fabric, it required no more than three seconds to slip her panties over her thighs and down to her ankles. He studied the black triangle, ran his fingertips over the satiny growth of fine curls, placed a thumb at the top of the labial joining. He thought of the Dallas whore, of her ineffectual mouth and wondered why his penis now stirred, stiffened, tented the front of his loose trousers. There was, in the end, no explaining, even to oneself, the conduits that led from the human mind to the sex organs. Grasping a small tuft of curls between thumb and forefinger, he jerked suddenly. She groaned and tried to claw his rigid forearm as she rose, but he merely worked it free of her grasp and back-handed her across the forehead. Tears welled in her eyes. It was the coming of The Sign. He looked at his watch and saw that he was now four minutes into it.

He pulled the tape from the side of her mouth and said, "If you scream I will tape your nose also. Do you understand?"

She nodded, inhaling noisily through the freed portion of her mouth. Once again she attempted to shove her skirt downward, but he seized the bound wrists and held them with the contemptuous ease of a boy holding a captured rabbit.

"Now listen to me," he said. "I am not here to harm you. It is true. It is also true that I would butcher an infant if it hastened my mission. The choice is yours. Now where is it?"

"I don't have it," she said, her mouth forming the words crookedly past the tape.

"Very good. You do not have it. Does Roger have it?"

"No. It isn't here. That's why he packed and left."

Firebrands of realization slapped his cheeks and forehead. His gut feeling was that she had just told a truth that he did not want to hear. But truth it had to be. While in the stairwell the thing about Wilder's suitcase had seemed to be an elaborate bit of stage setting for the trap. Since there was not a trap, the suitcase was . . . legitimate.

"Very well," he said, "then where is it?"

She leaned to her right, worked her tongue against the interior of her jaw, aimed, and spat in his face. The stringy, white cloud of sputum hit his left eyebrow and dripped onto his nose. Rolling her head back and forth on the bed she tried to scream but he was too fast and within a second the tape had been reattached to her flesh, covering her mouth. But, during that second, he was off balance and, with fingernails curved talonlike, she dug into the top of his taping hand and sliced away three inches of flesh, leaving narrow, elongated, shallow trenches that instantly burned like the fires of a miniature hell. Cursing at both her defiance and the pain, he massaged the injured hand for a moment and then tore her blouse away. It was the cheap and overwashed fabric of poverty and tore easily. He wrapped the injured hand and leaned into the cooling effect of the cloth. Blood stains welled through the fabric and she stared at him in triumph, her labored breathing causing her nostrils to flare.

"Good Jew," he said. "Fine Jew." His left forearm came down and pressed her wrists against her belly while his right hand unsnapped the hook at the front of her brassiere. As her breasts lolled freely she stared down at her nipples and began to cry again. Mucous began to form in her nostrils, and she instinctively closed her eyes and inhaled massively. It was at this instant that he reached into his shirt pocket, pulled out a book of matches. Holding the matchbook in his injured hand, he extracted one, struck it, and pressed it on her left nipple. A muffled scream rumbled through her chest. The odor of seared flesh cast its fetor over the bed. Her body now twitched with the heavy thrusts and throes of electric shock. He rolled off the bed, stood over her, and saw that a dark gray stain had formed beneath her hips. She had urinated.

He dropped the matches into his pocket and smiled. "When I remove the tape this time you will answer. Otherwise I will burn the other one."

He leaned and pulled the tape away.

"Water. Please." She stared at the ugly cerise-gray that was the burned nipple.

Ableiter went to the bathroom and hurried back with a glass of water. He poured a steady stream onto the burn and neither smiled nor frowned. The blouse was now more hindrance than comfort, and he removed it from his injured hand and laid it over the breast, pouring the remainder of the water onto the cloth.

"Momentary relief. Now, where is Wilder?"

She looked at his shirt, saw the outline of the matchbook through the exposed part of his pocket, and shuddered. "Arizona. That's all I know. God, please . . ."

Wrinkles appeared in his forehead. "Arizona? What about Arizona?" he asked, knowing beyond reason, or perhaps ahead of it, that she was telling the truth at last, knowing also that it was a truth that somehow mocked and belittled all that he had imagined, planned, venerated in fantasy. He stared at her and felt a dull, ominous sensation, not unlike that of standing alone in a great fenceless pasture.

"I heard them talking on the phone. Molly is not a person but a place. Molly is a mountain in the Grand Canyon. Gomez hid the thing there. Roger has left for Arizona." She tried to raise herself from the bed but fell back and, with her restrained wrists, moved the cloth over the burn, grimacing as she rubbed herself, pain and relief counter-balanced.

"Molly is . . . a mountain?" he asked rhetorically. He toyed with the word, rolled it over his tongue in the playful way of one who has just discovered that he has the power of speech. "A mountain."

Starla nodded. Her shame and her pain were as one. She closed her eyes; her face was expressionless. "More water," she said at last, the pain overwhelming what was left of her pride. "Please."

He moved like an automaton drawn by sound beams, the sound from his own lips being that which drew him, a self-perpetuating thing of movement whose code words were "*Bergig* Molly." He looked at himself for a time in the bathroom mirror, first smiling, then frowning, smiling again. He could have expected such foolishness from an American, but from a Mexican . . . never. The girl in Tijuana had screamed, while being beaten, that her father was a lovable man, a maker of jokes, a giver of candy to children. Maker of jokes, she had said, jokester, some such word or phrase that was buried among a million other words of the last week. But now it was a Laz-

arus word, rising from the tomb of memory to change the
whole threnodic pedal point of this quest. Gomez was a
jokester. He wondered how Wilder had taken the realization of having been fooled; Americans had a way with
foolishness that made it not only acceptable but desirable.
Americans—a strange race, full of surprises.

While removing the plastic cover from another glass,
he saw the bathtub reflected in the mirror. Fire would not
do here, even if he had the gasoline. Besides, he had all
the information that he wanted from this woman named
Starla, whereas the taunting of Jarvis had been pure
magic, an exercise in psychological will worthy of an Iron
Cross. He pressed down the tiny chromium lever and
watched the stopper drop into its round slot soundlessly.
After turning on the water full force, he rinsed his hands
and winced as the sting found the scratches and washed
away the drying blood. He stared at the running water for
a moment. So, Molly was a mountain.

He returned to the bed, found her staring yet with those
stupid, acquiescent eyes of a woman whose fate is in the
hands of another. After pouring the water onto the
drenched cloth that lay over her nipple, he tossed the glass
to the carpet, pressed the tape down tightly, and rolled
her over onto her side.

The zipper of his trousers made a sound like tearing
silk, and he moved close to her hips. He shoved once,
twice, adjusted her hips and shoved a third time. Either
in instinctive assistance or in an effort to minimize the
pain, her upper leg lifted almost imperceptibly and he slid
into the moist warmth to full penetration and lay very still
lest the explosion occur too soon. She had made no
sound. He retreated, thrust, retreated, thrust, felt the
hardening tingle in his testicles, grabbed her hips and
buried himself in her as deeply as was possible. The
throbbing went on for ten seconds and, at last, he heard
his own gasps. It was one of the more intense orgasms
that he had ever known. At sixty-four, beset by cancer,
he was yet quite a man. He felt it wither, heard it slip
out of her with that sound that was like an infant's suck.

Hearing his own breathing walk down passion's flight
to normalcy, he allowed himself a few moments to think

of infant suck sounds and running water. He stared at the back of her neck, at the incredibly tiny sweat droplets there, and was awed by water in its many forms.

His uncircumcised penis reasserted its foreskin over the glans, and a clear pool of effluvia formed a perfectly round little skater's pond of semen there, while down the wrinkling sides the juices of lust were drying whitely. Yesterday, in Dallas, he had been impotent, while today he had performed with the ruttings of a pubescent youth. Why? That, too, was one of God's mysteries.

Raising himself onto an elbow, he looked over at the woman's face. She was crying again. Women were incredibly ugly when they cried, but just now he felt a sense of tenderness toward this one. She would, after all, possibly be the last woman that he would ever fuck, circumstances being what they were. Cancer or Wilder would see to that.

Rising to the task at hand, he went into the bathroom and saw that the tub was three-fourths full. It was time. He approached the bed and saw that she had not moved, had ceased to cry, was again staring away at nothing with those doll's eyes. For the first time, he noticed fine, dark hairs at the base of her spine. These, too, would die, for they were life forms attached to the large life form, and he touched them and smoothed them against her body. Somehow, it seemed unfair that these hairs must die, just as in recent weeks it had seemed unfair that monkeys and parrots died in the jungle as they burned and searched for the Indian named Portillo. Over the years he and others had killed several Indians, recalcitrant bastards that they were, but it always bothered him to kill monkeys. The SS was known for its harshness, but it could never be said that they were not lovers of animals, of things that lived unoffending lives. Monkeys, and hairs.

He removed the dental floss from his pocket, broke off a two-foot section, and ran it between her ankles. Pulling her wrists downward, he attached the runner line and tied it off, so that she was now bent and tied in a fetal position, her feet and hands less than six inches apart. She did not protest, did not even look at him. Sliding his arms under her body, he lifted her and carried her to the bathroom. Suddenly aware of what was about to happen, she began to pull at her bonds and the keen floss cut red lines in her flesh.

"You have been most helpful," he said, leaning over, allowing her body to roll off his arms and into the water. The splash blasted outward and wet his lower trousers, and he cursed in German. Having landed face downward, she tried to balance on her tethered hands and as her back arched upward he pressed one hand on her neck, and the other on her lower spine. Her head went under for a second, and then the neck developed a superhuman strength and forced him upward, her drenched hair hanging in besopped ugliness at the sides of her face. With his fist he hit her twice in the back of the head, and she went under again. His hand went under with her and found the neck and held her there, feeling the instinctive lurching as mucous and water filled her lungs. Her hands fought against the floss, and blood's pinkness tinted the water. At last, her body relaxed, collapsed, stilled. A small opaque bubble floated about her hair, touched his coat sleeve, and popped into nothingness.

Numbness lay in the pit of his stomach and, for a full minute, he did not move. It was as though something deep inside him had been torn loose by the straining. Moving his lanky body in sections, he raised himself up from the tub and toweled off his wrists, being careful not to rub the scratches on his hand. His penis had returned to its lair, and now he smiled down at his unzipped trousers. The sex and revelry of moments before seemed as days ago, and there was a dreadful, indefinable feeling of emptiness in him. It was as the doctor had warned; he was becoming weaker.

Submitting to that eternal and ambiguous voice that calls certain of the higher animals, he conceded that he had time only to enjoy a good meal, acquire the plaque, mail it, return to Germany. It would be good to die in Mainz, just as it would be good to confront Wilder, a soldier. Die in Mainz, die in Arizona, but die a soldier.

He went back into the room, surveyed it for clues, for that last bit of insignificance that might disrupt his quest. The bloody and wet remnants of the blouse lay on the bed, and he picked it up, kissed it, threw it onto the floor. Starla's suitcase stood open like the mouth of a timorous bird. Without really knowing why, he closed it. It seemed the gentlemanly thing to do.

Nineteen

It was just after four in the afternoon when Roger parked the van on the north side of the Memphis air terminal. He got out, picked his bag up from behind the seat, and sat on a concrete stanchion for a long while. Not only did he feel a deep kinship to the ugly black box that had carried him a thousand miles in the past few days, but Starla was on his mind as well.

Taking a last look at Nicodemus and jingling its keys in his pocket, he considered floating a loan to buy it, if he made it back to San Antonio, and if the van did. With Henry you could never tell.

The elephant gray of the terminal's interior was sparsely populated for a Friday afternoon, the rows of seats holding two people here, one there, and the usual smattering of baby-faced Marines and sailors. The magazine shops were full of Elvis Presley books, each of which examined a decidedly inane part of the departed rock star's existence.

The purchase of his plane ticket added new colorations to his thoughts of impending mortality for, instead of buying a ticket to Flagstaff with a return to San Antonio, he opted for a straight shot to Flagstaff. Besides, the extra money might come in handy. He had just over two hundred bucks, more than enough if he played his cards right. There would be a car rental in Flagstaff, and at least one night in a motel, not to mention meals. Being on the road for a class outfit like the *Sentinel* provided the traveler no end of decadent options.

The first person he saw on his way to the lounge was Henry Underwood. The silly bastard was standing in the middle of the waiting area like a farmer in a ballroom, waiting, no doubt, to be told where to sit down. He wore a pair of gray corduroy slacks and a red pullover shirt with a tiny green alligator at the pocket. Roger smiled at him and once again remembered just how wonderful a face from the real world could look, even a face as empty as that which decorated the head of the Big H. As Henry loped toward him, Roger saw that he carried a ratty little suitcase from whose lower corner hung a bit of triangular cloth. Hen had packed in a hurry.

"Roger!" he bellowed. Several faces turned toward him lazily and then turned back to magazines and nothingness.

"How's the Hen?" Roger said, extending his hand.

"Jesus, Rog, it's good to see you! I'm a little drunk. They serve whiskey out of little miniature bottles at a buck and a half. I had six!"

"Uh, yeah," Roger said embarrassedly. "C'mon. I'll stake you to another. But let's hold it down, huh?"

When they were in the neon confines of a lounge, Roger said, "Bring me up to date. Has the paper been sold?"

"Sold? Nah. What're you talking about?" Henry rubbed his nose as if to assure himself that it was still there.

"Nothing, Hen. Just a rumor I heard."

"Guess what, Rog?"

"I dunno, Hen."

"Mister Mohler says I can have a crack at a story when I get back. Me and you babe. Won't that be something?"

"Yeah." It was all that Roger could think of to say. "How much money did Moe give you for the trip?"

"A plane ticket and a hundred bucks," Henry said with disgust. "Not a whole lot to do but get the van and go home. You got the keys?"

Roger dug into his pocket and handed the keys over, feeling again a twinge of finality. He wondered about Starla and hoped that his plane would get away before she got to the terminal. "No, it's not a lot. Just remember this, Henry, whatever happens: Voris Arnold Mohler is one helluva human being. When he does a thing, it's always for a reason. Got me?''

Henry looked at Roger, moon-faced and a little confused. ''Not really. Are you saying I might not get the job like he said?''

A wave of futility washed over Roger and he merely shook his head. ''Just remember what I told you. Would you like a drink before you start back?''

''No thanks, Rog. I've got a long way to pedal.''

Roger read the computerized flight board and saw that his plane was on time. Within forty-five minutes he would be in the air, and Henry and Starla and Memphis would be light years behind him. That old song by the Kingston Trio crossed his mind, something about walking a lonesome valley. For the first time ever the words made a gut sense that he could almost reach down and touch.

He said goodbye to Henry, rode the motorized walkway to his waiting area, and stared out the great windows at the failing sunlight. A terrible sensation of uneasiness seized him, and he turned away from the sun and tried not to think of Arizona.

Miles away, in a restaurant called The Knickerbocker, Ableiter perused the wine list and ordered a liter of red known for its rather pretentious ebullience. He smiled at the waitress as the woman walked away. These Americans had absolutely no knowledge of wines, and yet all professed a romantic entanglement with the blood of the grape that was ostensibly a marriage. Idiots. He thought again of the waitress's words: rather pretentious ebullience. The woman was patently stupid. Still, let it go; not a person in the restaurant could be as happy as Ableiter was just now. Not even the remaining dampness in his trousers was uncomfortable at this moment. For the first time in weeks he was able to relax for a few hours, perhaps even for the night. *Freizeit*, Leisure. There was not even a stir in his loins, his seed having recently been deposited, albeit secondhandedly, in a nearby motel bathtub. Yes, this moment was akin to euphoria. If only some of the Old Guard were there to sing with him. But, there could be none of that here, not in America. They were such fools, really fools!

When the wine was brought to his table and poured, he held the glass to the light, studied it, created movement within the glass. Adequate, at best. Seemingly unaware of the other diners in the room, he whispered a toast to Roger, bade him Godspeed in finding the plaque. He would enjoy his meal, take a room, read a paper, possibly even see a movie. Let Roger wear himself out doing the utility work now, for there was an end in sight. The scenario that Ableiter had planned was to be beautiful in its simplicity. There was no pain in his intestines, not just now.

Twenty

Railroad tracks, pines, darkness and dew. Flagstaff just before sunrise. Roger parked the rented Ford outside the cafe called Pete's and went inside. Several college students sat huddled over their coffee cups like palm fronds, their fatigued conversation concerning summer finals.

He ordered ham and eggs and coffee. While waiting he recalled the heat of Texas and Memphis and compared it to the blistering cold of this high pine country. If his skin was any judge, the temperature outside must have been in the low forties. He rubbed his neck, felt the razor burn, and wondered why God had made whiskers. A shave grabbed in the Phoenix airport had been a ghastly affair of hard water and hand soap, hardly the stuff for what Moe called "baby's ass smooth."

He noshed his food without tasting it and thought of the past twelve hours, a jangled and bedraggled time of tight plane seats and that hard chair in Phoenix. His flight from Memphis had gained him an hour, and he had been on the ground in Arizona at dusk. It was then that he learned that his connection to Flagstaff was going to be two hours late and, until one in the morning, he had tried to grab a few fitful winks, turning first this way and then that, his ass becoming one big dead bunion in the process. He barely remembered being called for his Flagstaff flight, could now recall nothing except the thrust as the plane had lifted off and headed north.

After leaving the cafe he found that the sun had just begun its feeling motions from the east, soft fingers of pink and blue touching the horizon. He found a gas station whose phone was mounted on a stand in the driveway, pulled in, turned on the car's heater, and dialed the operator. It was just after 5:00 A.M. in San Antonio, and he wanted to hear Moe's voice for what might be the last time.

"Yeah?" Moe answered groggily.

"Will you accept a collect call from Roger Wilder?"

Moe could be heard swallowing against the dryness in his throat. "Uh, yeah, sure operator. Put him on."

"Moe?"

" Yeah Rog. What's up? Jesus, what time is it?"

"Who knows? I'm in Kurdistan with the rebel forces. We ain't got no watches."

"Where are you, you asshole?"

"Flagstaff, Arizona. Where in hell'd you think?"

"Better lay low, Rog," Moe said ominously, without humor.

"Uh oh. What's up now?"

"I hope you're sitting down, because I got some bad news."

Roger swallowed heavily, and his temples burned. "Darlene got married or the paper was sold? Am I warm?"

"Starla is dead, Rog."

Roger felt his chin tremble; he found himself gasping. "Oh, Jesus Christ, Moe, tell me you're lying!"

"Sorry, pal. In a motel bathtub in Memphis. She was tied with dental floss. Sound familiar?"

"Yeah," Roger said almost soundlessly. He wiped his forehead and turned off the car's heater. All the thoughts that went through his mind, all the potential questions, all the sorrow, all seemed somehow foolish, blasphemous. He could not think of a thing to say.

"You there, Rog?"

"Yeah. God, she was a dumb, stupid nobody who never hurt a goddamn soul. Of all the people to die . . . " His voice trailed off.

"Sorry, kid. Long distance is not the way to convey such news. But it's all we got. You know what all this means, I guess?"

"Uh huh. Ableiter tortured her and got it out of her, and he is on my ass like white on rice."

"How'd you know she was tortured?"

"Because she was a gutsy little Jew who would have gone out swinging, that's why. So why do you ask?"

"He burned her nipple with a cigarette, or something. Willard came to my house at nine last night with the full details. The Memphis cops put some two's and two's together. There's an APB on you, Rog. They think you did it."

"Me? Jesus, Moe, why?"

"Because, dummy, Ableiter does not exist, remember? You and Starla checked in at the same time yesterday morning, and the desk clerk remembered it. Willard spent two hours last night eating my ass out about this weird turn of events. He still thinks we're holding something back from him, suspicious bastard that he is. And we are. Frankly, I chewed on my pillow for a while last night."

"Can we hold off the dogs for another day?" Roger asked. He wiped his eyes and mentally blamed his tears on the heat of the car's interior.

"Yeah. Willard told the Memphis flock that he'd handle it from here. Not to save your ass, but his own, which is understandable. I swore that you were innocent, that Ableiter was the prick in this one. Willard knows it, but he's got his own nuts in the fire if he doesn't look interested to the right parties." Moe stopped in the midst of his reasoning and inhaled noisily. "Anyhow," he said in summation, "do you see what a weird piece of shit all this is?"

"Yeah. I got nine monkeys on my back. If Ableiter doesn't get me, then the cops will, and vice versa. Frankly, the cops look good right now."

"No they don't," Moe countered. "You are within a gnat's nuts of the plaque. Goddamnit, Roger, puh-leeeze don't fail now. With the money I've been sending you and that money I gave Henry for this van job, Lynch is going to shit down both legs. I mean it, Rog, don't get caught by the cops. God, get off this phone rat now. Anything else you need to ask me?"

"Naw. I guess not." He paused for a moment and then said, "Moe?"

"Yeah?"

"All the shit aside—you are a great newsman."

"Yeah, Rog. You too. But let us not sound so goddamn funereal, if that is the word. I know you'll do well. If not, well . . . " The joking quality had left Moe's voice. "Get your ass back here, by God, or I'll have it on a tray!" he said suddenly.

"I hear you, Moe. See you in forty-eight hours."

"Can I count on that?"

"You bet your ass. After what happened to Starla, I just got back my Marine guts. This Ableiter sonofawhore has his work cut out for him."

"See you, Rog."

"You bet."

Roger hung the phone up and wondered if indeed he had regained his guts. The world as he knew it seemed to have fallen apart in the past five minutes, and his only thought at this moment was of Starla.

Roger shook his head and rubbed his eyes. A horn sounded from behind. He looked in his mirror and saw a work gang in a super cab pickup; they were glowering at him. He started the engine and drove away. God, hopefully she was dead or at least knocked out before it happened. He found himself wondering whether she had screamed. He remembered her voice, and tried to turn it into a scream. There was nothing there; he might as well have been trying to turn a talking voice into a singing voice. He was not able to cry at all, and he wanted to. Damnit, somebody had to, and he was all she had. The black pine tops became a sun-goldened green; it was as if the world was telling him not to give a damn.

Roger headed the Ford north out of the city, and the darkness appeared to prevail again in the rock and pine country. A family of deer scampered beside the car in a grove of cottonwoods and then were swallowed by the trees as quickly as they had appeared. Pickup trucks mounted with campers stood in dew-soaked stillness along the road, their noses pointed into alcoves of shrubs like marauding animals. He cursed and hit the steering wheel.

Now the pine forest fell away and the sun painted the scrub-brush world green, yellow, and rock gray. Traffic increased, and Roger pushed the car forward at sixty and seventy miles per hour. Signs began to appear along the roadside, each offering a tourist's diversion. Cactus candy, hot coffee, reasonable breakfasts. Roger frowned at that last one; Moe would have a field day chiding a reporter for writing such questionable English, for Moe would assume that a reasonable breakfast, like a reasonable wife, was one that did not argue. He window-dressed his thoughts with the signs for a long time for, by reading them, he did not have to think of Starla.

At the entrance to the Grand Canyon he paused behind a line of cars, allowed a U.S. Forester to read and record his license plate, then drove on into the main camp area. A great log edifice that stood off to his right identified itself as the El Tovar Hotel and, just beyond it, was the famous Bright Angel Lodge. Both towered over the tourist area like great birds having alighted at the canyon's lip. Stretching out behind the hotels was the great yellow and pink chasm that herds of tourists were already photographing even at this early hour.

Sighting a sign that offered, in no nonsense terms, *Information*, he parked the car and went into the Bright Angel Lodge. The uniform of the day seemed to be Bermudas, cutoff blue jeans, and rough boots. America at play.

"May I help you?" an ancient lady asked.

"Yes. How do I get to this place called Molly's Nipple? Where can I get a guide?"

She perused him for a long moment as though to determine whether he were armed. "Well," she said in her best Chamber of Commerce tone, "there is an old man named John Landers who might be available. He's . . ." she searched for the proper word, ". . . different."

Roger liked the sound of old John immediately. "How is he . . . different?"

"He lives along the rim about forty miles to the west. He has mules and dogs. I think he might be who you are looking for. Weird. A real coot, you ask me."

"How do I get there?" he asked.

She grabbed a yellow brochure and drew a map along its back. Her hands were mottled with age spots, and Roger gathered from her easy demeanor that she had seen and heard it all. "Follow this. You can't get lost. And good luck."

"You think I'll need it?"

She smiled sweetly and looked beyond him at another tourist. "May I help you?" she asked.

He left the tourist area, driving slowly to avoid the packs of sightseers who wandered like cattle and, within minutes, was back at the exit. The line of cars had grown colossally by now, and he felt a touch of loss at having come so close to a natural wonder without having paused for even a minute's gaze.

An hour later, following the crude map, he turned off the main highway and followed a dirt road for five miles. Bits of pine lay here and there uncrushed, unmoved, and it was obvious that Old John had the place pretty much to himself. The road soon became little more than a trail and, after two miles of easing among pines, he drove into a clearing. A tiny cabin stood with its back to yet another grove of pines and, beyond them, Roger could discern miles of bronzed and orange rock as the canyon again made itself visible.

There was a sudden din of yowling as a pack of dogs ran from beneath the cabin and headed for the car. Their sizes, coloring, and ancestry were somewhat pastiched by an obvious freedom of social life. Circling the car, they yipped and snarled for several seconds and then took turns sniffing and saluting tires and bumpers, their hackles at full staff. Roger eased his window down a bit and said, in his best liar's tone, "Nice puppies."

"You goddamn bastards is gonna get it!" a gruff male voice roared from the cabin.

Roger looked at the place and saw nothing but a screen door and two dusty windows. Forgetting the dogs, he decided that the place was one of the more eerie things that he had seen in a long while. In the noon heat the little house appeared to shimmy with the sun's rays. He opened the car's door slightly, placed a foot on the ground, and allowed a yellow and white mongrel to sniff his ankle. Convinced that the sweaty foot was nonlethal, the dog trotted back toward the cabin. The others went onto their haunches and lolled their sweaty tongues at the visitor.

"Safe to get out?" Roger called.

"Depends! Whattaya want?"

"You John?"

It was the screen door that answered. "Under the circumstances, who in hell else would I be?" John materialized behind the screen like a bolt of tapestry suddenly weaving itself into human form. Roger could make out khaki hat, suspenders, cowboy boots, and red shirt, all of which served to complement a pot belly and a white beard. The man wore no pants. Even from this distance, Roger marvelled that those skinny legs could hold up such an ample gut.

"Well, you comin' in or not?"

"You ain't answered me is it safe yet," said Roger, wondering why fear always did this to his use of the King's English.

"If'n it ain't, I been in danger for well over eighty years," said John. "Here Susie! Here Cloudy!" Two more of the dogs broke ranks and headed for the house and the others, convinced that the fire was out, imitated them in dog disgust.

Roger got out and followed, keeping a wary eye affixed to the dark area under the porch. When he was a few feet from the steps, he bolted forward and leapt onto the rickety porch, his leg hairs crawling against his trousers.

Old John was busy placing one leg into a pair of blue jeans as he held the screen door open. "Who you?" he asked.

"My name is . . ."

"Never mind! You got any tobaccer or whiskey? I been outa supplies for two days. Damndest thing, when some folks drink they hate food! Me, when I get to boozin' I eat up everthang they is—food, chewin-tobaccer, you name it. It's like I think I'm gonna die and I hate to waste food. I was raised that no matter what else you do, you don't waste food nor water. I got enough water, but food is somethin' else. What'd you say your name was?"

"Roger Wild—"

"Roger, huh? I knowed a Roger once. He had red hair, though. I don't guess you're kin to him." He looked at Roger's head.

"Roger Wilder. No, I'm not."

The old one finished the trouser pulling and hooked his suspenders into buttons of different parentage: one was brown, the other a stark, robin's egg blue. With the exception of purple, the oldster now wore about every hue in the rainbow. The red shirt and white beard created an image of a malevolent Santa Claus. When Old John was satisfied with his sartorial efforts, he motioned for Roger to sit. The location offered was a homemade chair, whose back and seat were inner tubing cut into long strips and threaded intricately among heavy pine saplings. Roger found the caress of the springy rubber to be an interesting respite from the seats of planes and cars. He fought down the urge to bounce up and down a bit. "Nice," he said.

"Not so nice, but adequate as hell," said Old John. He lumbered backwards and sat on his bed, a tautly-sheeted pad that featured an ageless cathedral bedstead of roseate iron. Roger let his eyes wander over the rest of the place: antique dresser, complete with mandatory cracked and age-smoked glass; rummage sale table with two chairs, age indeterminate; homemade, doorless cabinets whose barrenness bore out the old one's earlier nod to starvation. Seeing Roger begin to relax in these surroundings, Old John said, "Now what can I do ye for?"

"They tell me you're quite a camper."

The old one laughed. "Yeah, them up there at the circus thinks of me as the local yokel. Or more like the village idiot."

Roger dispelled this with a smile and said, "I want to go to a place called Molly's Nipple. You know it?"

John nodded. "Nothin' in this canyon I don't know." There was a slight edge of apprehension in his voice as he asked, "What in hell you lost at the Nipple?"

"I'm an anthropologist, and certain place names tend to catch my eye. That one did. Any bones up there, to speak of?"

"No. Where'd you say you was from?" John's frozen stare caught Roger in the center of his forehead, where sweat was beginning to form.

"San Antonio."

"That's nice. Never was there, but I read on it some. You ever do any stuff on Kaibabs?"

"Uh, no, not as yet."

"How about Hualapais? Ever study them?"

"No. Most of my stuff has been on Oriental cultures."

There was a rigid silence of about thirty long seconds before Old John spoke again. "Funny thing, I don't get a pack trip to the Nipple once every two years, and now inside of two weeks I get two offers. Coincidence, I reckon." He leaned back on the bed and rested on his elbows, his grizzled hands patting his tubby belly. His eyes had never left Roger's.

"So," Roger said huskily, feeling his throat tighten, "how do we go about it?"

"We pay me seventy-five dollars plus twenty for the food we'll eat tonight and tomorrow," said John.

"Where do we go to get provisions?"

"We don't. All we'll need is out there in back in the storehouse by the mule pen."

"But I thought you were out of groceries," said Roger.

"Damnit, son, I'm out of eatin' supplies, not campin' supplies."

"Pardon me. I wasn't aware of the distinction."

Old John leaned forward and said, "Out here, they's a hell of a distinction. Only once in my life I had to eat my campin' supplies, and that's when I had the flu. Puked up ever'thing that went down. No sir, when you live back here like I do you learn to distinctify your goods. They's enough out there for a three-, four-day camp," He lifted his hat and scratched a mostly bald head.

"So, when could we leave?" Roger asked, feeling a bit fidgety.

"We can't."

"But I thought---"

"Don't think," said John, not harshly, "just listen. I didn't get to be my age goin' off on fool's errands. People take me for a coot because of how I live. They think

I've never drunk whiskey, laid a woman, nor read a book, while the fact is I've done 'em all. You ain't been straight with me, have you?'' The question was cold, toneless.

Roger started to lie again, but felt the benevolent glow of confession starting to stir in his soul. "No, I haven't. How'd you know?'' He looked down at his shoes. They were dirty, and small.

"Several things. A Mexican comes, wants to go to the Nipple. We spent the night, and he leaves a suitcase in that cave up there. He thinks I don't know about that, but I do. Some days later, a guy comes who claims to be an anthropologist. He wears city shoes, city clothes, and his hands are baby soft. And he gets sketchy when I talk of Kaibabs. If you are an anthropologist, then I am Warren G. Harding. What are you? Police? FBI?''

"No. I am Roger Wilder, a reporter for a San Antonio paper. And that is the gospel.''

Old John hunched and knocked a bit of dirt from one boot. From beneath the house came the sound of a dog coughing, hacking. John listened attentively and, when the dog's distress ended, he again looked at Roger. "Okay, I believe you, I guess. Just don't never try to fool an old fooler. This Mexican, is he dangerous?''

Roger shook his head. "Not any more.''

"Dead?''

"Yep. Dead as a hammer. Probably less than two days after he left you. What can you tell me about him?''

"Do we lay our hands face up?'' John asked.

Roger nodded. "Face up.''

"Said his name was Gomez. Said he wanted to go to Molly's Nipple. Got here like at six or so in the goddamn mornin'. Looked bleary-eyed, but Mexicans always look bleary-eyed to me. Had two suitcases, three really, but I didn't know about that until later. Turned out one of the big suitcases held a smaller one. A heavy sonofabitch, too. Until the next mornin'. That's how I knew. When the bastard thought I was asleep he went up and deposited the smaller one in the Nipple cave.''

So Moe had been right. But, instead of jubilation, Roger was overcome with a dull melancholy. After all the travel, all the bullshit, all the deaths, and all the money spent, he was about to be declared winner. And it was strangely like ashes in his mouth. "And your natural curiosity didn't get the best of you?" he asked.

"Curious, yeah. Stupid, no. I got paid to take him up and back. You live out here long enough, the wind and sand tell you things. They told me to leave this thing alone, and I have."

Roger stood, rubbed his bottom, and sat again. He had forgotten how quickly rubber causes perspiration. "That was a good move on your part," he said. "What is in the suitcase, if indeed it is there, is a bitch in any sense of the word."

"You've got my cards," said Old John, "now let's have yours."

Roger talked for fifteen minutes, being careful not to leave anything out. He had by now reckoned John to be aboveboard all the way, and certainly not a man who would suffer a second lie casually. "As far as I can remember, that's it," he said at last.

"These other bastards don't bother me," said John. "It's the woman part I don't like. Any asshole that'd kill a woman is lower than snake shit. Somethin' I saw in World War----" His voice trailed off. Finally, he came back from the dark world of memory and asked, "This woman, was she yours?"

"Not really. We were together for a couple of days. We never even got close."

"Yeah, sometimes that's best, and worst. Always leaves a man wonderin' what he might have had, but doin' it would have made her one of the flock. Always works out that way; the best is what you ain't had yet. Life's a funny goddamn thing."

"Maybe so, but I haven't laughed in days. This whole bastard episode has made my nerve endings come unglued. By the way, I'm sorry I lied to you."

Old John waved the statement away with a rough palm. "One thing I ain't clear on: you said all these people was tied up with pornography in one way or another. Why would a Nazi statue be of interest to pornographers?"

Roger managed to chuckle weakly as he shook his head. "That, friend John, is the last part of the puzzle. Gomez knew, but it went with him."

John doffed his hat again and fanned himself. "You said somethin' about him bein' a sort of practical joker. Funny, I don't remember his bein' anything but damned serious. Looked over his shoulder a lot, if you know what I mean. I guess now I know why. But my point is, maybe this whole thing was a joke on somebody."

Roger framed his words carefully to avoid insult. "That has been taken into consideration. Having not been on this for the better part of a week like I have, you might come to that conclusion. But believe me, there are too many dead people around for this thing to have been the mindless prank of a jokester. It's more as if he wanted to work a joke into something serious, something that suddenly turned more serious than he was bargaining for."

"Pornography," said Old John, returning the hat to the back of his head. "It don't figure."

"I know. That's why I'm here, so it will." He pointed toward the wall in the general direction of the Canyon. "And it's out there waiting for us."

Old John got up, went to the rickety cabinet and knelt down on all fours. After a moment of rummaging among old sheets and tablecloths, he extracted an ancient, sweat-stained cowboy hat and threw it to Roger. "You'll need that bad," he said.

They went out into the raging sunlight, and Roger tried to block the hat into something chic. By the time they were at the mule pen, he had given up on it and placed the floppy crown low over his eyes, blinding himself. By the time he regained his sight, his cohort was well into the little shed that stood off to the left of a circular mule pen.

"One thing to always remember," said John, placing blankets on the back of a gray and two browns, "is that no mule wants his asshole touched. Goosiest critters the Lord ever breathed life into. I knowed a mule once named Horton. Some kids goosed him. The bastard did a swan dive over a cliff like it was the most natural thing in the world. Don't mess with their ass.''

"I promise," said Roger, trying to imagine a mule doing a swan dive. Somehow the metaphors were less than compatible. "Have they got any other pecadilloes that might interest me?''

"Bad to bite, sometimes. Especially old Bridey there. She's gonna be yours.''

Roger looked at Bridey. She had yellow teeth the size of matchboxes, and there was a flame in her eye that said just wait until you turn your back, you bastard. She gnawed on her lower lip and spit ropes hung from the sides of her mouth. Of all the animals that could be called domestic, mules had to be the ugliest. "We'll get along," said Roger, not too convincingly.

Old John spat a brown stream of tobacco at the assembled dogs. They merely leaned sideways and got out of the line of fire, their heads coming back to upright position like a girl's chorus after a low note. "They know we're goin'," he said to Roger.

"Are they going to make trouble?'' he asked.

"Nope. They always get real docile like this. You cain't tell me animals don't know stuff. Times, I think they are some ways smarter than humans.''

"Do they guard the place well?''

Old John looked at him, his hand hanging against a bridle in mid-motion as if a fist of thought had just tapped him. "Naw, not that good. They tend to be friendly. Too friendly.''

"Then what you're saying is that we don't have any backup for when we come out of the canyon. Is that about it?''

John resumed his tacking and said, "That's about it. Wish you hadn't brought it up. Comin' back tomorrow is gonna give me the willies.''

"What about at night?'' Roger asked.

"You just don't trundle around in the canyon at night, son.'' He spat again.

"I see. Where'd you get the tobacco?''

"Campin' supplies." He grinned at Roger and winked. "That is the thing that makes me gladdest you came. So's I could get a chew of this campin' tobaccer."

"Glad to be of service. When do we leave?"

Old John stared upward at the sun, his hand saluting the harshness of light with the practiced ease of a man who knew his elements. With that one lazy movement he proved to Roger that he was all that was at one with the environment. His arm crooked to knock away the sun's rays, John had become a Saguaro cactus. "It's between twelve and twelve thirty now," he said. "Barring snakes, broke legs, or heart attack on your part, we'll be at the Nipple by nine tonight."

In less than thirty minutes they were at the pines that fronted the lip of the canyon. Old John, mounted atop a mule named Pearl, turned around in the saddle, and looked at his little cabin before the trees swallowed it up. He hooked his leg over the saddle horn and rubbed the butt of his .22 rifle thoughtfully. The weapon, a scarred but well-oiled little instrument, appeared to be dominant in his thoughts, although his eyes roved elsewhere. Roger had seen this look before. It had belonged to a point man on a patrol; it was a gaze of thinly-concealed fear. He eased Bridey along, third in the convoy behind the heavily-laden brown called Wiley and, just before the pines moved as though to close ranks behind them, he, too, took a long last look at the cabin. The other mules and the dogs stared after them and were still and silent.

The descent was immediate. The little trail was no more than four feet wide and was walled for a few yards by tortured and convoluted sand formations. Suddenly the right wall was gone, and the magic canyon lay before them in oranges and browns that stretched away to the horizon. Roger felt his legs tighten against the mule's body as he looked away from the crevasse that beckoned mere inches from the trail's lip. There were no guard rails here, no Smokey Bear government employees. This was raw nature, silent, open and deadly. He released the reins and clutched at the saddle horn. The first bounce point off the trail was at least six hundred feet down.

When they were less than three hundred yards down the trail, it arched upward again and opened into a spot that was ten yards wide. Standing to the left was a clutch of boulders. Old John reined in his mule, dismounted, and pulled out a small shovel. "Wanta get off and rest a spell?" he asked.

"Not especially. Anything wrong?"

"Nope. These is Shit Rocks. Ask me why I call 'em that."

"Why do you call 'em Shit Rocks, John?"

"Because I always get of here and take a shit." With that, the old one disappeared behind a boulder and was gone for three minutes. When he returned to his mule, Roger noticed that the shovel was clean.

"Any luck?" Roger inquired whimsically.

"Nope. I ain't et since yesterday, so I didn't need to go nohow." He replaced the shovel and looked upward at the pines. "Thing is, I stopped here once to take a shit, thirty-, thirty-five years ago. While I was squatted I remembered that I had left my canteen back at the place. It's become a ritual of sorts. Whether I need to go or not, I always stop here and think for a minute or so." He cocked his head sideways to determine Roger's attitude regarding this information. "Our German boy, if he's real sharp, will be in those pines up there. I want you to get a good look at this place, cause tomorrow, or whenever we come out, we'll be most open right here."

Roger complied and saw that the pines that now stood just above and to their left were the perfect lair for a sniper. How serene they had looked behind the cabin in their darkness, and how evil they were facing the sun. He looked around and saw that Old John had led Wiley on down the trail, and he urged Bridey onward, his neck hairs tingling.

There was no more foolishness now, nothing to do with hats and rock formations with scatological nomenclature. The old man did not look around for the better part of an hour, and the only movement that his body offered in and of itself was the steady bobbing of his head, a motion that caused his cowboy hat to often affect the mannerism of a lazy hawk. Roger had once interviewed an old farmer who tilled with a horse and single-blade plow, and the man's steady, tireless motions were the same as John's now were, methodical, timeless, powerful. His own ass was killing him, tailbone connected to de brainbone, as it seemed, and when they had gotten down to the wide place in the trail that fronted the Colorado River, he allowed himself to stand and rub his numb buns.

Without even looking around, Old John led Pearl and Wiley into the wide, shallow part of the river and surged on across. Roger sat down and let Bridey have her head. Grabbing the saddle horn, he saw that the Colorado was enraged even here in this wide and relatively quiet area. He had seen photos of the rapids, of the Kennedys shooting along in a blast of brown geysers, and he had always thought of this river as being twenty feet wide and roaring. Here, it was a half mile wide and merely snarling.

When they were across, John looked back, gave a V for victory sign, and moved on. The shadows of afternoon were probing and widening as John started into the high cliffs on the other side and, even Roger, tenderfoot that he was, knew that it would be well after dark when they arrived.

He thought of Starla, and tried to imagine where her body was at this moment.

The feet of Bridey made clicking sounds as they came out of the river sand and moved onto the shattered rocks that led them to the upward trail. Old John was a good hundred feet ahead, and Roger nudged Bridey on. He did not want to be left behind, not even a little distance. Not really knowing what he was looking for, he turned in the saddle and looked back across the river and at the awesome moonscape from which they had emerged. There was nothing there but hot orange and hot purple. The river blew its breath against his back and chilled him.

It was past ten, and they were ravenous. Roger had forgotten just how involved the setting up of a campsite was, how necessary were those dozens of picayune and pernicious little tasks that stood like rungs on the food ladder. Wood and pots and water poured here and there and sleeping gear and eating gear. And, for all their efforts, all that Old John put on the fire was a two pound tin of government beef. It sizzled and spewed until they were satisfied that the trichinosis was murdered and then they ate silently out of metal plates. The few shriveled and arthritic little sticks that fed the fire were hardy and burned slowly, and when they had eaten, each of the men leaned away from the fire and studied his own fantasies in the embers.

"The dogs," Roger said, rubbing his numb rump, "how do they make it while you're gone?"

"Just fine. Rabbits, gophers, a garter snake here and there. This place is more alive than outlanders think. Lots to eat here. Rabbit, done right, tastes like chicken."

"Better than Spam cooked over rice straw, I hope," Roger said.

"Damn sight better. Nam?" When Roger nodded, the old one continued, "I was in the big one."

"The one a guy was in was the big one. So you've been shot at?"

"Yep. Skybursts, mostly. Hun artillery. Never been so scared. No real place to hide from a skyburst, unless you tunnel down and in. Knew a guy named Hunsecker, digginest sonofabitch you ever seen. He could dig a three foot hole and tunnel sideways two feet in less than twenty minutes. Try that sometime."

"What happened to him?"

Old John laughed, and the orange glow made his teeth even more yellow. "Got it from a sniper. Second Marne. That's war—the thing you plan on don't happen; the other one does."

"That's life," said Roger, "not just war."

The fire had drawn them together, as campfires always draw people together, and Roger felt a masculine comradeship that he had not known since the war. He reflected on the fact that people are truly close only when there is nothing to fight over. "You're quite a philosopher, in your own way," he said.

"Maybe. And maybe I've been alone so long I'm just plain crazy. Ever'body's crazy, anyway, only in different ways." He leaned forward and spat tobacco juice into the coals. "Like my campin' tobacco, here. You probably think it's nutty to starve myself with tobaccer right out in the camp shack, but, nosir, I wouldn'ta touched this plug for hell.''

"Why do you do it, John? The tobacco and food thing?''

"Ran out one time in a rainstorm, about thirty miles over.'' He pointed to the darkness. "Holed up for two days waitin' for the river to go down. Decided I'd run out because of bein' greedy. It taught me somethin'.''

"Which was?''

"Which was, when you come right down to it, greed is the one thing that causes a man all his grief. Greed is what makes it all go, and what tears it all down. You understand?''

Roger gave an unconvinced nod. "A word here and there. Maybe you could be a little more specific.''

"Take that mountain peak there,'' he said, waving to the apparitional heaviness off to his right. "Molly's Nipple. Been there four million years. No value. But now they's somethin' in it that we think has a value. That's greed.''

"Maybe it's survival,'' Roger countered. "You get the money for taking me there, I get money for going there. We both get to eat another meal. Right?''

Old John said nothing. He folded his hands over his knees and looked at the fire, at the sum and substance of his existence. A warm breeze drifted through the camp and sparks rode up and away with it. The eyes of the mules glowed in bronze emptiness.

"This was a garden, once,'' the old man said finally. "Not the kind of garden like you know, but a garden all the same. It was life and time and goodness like the Lord meant. Now it's gettin' to be helicopters and campers and them key tops they pull off of beer cans and throw ever'-place. Greed wears a hundred faces, Roger, but it's the same body.''

Roger studied the words for a time and said, "You make me feel like an intruder.''

Old John stood, and his legs shuddered in their stiffness. "Nope, not just you. Us. Me and you. We're all intruders. What say we get that thing and be done with it.''

Pulling himself to his feet, Roger dusted the sand off and watched as the old man took a shovel and a flashlight from Wiley's pack. John walked back to the fire and threw on the few remaining sticks. He and Roger stared at each other for a short time over the glow and, for each, the staring was sinister and dreadful and indefinable. The moment of truth was at hand, and they knew that their conversation had been strained through the mocking fingers of the mountain's grasp. The stillness about them held up to their firedappled faces the terrible mirror of finality.

"Let's go," said Old John.

They moved cautiously at first, their eyes and feet making tenuous and unnatural movements as they adjusted to the desert's darkness. The beam from the light made little sweeps along the upward swell of the peak as John played it along the boulders. Occasionally something scurried out of the punctured night and then disappeared into the walls of darkness. Although it was an easy trail, Roger found himself breathing heavily; his heart was pounding, and he continually wiped his palms against his pockets. When they were less than five hundred yards from the camp, John stopped abruptly and said, ''There they are.''

Roger looked at the point of the light's beam and saw a series of irregular holes in the side of a thirty foot cliff. At the top of the cliff, the mountain moved back for some fifty feet and then arched upward out of the light's circle. The result of eons of wind and sandblast, the caves glimmered blackly in the light, a horribly melancholy and morose coupling of shine and shadow. As the light beam moved about, the caves seemed to swallow themselves, to change shapes, locations, moods.

"Jesus," Roger whispered.

"Yeah," the old one answered quietly, "maybe now you know why I didn't come up here alone. It looks like hell's own doorway." Handing Roger the light, he said, "It's your find. Lead us on in. If it's there, it'll be in that bigger hole in the center."

Roger moved forward with measured steps, his cadence checking off roll call of the names of those who had partaken of this minute: Moe, Gomez, Bond, Tatum, Jarvis, Ableiter, Starla. There was a winner's emptiness in his soul, for the prize, if it were indeed in the cave, was inadequate to compensate for the blood it had shed.

"There it is," he heard himself whisper drily.

Gomez's footprints lay starkly defined in the gray dust of the cave's floor. Like the steps of a ghostly, invisible dancer, they moved halfway into the interior of the shallow cave and ended. At the terminus of the footprints, standing heavily in the gray dust about halfway back, was the suitcase, a small rectangle of black or navy blue. Roger had imagined, hoped really, that it would be somehow phantasmagoric, sinister, evil, but, in the stillness of the timeless rock layers, it resembled a rather mundane bit of baggage standing forlorn in a small town's bus station.

"Whattaya think?" John whispered.

"About what?" Roger whispered back.

"You think it's wired, or something?"

An interesting thought, Roger had to admit, one that had not occurred to him. If Gomez the jokester had run true to form, then perhaps the biggest joke of all would be blast and burial of the thing in the cave, provided something was truly in the case. Again the winner's emptiness hit him, made his guts a bit queasy, caused his palms to sweat with the immediacy of all that was here and now and no longer speculative. Mentally offering up a prayer, Roger made a tentative step in to the cave, then another. When he was within two feet of the case, he dropped to his knees and played the light against the walls and the gray dust of the floor. The only sound was of his own breathing, its counterpoint being John's muffled footsteps.

When John had knelt beside him, Roger placed the light in the dust and said, "Ready?"

The old man nodded, the shadow of his hat waving ethereal wings against the walls.

Roger touched the leather gently, his damp fingertips feeling the dull richness of the sides. There was no evidence of dangling wire, of trip lever, of mine prong. He leaned in and smelled, remembering that certain explosives gave off a distinct odor. His fingers lightly massaged the small silver hasps for barbs of impending disaster but found only the indentation caused by the brand stamp: Vuitton. Gomez had gone first class.

"Open 'er up," said John.

Roger's thumbs moved against the hasps with methodical strangler's force, and the case responded noiselessly. Roger inhaled deeply and allowed the lid to ease down into the dust of its own weight.

"My God," said the old one, speaking for both, his eyes adjusting to the reflected glow.

The Himmler Plaque was a slab of dull gold, not more than eleven inches high, eight wide, its top adorned with the head of a diamond-studded silver eagle. It stood on a base of silver that incorporated the eagle's feet, and the toenails were inlaid with oval diamonds. The center of the plaque was a bedazzling swastika formed of perfect diamonds and, on either side of the delicately etched body, were lightning slashes, these, too, inlaid with diamonds. Roger guessed the assemblage to be something like two hundred carats, perhaps more.

As though responding to a silent command, the men moved backwards on their knees and sat in hypnotized silence. The eagle's diamond eyes threw a ghastly and cruel coldness toward the intruders. It was as though the bird had been awakened from its own malignant dreams, such was the pervasive malevolence that emanated from the dead white stare.

"You can almost hear their screams," said John.

Roger nodded. Here was not the blood of European Jewry, but its nerve endings. Here were the screams of old men watching their children led to gas chambers. Here were the cries of women who might have resisted only to have their ring-fingers cut off. Here was gold ripped from yet-warm jaw sockets as the cadavers were carried by carts to the ovens. Here was the shining and glinting heart of Cruelty itself.

Looking up and away from the thing, Roger blinked his eyes several times and hoped that his companion did not see his tears. Feeling a rage that he had never known, not even in the darkest memories of what he had seen in his own war, he crawled forward and grasped the plaque at its sides. Lifting it cautiously, his fingers came in contact with a texture that was not gold at all but the smoothness of polished wood. The object weighted fifteen pounds, possibly twenty. When he had placed it in the dust to the front of the suitcase, he leaned over and saw that the metal was set into a small case of burnished teakwood. An inch thick, six deep, five wide, the backing clung to the eagle by a series of steel brads. He tapped the wood almost as an afterthought; the hollow sound came as something his subconscious mind had already told him to expect. He now knew that the secret of the Himmler Plaque was not in and of the plaque itself, but in what lay within the dark wood. Touching the wood on all sides, he discovered that the topmost bit was joined to the body by a master carpenter's exercise known as tongue-in-groove. He pressed down on the top, eased the small rectangle of wood outward. It slipped and fell into the dust.

"Pictures?" Old John asked absently.

Roger nodded. There were several pieces of heavy paper inside, their tops standing stiffly and whitely. At their sides was excelsior stuffing, the yellow-hair fabric placed there for cushion and moisture retardance.

"Ease'em out slow. They look old," said Old John. He moved the light an inch to the left, and the eagle's eyes glinted fiercely.

Roger touched the top of the paper gently and lifted. It was a black-and-white photograph with intermittent grays, its content too small and too dark to be readily discernible. He blinked twice to adjust his eyes to the scene and then said, "Oh, Jesus Christ."

A man in a white coat was smiling into the camera, his moustache hanging over his curled lips as obscene camouflage. On a table to his immediate front lay a pair of twin babies, female infants whose vaginas had been penetrated by daggers. Both were emitting large pools of blood, and one tiny face was contorted by its screams of agony. The other infant's face was partially obscured by the man's penis, an organ of common size that was just beginning to droop following orgasm. The tiny mouth was dripping semen and from the blurred effect of arms and legs Roger assumed that the child was strangling to death. His brain rioting hotly, Roger turned the picture over and found, written in precise hand: Mengele, 11 Juni 44.

Doctor Josef Mengele at work, June 11, 1944.

"How could they?" Old John asked, his tone diminished, bland, a bit fearful.

"The selection doctor of Auschwitz," said Roger. "He had a thing about twins, made a study of them. He was a sonofabitch of the first water. Word is, he drowned somewhere in South America, probably Paraguay. I'd bet he's alive."

"How can it be?" John asked, his old eyes registering bewilderment not experienced before in his life. "I mean, how could a pukesnake like that still be alive? Free? Still loose?"

"A good question, thirty years ago," said Roger. "But not so good now. Law and extradition and apathy and a whole lot of things about the outside world that would confuse you if I tried to explain them."

"I ain't exactly stupid," said John. "I do read a paper now and then. Not that I understand what's what, though."

Roger laid the photo across the butt of the flashlight gently and with disgust, as though it were a rotten egg that had maintained its value in spite of its rottenness.

Old John was breathing heavily. "Get the next one," he commanded. "It cain't be that bad."

But it was. The second photo featured Mengele in a supervisory capacity. Naked still, holding a short, stiff black whip, the good physician stood beside a mattress and smiled down at the activity thereon with an excess of glee. A blonde girl of about eighteen was being raped by a Doberman Pinscher, the animal's neck attached to her own by a three foot length of silvery chain. The animal's glistening penis had caught the brunt of the camera's flash and, even in black and white, the pinkness was revealed, the result of some phenomenon of light perfectly attuned to celluloid.

Bloody scratches on the girl's hips and lower back assured that the dog's legs had been active in his frenzy, and the blurred hind quarters indicated that the picture had been made at the moment of climax. But, it was in the girl's eyes that Roger found the focus of the scene; dull, staring, horrified, and beyond shame, she wore the look of one who had entered the room of human degradation, only to emerge at a distant door without the ability to comprehend the senselessness of what had happened. She appeared to stare at the delicate striping on the dirty mattress, as though hoping to be absorbed by it.

"I wonder where she is now," Old John said quietly.

"Gassed, probably. Hanged or shot. Who knows?"

"I remember readin' about the trials, some of the things the witnesses said. It never sunk home until now. About the medical experiments, the mass graves, the castrations. You hear about shit and it's just words. And words don't get it. It takes this." The old man tapped the picture.

A dull rush of nausea tugged at Roger's guts, and he looked up and away. The intensity of it was such that he remembered another time when it had been this bad. On returning to base camp from an inspection of a radio bunker he had, by dawn's early light, stepped into the mouldering and sloppy chest cavity of a sun-ripened Cong. That was scent; this was visual; the result was the same. The picture of the dog rape began to flutter in his hand. The old man took it and laid it with its mate.

"Go on to the next one," said Old John. "You gotta do it all. If you don't, you'll never feel right."

Roger wiped his forehead with the back of his hand, rearranged his throbbing knees in the dust, and took out the third picture. This one resumed the sequence of the first, and Roger placed it atop the other two, his movement not quite fast enough to blot from his eyes and his eternal memory the sight of the twin's severed heads on the table, the shapeless lakes of blood, the innocent and dead eyes of the babies beaming roundly from beneath hairless eyelids. Mengele was in that one also, the same cruel and bemused smile playing for the camera.

"Do I want to see that one?" the old man asked.

"Not no, but hell no," said Roger. "You want to pull out the next one? I don't think my hands will move just now."

John crawled closer to the plaque, and the diamond eyes glared at him as the light adjusted itself in his wake. Brushing the dust from his hands, he withdrew the fourth photo and stripped away a bit of clinging excelsior. Roger watched as the old eyes looked at the scene. Suddenly John's mouth opened, and his eyes squinted in the unmistakable manner of realization. "I ain't believin' this shit," he said at last.

"What is it?" Roger asked, leaning to spit toward the wall, fearing that he might yet vomit.

"Not what, but who. Look." Old John thrust the paper toward Roger and settled back on his knees.

A blonde man lay on a bed with his hands folded behind his head, the epitome of comfort and pleasure. He was naked, except for a portion of sheet that had wrapped itself around his right leg. His massive penis, some eleven inches in length, was inserted at the glans into the mouth of another male, the latter a dark haired, moustachioed and heavy set person who was also naked. The fellator hovered about the blonde's lower quarters and his eyes were closed. A dark, circular blur encompassed the periphery of the photo, and Roger surmised that the shot had been made through a peephole.

"So what is it you don't believe?" Roger asked "You never heard of queers?"

"Better look again," said John. "See anybody you know?"

Roger complied, feeling a little disgusted by this oldster's first foray into the pink world of homosexuality. He had seen countless gay publications but, not only was this one poorly done, it was at best a technical disaster. Roger's eyes skimmed the young man's features, the close blonde haircut, the folded hands. His senses a bit dulled by what he had seen heretofore, he looked away, blinked his eyes, looked again at the photo. And then like a fist hitting him in the chest, he realized what had so provoked his companion.

"My God! It's Adolf Hitler!"

Old John nodded. *"Der Schickelgruber* himself."

Roger held the picture closer to the light, an action that only distorted the grays, lightened the whites, nocturnalized the blacks. Bringing it back up to his original sight line, he asked, "You think there might be some mistake?"

"None. It's him, take my word. I might be crazy, but both of us ain't."

Roger lay the picture with the others and greedily reached for the fifth, his heavy breathing off tempo with that of Old John.

This time all doubt was dispelled. Hitler had leaned away from his pleasure and held the young man's penis at the base, his hands squeezing, the dark tip arching over his grasp plumlike, bloodgorged. Hitler had left his own member open for scrutiny by changing position, and Roger noted that fame and power do not a large dong make. He found himself almost chuckling at the brevity of it, the uncircumcised head revealing that der Fuhrer indeed possessed something denied all Jews. Already writing the story, his reporter's mind taking possession of the instant, he relinquished any reference to this ritualistic bit of skin, his worry being just how in hell these photos could ever be shown to the world. The word "world" rotated and fizzed about his mind like an insane balloon of success suddenly freed.

"People's wondered for years," said the old man.

"They don't have to wonder any more," said Roger.

"Could they be fake?" Old John suddenly asked.

A cloud of despair settled over the moment. Roger looked at the gray periphery of the photo, saw that it was smaller, took up less of the picture's area. A simple thing, a totally human act of an SS man's moving closer to the peephole, but it was enough. "No, it's not fake."

"Why not?"

Roger explained, hoping that the old one would go along with it. For ballast, he added, "Too much money, too many bodies."

Old John removed his hat and rubbed the brim along his chin. A dark splotch appeared, and Roger realized that they both were sweating gallons. "Yeah, you got me convinced," John said at last. "How many more we got left?"

Roger flipped the tops of the remaining pictures and said, "Four."

John replaced his hat and suddenly grabbed Roger's poised wrist. "Not yet," he said cryptically.

"Oh? Why not?" Roger shook free with gentle disdain.

John tapped the pictures. "Because this is all goin' to change things. It ain't a thing I can get a tush into just now and explain just right, but I'll try: I'm in the middle of somethin' that'll get me rich or famous or dead or maybe all of 'em. The one that's on my mind most is dead. Two hours ago I was a mule tender with a pack of dogs and a cabin and a Social Security check. Until I seen them pictures, this was all bullshit. But it's real! Do you know what I mean? It's real! Me and you and them mules is the middle of the whole goddamn thing right now. But, after tonight, it ain't gonna be just us. Know what I mean?" He shuddered and looked at the cave's opening. There was nothing in the distant night but a single star.

"You want to back away from it?" Roger asked, wondering why an eddy of anger was beginning to roil within him.

"I don't know," said John, his words reedy and fearful. "All I'm sayin' is, let's think about this."

Roger lurched forward, grabbed the old man by the collar and shook him viciously for five seconds, his knuckles pressing into the wattled neck. Realizing that it was a spontaneous, Marine Corps killing hold, he relaxed the pressure and roared: "Now you listen to me, you goddamn sonofabitch! You're full of fucking platitudes about the fucking Grand Canyon and Americana! These ain't no goddamn Norman Rockwell paintings! You want to be a goddamn failure all your life, then go ahead—but all that I'm ever going to have, all that me and Moe have worked for, that Starla died for, is lying right there in that goddamn dust! Now listen, motherfucker, you're in for the ride, so don't you forget it!"

Old John sagged backward, his face ashen, lips trembling. He lifted his hands and grabbed Roger's own, a touch of terror, one that he might use in removing a rat-tlesnake from his bed. In his old eyes lay the mirror image of the very evil greed that he had known the outside world to be, and it was as if he were seeing it up close again, that very thing that he had so long ago come to despise. And, too, there was the horrid knowledge that he had brought it into the canyon with him.

"Forget . . . " he said, rubbing his neck, coughing softly, ". . . forget what I said. I was just scared."

Roger wiped his hands on his thighs and felt perspiration forming hotly through the soft fabric of his trousers. It was a thing that he had done often in Nam, a reflex action that symbolized the psychological wiping away of the moment. Still, staring at the Jewtooth eagle and its malignancy, he could not bring himself to apologize. If this went well, he would never have to sweat again, never worry about rent or pussy or whether a set of tires would go the forty thousand as promised. The eagle and its pictures were silk shirts and a job in New York and telling Lynch to go fuck himself in the ass with an ice tong. There was no Starla here, no failing newspaper, no Moe with his goddamn toy airplane and doubts—no, this was the real Roger Wilder, an aging and frightened nonentity who sagged as he felt the purple ghost of raw greed settle coldly on his shoulders.

"Look," he said, lifting his eyes upward almost laconically, studying the walls of the cave, wondering whether hell indeed looked this way. "When it comes to a story I can be a real jackoff. But this ain't a goddamn cat up a tree with a fireman falling out. You gotta understand. You do understand, don't you?"

The old man nodded. There was rage in his eyes, but it was tempered by memory. "Yeah, I understand, I reckon. I was like you, once. The difference in forty and eighty or ninety, is more than just numbers. You'll understand that someday." He rubbed his neck and nodded at the plaque. "See what that thing's already done?" And then he laughed a hollow, sham laugh and said, "Let's see another picture."

Roger extracted the fifth photo and gazed into the face of a lady who was young and blonde and whose blue eyes stared into the camera with a wanton, but coquettish, simpering. She rather resembled that cartoon character in *Playboy*, a big-titted angel whose naivete was one of her more stimulating qualities. Roger thought of her for a long time before it occurred to him that the name was irrelevant. He was very tired and the photo made him chuckle. He had seen enough of human folly to last a lifetime, but this girl and what she was doing was a new splinter from the barrel's bottom. Hitler and the young man were attempting to place their thighs and hips into a crosslock that would bring their phalli to equal heights but, from the way that Hitler's left leg jutted out and away from the crux of the activity, it was apparent that this was a learn-as-you-go matter. The woman's hands—dainty, childlike, silken—were folding over the Furhrer's pubic hair as the wings of a dove might settle over a frightened rodent, such was the tentativeness of her gesture. Roger concluded that the purpose of all this shuffling of hip and thigh was to effect a double fellatio.

"Three to go?" Old John asked.

Roger shook his head.

"Why not?"

"Because we've seen enough," Roger said at last, aware of the worldweariness in his words even as he spoke.

"I wonder who she was?" John asked, trying to keep the moment alive.

"She wasn't Eva Braun. Too young. Probably a nice Jewish girl from one of the camps. She's dead now. They're all dead now. In the end, that's all that matters."

John cocked his head to one side and offered his words cautiously, lest Roger explode again. "What do you mean by that?"

"I mean that one of the greatest quests of my life is over." He looked at the old man's eyes and saw all the pluses and minuses of humankind there— greed, sexual stimulus, stupidity and, yes, an open-faced kindness that was uniquely American in nature. He loved Old John Landers, and he hated the human race.

"I guess I know the feelin'," said the old man. "Worst part of any hunt is pickin' up the body of what you've killed. Somehow it ain't as big as it was when you was after it. Am I close?''

Roger smiled and thumped John's hat brim playfully. "Yeah, close. There was a man named Gomez, and he wanted money. There was a man named Blaustein, and he wanted money. They all wanted something: Tatum, Jarvis, Starla, Sturbridge. And Lynch and Mohler and Roger Wilder. They all wanted something, and here I am kneeling over it in a musty cave. If only I could tell them right now how worthless it is; if only I could go back in time about seven days and tell Gomez to stay in Mexico. But that can't be, can it?'' The question was pallid, academic, somber, ridiculous.

"You forgot to mention them," said John, indicating the plaque. "A lot of dead Jews. It's easier to think of death when you say 'a lot.' One person's scream will go through your dreams like a lightnin' bolt for a lifetime, so it's best to say 'a lot.'"

He reached forward and stroked the eagle's stomach, the diamond lightning of the SS insignia. This time the diamond eyes did not respond; they too, were dead.

Roger gathered the photographs and returned them to the teakwood back. When he had carefully replaced the excelsior and reaffixed the cover, he stood and looked down at the eagle and the suitcase. "A lot," he said. "That about sums it up."

They went back down the hill slowly and without speaking, Roger lugging the suitcase, John leading the way with the flashlight. The mules were huddled about the campfire in an attitude resembling a miniature Nativity scene. Shifting the weight from his right hand to his left as they trudged downward, Roger knew that somewhere the man called Ableiter was waiting for them, and he felt a cold and delicious tingle of anticipation. It was going to be such a pleasure to kill the goddamned sonofabitch.

Twenty-one

The morning light followed the top lines of the ridges at first and then spilled in orange and yellow into the gorges. The blacks became grays and then yielded and went away toward the west. By the time they could see all about them clearly, they were three miles from the campsite. The breakfast beans, eaten cold, hung in Roger's belly like the very boulders in the river's bottom. When they came back down to the great river, they went across hurriedly and, when they were on the other side, Old John removed the bridles and let the mules drink. The sand here was wide and white, and Roger was reminded of certain beaches in Southeast Asia.

Removing a shoe, shaking out a pebble, Roger said, "So far, so good." It was a foolish comment, but it was better than silence.

"It's all good right now," said Old John. "She's like she was when Cardenas found her. He was the first European. You scared?"

Roger lifted the brim of his hat, stared at the old man, and nodded. "Let's say I'm aware, about as aware as a person can get."

"Caution is a good thing," said Old John. He waded into the river and patted Bridey on the rump. The river licked at his boots and moved on.

"Maybe we could hole up at Shit Rocks and then go in after dark," Roger suggested.

Old John replaced Bridey's muzzle and led her out of the water. There was dignity and deference in the way he attended to her. He touched her ear and looked at Roger as if to bridge the essences of good and evil. "Like I said last time, that ain't such a good plan. This place will swaller you whole at night. One slip and you buy the farm."

"Is that final?" Roger asked coldly.

"I'm open for suggestions, provided they are good ones. You was an officer; I was a corporal. You got paid to think, so think."

Roger watched as John bridled the others and led them from the shallows. It was no wonder the old man lived alone; he could be contemptible to the point of mentally aligning with his mules.

"If I were a man with a gun, why would I not pick us off at about the Shit Rocks?" Roger asked, making sure his question was pure conjecture.

"Because what I was shootin' about would be astride a mule, and the mule would be astride a thousan' foot drop. If he's good as you say he is, he'd think of that."

Roger merely looked away and thought of the old one's words. There was definite merit in them, but the introduction of military rank into the matter had created a chasm of sorts. Here was new guerilla method clashing with a trench mentality. But these canyon trenches belonged to John Landers, and Roger opted for discretion.

"Good enough," he said at last, "but what if he gets the last minute sweats and doesn't think of that?"

John strung the mules together and looked at the high and distant rocks that were to be climbed. "He's as scared as we are about now, I'd figger. He don't know but what I'm a mean old sonofabitch. " Turning toward Roger, fixing him with an impish grin, John said, "and he'd be right. For all I know, I killed his daddy in France. And for all he knows, I'm still just as good now as I was then."

"Not pointing uphill with a .22 rifle, necessarily," said Roger.

Old John Landers, king of the canyon rats, hooted at this and swatted Bridey across the tail. She led the others up the beach from whiteness of sandspit onto brownness of canyon dirt. The watering was done, and Roger watched for a full minute as his friend and the mules trudged into an incline that threatened to arch straight upward. His eyes followed the ugly rib cage of the canyon, and the reds and oranges went upward and onward for what seemed to be a rocket blast into eternity. Just as he thought that his eyes would be forever seeing feral formations of dust and wind-clawed rock, it all broke at the top of his vision and the great blue sky was there. A lone bird semaphored against the emptiness, and Roger knew that it was going to be his day. He was not given to praying, as such, and runes and signs were the stuff of old women and wild-eyed preachers, but here was a simple bird whose majesty was such that the moment was his forever. Whether he lived for an hour or for half a century, this instant belonged to Roger Wilder as an unquestioned gift from the Almighty. His legs and spine tingled with an extraordinary fervor. He trotted off the beach and toward the little plodding caravan.

For two hours they coursed upward, this trail being some three hundred yards to the right of the one they had taken downward. For a time this puzzled Roger, but he was too winded to question or to protest. It was only after seeing the mules lock their hooves onto the rocks for traction that the laws of physics presented themselves, and he remembered that yesterday's trail had none of these little stepping stones. Indeed, John Landers knew his business. Wheezing, rattled by chest pain and quaking legs, Roger decided that his own plans had been basically bullshit. Let the old fart have his way; Roger was too tired to argue.

They paused a mile up from the river. The oasis was a ten-by-twenty-foot ledge that widened beside a growth of dwarf shrubbery; at the far side was a sheer drop of five hundred feet. They could no longer see the river.

"How much farther?" Roger asked. He removed the hat and fanned himself with it.

"Four hours, five. Maybe seven." Old John emptied one of the canteens into his hat and gave each of the mules a sip.

"So we've got four hours to live. Maybe five, maybe seven. That about it?"

Old John laughed. "Maybe. It's about three miles to Shit Rocks by this trail. Little steeper, but closer."

"Little steeper. I like that. I've seen tree frogs that couldn't get up these hills."

"You'll make it. You'd make a fine climber. I've been watchin' you. You don't complain. Old Gomez, he raised hell all the way back up. You about ready to hit it again.

"No."

"Good. Then let's hit it."

Before Roger could emit even the lowest of groans, the trip was resumed, the tenor of the journey underscored by a trombone-ripple fart from Wiley. The sound reflected Roger's sentiments.

By noon they had risen out of the bowels of the canyon so that distant peaks were again within view. Without ever breaking stride, Old John opened a can of Vienna sausages and passed them to Roger. The mingled scents of mule sweat and greasewood joined the aroma of the questionable ingredients, and Roger thought that he would swoon and go over the side at any minute. The mules moved their rumps in an undulating rhythm, and he rememberd a cooch dancer in Saigon who moved about the stage with the same motions. The sun bore down, drove lancets of angry light into their necks and backs, and still the walk upward never ceased. No route march at Pendleton had ever been like this, and Roger privately swore that if he survived this hike he would pay any Mexican whore in San Antonio five hundred bucks just to rub his feet. And on they walked. And upward they walked.

"There they are," said Old John. It was mid-afternoon.

Roger looked up from his dreamy fatigue, focused his eyes and saw the pines at Shit Rocks. They were some five hundred yards up and to the left. He looked at Bridey's empty saddle and fought down the urge to mount. Money meant nothing. Success meant nothing. Mohler and the plaque were a bad dream. He knew at last why the old and the sick lie on their beds and go gently into that good night. "So what're you waitin' for?" he asked, arrogantly. "Let's hit it."

The time of caution arrived unspoken, and they stayed closer to the mules. The first fringes of the pines beyond Shit Rocks came into view, those being the trees behind John's cabin, and both men walked without taking their eyes off the distant point. The old sniper itch developed between Roger's eyes, and it bore into his brain with a million unrelated thoughts and memories.

When they were within two hundred yards of the rocks, Old John slapped Bridey's rump, and they went the distance wheezing and sweating. A soft yellow dust rose from the hooves, and it looked as if the animals were swimming in a turbulent brown river. The mules, sensing discomfort in the men, brayed humbly, fearfully. In the last ten feet Roger and the old man ran in a low crouch and collapsed onto their knees behind the largest boulder. For a long while they gasped and sweated, their ears attuned to the trail beyond.

"That last hunderd feet was a booger," said the old one at last.

"It always is," said Roger, recalling the mile run in high school.

"Think he seen us?"

Roger removed the hat and wiped his forehead. "If he did, he didn't let on. Next fuckin' time I offer to make this trip, tell me no."

Old John laughed wheezily, his turkey-wattle neck dripping sweat. "One thing I want you to know, if anything happens to me, they's some money in my name in the bank in Flagstaff. It goes to Mrs. Sally Witherspoon in Lawton, Oklahoma. Can you remember that?" His old eyes were hautingly empty, but there was a hint of pleasure in them.

"You sound downright thanatoid," Roger said.

"Damnit, can you remember?"

"Sally Witherspoon, Lawton." Roger tapped his sweaty temple. "Consider it salted away." But he saw that the old man was about to become hostile, and he delved into his coat pocket and took out a well-chewed stub of a Mirador. After writing the name and address on a matchbook cover, he nodded and smiled. His hands were incredibly grimy and not at all befitting his sudden power of attorney.

"Anything happens to me, just drop my ass over a cliff," Roger said. "It'd be a better funeral than I'd get in San Antonio. If I know Moe, he'd leave me in the back of a '56 Dodge and let the city tow me away."

"Gallows humor," said John, laughing. He crawled on hands and knees to Pearl's side and turned her toward the distant pines. Rising slightly, he pulled the .22 out of its scabbard and crawled back toward Roger. It was at that moment that a mild and cold zephyr drifted out the canyon and raised a gritty dust. The mules stirred and the men felt chilled. They looked at each other, and the ominous breeze held for a few seconds and then went on.

"He's close," Roger said quietly. "I know it in my guts."

"Yeah, me too," said Old John. "I guess I've knowed it all along."

"I owe you money. If anything . . . happens, feel free to get into my wallet."

"Good enough. And if it happens to me, just feed my animals. Funny, I ain't had one of these conversations since the trenches. The words are always the same."

There was a minute of silence as the men retreated into private thoughts. They did not wheeze now, and this meant that the time of decision was upon them. It was Roger who broke the silence. "Give me the rifle. If I stay in a low crouch I can get to within a hundred yards of the cabin pines."

"Why you?"

"Because you know more about mules, and that is a mighty important mule just now." He nodded at Bridey and at the suitcase that sagged heavily against her right side.

"Bad move," said Old John. "Let's just say for the hell of it that he came down the trail a piece. You're movin' and he's still. That makes for bad odds."

"Maybe. But all that's left is that we wait for night and go up amid the mules. Then he'd nail us at the house from any direction. No, this way he's got to be on one azimuth and one only: straight up this trail.''

Old John grinned. "Looks like he's got us by the short hairs any way you cut it. So that leaves one choice: we draw him out.''

"And how do we do that?''

The old man took a dime from his pocket and said, "Call it." He flopped the coin upward.

"Heads," said Roger, automatically.

The coin fell into the dust, tails up.

Old John smiled, raised himself in a half crouch, his legs quaking slightly. The top of the boulder passed below his vision, and he viewed the ragged red cliffs and the overtowering green pines beyond. He held the small rifle at high port, head and chest exposed. A belligerent grimace crossed his lips. Here stood the last of righteous Americana, a man defending his home.

Roger had just begun to come up off his rump, to whirl onto his knees, to pull the fool down, to protest, to say something, anything, when he felt the bloody spray hit his hat, rain over it like a fine, wet silt. The sound was a butcher block slap, followed by a terrible whirring, the song of an angry bee, a sound that he had heard a million times during the dozens of target pulls that he had supervised at Pendleton. By the time he could pull himself around, the old man's shirt was already settling back against his body, the ragged hole spitting gore high and just to the left of the spine. It was pink blood, a lung shot. Bits of rib made clacking sounds in rocks and the mules screamed. Roger saw that the tops of his hands were flecked with pink. Old John placed the butt of the rifle on his toe, made two steps backward and fell at Bridey's feet, his eyes staring at her bridle in the unmistakable dullness of death.

The shot and the fall and the blood had happened in a matter of three seconds but, for Roger, it was a horror of slow motion. He blinked his eyes and wiped his nose, his fingers finding a bit of cartilaginous tissue as hard and as white as an ice crystal. Now the marine in him came forth, and he crawled over to the old man and grabbed the rifle. Gathering the tethers of the animals into a leather bundle, he pulled the trio together around him and started to lead them back down the trail. He felt no emotion but to survive, had no thought but victory. He recalled the bird in the morning sky, its promise. When he was less than ten feet from Old John's body he heard the voice.

"Come, Mister Wilder, let us reason together!"

Roger stopped and looked under Wiley's belly toward the rocks, on toward the cliffs, on toward the high pines. The failing light of afternoon had added shadows that lay against the landscape like fallen buzzards. The mules burped quietly, and the click of rocks against their hooves was the only sound. Roger licked his lips and remembered the sweet and deadly greenery of Con Thien. He did not want to die on sand; there was just something about dying while feeling gritty that did not appeal to him. The belly of the mule twitched, and he continued to look at the shadow buzzards and the hot orange cliffs. And the seconds ticked by.

"Whattaya say, Kraut?" he called. The mules protested in startled grunts, and he pulled down on the tethers.

"I say, let me approach you. It is over for us. And there is enough for us both. The time for killing has ended."

Roger felt that he had a fix on the sound. The Nazi was approximately forty yards away and on a right angle line to the boulder at which Old John had died. That meant that he was inside one of the shadows that was formed by the swirls and convolutions of the vertical gullies at the cliff's side. That was why Old John had made such a perfect target; hell, they had been wide open for the last mile. So, why hadn't the bastard shot them on the way up? Old John's theory had to have been right: the man knew nothing about mules and was fearful that they would panic over the side. Mark up one for John Landers. He looked at the old man's body and saw that a fly walked across the left eye. Incredible how flies always found bodies.

The ball had been thrown into Roger's court. He could think of nothing to say or do. It was as though he had been frozen in obscene bas relief, like one of those characters who sucked and fingered each other in that famous bit of friezework in India. They, at least, were involved in unquestionable pursuits. The seconds ticked away, and he chose to say something, anything even if it was wrong.

"What's your plan, Kraut?" he called.

"There is no plan, Mister Wilder! As one soldier to another, I offer you momentary truce."

The voice was a stiletto, snugly wrapped in cocoons of blandness.

"Step out where I can see you!" Roger called. Still hunkered, he was beginning to lead the mules back toward John's body. The big rock beyond was looking good again.

Like a flower easing itself out of the dead sand, a human hand emerged holding a rifle. It was closer than Roger had believed, a good fifty feet closer. The sounds of the canyon had proved as pervertable as everything else. As if taunting Roger to fire, the hand and the rifle stood serene and immobile over the orange sand.

"One wrong move Kraut, and I heave the thing over the side. You got that?"

The hand and the rifle disappeared. There was a five second pause, and then Ableiter stood and began to walk toward the boulder, the weapon held outward stiffly in his left hand. Roger was amazed at his height and at his leanness; it was momentarily difficult for him to believe that this was the person who had killed Starla and all the others. Rather than suggesting the head of death, the shock of white hair and the smiling mouth were the facial trappings of a kindly, middle-aged minister. He wore a dark suit, gray tie, and white shirt, exactly the sort of clothing not to wear in such a grainy terrain.

Roger stood, dropped the tethers, and left the mules behind, the .22 held at high port. He was within ten feet of the boulder now and was perfectly capable of putting two, maybe three bullets in the man's head before the bastard blinked his eyes. But, he could not do it. There was something in the man's use of the word soldier, the bonding of bloods that it implied, that prevented wanton murder. Roger tried to think of Auschwitz, of corpse piles, of Starla, of the ease with which he, himself, had burned little brown men in Nam, but the distorted and lunatic haze of the moment froze these visions, rendered them moot.

"That'll do," said Roger, coming around the boulder, stopping.

Ableiter leaned to his left, dropped the weapon soundlessly onto the sand. As he regained his posture and began to remove his coat, Roger noticed the fan-shaped scar on his cheek, the mark of the Junker. Having removed the coat, he turned slowly so that his back was exposed, faced Roger again, dropped the coat on the rifle.

"As you see, I am now at your mercy," he said.

Roger placed the .22 against the boulder and motioned for Ableiter to approach. When they were within five feet of each other Roger extended the palm of his right hand outward and his adversary stopped. They looked at each other for ten seconds, each searching behind the eyes of the other for those enigmatic purposes that had caused this confrontation in this desolate place. They were alone in the world, and each knew that only one would ever walk out of here.

The German flexed himself to his full height, placed his heels together, and saluted, with extended right arm. "Allow me to introduce myself. I am Obersturmfuhrer Gerd Renck, Totenkopf."

In his slovenly American way, Roger lifted the brim of his hat in a perfunctory salute and said, "Wilder, Roger T., Captain, U.S. Marine Corps."

Ableiter dropped his hand and looked out at the majestic vista to his right. There was fulfillment in his eyes and a certain nostalgia in his voice as he said, "The photographs do not do it justice. It loses something in its transference to paper, don't you think?"

"I don't think," said Roger, "Renck, huh? I've wondered all along what your real name was."

Still facing the canyon, Ableiter said, "I admit to having wondered about you also, Hauptmann Wilder. Tell me, were you and your old friend successful?" He turned and looked at the body of Old John and then at the mules.

Roger nodded. "We were successful. The Himmler Plaque is in that suitcase over there. It's mine." The truth rolled from his mouth as a sweet, vindictive taunt.

"*Au contraire*. It is ours. My presence here connotes ownership, albeit only by half, and there lies the pact that I came to speak of."

"I'm listening."

Ableiter leaned against the boulder and pressed his right hand against his belly. "There are certain . . . difficulties . . . which make a return to the jungle less than desirable. I need your help, you need mine."

Roger smiled at the Scots burr in his voice. He had pronounced mine as may-un. "I take it we are speaking of money in one form or another," he said.

"There is only one form of money, Mister Wilder, that form being possession."

"And I possess the plaque. So why should I bargain?"

The German looked at him incredulously. "Because I came to you as a soldier. With honor, I spared your life so that we might retire from the field with honor, both victorious. We are of the same blood; you of Viet Nam, I of Russia. You had My Lai, I had Babi Yar. We are men of blood and iron, your American hypocrisies notwithstanding. We have gone to war against vermin, and the vermin lives on. Can you not see that? I can make one phone call to Montreal and we can be wealthy men. We did not eradicate the vermin, but we can rise above it. It is purest reason!"

"What'll bring the most, the gold or the pictures?"

"Pictures?" Ableiter asked, stunned, bemused. "What pictures?"

"You're kidding," said Roger.

"The Himmler Plaque, as you call it, until recently, had lain in a trunk in a tool shed in Paraguay for the past thirty-one years. It has never been photographed, to my knowledge."

"Then you really don't know," said Roger, sighing heavily. "Jesus, all those dead people, and you didn't know the secret of why."

"Perhaps you should enlighten me." Ableiter's words were uttered in a schoolboy's tone of astonishment.

"Hitler was a queer. Gay. Homo. Get it? He sucked pricks. That's what your honcho back in the jungle wanted to save, not some goddamn slab of gold. There are pictures in the back that prove it."

"It is a lie!" Ableiter grimaced and pressed his stomach harder.

"You should know about lies. You call yourself a soldier, a man of iron, and then you kill a drunk who's hung over a commode. You kill a sleazy rock and roll singer who's strung out on dope. You tie a man up and burn him to death for your own pleasure. God, man, don't speak to me of honor!"

The German moved with leonine rage. He was off the boulder and at Roger's throat before the younger man could move backward. His hands closed in, the thumbs sliding upward in the sweat and seeking Roger's adam's apple. Roger brought up his knee, and it went into Ableiter's groin, glancing off his pubic bone. The German flinched, groaned, and loosened his grip for a second. Twisting his body sideways, Roger lifted his right foot and slammed the side of his shoe into a leg just below the knee, thrusting downward against the shinbone all the way to the top of the German's foot. Ableiter screamed and attempted to step backward. It was exactly the movement that Roger had desired, for now he was able to swing his left arm from outside the periphery of combat and slam his open palm into the tall man's face, the bottom of his hand savagely whipping into flesh just under Ableiter's nose. Eyes staring foolishly at nothing, the German fell back against the boulder and licked at the gore that poured from his nose and onto his chin and shirt. Wheezing, his legs and arms quivering from a decade of soft life, Roger knew that he had to make the kill fast. Even as he moved toward the boulder he saw that the fight was far from finished, for the tall one had reached into his shirt pocket and had taken out a small plastic box. In the insanity of the moment Roger recalled that all the others had been tied with dental floss, the gentle weapon of the coward, and he knew beyond conscious thought that this was the fine thread that had tied Starla. Be a Marine, he heard a voice call from his past, but the voice called to a hard body that was no longer hard. There is always a weapon handy! Find it! The voice screamed, trailing away into the neverland of memory. The German was already coming off the boulder, his hands making a double strand of the fine thread, his breath making tortured gasps that echoed Roger's own. He lunged, and Roger slipped under him as he passed over, the rush of air slicing coldly against the back of his neck. Now Roger was on his knees, his knuckles screaming against the bite of sand and chipped rock. Figuring that he had less that two seconds, Roger seized a bit of rock that was thin and tapered, three inches long and jagged. He rolled to his right just as Ableiter dived toward him, and the German came down heavily, his hands holding the floss in the practiced manner of extermination, tautly, easily, almost lazily. It was as if a smile formed beneath the blood that drenched the mouth and chin, and Roger smiled back through clenched teeth as he drove the ragged end of the rock into the high part of the left cheekbone and pressed it into Ableiter's horrified blue eye. Blood and screams tore out of the tall man's ruined face, and milky liquid slopped down over Roger's hand as he continued to twist the rock, to drive it more deeply into the socket where the eye had been. He shoved with his body and Ableiter went over onto his back, his hands trembling as they reached upward toward nothing. The remaining blue eye stared in beseechment as Roger moved like a splendid predatory beast, implacable, deadly, passionless, committed. When he was over the German, he wrapped both hands around the rock, lifted it over his head and slammed it downward, the point going into the other eye with a sickening dull sound of crushed bone and lacerated tissue. Ableiter screamed and grabbed Roger's wrists, but the hands of the younger man rolled the rock like a pestle until there was nothing left in the socket but a crimson paste, roofed by a sliver of haired flesh that had once been an eyebrow.

Roger cast the bloody rock aside, rolled over onto his back, and let his eyes suck in the azure liquidity of the sky that was, at this moment, all that was life and all that would ever be meaningful. From somewhere nearby someone was screaming, but it was merely a sound, an auditory proof working in tandem with the sky to assure him that he was alive. Hundreds of feet above, a bird hung on catamarran wings, semaphored, and was gone. Roger lay for a long time, long enough for the screams to become a groan.

Coming out of it, relinquishing the post combat trance that is known to all warriors, he saw that the sky was empty. No bird. No cloud. He smiled that smile of acknowledgement that he had seen on hundreds of faces in another time, faces emerging from jungles and from rice paddies.

Ableiter sobbed. His bloody hands were pressed against the fleshy excavations where his eyes had been.

Roger recalled a blinded Cong who had wandered for days before his capture, a little brown man whose hells had been accented by his sightlessness. By cliff, by sidewinder, or by thirst, Ableiter's death in the next two hours or the next two days was assured. It would give the son-ofawhore time to think. The Nazi had been right about one thing: he and Roger were basically of the same blood. But the difference was that Ableiter's cruelty was the cruelty of aggression while Roger's was the American cruelty of vengeance. The deadliest weapon in the world, someone had once said, was an outraged American. And the most unforgiving, the speaker might have added.

Roger pulled himself out of the sand, picked up the old hat, and dusted himself off with it. Lifting Old John's body with a gentleness born of respect and gratitude, he placed it on Wiley's back. When he had picked up the two rifles and secured them to Bridey's saddle, he gathered the tether lines and led the animals past the prostrate German. One hand now covered the upper part of the face; the other massaged the stomach. Roger fought down an impulse to kick the man in the balls.

Now, he led the mules up the trail and wondered what to do next. There were so many things to think of, so many things to do. The Arizona cops would probably nab him before he could get to Flagstaff, and it would be hours before Moe and the Ranger could clear him in the matter of Starla's death. Somewhere between Flagstaff and the entrance to the Grand Canyon he had seen a natural landmark, a place untrod by human feet, a place that would not be altered by any war page of memory. He would hide the plaque there, put the damnable thing out of the way forever or until his thinking was clear enough to justify its retrieval. Because of their nature, the pictures could not be shown to the general public and, because of its origins, the plaque would be the natural object of Semitic outrage, a justifiable outrage. No, too many had died already, too many had wept already. He would tell Moe that the thing did not exist, had never existed. There would be hell to pay, but for the first time in months, he felt clean. Roger Wilder, reporter, millionaire with no way to divulge his wealth, was a very rich man indeed, provided the plaque was never found again. He wished that he had looked at the remaining pictures, but not doing so would only add to the mystery, the sense of expectancy.

Yes, damnit, the thing had been done for all the wrong reasons. Old John had said something about it just last night in the glow of the campfire, something about greed. Roger could not remember the words, but the message was there. Blood and honor were the stuff of dreams, and only individual dreamers could know them, define them, enhance that thing called the soul with them. He would bury Old John, feed the animals whatever could be found, notify the authorities, and transfer some money to one Mrs. Sally Witherspoon of Lawton, Oklahoma.

When Roger had led the mules to the crest of the ridge, he paused and looked out over the endless swells of red and orange and purple. The sun pained his eyes after a time, and he led the mules on into the cool greenery of the pines that stood between the cabin and the canyon. Removing packs, saddles, and the old man's body, he let the mules wander down toward the cabin. He took the shovel from the pack and placed Old John against a tree in a lazy attitude and then leaned back with the old man so that they could watch the sun go down together.

He waited until well past moonrise before he began to dig.

Novels of Suspense
JAMES ELLROY

CLANDESTINE   81141-3/$2.95 US /$3.75 Can
Nominated for an Edgar Award for Best Original Paperback
Mystery Novel. A compelling thriller about an ambitious
L.A. patrolman caught up in the sex and sleaze of smog city
where murder is the dark side of love.

SILENT TERROR   89934-5/$3.50 US /$4.75 Can
Enter the horrifying world of a killer whose bloody trail of
carnage baffles police from coast to coast and whose only
pleasure is to kill...and kill again.

FEATURING LLOYD HOPKINS

BLOOD ON THE MOON   69851-X/$3.25 US /$4.25 Can
Lloyd Hopkins is an L.A. cop. Hard, driven, brilliant, he's the
man they call in when a murder case looks bad.

"A brilliant detective and a mysterious psychopath come
together in a final dance of death."
The New York Times Book Review

BECAUSE THE NIGHT   70063-8/$3.50 US /$4.95 Can
Detective Sergeant Lloyd Hopkins had a hunch that there
was a connection between three bloody bodies and one
missing cop...a hunch that would take him to the dark heart
of madness...and beyond.

AVON Paperbacks

The Provocative National Bestseller

WHO'S ON FIRST

WILLIAM F. BUCKLEY, JR.

"Timeless thriller ingredients: murder, torture, sex...
Soviet defection, treachery. And there in the middle of
it all is good old Blacky: charming, insouciant,
escaping one dragnet after another without rumpling
his trenchcoat." *Boston Globe*

The cunning and sophisticated hero Blackford Oakes is
back in a new adventure involving a beautiful
Hungarian freedom fighter, Blacky's old KGB rival,
a pair of Soviet scientific geniuses, and the U.S.-
U.S.S.R. space race.

"A fast-moving plot.... As in all good espionage novels
there is thrust and counterthrust.... Mr. Buckley is an
observer with a keen wit and a cold eye."
Newgate Callendar, *New York Times Book Review*

"The suspense is keen and complicated.... Constantly
entertaining." *Wall Street Journal*

"A crackling good plot...entertaining."*Washington Post*